CUTS THROUGH BONE

ALARIC HUNT

MINOTAUR BOOKS

A Thomas Dunne Book

NEW YORK

M

A THOMAS DUNNE BOOK FOR MINOTAUR BOOKS.
An imprint of St. Martin's Publishing Group.

CUTS THROUGH BONE. Copyright © 2013 by Alaric Hunt. All rights reserved. Printed in the United States of America. For information, address St. Martin's Press, 175 Fifth Avenue, New York, N.Y. 10010.

www.thomasdunnebooks.com
www.minotaurbooks.com

ISBN 978-1-250-01330-9 (hardcover)
ISBN 978-1-250-01331-6 (e-book)

Minotaur books may be purchased for educational, business, or promotional use. For information on bulk purchases, please contact Macmillan Corporate and Premium Sales Department at 1-800-221-7945 extension 5442 or write special-markets@macmillan.com.

First Edition: May 2013

10 9 8 7 6 5 4 3 2 1

For Dean Hill, Russell Spitzer, and Darriel Maner:
three determined old men.
And the original determined old man:
my grandfather.

CUTS THROUGH BONE

CHAPTER ONE

The blare of car horns from Thirty-fourth Street in midtown Manhattan leaked through two tall windows on the far end of the rectangular office. Rachel Vasquez was annoyed, but she only glanced across her jumbled desk at her boss, Clayton Guthrie, before turning back to her computer monitor. In the three months that the young Puerto Rican woman had worked for the little detective, he hadn't done much detecting. The job that started the spring as a godsend was becoming a curse. Clayton Guthrie was crazy. Three days before, Vasquez had gone home intending to quit, but intention was as close as she came.

That morning had started easily. Vasquez drove Guthrie's old blue Ford while they followed a couple around downtown Manhattan. The man was a short, muscular Italian, with gold chains glinting on his dark, hairy neck. He had a prize-winning glare that moved people around him like chess pieces. Vasquez found him easy to dislike. The woman was taller, with light brown hair that glowed like butter when the morning sunshine touched it. She dangled her rounded curves before the Italian like presents, gift-wrapped in a short white skirt and a clinging blue top, but her pinched expression changed to a smile only when he was looking.

Vasquez thought the couple was gangster-movie comic, but Guthrie watched and filmed with the soberness of a government employee. The detectives wore walkie-talkie earpieces like Secret Service agents, and Vasquez had a second camera tucked into her jacket pocket while she drove.

After a morning spent slowly shopping boutiques in SoHo and TriBeCa, the couple stopped for lunch at an upscale grill on a corner of Broome Street. Their table was on the outside corner, and visible through front windows on both streets. Guthrie left Vasquez to film from the front of a shoe store on Broome, and he hurried around the corner to shoot from the other side. The angry Italian and his simpering mistress settled at their table and ordered. Vasquez filmed. Her view was so clear, she could see every gold tooth in the man's busy mouth.

Partway through lunch, the Italian made a phone call. The street traffic was light, mostly Yuppies taking their cell phones for a walk. Vasquez filled her time by guessing whether passersby would enter the grill, and counting the number of taxis that passed without a fare. She despised surveillance. Guthrie tired of her monologue, and reminded her she was on a mike by asking if she would rather be driving a taxi. Several more minutes passed before Vasquez understood that the Italian in the restaurant had spotted her. He started laughing and pointed at her. His mistress turned around to look; the last thing Vasquez caught on video was the woman's terrified smile.

A heavyset young Italian gripped Vasquez's right arm and whipped her around. "Hey there!" he exclaimed, a happy note in his voice. "Whatcha doing?" A drooping mustache concealed most of his mouth. His face was rough like a concrete block, and his shoulders had layers like a vault door. Another young Italian in a jogging suit stood beside him. He wasn't as big, but he looked equally amused.

"Let me go!" Vasquez demanded. After a moment, she emphasized with a knee aimed at his crotch, but he turned it aside with his thigh.

"We got a fighter here," he rumbled. As always, some pedestrians hunched their shoulders and hurried away, while the others craned for a better view. The scuffle was brief. A skinny teenaged Puerto Rican girl with a long black ponytail didn't burn much time on the fight cards of two Italian heavyweights. They wanted the camera; they took it. Vasquez's ears were ringing before Guthrie arrived, but she held a grip on the bigger thug's wrist, trying to reach past his long arm with a punch.

The big Italian with the mustache tossed Vasquez against the window of the shoe store, but he stumbled as he rushed Guthrie. Vasquez watched as the little detective drew back an open hand. After a thunderclap, the big Italian slid to his hands and knees.

"Yo, Dave, what happened?" he muttered.

Guthrie stepped over to the other thug and snatched Vasquez's camera from his hand before bending to pluck his crumpled brown fedora from the man's face. Vasquez pushed herself away from the storefront window as the Italians struggled to their feet. She could hear the sounds of traffic again. She aimed a few cheap kicks at them as they scrambled down the sidewalk. Bystanders hooted and catcalled, and a clerk rushed out of the shoe store.

Across the street, the couple was watching from the window of the grill. The Italian was livid, pointing at them while he shouted into his phone. Standing on the sidewalk, just inside the edge of shade from the strong July sunshine running down the middle of Broome Street, Guthrie dusted off his fedora and punched it back into shape. His face twisted in disgust when he glanced inside— fresh speckles of blood decorated the silk. He flapped it against his leg instead of putting it on his head.

Once they were back in the old Ford, the little man caught Vasquez's chin and held it while he scowled and inspected her face. "You ain't too bad," he said.

She shook him off and started the car, pulling out just before a patrol car turned into the intersection at the corner of Broome Street. She wiped her stinging nose with the back of her hand and checked for blood.

"How in hell did they sneak up on you anyway?" Guthrie asked. "I thought you grew up on the Lower East."

"You're *loco, viejo*," Vasquez barked. "They got up on me since you didn't warn me I should be looking! Who the hell was that?"

"Or maybe you were too busy counting taxis?"

"Screw that. You should've told me he was connected. Why are you watching him anyway?"

"We were watching *her*."

Vasquez pounded the steering wheel and poured out some rapid curses in Spanish. The detective laughed at her, and fired some more that she hadn't used. Discovering that he spoke Spanish startled her into quiet.

"Maybe I should have warned you about my suspicions," he said after a minute. The old Ford rolled past Washington Square. "And maybe you should've just paid attention. He spotted you, so you blew it—hugs and kisses won't make it sound better. You gotta see that, Rachel. This's a tough job, but I got faith in you. You're a smart girl. You'll figure it out."

Vasquez went home angry, intending to quit after her next check, but she had forgotten about the marks on her face. Billboard advertisements would've drawn less attention in her parents' tenement apartment that night. Even her brothers kept quiet, staring at her face with shocked and angry looks. Papì recounted his top twenty-seven reasons she should be applying for college, finishing with a final silent finger gesture at her face. At that point, she discovered she was determined to keep working for Clayton Guthrie. Late that night, after the apartment was quiet, Vasquez's mother came to the open door of her bedroom. She stood silently, as if thinking of something to say, but only sighed and walked quietly away.

So Rachel Vasquez didn't quit, and her immediate reward was returning to the study of video-surveillance tapes. After which the little man grilled her like a sandwich to see if she had noticed everything he wanted her to notice—*without* telling her in advance what he meant her to notice. Clayton Guthrie was crazy. The quiet in his office was driving Vasquez crazy. At least the blare of horns on Thirty-fourth Street below them meant something was happening—kids were pushing racks of clothes on the street and slowing the traffic. That was an everyday occurrence in the Garment District. She glanced across the jumbled desk at Guthrie again. Then someone knocked on the office door.

Beyond a square of mismatched furniture, a shape behind the frosted glass window filled it almost completely. The door swung open after one brief knock. A tall silver-haired man in an ash gray suit stepped inside, followed by a young woman in a navy dress. Guthrie dropped his magazine onto his desk blotter. "Good afternoon, Mr. Whitridge," he said.

The office was well-lit. The desks each faced a couch, squared across a low coffee table littered with books and magazines. Vasquez's desk faced a wall of green paint over plasterwork, split by the frosted outer door, and an oxblood leather couch that belonged to a bygone era, when the entire room had been better dressed. The other couch, overlooked by the tall windows, was ratty brown faux fur. Another remnant of the previous aristocratic era was dark wooden wainscoting on the walls, interrupted by the outer door, and a pair of dark wooden doors behind Guthrie's desk—a supply closet and a bathroom.

The tall silver-haired man, Mr. Whitridge, seemed about the same age as Clayton Guthrie—in his middle years—but he was tailored and distinguished. His gray suit fit him as neatly as a general's dress uniform. A similar number of years left Guthrie rumpled. He was short and slight, and though his soldier-length hair was mostly dark, a dusting of gray seemed to load him down. A dark brown fedora rested on his desktop, and he wore a long-sleeved white shirt tucked into dark trousers. Whitridge stepped around and sat down on the oxblood couch. Moving and seated, the tall man had the perfect carriage of an aristocrat; Guthrie was his working-man opposite, down to the final detail of a relaxed slouch.

Vasquez wore a Yankees cap set crooked on her head, blue jeans, and a red windbreaker with the cuffs pushed up to her elbows. Her ears jutted like open car doors, because her long black hair was tied in a ponytail. The young woman with Whitridge was wearing a loose navy tea dress that couldn't hide rolling curves that had gone out of fashion after Marilyn Monroe. She was pale and blue-eyed, with chocolate brown hair pulled into a short tail with a navy ribbon, like a bloom behind her ear. Despite the curves and clothes, she was plain. Vasquez was dressed like a boy, and slim as a whip, but her dark eyebrows and sharp jaw took her long steps past merely pretty, into the realm of beautiful. The fading marks on her face only made her seem determined, not breakable. The young woman hesitated, then sat down on the brown faux-fur couch.

"Where's Weitz?" the tall man asked after glancing around the office.

"She had enough, I reckon," Guthrie said. "This's Rachel Vasquez, my new operative."

Whitridge measured the young Puerto Rican with a glance, then tipped her a diplomat's smile. "I think Michelle may explain this situation better than I would," he said.

Guthrie nodded.

"You're a private detective, right?" the young woman demanded.

"Sort of," Guthrie replied.

Michelle frowned, thinking about it. Her face came to life and she suddenly became more than ordinary, while deciding that "sort of" was good enough. "I need you to find out who killed my cousin," she said. "The police think they know who did it, but they're wrong."

The videotape on Vasquez's monitor continued running, but she paid no attention. She was listening hard. The job she had taken that spring started with her expecting something serious. Clayton Guthrie was a private detective, and somewhere he found enough power to break laws—enough to buy a teenager a gun and supply her with a carry permit. The first month, she spent six hours a day at an indoor pistol range. The little detective drank coffee, loaded bullets into clips, and timed her with a stopwatch as he flipped targets and shouted "Draw!" Vasquez fired the Smith & Wesson Chief's Special until both of her wrists ached, because he made her switch hands. The practice suggested something serious in the future, with the same kind of unspoken language as the revolver Guthrie kept hidden in the bottom drawer of his desk.

Then more months passed watching surveillance videos, or sitting in a park or on the street watching passersby do nothing. They ran background checks, which meant finding people and asking them what they thought of someone else, investigating references on résumés to see if they were real people and real companies, and determining whether people paid taxes or had criminal records. Vasquez supposed that was detective work. Maybe people could earn a living doing that. But that wasn't the job she'd expected when Guthrie had handed her the pistol and said, "Hitting what you fire at should be as easy as drawing breath." Now two office visitors and one asked-aloud question were enough to erase Vasquez's boredom and awaken her expectation.

Guthrie gave the young brunette a surprised look. He glanced at Whitridge, then asked, "You mean the Bowman murder?"

"That's right! No *way* did Greg kill her, but they arrested him last night. . . ." She trailed to a stop, puzzled.

Before she could ask another question, Guthrie said, "It's a society murder—you're society." The detective threw another incredulous glance at Whitridge.

"Oh. I asked Uncle Harry for help, and you're the help. I suppose you'd better be good." She gave Guthrie the once-over, measuring the small man against his advance billing. "Well?"

Guthrie nodded. "I hear you, miss," he said, "but I wonder if you're reading the papers. This guy, they took him in on the Bowman murder, but I shouldn't need to say they're looking at him for all of it."

"But he *didn't*!" she insisted.

Camille Bowman's murder had been the lead headline in every city paper for a week, the latest in a dead cast of characters. She was eye-catchingly blond and beautiful, another young woman murdered and dumped, without an obvious suspect. The newshounds called them "Barbie doll murders," because the victims had been beautiful. For the media, the killings were a carnival, complete with lurking villain, the smell of sex, and a paper chase. New developments were impossible to miss.

"I have sent the young man a lawyer," Whitridge volunteered.

"The lawyer doesn't have a guy? What about him?"

Whitridge smiled. "The law firm doesn't specialize in criminal matters, I'm afraid. That isn't ordinarily useful to me. Then the police found a gun."

"A gun?" Guthrie asked, settling back into his chair.

"See, you think he's guilty," the young woman said. "The police are wrong, too! Greg didn't do it! He loved her!" She dropped back onto the furry brown couch when Whitridge patted her shoulder a few times.

The silver-haired man's face was grim, his thoughts unvoiced. "Can you take care of this?" he asked.

Guthrie nodded. "I'll be all over it."

"Thank you," Whitridge said.

Vasquez went to the office window and looked down at Thirty-fourth Street in time to see Whitridge and his niece climb into a chauffeured Town Car. For once, the street hadn't been blocked by kids trucking racks of clothes. The horns stopped blaring when the Town Car pulled away. "Who the hell is he?" she asked.

"HP Whitridge," Guthrie said. "Harry Payne Edward Whitridge."

While Guthrie made phone calls to the lawyer and some police detectives, Vasquez paced the office impatiently. She didn't know what to do, but she wanted to be doing something. Camille Bowman's murder was the leading item on the television news, in a city already burdened with a string of similar killings. For seven days video clips of a filthy shoreline ran together with sequences of an ambulance, a gurney, and head shots of a beautiful blond Columbia coed. Like the other murders, there had been no witnesses to Bowman's murder. An army of reporters with no facts at hand manufactured a story from Bowman's shiny would-be future and screamed about tragedy.

Between his phone calls, Guthrie explained that a recovered gun, followed by an arrest by the NYPD, might mean a finished case. HP Whitridge wanted him to backtrack the police detectives' trail to reassure his niece, but he hadn't seemed to possess her faith in the suspect.

"We're smoothing over hurt feelings?" Vasquez demanded.

Guthrie shrugged. "Maybe. The Ds at Major Case aren't idiots, but they can make a mistake. I reckon they were careful with this one, and they want a slam dunk with the lawyers watching. So we walk up to it carefully. This time, it's about the client."

"HP Whitridge?"

"That's right. He manages a fair-size piece of the Whitney fortune. Some of it's even his. He's the family fixer, and he don't like anything less than he likes pictures in the paper, unless they're in the style or society columns, right?"

"Screw that," Vasquez muttered. "My first case is a loser."

"Don't worry about it," Guthrie said. "You're gonna see how this is done. Before, that's all been playing. This time will be for real."

She gave Guthrie an ugly look. "Playing?"

"Why do you think I hired you?" he countered.

"To do detective work, right?"

"No, not *what*. Why *you*?"

Vasquez's face twisted with a scowl. "*I* know?" she asked. Papì was right, she thought. This blanco is crazy. Everyone in her family had a different answer to that question—but they all had one. Who hires a Puerto Rican girl fresh out of high school and gives her a pistol? Papì didn't care about the job. He wanted her to go to school, school, and more school, so she could be a doctor. His eldest son had an education and a white-collar job in New Haven. His daughter could have that, too. Forget his two useless middle sons, Indio and Miguel. They had darker things to say. Indio suggested, maybe joking, that the little detective wanted a pretty young Puerto Rican girlfriend. A few weeks of watching damped that suspicion. Guthrie didn't seem to notice her. The question kept her wound up, fueled by Papì's continual suspicion and disappointment.

"I don't know," Vasquez said, leaning against the outer door of the office. CLAYTON GUTHRIE, DETECTIVE AGENCY showed faintly through the frosted glass, reversed in gold lettering.

Guthrie grinned. "You're a smart girl," he said. "You'll figure it out." That was his favorite reply to any question he wouldn't answer straight. "Come on, we gotta go downtown to the Manhattan House. That's where they're holding Greg Olsen."

Vasquez drove south on Broadway. The sky reappeared after they left the shadows of the big buildings in midtown, but it was soon blotted out again when they reached the downtown tip of Manhattan. Traffic was light. Bright afternoon sunshine at the end of July left the gray marble buildings looking dreary and grim. They parked on Canal and walked to the Criminal Courts Building, moving against the crowds that were flowing out of the area in the afternoon.

The lawyer's investigator, Henry Dallen, was waiting for them outside the bull pens. He was a heavyset white man with a mustache, wearing a dark gray suit. While they waited for Olsen to come out, he outlined the facts in the case. Major Case had served a search warrant the previous day for a registered .44, and left officers to baby-sit Olsen in case he tried to run. Two hours after they had the pistol, they made the arrest. Olsen was the dead woman's fiancé; they were attending Columbia together. Once the police started making accusations, he had lawyered up, but in an initial interrogation, he had admitted ownership of the pistol and claimed innocence. Major Case wasn't suggesting motive. The arrest sprang from the pistol.

Olsen shuffled into the interview room, escorted by two guards. The big blond man seemed stunned. Being arrested had turned his world upside down and he was suddenly unsure of what he was seeing. The guards watched him cautiously; he was shaped like a lumberjack, broad in the shoulders and narrow-waisted. Even with an unsteady gait, his size was menacing. He slid down into a chair and sat forward, cupping his chin with one hand, but the other one stayed below the steel table.

"I didn't do this," he whispered. He glanced at each of them, his eyes full of questions. "I didn't kill Cammie. I *couldn't.*"

"What'd the detectives say to you?" Guthrie asked. "They said things meaning to rattle you. What were they?"

Olsen frowned. "They showed me pictures," he said softly. "They asked how I could bring myself to mess her up like that. Someone beat her." He had a slow, measured way of speaking, taking care to make himself understood. Everything about the big man was handsome, without being pretty. Even his frown and his pauses were handsome, and the way he rubbed at his chin while he thought earnestly. He didn't seem calculating. He just wasn't moving at the speed of the city. Olsen was slow, from someplace slower than the city, where clear was more important than quick.

Guthrie nodded as if he were hearing it all for the first time, but pictures were a standard police tactic. The police often flashed pictures of bloody messes, trying to dig up a reaction. Olsen was wound tight, but he wasn't frightened.

"So they kept asking why I killed her, even though I told them I hadn't. They said a reason would help me, like if she'd been sleeping around and I was jealous. They could see that, as if I had had a fit then." His big hand rubbed at the tabletop slowly, or at his chin during pauses, and sometimes it seemed that he was applying tremendous force to wipe something away.

"They said my gun killed her, that little gun I bought her in case of a burglar, and they could prove it was fired. And they said they had a bullet to match it, but those were lies. She was the only one who fired the gun after I zeroed for her. I didn't need to practice like she did, and the other was a lie, because *I didn't kill her.*"

"Easy, Mr. Olsen, easy," Guthrie said. The big man was tense in his seat, red-faced as he spoke about the pistol. He looked down at the tabletop while he recounted the detective's accusations, then up at Guthrie as he explained.

"You do own a forty-four?" the little detective asked.

Olsen nodded mutely and looked down.

"Do you know who Camille Bowman was, Mr. Olsen?"

"I know she was rich." He stopped, reddening again. His hand crushed slowly on the tabletop. "That never bothered me, that she had money, though. I had enough to do for all that I needed. She didn't make much of it."

"Who would kill Camille?"

"Nobody! Everyone liked her!"

Guthrie nodded grimly. He handed Olsen his card before the guards knocked and came to take the big man out. The way Olsen tensed when they drew near made the guards hesitate about touching him. He tucked a hand in his waistband as he walked out. Henry Dallen shrugged once Olsen was gone. The lawyer's man had heard the same story twice, and he had no opinion.

CHAPTER TWO

"You can't talk about a case with nobody," Guthrie said after he closed the passenger door on his old blue Ford. "You can't talk about a case in front of nobody, neither."

Vasquez started the car and frowned.

"*Especially* if it's got anything to do with Whitridge."

She turned south off Canal onto Broadway. Most of the traffic poured north. The city was emptying. The big buildings loomed like mountains around them, with the hot summer sky burning through in the creases. The rushing crowds and blurring cars around them resembled slowly settling confetti—a whirl of movement with a visibly approaching end. Vasquez cruised straight down Broadway to Battery Park.

"Or in this case, his niece," she said.

"Yeah?" The old man glanced at her before turning back to watch Broadway glide past.

Vasquez smirked. "That was the first thing I thought when I saw him. She's got a reason for wanting him out of jail. . . . *Wait*. What if she—"

"Yeah," Guthrie said. "That makes her the first person we have to cross from our list. Dead woman, and she shines on the fiancé, right?"

"But what if she is—"

"Is what?" Guthrie demanded without meeting her gaze. "We ain't the police. We work for Whitridge."

Vasquez frowned and drove silently into the park. She found a space and tucked the old Ford in tight. "You're saying we might be covering up?"

"Welcome to the rest of the world. Maybe refusing to uncover ain't the same thing as covering up. Then what if she didn't? Don't go wringing your hands until then."

Vasquez cut a glance at the detective. "You done that before?"

"Not for murder." His mouth set grimly. He looked old.

"Less than murder, then," she murmured.

They walked into Mako's, a working-class pub on the edge of the park. Inside was dark except for the televisions showing baseball games, and empty except for a few middle-aged men tipping mugs. They took an empty booth in the back. Guthrie ordered steak fries and a pitcher of draft. The dark-haired waitress brought two mugs. Vasquez grinned, and Guthrie shrugged. They weren't leaving for a while. Slow conversations and the occasional clink of silverware washed over them.

Vasquez watched him eat potatoes for a minute, then asked, "You think he did it? And don't say it don't matter."

He grunted. "He's a soldier—that's a tough read." He shrugged at her surprised look. "He's carrying the stamp of it. But I say no, or at least he didn't plan it. He talked about their relationship like it still is, not was. He wasn't rattled by the pictures, and he remembered what went on at the interview. He's been in some hot spots before. To me, that says clean on the rest of it."

"You cover your ass like a council candidate," she said.

"Nobody wants to be wrong."

"But everyone wants to get paid," Vasquez said. She poured herself a beer. "So what am I missing?"

"Nothing. You caught me there, so here's a real answer. He didn't do it. I don't know *how* he didn't do it, but he didn't do it. Is that better?" Guthrie grinned.

"No, because I still don't know why," she said.

"Well, this's what we can do—we trade," the little detective said. "You tell me what was wrong with Olsen, and I'll tell you why he didn't do it."

She laughed. Guthrie eased the plate of fries toward her, then glanced at the beer she was drinking. She waved the food away. "*Viejo*, there is *nothing* wrong with Olsen. That's the best-looking man I've ever seen in my life—maybe not enough to kill for, but I can see why the muchacha is hot to prove him innocent. *Wrong* with him? Are you crazy?"

"Then you didn't notice he was crippled?"

She ate some steak fries. He let her wait for a while before he let her off the hook. "Olsen's left arm is crippled," he said. "He never used it, not even once. He's been practicing that for a long time. Maybe it's disfigured, or maybe it's dysfunctional. That's something he brought back from overseas, I reckon."

Vasquez put it together suddenly, why she'd been looking at point-less surveillance videos. She'd been practicing looking for things that she wasn't looking for. The little detective was willing to waste her time, and his money, seeing if she would learn something that she didn't even know he was teaching. She was glad Mako's was dark; maybe he wouldn't be able to see the look on her face. Three months, and it wasn't the first time she'd wished she was back in school, where everything was safe and expectations were carefully spelled out. She realized that Guthrie was waiting on her again.

"So he got wounded in the war," she said thickly. "He was a soldier." She paused. "He took it hard that somebody hit her. Maybe he's got some kind of history with that."

"Sure," Guthrie said. "And you're saying you believe he's clean."

"I better believe it," she muttered.

The little man laughed. "You like him."

Vasquez shrugged. "You said you know why he didn't do it."

He scanned the thickening crowd and frowned at the door. "I could be wrong." They were waiting on someone, and the wait was stretching. "Anyway, he didn't try to blame anyone. He's been sitting in a cell for hours, knowing the police say he did it. If he shot her, he would have spent that time thinking up a lie. For him, she was Little Miss Perfect. Nobody could want to kill her—and that's that."

A stream of people slowly filled the bar. Guthrie kept scanning the crowd. At the bar, men shouted indiscriminately at the televisions and one another in an incoherent roar that even music wouldn't have covered. Three waitresses rushed back and forth with pitchers and platters. Two men emerged from the crowd, snooping among the booths, and Guthrie relaxed. One was older, with a full belly and a haphazard stride, as if he couldn't decide which part of a sore foot to settle his weight on. Maybe he had walked too far in bad shoes. His hair was ginger and gray; his wire-frame glasses were taped together. An angry younger man trailed him, tall and imposing, with a Dodgers cap set square on his head like a battle flag. The older man spotted Guthrie in the booth and lumbered back to sit down.

"Evening, Guthrie," he said. He gave Vasquez a puzzled glance. "Where's Wietz?"

"She moved on," the little detective answered. "This's Rachel Vasquez." He shrugged, then waved at one of the waitresses, pointing at the pitcher. "This's Mike Inglewood. He—"

"Don't listen to him, little girl," Inglewood said. He pushed his glasses back up his nose. "I known this one since I was in MTS. He's no good. He'll lie to you every time."

The younger man sat down and scowled generally at the table. Inglewood raised an eyebrow at him. "I told you she was pretty, and this ain't even the one I was talking about. But you gotta do better than that—" He turned back to Guthrie. "I told the boy to grow a mustache, and maybe it'd do something to cover that ugly-ass smile."

The waitress brought a fresh pitcher and some more fries. Inglewood broke a few more rough jokes to settle himself. His partner, Eric Landry, was new to Major Case, the downtown squad of detectives that worked high-profile crimes in the city. Guthrie and Inglewood had known each other for several years. He and his partner weren't working the Bowman murder directly, but the older detective collected squad room gossip like a bathroom drain. A bit of everything stuck on him on its way down.

Inglewood knew Guthrie had called him wanting information. His trade-off was a pitcher and a burger, and finding out why a private D was interested. He quieted when the little man told him he was hired, not curious. He tore up fries and a burger while Landry sipped a beer and tried to avoid looking at Vasquez. Inglewood's shrewdness showed in how he listened without interrupting, and left off the banter when the conversation turned serious.

"So you don't mind if I give a heads-up to Barber?" Inglewood asked. "He caught the squeal, or got it pushed in his lap on account of being prettier than anybody but Landry here. Then he's our new prima donna, with gold in record time, and like that. So?"

"I don't see that it'll hurt," the little old man said. "I signed in and out of the Tombs today. He's such a good D, he might catch on to that anyway."

Inglewood grinned and pushed his glasses up his nose. He finished his mug and clapped it down on the tabletop like a punctuation mark. "You trust your new girl, Guthrie?" He studied Vasquez.

"I think that's a compliment—he can see you," Guthrie said. "But yeah, I trust her. She's a straight shot. She hangs in there."

"Just like Wietz," he said, and chuckled. "You remember the time she got hauled in for bombing that pimp on Lexington with her cannon? That's a mean woman." He stared at Vasquez again, his face serious. "All right. This gets out, the rest of your short life is a nightmare. Got it?"

"Sí, for sure," she said.

The detective nodded. "Listen, Guthrie. You've talked to your guy. I ain't. I don't know what else is going on here. Maybe you do. I do got this much, in this particular case. Your pretty boy had a pretty girl. She was shot with a forty-four. What d'you know, pretty boy owns a forty-four.

"Barber, my prima donna, talks his way into a warrant, and goes and gets pretty boy's forty-four. The pistol is right where he says he keeps it, locked away safe and sound. The pistol smells like fresh powder. Barber carries it downtown and IRD runs a bullet.

"Guthrie, you know it's the gun, the same damn forty-four, under your pretty boy's lock and key. So you talked to him, and he don't sound guilty. Maybe he's got two, three more personalities, and one's the good talker you spent time with. Maybe one of the other ones is GI Ken. Get it? See, Ken and *Barbie*, and this guy is some military guy. GI Ken, I just made that up. . . . You don't like the ring it's got? Don't matter. This is him"—the ginger-haired detective's hand floated above the table, then dropped suddenly—"going down hard."

Guthrie drove on the ride back to the office. Inglewood's information was a challenge. The little detective trusted his judgment of Olsen, but that wouldn't be enough to convince the NYPD. The switch caught Vasquez off guard. Guthrie was always relaxed. Even when they had scuffled with the Italians in SoHo over the camera, he didn't flare up. Now an edge of determination and purpose showed.

Once they were back in the office, with the building as quiet as a grave around them, Guthrie opened a bag of dirty tricks he had kept hidden. Vasquez thought it was fitting that they were doing it after hours. He had brand-new laptops and phones—not expensive, but good enough for digging. He turned the phones on with names from a Hemingway novel. Then he brought out electronic keys that opened database doors in some unlikely places. He called friends and set up appointments for the next day. She dredged in computer files. After he finished with the phone, he joined her.

Guthrie wanted background. His process resembled picking apart a résumé and looking for what had been deliberately omitted. This time, though, they had to supply everything. They had only names. The real information had to be pulled from the air with only a few starting points. In a few short hours, Vasquez saw a dirtier side of what he did.

"Some of this shit ain't legal, is it?" she asked while she scrolled through a list of ATM withdrawals.

The little man shrugged. "It's fast. I want to know where they were at, when, all that. Copy anything with one of the names on it. That dumps to a disc and holds in a file. That file gets searched for what leads elsewhere, like SSNs."

While they gathered data, they quietly announced back and forth when they found something. Guthrie was beginning at the beginning. The victim was Camille Bowman. The suspect in her murder was Greg Olsen. Michelle Tompkins was the only other person they knew with a possible motive. All three attended Columbia University. That was the beginning.

Bowman was simplest, partly because she was the youngest. Young people haven't had years to leave fingerprints on the world around them. She'd been a sophomore without a declared major, had gotten mediocre grades, and came from a society background. The world mostly noticed her after she was dead, and then she provided a sensational arc of pictures and thoroughly chewed information. Death was her moment in the spotlight, as if twenty years was the exact time required to groom her to be a victim.

Tompkins was older—easier—and in a social register far higher. *Who's Who* listed her birth. Her grades at Columbia were impressive, even as a graduate student. She had studied overseas. Both of the young women had unblemished records, but Guthrie was quick to point out that no amount of superficial scanning would reveal anything that had been deliberately hidden. Some things became obvious only after thinking and back-checking.

Greg Olsen was the mutt of the group, only partly from being the eldest. The slow voice came from Wisconsin, and his military service was long and distinguished. He was discharged as a lieutenant colonel, then resumed his interrupted education. Guthrie was puzzled by the rank, because Olsen was only twenty-eight. The big man had played hockey for the Wisconsin Badgers, and Uncle Sam was paying his way at Columbia.

Until the murder, and then the arrest, all three had led ordinary lives. They did the things everyone else did—bought CDs and books, had traffic tickets, and went unnoticed by the people around them. Bowman and Olsen had the distinction of having faces that caught attention. Tompkins was invisible, protected by a machine that would keep her overlooked forever, if that was what she wanted. The night had grown old and died into morning before Guthrie was satisfied and called a stop.

By then, Vasquez was sober and frustrated. "What's this going to do for us?" she demanded.

"Maybe nothing. But suppose I wanted to ask one of Olsen's old girlfriends if he's a jealous type. How do I find her?"

She drummed a pencil on the desktop for a moment. "We go to Wisconsin?"

"That's right. Or we could make some calls, or I could hire someone out there. But eventually we knock on a door, ask a question, and decide if we believe what we hear. But anyway, how do you know about Wisconsin?"

"Okay, you win that one," she said. "It's quitting time?"

"Not yet. Now we take a little ride. I think it's finally late enough."

"Late enough? We going to work all night?"

Guthrie grunted. Sometimes, late nights or all nights were part of the job. "You're driving. We're going to Washington Heights."

Once they reached Highbridge Park, the night seemed eerily quiet. The Harlem River was hard by them, lapping away slowly. Vasquez needed two passes to find the scene, hidden behind a hairpin turn around a hurricane fence that was a magnet for trash. The old Ford's headlights lit up some strands of crime-scene tape, waving idly where they had been broken, but still long and bright. Guthrie had her douse the lights before they climbed out, and then they stood for a minute, allowing their eyes to adjust to the gloom. Bowman had been murdered in a quiet, dark corner of the city.

The river added a tangy smell to the garbage. Cars buzzed and whirred distantly on the bridge. In the darkness, the lined columns could have been the arched nave of a church, with the insects quietly whispering prayers. Fragments of tape formed a communion rail around the altar of a green Dumpster. Graffiti made a resplendent iconostasis along the columns and abutment. Guthrie used a small flashlight. They searched the ground around the Dumpster. Amid the broken glass and litter, a few evidence flags remained pinned around a dark stain in the thirsty dust.

"See anything else?" Guthrie asked.

Vasquez shook her head. She kicked a bottle.

A laugh floated from the darkness. "Expecting a party?" The voice sounded half-cracked and drunk.

"In this part of the city, a wake, at least," Guthrie called back.

"Them tight-ass micks don't drink to the dead no more."

Quiet followed. A bottle gurgled faintly.

"You're out here a lot, aren't you?" the little man called. Some gravel rattled. "You ain't no cop."

"No."

"Didn't think so. Cops ain't got pretty girls for partners."

"You got a face out there?" Vasquez demanded.

"What? For you to punch? Too drunk for that." More laughter.

Guthrie kicked slowly through a pile of trash while Vasquez muttered threats.

"So? You want to know about the little girl? That's it?"

"You know something?" Guthrie called.

More laughter, and then the thud of an empty bottle. "She had a wad in her pocket. I been drunk all week."

Guthrie's face tightened; he waved at Vasquez to stay out of it. "You came on it after, or were you near when it went down?"

"This my spot, little man." For a minute, silence threatened. Then gravel sounded from another direction. "He came in here slow. I felt he was creeping ill, so I dee-deed. I look back, he's already playing with the girl. He's posing her for the fashion show. I didn't know he had the pistol, then, *bang!*" Stones rattled, and something heavy slid in gravel. "*Bang!* Not little firecrackers, something heavy!" Footsteps followed after cracked laughter. "He looked around, after. That kinda spooked me, like he could see or something."

"What he looked like?" Vasquez demanded.

"Looked like?" Laughter was punctuated by gasps and rattling gravel. The voice was farther away. "I ain't no wit-ness!"

"We gotta get him!" Vasquez hissed.

Guthrie shook his head. "Relax, will you? Don't chase squirrels. Squirrels come back for nuts." The little man strolled back to the car. Vasquez hesitated a moment, then followed.

CHAPTER THREE

Early the next morning, Guthrie picked Vasquez up in front of her parents' tenement apartment on Henry Street. The traffic on the Lower East Side was as thick as cool syrup on the streets and on the sidewalks as the workingmen walked to catch their trains. The tenements emerged from darkness as shades of gray, sparkling slowly in the sunshine. On the way downtown, the detectives drank coffee, and Vasquez finished waking. She aimed a few scowls at the little man while she searched for the bottom of her cup.

"*Viejo*, that was crazy to let the drunk get away," she said.

"Maybe," he replied. "But I need some convincing about him." He parked in the shadow of the Brooklyn Bridge, a few blocks from Police Plaza. "We heard enough details to check his story against the newspapers, and we could save getting excited by finding out first if the NYPD talked to him. Right? That works out, we'll talk to him again."

Vasquez grunted; the little detective had good reasons, but reasons wouldn't catch a drunk. The Lower East sheltered plenty of drunks and crackheads. She knew enough of them. They could get low and dodge cops better than anybody but a priest. The detectives locked the old Ford and walked, pausing to wait on the south side of the plaza.

Downtown Manhattan filled with people while they waited. Trains and taxis poured forth rushing torrents of busy professionals. Women held purses clamped beneath their arms and phones to their ears. Men uniformed in dark suits and wing tips wielded briefcases and folios like shields. Offices and cubicles awaited them, each with an appointed place at the end of the scramble of rush hour.

The detectives waited, as invisible as lampposts, while the rush slowed to a trickle. A tall young man wearing a dark blue NYPD jogging suit leaped from a taxi on the south side of Police Plaza. He rushed the entrance like a linebacker chasing a ball carrier, but stopped suddenly when he saw Guthrie.

"Yo, Guth! I should've known you'd wait here. You need a pass—" He gawked at Vasquez, pulling off wraparound sunglasses. "Geez! How old are you? Twelve?"

The young Puerto Rican laughed, looking up. He towered over her, but he still didn't have a beard.

"Tommy, I know you're a blond, but seriously," Guthrie said. "She's Rachel Vasquez, and she's, like, fourteen at least. Ask her if she wants to go roller-skating, why don't you?"

"All right! Don't get upset, Guth, come on."

"This's Tommy Johnson," the little detective said. "I changed a few of his diapers when he wasn't so big—his folks are from Ohio. Now he's some hotshot engineer who plays with the chemistry sets they keep in there."

"I'm just a tech," he said with a shrug. "Guthrie kind of helped me find a job while I'm finishing school."

The young man secured passes, then ushered them through the glowing marble lobby. The elevators opened into a different atmosphere—less impressive but more human, without any feel of their being watched. Glass walls in the work spaces allowed an illusion of depth, but the sight lines were cut by moving people, banks of tables and machinery, freezers, racks, and darkened spaces. The ISU processed evidence for the NYPD. Almost all of the investigative threads in the city passed through the ISU lab.

Tommy Johnson's boss was Beth Whitcomb, a first-grade in her mid-forties. Locks of dark hair peeked from behind her ears, escaping from her paper cap. She sighed impatiently when she saw the young man and his visitors.

"You're who wants a walk-through on Bowman?" she asked.

"Yes, ma'am," Guthrie replied. "The papers haven't had much, and now that you have a perp—"

"About a perp, I'd say maybe," Whitcomb interjected. "Anyway, we're off the record *and* we're not talking about a perp, only a crime. Only *this* crime. What we do is about the crime, not the suspects. Right, Tommy?"

"Yes, ma'am," the young man intoned dully.

She smiled. "Good. Now you're having all the fun I'm having, and that makes us even." She waved them all into her office. Tommy closed the door. Beyond the glass on the other side, a long table held a bank of microscopes. Two techs worked repetitively at sample cases. Faint chemical odors and ozone mixed, giving her office a spicy smell.

"We have a bullet and we have a gun," Whitcomb said. "That's the end result, but not the order they came to us." She opened a laptop on her cluttered desk. "Here's my time line. On the twenty-fourth, we receive a body, petite Caucasian female, blond/blue, a well-kept Jane Doe—probably not a runaway. Her face is marked up with undarkened contusions. Nice clothes but no other personal effects. Two bullet wounds. One wound is ragged. The other is entry only. We work the body up as a homicide. At the scene, we find a small amount of blood. The body may've been dumped."

Vasquez scowled at Guthrie, thinking, the drunk vagrant is three for three already.

"Something to share with the class?" Whitcomb asked. "No?

Okay, on the twenty-fifth we have a provisional ID. Our Jane Doe may be Camille Bowman, a missing Columbia student. We confirm by one P.M. and move on to the ballistics. One bullet is battered; it entered the body and passed through, struck the ground, bounced, and reentered the body. That sequence explains the wound channel and the condition of the bullet. Trace from the scene entered the wound channel—she was shot in situ. Minor blood pooling under the body indicates the bullet was fired from *above* the prone body. That particular bullet pierced the heart twice, but it still wasn't the fatal shot. The first shot killed her, and prevented bleeding. That bullet entered at the base of the neck on a plunging trajectory. The wound channel stopped at the diaphragm. We recovered a pristine bullet. Two bullets—one smashed and one clean, both forty-four caliber. This was a small woman. The forty-four was massive over-kill. Her blood alcohol was point oh-two. No other chemicals."

"What about the beating?" Guthrie asked.

"Some argument about that, but no disagreement that it was only a few blows shortly before TOD. Slapping or punching, no indication of a weapon. The contusions are too diffuse for a weapon—no edges or lines. This happened ten or twenty minutes before TOD." She drew a long breath. "Negatives—no ligature marks, so she was never restrained. No sexual assault apparent. The only thing disturbed was her pockets—could be a robbery motive, that being speculation, but it was evident that something was removed from her possession."

Whitcomb sighed and tapped keys on her laptop. "So, a few days, no significant trace, but we have a bullet. Early on the thirtieth, we receive a gun by warrant, a forty-four Smith & Wesson Chief's Special five-shot, recently fired. We trace ballistics. The weapon is a perfect match for our clean bullet. We have the gun that fired the bullet—" She studied Vasquez. "You need some water? You look like you're choking."

The vagrant witness was four for four; the pistol was tiny. Vasquez knew because she carried the same pistol in .40 caliber. Guthrie glared at her, but it was too late.

"What the hell is going on?" Whitcomb demanded. "This is some sort of circus? Tommy?"

"Guth, what the hell?" the young man asked.

"Some people will be looking at this," Guthrie said. "You already knew that when you pushed the first ballistics test up the list, right?"

Whitcomb slid Tommy Johnson a sharp glance. "I guess we're done here," she said. "Walk them out, Tommy; then come back up here."

The elevator ride down was silent. Several times, Guthrie or Tommy Johnson started to speak but subsided before words broke out. Vasquez studied their reflections in the brushed stainless-steel elevator door. The two men were made from the same mold; even the way they held their heads when they brooded was similar. Vasquez kept quiet because she knew she'd screwed up. She had been excited. The NYPD didn't need to know they had something to work from, because they weren't on the same team. While the elevator was sinking, she realized the only worse thing she could've done was blurt out anything about the witness.

Outside, the morning was already warm. Traffic poured around Police Plaza. Guthrie and Tommy Johnson shook hands. "Don't mind her," the young man said. "She acts like my boss sometimes." He glanced at Vasquez. "Maybe I'll see you around, but it'll probably be hot around here for a while."

"Maybe," she said.

Vasquez hurried after Guthrie before Tommy Johnson went inside. The little detective was marching fast toward Barclay Street, where he'd parked his old Ford. She brushed past a string of messengers to catch him. "I'm sorry," she said. "I wasn't thinking."

Guthrie shook his head. "That was on me, Rachel. I knew I might be putting him in a spot, having already talked with Inglewood, see? I just wanted more time. I wanted to get away with it. Now I gotta try to get in front of this mess with somebody else I know downtown." He kept hurrying. The sidewalk crowds had a monotonous sameness. At the car, he tossed her the keys, then made a phone call.

They went down to the Battery and waited for the lunch hour in a shallow-lot fry shack called Tony's Fillets. Guthrie gave the waitress a sawbuck for holding up a booth. They watched ferries plow across the harbor, and scanned the news clippings on the Net to see if the vagrant might have picked up his details from someone else. Tony's filled up with a lunch crowd, and Guthrie ordered three platters and an extra lemonade, no ice.

Before the fish could cool, a dark-haired woman appeared suddenly at their table. She paused to study Vasquez, then gave a dismissive shake of her head before she sat down. Her hair was cut bluntly across her forehead, and she slipped off dark glasses, revealing blue eyes. She was pale and thickly built, while still having a waist she could show off with a slender belt. Her dark pantsuit proclaimed office drone, but her smile when she looked at Guthrie said hungry shark. "Hello, Clay," she said.

"Sorry about the rush," he said. "Monica, this's Rachel Vasquez, my new operative." He pushed a platter of fish across to her, and the glass of lemonade.

Monica shrugged, glancing again at Vasquez. She ate with neat, quick bites while Guthrie watched her. They laughed back and forth, not saying anything. Vasquez studied news clippings on her palmtop and ignored them almost as well as they ignored her. When she was done eating, Monica handed Guthrie a disc and ran her gleaming fingernails down his arm.

"All right already," he said. "What's on it?"

"Just the files on Bowman," she replied. "The rest of that stuff is radioactive." She smiled. "Actually, I rubbed my trail off on the captain of the one-nine—he's a shit—but it was still too risky to try for the other stuff."

Guthrie grunted.

"Don't be like that, Clay," she said, then paused. "You think they have the wrong man?"

"That's what I get paid for," he said.

Monica stood up and slid on her dark glasses. The little detective smiled. "You like that, huh?" she asked.

"As much as you like fish."

"Meow," she said before gliding out.

Guthrie tucked the disc into his pocket. "NYPD has something big going on," he said. "Monica's on the inside. She usually gets everything. I know they're looking at Olsen for the Barbie dolls—that just makes sense—but without some details to examine, we're gonna end up focusing on the Bowman murder."

"How's that a problem?" Vasquez asked.

"Maybe it ain't," Guthrie replied as he chased some catsup around his plate with a french fry. "I reckon it'll keep me honest."

After lunch, Guthrie called for an appointment with Olsen's lawyer, James Rondell. The law firm had Wall Street offices, tucked among other elderly buildings holding aristocratic chins high beneath the shadows of the downtown skyscrapers. Reed, Whitaker & Down had a street entrance, with a lobby cut from marble polished to a mirror sheen. Thick walls produced an awesome quiet. The city seemed miles away.

Rondell's office featured a window looking directly down onto Wall Street. Even without a partnership, he had arrived. Leather chairs, old wood, and molded plasterwork made the office smell like a gun club. Books marched along the walls, but the desk was bare of paper. The lawyer was an electronic worker. A desktop computer shared the blotter with an open laptop. James Rondell was neat and dark-haired, about midway into his thirties. He had a cleft chin and square jaw, unremarkable features, and a lean build wrapped in a charcoal suit.

Without preamble, he said, "George Livingston recommended you." He struck quickly at the keyboard of his laptop. "I have to admit I have some qualms about using an outsider, but Henry Dallen is mostly good for watching old apartments and driving people back and forth. I need a sharp knife for this one." He frowned at Vasquez.

Guthrie sat down and gestured for her to join him. The lawyer wasn't going to waste breath on an invitation.

"You spoke with Olsen," Rondell said. "Did he give you an angle?"

"He's stunned, Mr. Rondell," Guthrie said. "He might not be any use until after he settles down. Right now, though, I'm looking for an eyewitness it seems the NYPD missed on canvass."

The lawyer's attention focused on him. "You're kidding?"

"Not so fast," Guthrie said. "I had part of an interview before he spooked. That was enough to establish his bona fides—the number of shots, small heavy-caliber pistol, and he robbed the body—but he bolted without describing the shooter. The witness is a vagrant—street type. I have to run him down."

The lawyer eased back in his chair. "So how long will you need to find him?"

Guthrie shrugged. The lawyer was disappointed, but a glance out the window seemed to encourage him. Like anyone else, he wanted things to be easy, but it didn't get to him. He could look *down* on Wall Street. Rondell typed on his computer for a minute, nodded, and announced that a witness might not matter. For the moment, Olsen was charged only with Camille Bowman's murder, but the media had their hearts set on an alignment with the other murders. If Olsen lacked alibis, he would probably be charged. Even without more charges, Rondell thought Olsen's best chance at the moment was to angle for a deal. The lawyer didn't see a bright outcome for Olsen on a plea of not guilty. If an eyewitness changed matters on the Bowman murder, they would still need to deal with the others afterward.

Guthrie asked for details on Olsen's alibi, despite the fact that the NYPD had arrested him anyway. The lawyer tapped on his computer, then outlined his notes. Olsen was sitting with a drunk veteran named Philip Linney on the night of the murder. Linney was his alibi for several nights, but the NYPD tripped the vet up during an interview. The cell phones showed calls spanning days before and after the murder, but Linney admitted he'd been stinking drunk a lot of the time. The alibi was good until the NYPD zeroed in on the .44, and then it sank.

"Maybe it's an angle," Guthrie said after jotting in his notebook.

"Along that same line, I want to see who gets Bowman's trust fund. That's motive, and maybe another suspect."

Rondell's mouth hardened into a grim line. "Camille was an only child," he said. "Without checking, I'll venture that her trust reverts to her parents, or someone higher up." His fingers rapped out something on his laptop keyboard while he spoke.

The lawyer fell silent, but Guthrie outwaited the younger man without betraying impatience. Rondell's annoyed glance didn't deter him.

"I'll put a number on it," Rondell said finally. "I'm afraid the Bowmans left the city after the funeral. Dealing with the police was quite enough for them." Unspoken, but implied by the lawyer's tone, was a suggestion that someone owned a piece of the street they were on—including the buildings and everything in them.

"I got reasons," Guthrie said.

"I'll make the calls. It'll be your business what you can do with it."

After they were downstairs and had passed from the tomblike quiet of the marble lobby back into the city's noise, Guthrie seemed to walk a bit taller. Some burden was gone. Around them, businesspeople rushed along on the sidewalk. Vasquez and the rumpled little detective didn't match the surroundings. If they'd been raindrops, they wouldn't have lasted long on Wall Street. They would've gone quickly to the darkness of the storm drains. Vasquez drove the old Ford back to the office.

They stopped working early that evening, and Guthrie drove Vasquez home. Henry Street was hot and crowded. Young people were in the street and on the sidewalks, listening to music that blared from parked cars, drinking, and throwing insults back and forth good-naturedly. The old people were on the fire escapes, and peeping from windows. Rachel's middle brothers, Indio and Miguel, called the old ones "sky boxers," like they were at Yankee Stadium, sitting above everyone and watching. The old people sat still, and the young people hustled back and forth below them in the street.

For Vasquez, that was the natural order of the universe, and so being still and quiet was the closest thing to being dead. Old people were still and quiet. That gave her trouble with the hours of watching, reading, and writing reports she did, working for Guthrie. Working on the new case made it seem not so pointless, suddenly, and Henry Street looked different. The young muchachos stared at her, like always, but didn't say anything like always. She was singled out for silence, and that was because of her brothers. They were loco; nobody messed with them.

Vasquez paused on the stoop to enjoy the heat for a minute before she went inside. Papì had already swept the steps. He liked to come out and sit when the afternoon was nearly over. Inside, Mamì was cooking and talking on the phone in a hushed stream of Spanish. Some music was playing in the big bedroom; that was Papì.

When she came inside, the phone conversation paused in mid-phrase. That was an unmistakable signal. For good or ill, Mamì was talking about her. She set her palmtop down in the living room, atop the overloaded coffee table, then went into the kitchen. Mamì signaled her furiously when she came into sight, indicating the phone.

"Roberto has some good news," she hissed, covering the mouthpiece with one small brown hand. "This is perfect, at just this time. You have to talk to him."

Vasquez's stomach churned. Her appetite disappeared, and she wished she was back at work. Even so, she took the phone. "*Sí?*" she said, unable to disguise her weariness.

"*¿Cómo estás*, Rachel?" Roberto asked. Her eldest brother always spoke Spanish to the family. Language was one of the few things he ever argued about with Papì.

"Ay, nothing. I just came home," she replied.

"From work?"

"Yes."

A pause stretched before snapping. Roberto was measuring his next sentence to see if it would come up short. He was the perfect one, Mamì's white boy. He could spit English like a professor, but not to the family. Probably he needed a reminder that he was Puerto Rican, because he looked so much like Papì. He had golden-brown hair and eyes flecked with green and gold, just like Papì, and he shined even next to Rachel, who was next lightest, a splash of coffee in a cup of cream.

"I know you still haven't signed up for school yet," he said, "but I know from a friend at Fordham that they could waive preregistration. You could still get in for the fall semester."

Vasquez turned so that she wouldn't be facing her mother. She didn't want to show how angry she was about needing to repeat what she had said since school ended. She was not going to college. The conversation had layers of stupid repetition, like an archaeological excavation. "I got a job, Roberto," she said. "I'm not sitting at home being bad, you know."

"I didn't say that," he insisted. "No one is saying that."

Insinuations don't count, Vasquez thought bitterly. Her family meant her to do what was expected, exactly the opposite of her other two brothers. Some jokes they made about that. Years before, they had dressed her up with a crown and called her "Princess," and she was fine with that until she realized the crown was a ratty old pair of rolled-up underwear.

"Fordham has a satellite campus right in the city," Roberto said. "You don't have to ride up to the Bronx. You don't even need to choose a major right away—mostly, freshman year is for mandatory courses."

Vasquez wanted to scream. She had been hearing all of this from Papì since the beginning. He'd pushed her to take the tests. That was where she should have said no. Once she got the scores that would earn her a scholarship, a golden ticket that she didn't want, her life started breaking apart under the jabs of insistence. "I have a *job!*" She darted a glance over her shoulder at Mamì, and repeated more softly, "I have a job."

"Forget medicine, okay?" Roberto said soothingly. "I wouldn't want to be a doctor, either. But that job, come on, Rachel, that's not a job. What are you doing, typing? You're wasting yourself. Being lazy is one thing, but hurting Mamì like this—"

"You don't hear what I'm saying, Roberto. You don't get it." Vasquez was furious; she wanted to say ugly things, but she was neatly trapped. Roberto could provoke her however he wanted, because Mamì couldn't hear him. She wasn't so lucky. Angrily, she fired a bullet she had saved from the beginning. "You don't even know what I'm getting paid, Roberto, for this job where maybe I do nothing."

"It's not worth your future," he said, but more weakly, because she had hit him solidly. He turned it around quickly. "So? How much? How much is your life worth?"

She shrugged, biting back insults. How good would it feel to ask him what his dignity was worth? "Twelve hundred a week," she said. "I'm not doing nothing, Roberto. It's serious stuff, even if I don't have it all figured out yet."

"Twelve hundred? You could get that in an *hour*, Rachel."

After twenty years of school, she thought, and laughed. "What hour you ever make twelve hundred, Roberto?"

"When did we start talking about me?" A barrio edge chilled his voice; the resemblance to Papì was uncanny. "What are you doing, then, that's so important? That's pushing you to the top of your profession? Typing? Polishing shoes?"

Vasquez flushed. "It's confidential," she said. She wasn't allowed to talk about the cases, especially now that they had a case to talk about. Guthrie had made sure to drive that point home while he was driving her home.

The mess at the ISU lab that morning was fresh in her mind. They had a client to think about. Part of the pay was for confidentiality, especially for this client.

"You're dropping down to lies now?" Roberto asked. "That's where you're at? A half-grown girl living at home, pretending she's doing something—"

Vasquez handed the phone to her mother. "Tell him to shut up, Mamì," she said. In her mother's dark eyes she could see doubts warring with doubts.

CHAPTER FOUR

A hazy sky covered Manhattan in the morning. Thick, humid air promised a scorching, sweaty day. Guthrie drove uptown after he picked up Vasquez. He passed Thirty-fourth Street while she was still drinking her coffee, and she decided that they must be going back to the crime scene.

"We gonna catch that drunk asleep?" she asked.

The little man shook his head. "Never try something like that until you're desperate, or you know your man real well. You spook a vagrant, he might go up to Boston, or down to Philly. You'll never see 'im again."

"He's an old drunk," Vasquez said.

"A drunk, sure, but his head ain't gone. He said something that made me think he was a vet, or been running around with vets."

"That guy sounded old, Guthrie. Too old for the war."

Guthrie laughed. "Iraq ain't the only war this country's ever fought. Ever heard of Vietnam?"

She frowned. "You're kidding. All those old guys are dead. Except for John McCain, and he's, like, a hundred."

"Not hardly." He pulled a disc from his pocket and dropped it on the console. "Load that behind the kill switch on your palmtop, okay? That could get you into trouble. It's the police reports."

The vagrant was a priority because he wasn't mentioned in the canvassing reports. Guthrie had spent hours combing the material. The NYPD had turned up one witness Guthrie did want to interview, but they'd missed the vagrant at the scene of the shooting. The investigation by Major Case had focused on Olsen almost immediately, because detectives usually follow the path of least resistance on a homicide. Murderers are usually obvious. Husband shoots wife or wife shoots husband, robbery, rape—these motives are obvious. Suspects leap into the net. Drug or gang shootings are tougher, because more suspects share the same motives. So the NYPD had no hesitation about Pin the Crime on the Fiancé. They had a registered gun with matching ballistics. The assistant DA would close the case by selling it to a jury. Mere suspicion to the contrary wouldn't derail a conviction. Guthrie and Vasquez needed something beyond solid, since they believed Olsen didn't murder Bowman. By the time they cruised into Washington Heights, Vasquez had glimpsed from Guthrie's explanations the enormity of the task before them.

The little detective parked his Ford in a gravel parking lot shaded by a long redbrick house. Dormers peered out at them from the high peaked roof. Below the eaves, it wore a sign that read: SALVATION SHELTER. On one side a hurricane fence edged the lot, clogged by isolated runners of ivy where the building's shade fell. The Harlem River was nearby, and the morning was still cool.

Some dirty, ragged kids tossed a bottle back and forth in one corner of the lot. Most of the windows above them were open, laundry flying out like flags to dry. The other loiterers in the lot wore a long-time-without-a-job look of scruffy and mismatched. They watched suspiciously as Guthrie and Vasquez climbed from the Ford. The kids poised for a long handful of moments before deciding they weren't cops. The nearby fence had well-worn marks of passage. The ritual of running was so practiced that it had scarred the landscape.

The ambitious people were already gone from the shelter, looking for work at day jobs or hooking cans. A man along the edge of the lot drifted toward them. He had dark, wavy hair, a pale and sunken chest, and icy blue eyes with a fanatic stare. He was clean-shaven, almost baby-faced. His intense gaze slid across Vasquez as if she wasn't even there. He slowed in front of Guthrie but didn't quite stop. His feet kept shuffling, turning him in an orbit that would have circled a manhole, if the manhole could slide along the ground at random every few seconds.

"Ain't seen you since before the summer started." The man's perfect teeth seemed wildly out of place. Looking at his ragged clothing and bent posture simply created an expectation of broken, dirty fangs.

"I been busy, Black-haired John," Guthrie said.

"We been hungry this summer."

The little detective looked skeptical. "You could've called."

"Maybe." Black-haired John kicked at the gravel crunching beneath him. "If we still had that phone you give us."

Guthrie folded his arms and frowned.

"I give it to Cindy! I don't know what she done with it. Probably throwed it at somebody."

"Figures," Guthrie said before pulling a cheap cell phone from his pocket and wrapping some fifty-dollar bills around it. "Here."

The drifter edged forward and took the package on a pass-by. He stared at it, then looked mistrustfully at Guthrie. "We ain't hungry right now."

"Buy ice cream for the kids, John."

He nodded slowly and examined the phone. "Press *one*?"

"Just like always." Guthrie shot a glance along the fence line, then continued: "I'm looking for somebody."

"I know 'im?" His gaze drifted aimlessly, like a cloud.

"You might. He's on the streets, drinks, maybe by the bridge down from the Polo Grounds. Where that girl was just killed."

"Seen plenty of dead girls. We all have. Young ones, old ones, pretty ones, yellow ones . . ." He paused for a moment, then reversed his orbit into counterclockwise circles. "Cindy! Come here!"

A slender young woman with dirty blond hair detached herself from the shady fence and walked over. Black-haired John handed her the money. "Maybe some ice cream?" he said.

The blonde smiled. She was pretty in a dreamy-eyed sort of way. She tucked the money into a pocket of her ragged jeans. "Sure, John. Soon as you ready." She eased away, pausing to scowl at Vasquez.

Black-haired John reverse-orbited. "Where did you say?"

"Down from the Polo Grounds—"

"Yeah, lots of lights a week ago. I remember. Screaming racket and whines near dawn."

"Okay, that's the place. Is someone over there?"

He nodded. "You're looking for Ghost Eddy. He ain't friendly."

"I don't want to run him off; I just want to know what he saw. No police."

"Huh."

Guthrie watched him orbit for a minute. The young blonde was surrounded by a cluster of kids. Some old people peered down at them from the upstairs windows of the shelter.

"He's an old solo, Ghost Eddy. Big white beard, stiff like hog bristles. He's a heavy man, but he's fast. Don't mess with him." Black-haired John wiped his mouth, then continued: "We'll look for him for you. You been good."

"All right. I'll come by in a day or so."

John nodded, but he was already moving away. The kids closed around him, trailing the young blonde. Guthrie gave Vasquez the keys to the Ford and climbed into the passenger seat. He pointed which way he wanted to go, and she went south on Amsterdam. The morning was still young.

The little detective had been working with the street families for years. He warned her that they could smell bullshit. Luckily, Black-haired John had given them a handle to work from; that would help when they asked around. The drifter would look, too. He had a big family among the hard-core faction, because he didn't abuse or use.

Cindy had John's back. She threw rocks, and could knock the cap from a bottle at a hundred feet. The kids had her back. On the north end of Manhattan, not much moved around without their seeing or finding out.

"They were strange," Vasquez said. "I thought they were crackheads."

"No, they just don't fit into the machine."

Vasquez drove down into Morningside as the morning stretched out. Soon, she felt like a pinball, because Guthrie kept chasing from corner to corner and pausing to peer down alleys and into lots. She crossed and recrossed Broadway and Amsterdam Avenue between 170th Street and the mid 140's. The little detective found the street people he knew would talk—and have something to talk about. Along the way, he broke fresh ground where he could. He handed out sodas, cigarettes, and small bills. The street people knew Ghost Eddy's name. He was a mean drunk, and drew careful watching. Even garbage gangsters that faked bravado backpedaled their feet while they talked about the big graybeard.

On the corner of 153rd and Eighth, they found Mother Mary, a fat old woman in a paisley dress. She made hex gestures over the drifter's name. No good would come of looking for him, she warned—or, worse, finding him. She gave Guthrie a pat on the head, picked up her bags, and hustled down the avenue. The little detective shrugged. He kicked around on the corner for a minute, as if she might come back, but she didn't.

Later, Guthrie gave a half carton of Camels to a skinny old man named Wheezy. The vagrant wore suspenders and short-legged blue jeans that showed off mismatched socks. His voice was a breathy rasp, almost completely covered by the noise of traffic. Ghost Eddy wouldn't catch easy, he said. A pair of patrol cops tried to take him in one time. The gray drifter waited until one of them had a grip, then suddenly used him to bludgeon the other cop. He trotted away while they were dazed. The skinny old man laughed and rubbed at his unshaven chin.

Guthrie left behind a trail of promises from people to keep an eye out, but the morning didn't seem encouraging. He pointed Vasquez to turn from Broadway a last time and park in a visitor's lot at Columbia University. The campus seemed cool and inviting after the hardscape in the Heights. The little detective began his search with campus security.

The campus cops in the administration building started an immediate whitewash when they heard the names Bowman and Olsen. After all, the killing didn't happen on campus. Guthrie went along with them without objecting that the victim and suspect were both students. The oldest campus cop held back, catching Guthrie's eye a few times while he pulled permission to examine Olsen's dorm room and took some visitor passes. The cop made grim faces when the rest of them joked about Olsen, then volunteered to show them the room in Livingston Hall.

"Mike Hines," he said, offering a handshake to Guthrie after they were outside. The campus cop was tall and a little overweight. A bushy gray mustache underlined a red nose that came from years of heavy drinking. He slid a hat onto his head and squinted at the sunshine.

"They went over the line, trying to make Greg Olsen seem obvious," he said. "We never had a complaint about him, though you could say he hadn't been here for long." He frowned.

"Is there some more to that story?" Guthrie asked.

"I don't figure him like that," Hines replied. "Come on, let's walk over. I'll get it lined up in my head."

Guthrie and Vasquez followed him. The campus was lightly populated. Most of the undergraduates avoided the summer session unless they needed to make up course work. Livingston Hall was quiet because of that. Over the summer, the students remaining were usually more serious. Hines paused once they were back inside the air conditioning.

"Olsen's a good man," he said. "I guess I got to explain that. Most of what we got here is kids. They don't know who they are or what they want. Olsen does. He's not a girl-chaser type, or a partyer. He was real focused on his studies."

"Yeah?" Guthrie asked. "Where do you get that?"

Hines shrugged. "We got a support group that runs out of the One hundred and Eighty-third Regiment of the Guard. That's where I talked to him the first time. I kinda realized he was a student, but he didn't know I worked here. He saw that later. But the group isn't for the school. It's vet stuff. The young wolves I work with, they're quick to pile on, even when they don't know what they're talking about."

"You figure him for that solid?"

"I ain't the only one. Ask around. I'll be seriously floored if he did kill that girl."

"What about her? You knew her?"

Hines shook his head. "Never noticed. Sorry."

The campus cop led them upstairs and opened Olsen's dorm room for them. After a glance around inside, he shrugged. The room was almost entirely bare. He explained that the NYPD had come and gone. The school administration hadn't decided what to do with the room, now that Olsen had been arrested, but they would probably pack his meager belongings and store them until they were claimed. He shrugged again and told Guthrie to lock the door once he'd nosed around.

Guthrie and Vasquez needed only a few minutes to search the small room. Olsen had a single because he was older. A few books, notebooks with classwork, some clothes, and a few toiletries were the only signs of habitation. Olsen traveled light, or he actually lived somewhere else. Vasquez dropped his notebooks back onto the desktop just before a big young man rushed to the door.

"Yes!" he said. "I missed you guys last time." He stopped suddenly and stared. He wore dark sunglasses, jeans, and a T-shirt. A shock of unruly black hair made him seem as tall as the door frame. His gaze fixed on Vasquez. "You're here about Holy, right?"

"You mean Greg Olsen?" Vasquez asked.

The young man grinned. "Yeah. You guys got that all wrong. No way he killed Cammie."

"He was with you that night?" Guthrie asked.

"No, man. I'm just saying he wasn't like that. I mean, other nights we clubbed—he was like my wingman."

Vasquez challenged him with a look. "Okay, so why'd you need a wingman?"

He smiled. "That wasn't the plan—it was just how it worked out, you know? Holy didn't run with the Greeks—frats—so he was like a godsend. Man, they hated him. They wanted him, and so they hated him. I was just lucky he liked me, you know?"

"How's that?" Guthrie prompted.

"The girls chased him." He looked at the little detective like he might be retarded. "That's why I started calling him Holy, because he didn't mess with them. And it rhymed with Oly, like Olsen."

"So the girls dropped off on you?" Vasquez asked. "You were good with second?"

He laughed. "This is college, Dick Tracy. It's all fun except for class. Anyway, he didn't kill Cammie, for real."

"That's what we're here for," Guthrie said. "Didn't catch your name, by the way. We work for Greg Olsen's lawyer."

"Whoa!" the young man said. He took off his sunglasses and looked at both of them again. "You're not cops?"

"No. We're working for his lawyer, James Rondell," Guthrie said. "That change your mind about talking to us?"

"No way! Maybe that's better, you know?" He frowned. "I'm Robert Deaton."

Guthrie handed him a card. "Maybe you got some foundation for saying Olsen didn't kill Camille Bowman?"

Deaton paused a moment, then stepped in and closed the door. "He didn't need to freak over her, because he had her. She was serious about him, right? She dumped all that Greek stuff for him, and she was like a serious princess."

"So he was a good guy, and like that?"

"Okay, I get it," Deaton said. "Just the facts, man. Right? Holy had one weird thing about his scene—the mouse." He took a long look at Vasquez, and continued: "See, you're not a mouse."

Guthrie shrugged. "Okay, I'll bite. What's a mouse?"

"A plain girl. Holy drew girls, you know? Some girls just know they ain't got a chance with some guys, you know? Too much competition. So they fade when the pretty ones show up. But Holy had a mouse." He frowned. "Or maybe it was Cammie. I don't know. The mouse was always running behind both of them, so I guess I really can't say who she was chasing."

"The mouse have a name?" Guthrie asked.

"Michelle something. She was a grad student, I think, because I never ran into her in classes."

"Maybe she was a friend?" Vasquez suggested.

"No way. After he hooked up with Cammie, Holy didn't use this room much. So I noticed when he did, you know? So when the two'd go in, cuddled up and making out, the mouse would tumble after. They were cramming, but not for a test. That wasn't like Holy, except for Cammie and this mouse."

"Maybe that's what you wanted to see?" Guthrie asked.

Deaton frowned and ran a hand over his unruly hair. "No way. This was just the one weird thing. Don't matter if he got something going—it's just how I saw it, you know?" He shrugged. "Anyway, what's going to happen to Holy?" He aimed the question at Guthrie.

"We're looking at it," Guthrie said. "Don't be shook up if the lawyers give you a call."

CHAPTER FIVE

The midday sunshine was blinding after the darkness of Livingston Hall. Guthrie was quiet, thinking to himself, while Vasquez had a quicker step. She wanted to move faster, but the little man kept pausing to rearrange his fedora on his head. She took their visitor IDs and ran them to administration to give him time to reach the car without making her wait. The detective was sitting in the passenger seat when she walked up to the Ford. She climbed in, watched him for a moment, and decided he was bothered about something. His expression was the same as on the elevator ride down from the ISU lab, after Tommy Johnson landed in the crosshairs.

"How often do you get something like this?" she asked quietly.

Guthrie didn't hesitate; he might've been waiting on her question. "You thinking about bailing?"

She laughed. "Are you kidding? This's what I took the job for."

"So you'll be thinking about bailing," Guthrie said gloomily. "If you're looking for murder cases, you want to be a cop. Because this ain't normal for a PI." He sighed. "Pick a place to eat, someplace we can sit for a while."

Vasquez started the Ford and pulled out. She drove past St. John's and turned onto 110th Street. The traffic was light. "You didn't answer my question, Guthrie," she said. "How often?"

The little man smiled. "You've learned some things in the past few days. I gotta give you that. Anyway, every few years something serious like this comes up. Sometimes back to back." He shrugged. "This isn't where the money is at, you know. It's just where the reputation is at. You make a mark on something like this and people don't forget it."

"But it's not where the money's at?"

"You gonna drive all the way to the East River?"

"Just down to the barrio, boss. I know a place where the burritos are so fat— What?"

"Nothing. I was just thinking about where we go after lunch. Maybe we should go over the river anyway, but it don't matter."

She nodded. "The money, follow the money."

"Most PIs do divorce, custody, insurance—that's steady money. You notice we do background checks, a little camera work, and sometimes just sitting and watching?"

She frowned, threw a sharp glance at him, and changed lanes to pass a truck dawdling on the inside lane. "Whitridge and his niece are the only two clients I've seen come through the door," she said.

"Exactly. I don't do nickel-and-dime work. Retainers and recommendations only."

"Whitridge has us on retainer?"

The detective nodded. Brownstones slid by outside the Ford's windows. Kids clustered on the street, waiting for cars to pass.

"So how is that?"

"People don't forget when you make a big mark," Guthrie said. "Once upon a time, I was in the right place at the right time—and did the right thing."

"So you were lucky?" She laughed.

"Sure. And I did it. These people know what I'll do, and they trust me to do that. It ain't hard for them to choose between me and calling a big agency where the operatives come and go."

Guthrie and Vasquez parked down the street from La Borin-queña, a café in Spanish Harlem. The grill had a sharp smell of meat rescued just before scorching, mixed with peppers and tomatoes. The booths had a scattering of customers, and four old men sur-rounded one table, playing dominoes. Soft music played on a box-top radio. Vasquez took one of the window tables and fended off some razzing from the old men before she ordered.

"Papí always brought me here," she said after the café settled back into rhythym. "These old guys all know me from when I can't remember. It looks just the same now as when we used to take the train down." Art Deco tables from the fifties looked old on the red-and-white tile floor. She smiled. "You know I got it figured out now, right?"

"What's that?"

"Why you hired me."

"Do tell," Guthrie said, picking a tortilla chip from the basket on the table, then testing it for crunch. He nodded approval.

"You wanted me for a distraction when you interview."

The detective laughed. "You saw that, huh? Little boys are so easy. And you did real good, challenging him—he wanted to con-vince you. You're learning." He paused to eat more chips, and let her enjoy her victory. "It's a good thing that ain't all there is to it, right? When I knocked on your door, I didn't know you were pretty. *That* was lucky."

"Ay!" she cried.

"Thought detective work was that easy, huh? Not a problem. You're a smart girl—you'll figure it out."

By the time they'd finished eating, Guthrie had decided that their next move would be to examine Olsen's alibi. The NYPD interview report had a Westchester address. The afternoon was flaming hot, a typical dog day afternoon in the city. Vasquez drove past the Triborough to take one of the little bridges across the Harlem instead. The neighborhoods were empty except for the kids, and mostly they were packed into slim slices of shade. Vasquez whistled when they pulled up on Linney's address. The front of the tenement was sprinkled with bleary-eyed men nursing lunch from bottles wrapped in brown paper. There were no children, and only a few women. Philip Linney lived in a flophouse.

The veteran's room was on the third floor. A patch of fresh plywood subflooring, not yet carpeted, was the only clean smell in the hallway. Men stared at them through open doorways. The little rooms had twin beds and tiny matching bedside dressers. In most rooms, the decor favored empty bottles, overflowing ashtrays, and crumpled fast-food wrappers. One old white man, with nose and ears almost as large together as the rest of his head, shuffled into the hallway in a bathrobe when they were passing and unceremoniously dumped his small wastebasket onto the hallway's floor. He grunted a sullen greeting before turning around. His tattered bathrobe nearly left his ass uncovered.

Philip Linney lived in room 318. He shouted at them to come inside when they knocked on his door. The slim, dark black man was sitting slumped on the twin bed, peering out the window. A faint mustache rode his upper lip, and his hair was wild. An overlarge T-shirt sagged around his torso. He clutched a bag of cookies with one hand, leaving the other free to move them to his mouth. In one unswept corner, a small fan with a wire-head basket labored slowly atop a milk crate, but the room was still hot and sour-smelling. Light reflected in from the window without brightening the room.

"You're the detectives from the lawyer, right?" he asked.

"That's right."

He studied Vasquez intently and then looked down into his bag of cookies. "You know the cops don't believe me," he said bitterly. "They got Captain locked up."

"I know. That's why we're here, Mr. Linney." The little detective looked around at the wrappers and containers in the room. The smell was sour, but not from alcohol. "You been drinking, Mr. Linney?"

"Hell no," he said softly. He ate a cookie. "Not in two days. I done stopped seeing shit."

"You were drinking before." Guthrie left it hanging in the air like a question.

"I know. Fucking dumbass, like a kid. My chance to take point for Captain, and I blow it." He scrubbed at his face with his sleeve. "Captain called from the jail. *He* keeps calling to check on *me*. He ain't done this shit, man. He was *here*. Trying to straighten me out. Moms got killed, and I started tripping." He scrubbed at his face again.

"So you're drying out?"

"Dried out. Just too damn late. Captain was talking me through." He ate a cookie. "Paid for these, even." He gestured at a stack of bags along the window side of the bed. "Juice and cookies, the Captain's prescription. Said nothing takes care of you like a cookie."

"The lawyer said the cops tripped you up on days," Guthrie said.

"On *days*," Linney said, "but that don't matter. It's nights that matter. He was here every night. That's when things get bad." He glanced at the window and shivered. The light seemed to reassure him. "I served under Captain for two years. They say Afghanistan's worse now, but that's bullshit. Just more people complaining makes it sound worse, because the bitching's coming from more mouths."

Guthrie turned a milk crate so he could sit on it. "Can I get some cookies, Mr. Linney?"

"Yeah, sure." He jogged at the bags. "You want chip or peanut butter? I ain't decided which juice I like best with each. I got lemonade, apple, and orange."

"Lemonade and chocolate chip," Guthrie said. When he stepped over to take the proffered snacks, Vasquez looked hard at a wall before settling into a lean against it. "So Olsen was here every night. What was the problem with the days?"

"I used to get loaded before sundown, okay? That was trying to get through the night. I couldn't remember which day Captain brought the cookies, so I picked one—and the receipt's in the bag. I'm wrong." He glanced at the window again. "But he was here every night. All night. That's a fact. Captain always finishes the mission. There were times I hated that. Even hated him, but I'm past that. Captain is the real thing." He watched Guthrie follow a cookie with lemonade.

"You know an AK makes a particular sound? I can pick it out on the street, when the stupid kids play games. It's got a heavier slug, too, sounds different when it hits. Splatters on rock like a fat raindrop." He laughed. "When I first went in-country, they posted me up north. Mostly Euros up there, in the coalition, right? They hate the sound of guns going off. I had a street attitude—I'm tough, this shit's nothing, all that—just like the kids outside. Now I know better. A drive-by? See, it all changed when I shipped south. Over there, they build units that don't exist over here. You can be detached this, brevet that, temporary duty, stop-lossed. Supposedly they had a system once upon a time, but that went out when they started hurting for infantry. Once you go south, you find out why.

"Once I was temporary to Alpha Strike, I broke in quick," he said. "Snipers down south are like flies—they'll drive a fucker crazy. Whole units have flipped out—massacres, called air strikes on ghosts, like that. The Pashies hate us. I mean, they hate everything, even the air they breathe, but right now Uncle Sam is at the top of the list."

"So I ship in to Alpha Strike. I'm a newbie; I'm pulling perimeter. The snipers come out at night. *Bang-splat, bang-splat.* That's an AK, then the bullet striking. An hour into the duty, I'm huddled down like I'm getting rained on. Two pairs of boots walk up. It's Captain and Slip. Slip don't say nothing, just like normal. Captain goes, 'So you don't know they can't hit you, then?' Big dumb bastard looks like a tree standing there, dripping that slow shit from his mouth. It takes him ten minutes to say anything.

"So he gets me up and starts pointing into the dark. 'Where is he, Linney? Show him to me.' I look. *Bang-splat.* Captain don't even flinch. I don't see a flash. 'He can't see you either, Linney. He's shooting the building, because he knows it's getting to you. They're out there taking turns, laughing.' *That's* the Captain. When he's standing there, you can feel your balls get bigger."

Linney stood up slowly, like it hurt him to change positions. Once he stretched out, he was a slim six feet tall. He crept to the window and squinted into the daylight. "Long time until nightfall," he said softly. He turned back around. "Are you doing something to help Captain, or is he fucked?"

"You're talking to him every day?" Guthrie asked. "And you're not keeping anything from him?"

His questions fell into the silence of the darkened room.

The vet went back to his bed and reached into his cookie bag. "You on some operational security shit, man. Go ahead, then," he said. "But you better remember Captain ain't done it."

The little detective stood up and turned the crate back onto its bottom. "Thanks for the cookies," he said. "Keep yourself together, Mr. Linney. Olsen might still need you. The shooting was after nightfall." He paused "Tell him to call me, will you?"

Linney nodded. "He better still need me. I give up drinking." He laughed.

Guthrie and Vasquez entered the city again. The flophouse was like something that needed to be rubbed away, a sheen of sweat that lingered, unwelcome. The darkness, stench, and ticking quiet was the opposite of the city. Guthrie's old blue Ford wasn't fast enough to outrun the memory. He brooded as Vasquez drove back to Morningside Heights.

Crossing the Harlem, she asked, "You think maybe Linney got it mixed up?"

Guthrie shrugged. "I knew a vet like him, before—bright, funny, when he was sober," he said. "'Big Tom,' that's what everybody called him. Before the war, he was a boxer. Silver, gold gloves—he looked good. After the war he ain't had no legs, but he still had a fist like a ham. The VA put him to work making prosthetic arms and legs.

"Big Tom kept extra legs. He had one he drank beer from, and another he made special, he said, just a bit longer, so he could kick somebody's ass from farther away. Tom drank a lot after the war. He would get so drunk as to lay in bed and shoot holes in the walls with a Colt. He always said he was shooting at cockroaches, but I guess he was shooting at the ghosts he saw at night." Guthrie fell quiet and started brooding again. He looked old, hiding under the brim of his brown fedora.

"So what happened to him?" Vasquez asked.

"He shot himself in the head in 1975."

The night before, Guthrie had read the NYPD reports, but only found one witness he wanted to interview. He considered the file to be surprisingly thin. The detectives had done little work before pegging Olsen. A passerby had found Camille Bowman's cell phone on the sidewalk outside the Long Morning After, a dance club on 124th Street. The detectives talked to the bartender, and the interview impressed the detective enough that he included it in the daily report. Incidental interviews didn't usually cross over to the reports.

They walked over, after parking on 123rd, and Guthrie took a look at the exterior of Long Morning After. The windows were blocked out with lemon and orange floral designs, thickly painted on the inside of the glass. The neighboring frontage was boarded, and past that, an alleyway pierced through from the street. Bass notes thrummed the windows like a badly timed blinker. Guthrie watched two young men go inside, noting a locked-in vestibule with a concessions window. The little detective studied the sign like it was missing something.

"Pretty sure this was a pub," he muttered. "Some Irish place."

Vasquez grinned. "Back in the day?"

"Maybe," Guthrie replied. "These kids are drifting this way to get off campus. Them two boys ain't looked twenty-one, but they went on in. Let's see how they treat you."

The young Puerto Rican pushed up the cuffs of her red windbreaker and opened the street door. The man at the window gave her an appraising look, then waved her through. Guthrie had to pay

a cover. He pushed into the darkened interior, where she was waiting, muttering about a pretty pass. House music stuttered from
hanging speakers. The Long Morning After was warming up, the
same way a bar spends its early hours slowly winding down. An old-
style pub bar lined the right-hand wall, looking out onto stools and
a narrow strip of dance floor. The wall connecting the streetfront to
its neighbor was stripped out to piers, for more dance floor, sandwiched on the far side and end by a line of shadowy booths. Cheap
paintwork and dim lighting covered the rawness of the reconstruction. Lights above the bar, reflecting from the mirror and glass-
work, provided most of the illumination.

The bar was empty of customers when they came inside. The
bartender was polishing the top and waiting. She seemed small behind the heavy bar. Her dark hair was cut short, and her lip and
brow winked with silver piercings. She scowled at Guthrie when he
approached the bar.

"You're who called my boss?" she barked, glancing briefly at
Vasquez.

"Sure, if you're Sand Whitten."

She shrugged, glancing at Vasquez again. "That's me. But I'm
not taking my break to talk to you," she said. "The party rooms is
up the stairs, unless you want a drink?" She pointed with her chin
at the back wall.

Vasquez paused to turn her Yankees cap around, then said, "I'm
with him."

"Damn, really?" the bartender asked. "You came in the door
separate." She kept buffing the bartop with her rag, and scowled
again. "I shoulda kept my mouth shut when the cops were in
here."

"So it don't bother you that girl was maybe snatched right outside here?" Vasquez asked, pressing against the bar.

"Should it? The guy's in jail, right? Or is the Barbie doll killer
gonna get me?" She smirked. "I don't think I match the fashion
show."

"Relax, will you?" Guthrie said. A pair of fifties appeared between his fingers. "Just tell us what you told them, then let us follow up, okay?"

"Neat trick," she said, and took the money. "Two house specials coming up." She smirked at something behind them; then her hands grew busy with bottles and glasses.

In the mirror behind the bar, Guthrie and Vasquez saw a trio of dancers—one girl with two boys. They all wore dark glasses. The girl had her blond hair waved and cut at her shoulders and wore a button-down shirt and plaid schoolgirl mini. She had a teddy bear in one hand, spanking one of the boys with it as if she had a riding crop while she rode his outstretched leg. He was synching inaudible lyrics that might or might not have matched the beat dropping from the speakers, while the other boy held a handful of the blonde's hair like a leash, tugging gently in time with the music and grinding his hip against her ass. All three seemed oblivious to the watchers. Both boys held clear bottles of water.

"Unbelievable," Vasquez said.

"Welcome to the market, girl," Sand said. "Go on out and roll with them—they'll give you some water. Or you like watching? Take a booth." She pointed with her chin at a few people sitting in the shadowy depths.

"We're not here for the floor show," Guthrie said.

Sand Whitten flashed a razor-sharp smile as she slid them two Shirley Temples. The smile made her look like a movie star. She told a simple story while they drank. Working at the Long Morning After, she was familiar with Bowman by face, not name. She discovered the name when the NYPD came with questions, and she put the glitter girl together with the picture and name in the newspaper. Bowman came in that night, butterflied from place to place, then left early. A dark-haired man trailed her around the club, trying to hook up, then was gone when she was. That evening, the city had a shower and cooled down. The weather kept her from mixing up that night with another.

"You remembered all that?" Vasquez asked. "After days?"

"Only because I wanted to kick her ass," Sand replied. "The man was cut from just the right cloth—short black hair, a glimmer of green behind long dark lashes, thick shoulders over a lean waist—you get the picture. I saw him first, and built up a picture. Then I saw what he was doing—chasing the little blond glitter girl, just like the rest."

"Did he get anywhere with her?" Guthrie asked.

The bartender shook her head. "Not dancing," she said. "He cornered her a few times for some mouth-to-ear, and she talked back, but she kept dusting him."

"You seen him again?"

"No! That's why he stood out. God don't make many copies of that model, then give them attitude to go with it. He had glitter-boy looks and boxer strut."

"What about her? She was in here a lot?"

"Yeah. She used to glitter all night, every night. The man wouldn't have gotten near enough to her to talk, back then. She was circled by a big crowd. Then she slowed down, and they fell away."

"You know the regulars with her?"

Sand Whitten smiled. "Glitter boys and glitter girls, they're bright. You always see them." Her eyes cut to Vasquez, and the smile sharpened for a moment. "That kind of bright keeps you from seeing the shadowy people standing nearby, unless you look hard."

Guthrie pointed at the mirror. More kids bounced on the dance floor behind them, grinding to a shifting beat. "She did like this?" He finished his Shirley Temple.

"Dance?" the bartender asked. "She used to. Not so much anymore. Or the booths, or the playrooms. Used to be all that *and* a bottle of water."

The little detective nodded, watching a girl in the mirror pause for a drink. The dancer was damp with sweat. That came along with ecstasy, just like a dry mouth. He slid another pair of fifties across the bar. He nodded to Vasquez, and they left. The city outside seemed quiet but blindingly bright.

CHAPTER SIX

On the morning of August 3, the stones of the city were crying out for rain. Night couldn't cool the city. A cloudless sky left Manhattan at the mercy of the sun. Even at dawn, the shaded pavement was eighty degrees. Guthrie idled his Ford on Henry Street, waiting for Vasquez to come down. Then they drove downtown to the Criminal Courts Building. Greg Olsen was scheduled for arraignment. The tall buildings downtown surrounded the courts like suppliants. Crowds of pedestrians moved among them faster than the cars.

Inside, Guthrie and Vasquez found Henry Dallen baby-sitting outside courtroom 11. Olsen was scheduled for Judge Patterson. Rondell was already at the court, juggling a meeting with clients for another case in civil court. The investigator said Olsen would be bound for supreme court, and Rondell expected a high bail that he might be able to reduce, eventually. They would play a waiting game while Guthrie chased his witness. Guthrie gave the investigator another copy of his card, for Olsen, with a scribbled note asking for him to get in touch. Guthrie and Vasquez had other things to do. Olsen had questions to answer, now that they'd seen the Long

Morning After, but it wasn't worth an entire day spent waiting for the ADA to orchestrate a media frenzy at his arraignment.

Vasquez was unsettled by visiting the courts. She always went when her brothers were in trouble; the sterile smell and tomblike quiet were a reminder. Dallen's nonchalant attitude resembled that of a public defender midwifing the state's efforts for conviction. Indio and Miguel always came out angry. They had to wait for a while before they rediscovered their laughter. She was glad to leave, even though the street smelled like burned tar and was crowded with empty taxis looking to hustle uptown fares.

While Vasquez drove up Broadway, headed for the office, Guthrie called George Livingston, HP Whitridge's hatchet man, to air his doubts about Olsen's lawyer. The conversation cut back and forth. Livingston had recommended Guthrie to the lawyer, and he had no hesitation about putting the shoe on the other foot. True enough, Livingston admitted, James Rondell worked in a firm specializing in tax, trust, merger, and other Money Street matters, but he was a big young shark, being groomed by heavy hitters at his firm to be their primary courtroom advocate, and eventual senior partner. His talent was unmatched in the city. HP Whitridge wouldn't accept less than the best.

"Okay, George, I get you," Guthrie admitted. "I could be wrong about him. Maybe I'm getting old and I need to see a bit of gray on a head before I can trust it."

"I am not going to rise to that particular bait," Livingston said, his voice audible on the cell phone.

"I went out and talked to some people yesterday, and now I need to compare notes. Where am I going to find Michelle Tompkins today?"

Laughter sounded on the other end. "That's your nice way of saying she needs to be available?" Livingston asked. "I'll do something about that and get back to you. HP has a thorn in his ass about her right now, you know."

"That's good," Guthrie said.

"You're working on something?" Livingston asked sharply after a pause.

Guthrie frowned. "Maybe this thing works out," he said.

"What's going on?"

"Now ain't time for details, George. I gotta firm it out."

"Okay, that's your thing."

After lunch, Vasquez and Guthrie drove to the Upper West Side. Michelle Tompkins had a walk-up apartment on 101st Street off Amsterdam. Old trees along the sidewalks grew from broad puddles of shade, pushed to the sides by a line of brilliant sunshine running down the street. The sun blew down hot breath in vain. In the landscape, the streets were skillet-hot, but between the park and the Hudson, different rules applied. Vasquez's red jacket glowed like a beacon among the gray and green as they walked over. A parking spot had been hard to find.

The building retained the solid look of prewar construction, even while the bones of modern infrastructure showed through. An unblinking camera peered discreetly onto the stoop from an ivy-wrapped perch, and doors with the feel of ancient wood seated neatly into aluminum casings veneered with molding. The pressure changed with an audible hiss when the outer door closed behind them. A gray-haired doorman waited in a foyer that doubled as a narrow lobby. He had the clipped certainty and hard eyes of a retired policeman. He studied Guthrie, but his eyes seemed to skip over Vasquez.

"Miss Tompkins is expecting you," he said, and glanced at the stairs.

Old dark wood on the stairs and in the hallway drank up the light from the fixtures and left the hallway dim. Guthrie knocked twice on the door before Michelle Tompkins answered. Bare toes showed beneath the hems of her faded blue jeans, but an oversized shirt covered her curves. Worn loose, her brown hair wasn't quite long enough to catch on her shoulders.

"I have a seminar at three o'clock," she said, still holding on to the edge of the opened door while the detectives waited in the hall.

"We ain't gonna need the whole afternoon," Guthrie said.

The apartment was small, and only its bareness saved it from being cluttered. One dark green couch and chair, along with a low table, were enough to fill the living room. A countertop served as a divider between this area and the kitchen, and three dark wooden doors were visible beyond. The far door was open, but only hinges and shadows were visible. A pair of tall, narrow windows lit the room.

"What was so important?" Tompkins asked as she followed them into the living room. She glanced at Vasquez as she passed her. She bent at the coffee table and closed a laptop with an impatient sigh.

"Greg Olsen is being arraigned today," Guthrie said, looking around the apartment again. A second look was quicker, because there was nothing to catch the eye.

"George Livingston mentioned that," she said. "Then he said you found something." She watched his eyes, then smiled. "It's better this way. Nothing to distract me when I'm studying. It's my safe house."

"Olsen's tied up in the system," Guthrie said, "and he's still in shock, or was when I spoke to him three days ago. I don't know if he can give me solid answers even if I could get to him. I've looked around a little bit, and I hope you can help me connect some information. He couldn't give me much background before, but I did get the impression that you're right: He didn't kill Bowman."

Michelle Tompkins's face relaxed while she listened to Guthrie. She lowered herself onto the arm of the couch and pulled a bare foot up so that she could rest it on her knee.

"So I begin at the beginning. *Someone* killed Bowman. Who? I can't work a random killing, so I need the background to fill in the motive."

She nodded. "What can I tell you?"

"Do you know how they met?"

"Classes. They're"—she frowned—"were prelaw." She stood and paced toward the window. "But they met in a weeder—Professor Wyatt, he's a major ax. They started with a tactical alliance, and then it grew from there."

Vasquez threw Guthrie a look that said, What's that? He shrugged, turning his fedora in his hands. "You lost me, Miss Tompkins," he said.

"Oh." She turned back from the window. "Sorry, too much school talk. Call me Michelle, will you? Anyway, Columbia is a traditional school. It's not a diploma mill. The early years are meant to be tough. They mean to push you out of school, and I guess it's better that way. Not at all like Harvard, which is under a national microscope, so some students get an automatic pass. Columbia is tough because it's not as famous. Crazy, right? But a weeder course weeds out weak students, and an ax is a tough professor—they cut out dead wood, students who struggle to make good grades. Some of them really put pressure on the bright students, since it's not all about being smart. Toughness, grace under pressure—the axes are looking for that. Wyatt went after both of them, and they stuck together against him."

"How long ago was that?"

"Last semester." She smiled, and her eyes brightened. "Cammie changed her plans after that. She wasn't prelaw then. She was retaking a mandatory she'd flunked last year, and admin—administration, the deans—was making Greg retake the mandatories because of the time he spent away from school. See, he transferred credits from the University of Wisconsin. That's a good school, but he lacked his senior credits *and* it was years ago that he went there. He wasn't even prelaw at UW. So she was chasing him, and she was way behind. She didn't do summer sessions, except that she was trying to catch up with him."

"She was more relaxed before she met Olsen?"

"Absolutely. Cammie didn't have anyplace to be anytime soon. Once she started with Greg, that's when she wanted to keep up."

"The difference in age wasn't a problem? He's a lot older—"

Tompkins rolled her eyes, and Guthrie's question slowed to a halt. "That's true, but it didn't hurt him. He spent some years in the army. That's how he was paying for Columbia. Being older just made him a man in the pool of boys. A few years didn't hurt him a bit."

"With Bowman, you mean?"

"Her, too." Tompkins grinned, then eased away from the window. "Let me get you something to drink. You like juice?" She padded barefoot into the kitchen.

One small table filled most of the space on the kitchen's tiled floor, penned between countertops. Above the sink, a small window looked out onto the street. The refrigerator and stove flanked it in a tiny triangle. With tall glasses of orange juice, they crowded around the small table, and their voices dropped to the whispers of conspirators.

"You knew them both pretty well," Guthrie said, and gave Tompkins a moment to assent. "Where were you on the evening of the twenty-third?"

She frowned, realizing he was asking about the night of Bowman's murder. She tucked a lock of hair behind her round, pale ear and bit her lip. "I was here. I had to give an oral on the twenty-fourth, so I was prepping."

"What about them? Do you know where they were?"

"I didn't keep track like that."

"I've heard different from other people, Michelle."

She reddened. "That's crazy."

"People wouldn't notice you if you weren't there," Guthrie said.

"Not that. You can't be saying I killed Cammie."

The little detective shrugged and finished his glass of orange juice. Vasquez covered her mouth and pretended indifference. Guthrie had warned her he would turn the interview after he let Tompkins talk for a while. As a suspect, Michelle Tompkins seemed unlikely, but he wouldn't walk around it without looking to see if odd numbers added up.

"Maybe," he said. "I can't see your connection yet. You got some interest here, or this doesn't get pushed in the first place. My imagination is free to supply motives." Guthrie jabbed at the tabletop with a finger. "They're law students, but you're international studies—nothing there. Undergrads, you're a grad student. You don't match up in age with either one of them. They're Hollywood pretty, you're a step or two above plain—"

"Oh, you are so full of it!" she exclaimed.

"Then what puts you together with them?"

"I had something they both wanted! I know the ropes at Columbia."

Guthrie frowned and dropped his hat onto the small tabletop. "I'll accept that for a why—but not a how. That's why you had something to do together, not how you came to find out about it. How always comes along in front of why. You meet someone before you discover what use they are to you—"

"Cammie's my cousin. She's from the other side, my *father's* side," she said. "She's not a Whitney, but she has the curse—a trust, legacy, expectations. . . ."

Guthrie settled back into his chair, frowning. "Okay, your cousin."

"My cousin. I didn't meet Greg until after she did."

The little detective nodded slowly. "I get it. Olsen wasn't in the picture until last semester. Maybe that was around the time Bowman slowed down at the Long Morning After. Did you used to spend time with her there?"

"That doesn't have anything to do with this," Tompkins said, reddening. "It's illegal to get drunk?"

"Not at your age, but it was at hers. And X don't come from a pharmacy anytime—but that ain't what I'm after here," Guthrie said. "Bowman was a regular at the Long Morning After. I don't need you to confirm that. I got that. She was snatched right outside that place. Maybe somebody you know, or saw, knew her from there." Watching her expression, he stopped. "No, that wasn't on the TV, was it? You didn't know that. *Something* got her killed, Michelle."

"They said she wasn't raped," Tompkins whispered.

He shrugged. "Maybe college boys are smart. Maybe they learn things while they're watching TV instead of going to class, like being satisfied with just making somebody dead. But back to you. When you went to the Long Morning After with her, did you roll with her, or did you watch from a booth? Did you go upstairs? Is that where she really met Olsen?"

"They call it LMA—just LMA. That's *not* where she met Greg," Tompkins said. "Greg didn't have anything to do with LMA. If—" She drew a deep breath and glanced around the small kitchen as if she wanted an exit.

Guthrie watched her struggle for a moment, then waved a hand to cut her efforts short.

"I don't mind a whitewash, but I still got a problem. Somebody took Bowman outside"—he paused—"LMA. That doesn't look like coincidence. You're looking at it from a seat inside that angle. Who do I look at there? Who wanted her?"

Tompkins laughed, then stopped quickly. "You're kidding, right? Everybody wanted Cammie. You've seen some pictures." She frowned and studied Guthrie for a moment, sparing a glance for Vasquez. The question was serious because Camille Bowman was dead.

"Nothing's going to make this easy," she said finally. "You'll be walking out into a minefield. This's Columbia University in New York City. We have the best, the brightest, and the most powerful. If LMA was involved, then maybe it was one of the Greeks. She was a sister, and LMA is a Greek hangout. Outsiders do go to the club, but the Greeks are deep there. She went outside with Greg—he wasn't a Greek. They were scared of him, though. They didn't try any of the usual games with him. After I got to know him, I knew they made the right decision, to leave him alone."

Tompkins smiled, looking at Vasquez. "It just sounds complicated. They wanted her back with them, and maybe they would've done anything to break them up. Sport fucking, gossip, whatever would work. Greg was too old for games, though. And whatever it was about him, bouncing into him made Cammie grow up in a hurry."

"Then the Greeks it is," Guthrie said. He gave Tompkins a searching look as he plucked his fedora from the table.

"Do it," she said. "Greg didn't kill her. I didn't kill her. But she's dead. Next to that, nothing else matters. But if a Greek did it . . ."

The little detective nodded. "Maybe it don't matter, but it can stay in the dark."

The afternoon was even hotter when they went back outside. The air conditioning in Tompkins's building was a spoiler. They had a long walk back to the car. Vasquez was quiet because she was thinking. Michelle Tompkins had shown her a glimpse of college, and it didn't seem so different from the barrio. The muchachos in the neighborhood played games with the *chicas*, clowned their rivals, and tried to tear people apart with drugs and intimidation. That wasn't new to her. Seeing the *blancos* doing the same things behind their closed doors, that was new. Papì had that part wrong. That part of the world wasn't different, or safe. Just like the muchachos crossed the line sometimes, and somebody got killed, that could happen anywhere, to anybody. Guthrie had an angry look on his face. He was going to find out who killed Camille Bowman. Vasquez could see that in the firmness of his step. She understood then why HP Whitridge paid the little man money to sit around and do nothing. He wanted him nearby if something important came up. Money didn't matter next to that. Just like reasons didn't matter when someone was dead.

CHAPTER SEVEN

That afternoon, Guthrie's office in the Garment District seemed like a different place to Vasquez. Trucks thundered by with late deliveries and outgoing products; that was the same. Traffic piled up in a screeching battle of horns and shouts when the kids pushed racks of clothes in the street; that was the same. Vasquez sat still while she worked; even that was the same. The difference was that she could see something coming from it. That was enough.

The little man ordered bad pizza, like he always did in the afternoon. He wanted mushroom and sausage—Vasquez could hear him on the phone—and the pizza would come with that and pineapple. She didn't know, but maybe it was some kind of joke. Guthrie ate it and never complained. Tranh, a Vietnamese with a big hat, always brought the pizza. Guthrie would pretend to speak Vietnamese to him and he would laugh and accept an oversized tip. The pizza box-tops were like a portfolio of old record albums in the storage room in the back.

That afternoon, Guthrie showed her how to read the police reports from his contact at Police Plaza. After he explained, the jargon wasn't difficult to understand, and she could see how different things related to reveal a method. NYPD went by a system. Guthrie pointed out that they had blind spots and weaknesses, but in what they did, they were thorough.

Uniformed officers had canvassed heavily along the Harlem River, near the scene of the murder. They had some "shots fired" reports from the night of July 23, but all those interrogated had been noted down as "busybodies." Guthrie wasn't too interested in those, except for practice, because none of them really agreed on two shots—they claimed from one to five, seemingly at random. He made Vasquez push pins into a wall map of the city to locate the site of each report. A few days later, the uniforms had canvassed again, but in Morningside, in the area around the Long Morning After. They'd found nothing worthwhile but the bartender, Sand Whitten.

Tommy Johnson called while Vasquez was finishing a hardened crust of mushroom and sausage pizza. Guthrie usually put his calls on speaker to keep from handling the phone. The little detective spent the first few minutes saying "Uh-huh" and letting the young man calm down. Tommy was getting kicked around in the ISU lab for bringing Guthrie inside. His next stop would be typist or errand boy, and he didn't know which of those looked better. He wanted to take a bus back to Ohio.

Finally he slowed, and Guthrie said, "Boy, it'll get back better. They can't keep you down. I mean, who else over there can actually take that chromatograph apart and put it back together—"

"I put it back together wrong!"

"Well, you didn't have any leftover parts, like I do when I rebuild a transmission—"

"Guth, they want to *kill* me!"

The little detective made shushing motions at Vasquez. She was using her Yankees cap to smother some laughter. He threw a wad of paper at her, because some of Tommy's distress was her fault, for overreacting during the interview, even though Guthrie had accepted the blame at the time.

"The only good thing that happened that morning was meeting that girl, Rachel," Tommy said. Vasquez's laughter came to a sudden halt. "Do you think she might've liked me?"

"Boy—"

"She has *blazing* eyes! Green and gold! Maybe it was the light," he added more softly.

Guthrie glared at the young Puerto Rican, plainly meaning her to keep quiet. "Maybe," he said. "Who knows? I tell you what, though. I'm going to give you something, and then you can spoon-feed it to your boss. You tell her right where it came from, and you tell her she's got to lay off—"

"I can't say that, Guth! She's not doing anything official."

"*Listen.* You can tell her that, and then you tell her there's more, but I'm not going to give it to you yet. She'll respect you if you give it to her straight, and she'll respect you for having contacts that reach outside the office."

The phone was silent for a half minute. "You think so?"

"I ain't gonna bullshit you. The other morning was a disaster. We should've kept quiet better. But you're not gonna fix it by letting on that you'll get pushed around."

"I'm not getting pushed around!"

Guthrie sighed. "Relax. Everybody does. You pushed your boss into letting us in, because she wanted to keep you happy. She was getting something, or she wouldn't have gone along with you. Once you let her know what the score is, she can get back to where she wants to be—she wants you there, but you did something that she needs to make look good. You do that by giving her something. Get it?"

"You're saying that if I fix making her look bad, it'll go back to the way it was?"

"Maybe better, boy. After this, she'll know she can count on you to get square."

"I guess you got something big, then, because did I mention that they want to *kill* me?"

The little man laughed. "Come to think of it, I got something big. The uniforms missed an eyewitness to the Bowman murder when they canvassed. He didn't come forward. He don't like cops."

"He *saw* the murder?"

"That's right. That's why Rachel was gawking when your boss said things that corroborated his story."

"I wasn't—" Vasquez stopped suddenly when Guthrie gave her a hard look.

Tommy Johnson missed her voice because he was already speaking. "What the hell, Guth? You could've said this then!"

"No, I couldn't. And really I still shouldn't. This guy's in the wind, and maybe he ain't feeling like talking. I'm looking for him, and I don't need cops getting in my way."

Tommy set off a long string of fireworks, and Guthrie dialed down the volume on the phone. "He comes by that mouth honest," he said to Vasquez. "His mother talked just like that. I think it's an Ohio thing."

When the phone grew quiet, he turned it up again. "Here's the rest of what's going on. The witness spooked before he could finger anyone. I have to get a follow-up interview—and he don't like cops. His handle is 'Ghost Eddy,' and he seems to be mostly around Washington Heights and Morningside. They can check that, but otherwise they need to stay away. He ain't no drunk loser, Tommy. He's more like David Morgenfeld, you remember?"

"Holds his liquor. I got it."

"You got all that?"

Grumbling, Tommy Johnson repeated, and Guthrie corrected. "And you don't know if this vagrant saw Olsen?"

"Nope," Guthrie replied. "That brings me to my other problem, now that we've done a little something about yours. Olsen's in jail on the Bowman murder, but I'm pretty sure—"

"I hope you're not about to ask me for anything on the Barbie dolls," Tommy interjected.

"You could at least give me time to come out and say it."

"Wasting your breath."

"Boy, when I get something else to give you, you gotta give me that stuff."

"If this works," the young man said after a pause. "If I'm still getting walked on, you're getting crap."

The little detective frowned when he cut off the phone. "Major Case is laying on those files real hard," he said. "I guess we need to pull what we can pull from the newspapers."

Another search of the NYPD reports didn't reveal additional clues. The Garment District had closed down around them and become silent while they studied. Guthrie's cell phone chattered as he was gathering his things to leave. Black-haired John was waiting on 153rd Street, near the cemetery. The phone call lasted only a few seconds—long enough for the vagrant to give his location—and then ended abruptly. The little detective explained that they would have to meet him face-to-face. Black-haired John was afraid of telephones. Guthrie had seen him use one once, and he'd held it arm's length while shouting at it.

Vasquez drove. The traffic was light in the late afternoon, but the sky was cooling as slowly as a pan left carelessly on a stove. Along the way, Guthrie explained that John liked to keep his family close to the river, so he didn't often go below 130th Street. Vasquez turned on 153rd and cruised along the cemetery. Black-haired John slid from an alley alongside a bodega and turned to pull them back the other way. Vasquez followed him until he walked into an abandoned lot off St. Nicholas, and she parked. They climbed from the old blue Ford and cut across the lot behind him.

A couple of kids watched Guthrie and Vasquez suspiciously as they followed John into an alley on the far side of the lot. The alley was suddenly dark, long with winds and bends from jutting redbrick buildings on each side, which hid everything but a narrow slice of hot sky far above. Farther down the alley, they came to an open space that once had been a porch for one of the old buildings, long since enclosed from an ancient street. The door onto the porch, wrapped behind an iron railing, seemed painted shut. The sounds of the street were far away and faint. More kids lurked down the far side of the alley. On the porch, Cindy's slender form was wrapped around a huddled youngster.

Black-haired John slowed and began orbiting a crusted drain, a bit off center in the hidden space. "Ghost Eddy don't want to be found," he said.

"But you found him," Guthrie said.

John nodded. "He don't want to be found," he said again. "Ghost Eddy ain't friendly." He waved toward Cindy, shoulder-high above them on the porch. "She wants to hurt him now."

"Then maybe you all better stay away from him," Guthrie said.

The drifter relaxed but didn't stop moving. "I know," he said. "He woulda killed Danny. That's what he aimed to do. He aimed to teach us a lesson about following."

"What happened?"

"Like this," the drifter said, his orbit slowing a bit as he recounted. "Closer to the park, there's a drunk called Stoop-O, and he would cling like a crumb to Ghost Eddy's whiskers. I thought that out and Cindy agreed that been a good place to start. There's an old sandwich shop on One Thirty-eighth called Villa's. Stoop-O usually starts out there, digging for not good enough—leftovers, huh? Not good enough to eat. That's what's in the trash there. The river flows by the cans and drops off not good enough.

"So we went down early. The kids did a look-see, like they were searching for cops, and sure enough found Stoop-O. We laid on him and didn't say because—well, we could have given him an ice cream, even though they were all melted and he woulda had to drink it, but he's a craphead and he don't never share with nobody except himself—and so we laid and didn't say. One of the boys thought we should clean the cans in front of him, but I said he would just move along and we wanted to watch him. Cindy said so, too. We watched Stoop-O.

"After he filled his fat belly, he moved on. He was belching and rubbing his mouth like it was set for wine. That meant he was going to steal or bully, on account that Stoop-O is too lazy to bag cans. That be part of why he wants to sit beside Ghost Eddy, because he always has whatever he wants, even good enough if he wants, or so the story goes." The drifter frowned. "I didn't see until now, but Ghost Eddy must've liked him until earlier, because he never could've bullied Ghost Eddy for no wine."

Vasquez crossed her arms and started to say something, but Guthrie gestured for her to be quiet. The light was failing fast, and there was no streetlight in the alley. At full night, the alley would be almost pitch-dark. Black-haired John didn't notice. His orbit, and his story, rambled on.

"And we trailed Stoop-O. He didn't see nothing. He gets grabbed all the time because he can't see cops coming. I say he's too lazy to look. He moved along like he had something in mind, not like he was just going round somewhere to check, but knows it's there and where, and we follow him right into the trap because we're looking at him. How stupid is Black-haired John? So stupid he has to watch what anybody could see—Stoop-O—instead of watching for Ghost Eddy." The drifter's voice edged up and crested at an angry shout. Spittle flew from his mouth. His orbit reversed, then quickened.

"Down by the station on One Fifty-first, that's where he went. Ghost Eddy done gone mole, spooked before he knew we was looking. That's how smart Ghost Eddy is—too smart for Black-haired John. He seen Stoop-O coming. He seen us trailing Stoop-O. Ghost Eddy seen it all. Can't give him no ice cream to make it better!

"But anyway, we ain't knowed." The drifter's voice settled, and his feet slowed again. "Cindy knowed something was queer when Stoop-O stopped by that old lot with the manhole on One Fifty-first, looking round like his momma should be by, and puzzled. Then we heard Danny screaming like the devil had him. He was gone so quick . . . by me one moment, then down the street screaming the next, as if the wind gusted him there."

In the darkness, Cindy stood and peered down at them from the railing surrounding the old porch. On quiet feet, she slipped down the stairs. Her pale shirt was speckled with dark droplets. Dark puddles on the cloth trailed small, dark handprints on her body like a mockery of walking by someone with dirty hands.

"Then we forgot all about Stoop-O," Black-haired John continued. "You can recognize a scream, you know, if it's someone's voice familiar, near to you. So we all knowed it was Danny and we ran down the street—and damn Stoop-O anyway. Many's a night you can't avoid seeing him, as well he might be following you, as constant as the moon. We ran, and there's another lot down that way, where they's fixing something, or building on it. Danny's hanging high on the wall. He's screaming still, but softer. I climb up the scaffold there and catch him, 'cause he couldn't pull up on the bricks, nor jump back to reach the scaffold.

"He clung so desperate, he wouldn't let go even after I had him. I had to wrench him loose, and he left his nails on the bricks. Ghost Eddy had jumped out and got him. He kept Danny quiet and carried him off. When he held him out to the bricks, he told him catch on or get dropped, no matter which. Then he told him to hang on till we was close enough to see the drop, and laughed." Black-haired John's orbit stopped for a moment, and he looked directly at Vasquez for the first time. The alley was dark, and all of them were only dim shapes. Then he started moving again.

"Once we had Danny safe, some of the boys remembered Stoop-O. They went back and found him. He was stretched out like an old bottle, top missing. Back when I drank, that was the sorriest sight I could come upon. His face was touched up, and a good number of his teeth was gone. Once we was standing over him, Ghost Eddy started laughing out in the dark. He called out to me, called me a loser. Told me don't try looking for him in *his* city."

Cindy took something from her pocket and handed it to him. The drifter held it out to Guthrie: a cell phone and some money. "We can't look for him no more," he said gently, "and we don't feel right about it."

Guthrie grunted and took some more bills from his own pocket.

He pressed them atop the phone and other money. "Stay away from Ghost Eddy, Black-haired John," he said. "But you still need to call me when you need something."

"I guess," the drifter said, taking back the handful.

"Can I take Danny to a doctor?" Guthrie asked.

Cindy shook her head. "Done asked him," she whispered. "He ain't want to. Wants to be tough." John nodded in agreement.

The city was tough. It made the kids want to be tough. After Guthrie and Vasquez left the alley, noise and light rushed in to surround them. Black-haired John had a refuge in the alley, like an island away from the city, an island on the city's island. The kids watched them suspiciously as they walked back across the lot to 153rd Street. They were watching for Ghost Eddy now. The gray-bearded drifter wouldn't catch another.

CHAPTER EIGHT

"This morning I woke up and realized I was chasing the wrong rab-bit," Guthrie said after Vasquez closed the passenger door of the Ford.

The young Puerto Rican answered with a sleepy grunt and slid her rolled-up gun belt and windbreaker onto the floorboard. She added cream and sugar to a cup of coffee waiting in the console.

"The Bowman file is thin because Olsen had a registered gun," he continued. "Once NYPD put him with her as the boyfriend and looked into his alibi, the gun jumped out. That was the end of the Bowman investigation—about as quick as it began." Guthrie turned onto Clinton Street. His window was cracked for a hiss of air that included a faint whiff of car exhaust from the workingmen pouring from the Lower East Side.

"Wrong rabbit," Guthrie repeated. "That ain't the one NYPD started with, and it ain't the one they're hunting now. Bowman started out as a Jane Doe—a Barbie doll—and that's who NYPD's hunting now. Monica got what they threw in a file and labeled Bowman, but that wasn't all they were working."

Vasquez grunted again, drinking coffee.

"Burn yourself?" The little detective smiled as she gave him a sharp look. "Anyway, we gotta look at where NYPD found the gun. Someone used it. We gotta pick it up."

"We're not going to look at the students?" she asked.

The little man turned onto Canal Street. The sidewalks were crowded with people hustling in the soft morning light. Coming from the East Side, they were mostly Spanish, splashed with colors brighter than the gray and brown stones of the city. A bit of green or yellow, maybe some red, they were as necessary as an outthrust chin and a swagger.

"Sure," he said. "Just not yet. They ain't going nowhere."

Vasquez nodded. The night before, that part had seemed simple. Somebody had killed Camille Bowman. The college students had a reason to do it—motive. A bunch of half-grown men could push one another to do anything. She had seen it with her own eyes too many times. They would jump from fire escapes into trash cans, or whatever. One of them would brag about the killing, or one of them would feel bad and give the others up. That was barrio kids; rich kids wouldn't hold air any better. Someone would crack as soon as fingers began pointing. It was that simple, until she thought about the gun.

"Whichever muchacho thought to get his gun was a genius," she muttered.

"Unless it was Olsen," Guthrie rejoined.

She shook her head, then reached to the floorboard for her gun belt. She strapped up, tucking her Smith & Wesson into the kidney holster, and then shrugged into the windbreaker she used to hide it. While she rummaged in the backseat for the doughnuts, he drove into Greenwich Village. The town houses were tidy, the streets quiet. Pedestrians moved quickly, faces frozen and teeth clenched, disappearing into cars and taxis.

Guthrie shot into a parking place south of Washington Square, a beat ahead of a balding man in spectacles driving a Mercedes. The other driver honked in frustration, then roared away. "I hate this car," Guthrie said. "No, I hate driving in this city." He grinned when Vasquez shot him a look.

"You got powdered sugar on your chin," he said before handing her the keys to the Ford. "Wasserman said I was fixed on the notion of having a car. He said it showed how Middle America I was. He didn't mean middle class. He meant Midwest or anyplace outside the city. Wasserman always walked or rode the trains, but every once in a while he took a taxi."

"Wasserman?"

"The old man I started with. I think he originally came from another universe, because he sure didn't belong here. He said you gotta ride the trains if you want to be a real New Yorker."

They climbed out of the Ford into the morning sunshine. The old stonework in the Village glimmered. They walked across Washington Square and up to Grove Street. The traffic was thinner and people on the streets hurried by with only glances. Parking spaces were open like missing teeth; Guthrie sighed and touched the brim of his brown fedora each time he walked past one.

Number 33 was part of an old nineteenth-century brownstone. It had an underground alley entrance, surrounded by a wrought-iron railing with a swing gate. The door was built into an old window well, matching the others on the bottom story of the brownstone. A short, steep flight of brick steps showed signs of decades of passing feet. Guthrie was disappointed. The entrance was only partly visible from the street. He studied it for a while, checking it from different angles. He told Vasquez to watch, and settled down to wait for a while.

The sun climbed, glowering down, until the morning could no longer pretend coolness. Passersby ignored Guthrie and Vasquez, except for an occasional momentary puzzled stare. About nine o'clock, a white-haired old man marched from the front door of a narrow town house on the other side of the street, pulling a slender water hose and nozzle. He studied them placidly for a moment, then turned and began rinsing his stoop. He sprayed the front of his building, then chased the sidewalk debris into the gutter. Guthrie walked across the street to watch.

"Just giving her a bit of a sprinkle before the day gets too hot," the old man said to him.

The detective nodded. "You pretty much stay in?"

"Been pensioned off for a while." The old man smiled, taking a closer look. "You ain't too far off, with that dust you're showing. I'm Phil Overton."

"Clayton Guthrie." He nodded at the other side of the street. "I was having a look at that underground. I guess you really can't see it from here."

"A few steps down the alley?" Overton asked.

"Sure. You know who lives there?"

The old man nodded and wiped a palm on his khaki trousers. "That pretty little girl did. She got killed. Probably they aren't ready to let it yet." He paused to take a long look at Vasquez, who was standing on the other side of the street, her red windbreaker spread like a sail to catch the faint breeze while she looked toward Seventh Avenue. "Your daughter?"

"I wish. She works for me. Right now, I'm doing background work for a lawyer, relating to that young woman who got killed."

Phil Overton frowned. "They arrested someone, I thought."

"They did," Guthrie said, "and mostly that's why I'm taking a look. Maybe you know what kind of hours she kept? Did she have visitors, and like that?"

"I saw her," Overton said, "but it sort of runs together. Late in the day, mostly I rest."

"Sure. Okay," the detective said. "I'm going to take a longer look around, though, if something comes to mind."

Guthrie walked back across the street, beckoned Vasquez, and then went to the underground door. The seclusion of the alleyway suggested that anyone could have gone inside, and they wouldn't have been spotted except by going back and forth. Guthrie unlocked the door with a key James Rondell had sent by messenger. A simple alarm pad waited inside the door, and he disarmed it as

Vasquez came inside and shut the door. The apartment smelled a few days stale, from unwashed dishes, unmade beds, and cast-off clothes.

The apartment was surprisingly large. The underground door opened on a living room combined with a kitchen. A bathroom and bedroom opened onto the living room. A third door opened into a short hallway. A den, another bedroom, and a second bathroom lay beyond. The bathrooms and kitchen were away from the street, but each bedroom, the den, and the living room had windows looking out into bricked street wells, with wrought-iron railings above them. Careful remodelling hid the evidence of being an understory but left the apartment with a warm, lived-in feeling, with wooden floors and doors, well-used couches, and ranks of framed posters and photographs marching along pastel walls.

"This's the poor branch of the family," Guthrie muttered.

The front bedroom had an unused four-poster bed and a small desk with a stack of books, notebooks, and neatly arranged pens and pencils. The notebooks had the same handwriting as those in Olsen's Livingston Hall dorm room at Columbia. A laptop computer and cell phone sat on the desktop. In the closet hung clothes that might've come from a costume shop, and there were stacked boxes of hats, shoes, and smallclothes in different sizes. The boxes were labeled "Small," "Medium," and "Large"—seemingly for the sizes of clothing or shoes—with some jumbled inside and others neatly folded. The room was impersonal, perhaps even little used except for the desk.

The back bedroom was disarranged, the bed unmade. A number 42 red Wisconsin Badgers jersey was smoothed across one pillow. A single dresser held a mixture of clothing, for a small woman and a large man. A mirror looked over the crowded dresser top at an array of books, cologne, cosmetics, and loose change. In the closet, a bundle of records in a plastic case huddled among the shoes, and one class-A uniform still wrapped in a dry cleaner's bag fought with the dresses.

The den was an electronic paradise. Two wall-mounted plasmas overlooked the desk, with another wide monitor for the desktop computer. A second laptop was tucked into a cradle with a rack of cameras, recorders, and players. The room smelled like electricity. The wastebasket was filled with scraps of paper, each bearing an elaborately written piece of gibberish made from numbers and letters. Guthrie grunted as he shuffled through a handful before letting them slide back into the wastebasket.

Numerous photos decorated the apartment. Movie posters filled the broad spaces, ranging from 1920s silents with Valentino up to 1950s promos for Elvis and Monroe. The smaller pictures were snapshots of the city and anonymous pedestrians, except where they were pinned to the refrigerator or clustered in the den. Those were an album of Olsen and Bowman, at Columbia and elsewhere. Many pictures included Tompkins, or featured Tompkins. Some were of sedate studying, and others of drunken happiness, but none were suggestive.

NYPD's warrant for Olsen's .44 placed it in the bedroom, in a locked case in the bedside table. The case was gone, taken for evidence, but the police had seized nothing else. Guthrie gathered the electronics—laptops, phone, and hard drive—and the paper records in the back bedroom closet. They fit into a gym bag. He didn't seem encouraged.

"What's next?" Vasquez asked.

"We'll come back and canvass the neighborhood," he replied glumly. "I'll look around to see if somebody's security cameras caught anything. We could get lucky."

Vasquez nodded her way through his list. "What'd the old man tell you? Was he any help?"

"He sundowns," Guthrie replied with a grim look.

"What do you mean?"

"Sundowns—it's what people with Alzheimer's do. He's lucid in the morning, but he gets fuzzy in the afternoon. He don't remember nothing, so he thinks he rests in the afternoons." He let out a slow breath. "I had an uncle go down that way."

Guthrie reset the alarm on the door and locked up when they

left. The swing gate at the top of the brick stairs had a faint creak each time it moved, but not enough to call attention from the street. The apartment windows facing the outside had all been undisturbed, and the little detective thought a break-in unlikely. An intruder would've needed the expertise of a professional burglar. Walking away with the gym bag in his hand, he paused a few times to turn and examine the brownstone. Each time, he shook his head and started walking again.

Vasquez stopped him when he finally seemed settled on leaving, and pointed back down the street. Phil Overton was hurrying up the far side of the street, in their direction, waving a light blue hat. He shouted when they paused again, and kept coming. Guthrie and Vasquez crossed the street and went back. The old man wanted them to talk to his wife, but she was an invalid and couldn't leave their house. They walked back with him. The sunshine had baked Overton's stoop almost dry, but a faint dampness lingered, and it was cooler.

Inside the narrow town house, the bare wooden floors were spotless. Shaker furniture balanced neatly on slender wooden legs. Philip Overton took their hats and pegged them, then waited patiently for Vasquez's jacket. She was embarrassed, but the old man seemed not to notice her gun belt. He ushered them into the front room. A tiny woman with white hair pulled into a bun sat beside the large front window. She had a light green-and-blue shawl thrown over her legs. Another wooden-backed chair sat opposite hers at a small card table, with two hands of cards already waiting. Facing the window, a spindle-back couch had thin cushions, with a low, bare coffee table before it.

"Hello," she said in a clear, bright voice. "You're Clayton Guthrie. Phil told me you had some questions. I'm Jeannette." Phil sat down in the other chair at the card table, picked up his hand, and began to study it.

Guthrie sat down on the couch, leaning forward to put his elbows on his knees. "How long have you been married, Jeannette?"

The old woman smiled. "Phil and I have been married for forty years," she replied. "He took perfect care of me. I hope to return the favor for as many." She picked up her hand of cards.

"Okay. There's an apartment across the street. You can't really see the door from here, but you can see the gate, maybe. I wonder if you know anything about who lived there?"

"Phil told me you wanted to know about the pretty girl. I can see the street from where I sit, here. I don't watch television, so I watch the street. I suppose someone might call me nosy, but I'm really not. I don't bother people with questions. That's nosy, if you're not being paid to do it."

Vasquez laughed. The old woman was being polite to the detective.

"Did anyone live there with her?"

"I know you know that big young man did. You just came from inside, Clayton. I hope I can call you Clayton and not offend you. That's such a wonderfully old name. Couples don't name their children like that anymore. But you shouldn't play slow. The police say he killed her; that was in the newspaper. I don't believe that, because I watched them. They were in love, and they were nesting. He did not kill her. Nor did she sleep around on him. That's foolishness."

"That's a strong opinion from watching a doorway, Jeannette."

"I suppose you could say so. But if I watch a rock fall, can't I say how it came to be on the ground?" She glanced at Vasquez, who wore a frown. "She was a very pretty girl, like yourself, dear. She had many suitors. Until she met that boy, her suitors came and went at all hours. After that, she had only two visitors—that boy and the other girl. And she kept a regular schedule." She tapped her cards on the tabletop. "I suppose it's difficult to describe how they walked, how they paused, waited, or hurried to catch up with each other. I've been around long enough to know when two people are smitten with each other. That was them."

"You make a good argument, but those aren't the questions that need answers," Guthrie said. "Let me give you some examples." She nodded, and he continued. "When was the last time you saw Camille Bowman go in or out?"

"That was the morning of the day she was murdered, the twenty-third, a Thursday. She came out for school. The young man wasn't there that morning."

"You're *sure*?" Vasquez asked.

"Of course, dear. We have tuna on Thursday for lunch. She was going to school because she was carrying her books. Oh, do you mean am I certain I saw her? I always noticed her, dear. I would say it was jealousy. I used to be pretty myself, sometime long ago, and so maybe I see myself, or saw myself, in her. I always noticed her."

"She didn't come back?" Guthrie asked.

"No. The boy did. Of course, we didn't know she was dead, not for days. You should have seen the poor boy mope around. The dark-haired girl was just as upset as he was. I came to think those two were like sisters, the way they ran around together, and then she was the only one who kept coming back after the pretty girl met her boy."

Guthrie nodded. "So just those three came and went, and then after the twenty-third, just two of them?"

"Well, yes, of people who belonged here," she said.

"You mean people who lived in the Village?" Vasquez asked.

"Yes, dear. This was unusual. They had deliveries. They didn't ordinarily have deliveries. I suppose really it was an installer or a courier, not a deliveryman, but he brought a nice large box."

"When was this?" the little detective asked.

"Well, the first time was Tuesday, the twenty-first. I remember thinking that he *just* missed them. But one of them must have known that, and perhaps told him when to come. He went inside, because there's nothing else down the alley. Yes, I remember seeing him swing the gate."

"He left a box? He didn't take anything out?"

"No." Jeannette shook her head. "I remember thinking it must be some sort of computer thing, because he stayed inside for a while. I've read in the paper where they'll do that sort of thing nowadays—come to your home and install something electronic. I thought it must be a present."

"That was the first time," Vasquez said. "How many times did they get a delivery?"

"Once more," she replied. "At the same time of day. He brought another nice large box. That was Friday, the twenty-fourth. She was already gone, bless her. The boy must have felt horrid when he came back and found the present. I don't know which was giving it to the other."

"How long did the deliveryman stay the second time?" Guthrie asked.

"Not long that time. He finished quickly."

"Do you remember what he looked like?"

"He had a blue uniform with a cap. He wore dark glasses, like these kids do nowadays, but he wasn't really a boy, though he was a younger man. I could say the same of her boy—he wasn't really that young. He had dark hair and a clean chin. He had a smooth stride, very easy. Phil used to walk that way." She smiled at her husband, and he pretended to study his cards. "Oh, and he had a light green van. I thought he might get a ticket the first time, because he shouldn't have left it like that."

They sat quietly for a minute after she said that. The living room was dim with old wood. The light outside the window was very bright. "I didn't help very much, did I, Clayton?" she asked. "That's a shame. I wish I had invited her up here for cards, at least once." Her gaze fell gently upon her husband. "Bad things happen in life, and regret can't make up for them."

"No, ma'am," Guthrie said.

Jeannette Overton nodded. "If you're going to stay for cards, maybe Phil will get you some lemonade."

CHAPTER NINE

Guthrie ordered pizza once they were back at the office. Vasquez opened the laptops, discovering that they contained schoolwork and the traces of daily lives. Olsen used his cell phone for calls, but the laptops held the address books, mailing lists, and accounts. Only a few files asked for passwords. Guthrie wired the hard drive to his computer and drew a blank. After the pizza arrived, the little detective ate one slice, then let out a disgusted sigh.

"You finally realized that pizza's crap?" Vasquez asked.

"Huh?" Guthrie scowled at her. "So? My uncles flew most of that family over here in the seventies. They're family. And they don't have pizza on their menu—they make that because I ask for it. Anyway, I'm thinking about Olsen." He studied the directory on the hard drive. "Those are some huge files," he muttered, then stood and walked around the backs of the couches to look from the office windows.

"Watching people can make you chase your own shadow," he said. "You carry your suspicions around with you, and then you can end up seeing them everywhere—sometimes instead of what's actually there. That's why we can't tell Olsen anything, not even part of it."

The little detective studied Vasquez's blank expression and realized he wasn't making sense. While they finished the pizza, he tried to spell it out. If they told Olsen about the things they'd discovered—the eyewitness and the deliveryman—the big man wouldn't be able to think about anything else. He would start climbing the walls of his cell, and that would be as bad as his being shocked into silence. Olsen could know the killer. Left alone with his thoughts, he might realize it.

"*You* told the lawyer about Ghost Eddy," Vasquez said. "And you told Tommy."

"Maybe I'll come to regret that," Guthrie said. "Jeannette Overton stays in my pocket, though." He sat down again and picked up the phone. Vasquez went back to combing the laptops while Guthrie called downtown and talked a guard lieutenant into making sure Olsen contacted him. Then he began muttering about the size of the files on Bowman's hard drive. Ordinarily, casual users didn't fill drives with anything except for commercial software. Scratch files and databases took a small fraction of their space. Bowman's drive was loaded. The file names looked like gibberish.

Greg Olsen called from the Manhattan House, and Guthrie put him on speakerphone. After enough breath to say hello, the little detective said, "Mr. Olsen, we kinda need some background. Is it gonna be all right if we get some things from Grove Street?"

"Sure, if you need something," he replied.

"Rachel's gonna ask you about some people, then," the little detective said, ignoring her startled look and gesturing for her to get started.

While Vasquez quizzed Olsen about the names in the address books, noting down people from Columbia, Guthrie opened the paper files from the back bedroom at Grove Street. He flipped quickly through the financial records but slowed when scanning Olsen's military record. The big man had been discharged as a lieutenant colonel, wearing a chestful of decorations. His last was a Purple Heart. Olsen was stop-lossed for the final three of eight consecutive years in Afghanistan, without ever rotating for staff service. Guthrie extracted a single page from the file and smoothed it on his desktop.

The little detective waited for a pause to stretch after Olsen ran himself out describing to Vasquez what he knew about the people in Bowman's address book. "Mr. Olsen," he said, "you've had a few days to sit and think. Have you had any ideas about who killed your fiancée?" The pause continued, and the detective filled it. "Maybe I should phrase that a different way. *We* have some ideas about who might've wanted to kill Camille Bowman. That didn't need much digging. What's interesting here is that they decided to frame you for doing it. Do you see what I mean? After that, it occurs to me that I'm less curious about Bowman, and more curious about you. You've had an interesting life. Have you got any ideas about who would want to frame you for murder?"

Quiet drifted, faintly counterpointed by distant horns and the thrum of traffic. "So you think this could be on me, then?" Olsen asked. "I suppose the seat isn't hot enough unless it's melting through the ice at one and the same time. That's different. Then you might not be too far off, and a pretty good detective with it. I don't doubt plenty of people would want to kill me, and line up for a chance if the carnival sold tickets, but I don't suppose they could get to New York." He laughed briefly. "Then again, if they gave my name to Homeland, they might get a visa, with cab fare and directions to reach me. Is that who you mean, then?"

"That's better than what you were giving me, but you could start closer to the city."

Guthrie's question foundered on the rock of Olsen's determination that no one would've killed Camille Bowman for any reason. The argument was a whirlpool. After a few circles, Guthrie realized the big man was simply defending his memory. He needed to be led more carefully. The detective started over by asking how he came to choose New York City to finish school, instead of returning to

Wisconsin. Olsen claimed his primary reason was always at hand—with a bit of emphasis on *hand*—and pointed to Hillary Clinton as his model. She came to New York to enter the Senate. The state was forgiving of outsiders. He meant for Columbia Law School to be his springboard into politics.

Olsen volunteered for the army after 9/11. After serving, he felt the war was unnecessary. He decided Al-Qaeda was an idea that wasn't damaged by waging war against it. He knew that speaking up against the war wasn't popular. More Americans worried about lines at an airline counter than worried about soldiers fighting overseas. Coming back to discover the apathy was a rude awakening, but he had a constant reminder. That was enough for him. Then he met Camille Bowman. She was murdered, and now he was in jail.

"That's it?" Guthrie asked after Olsen came to an abrupt stop.

"Yes," the big man snapped. "That's it. Six months and seven days ago, I realized I had my arms wrapped around her. That was like getting cross-checked into the boards—you just hold on, skate hard, and pray you're still on your feet. I didn't know that could happen. Then just as suddenly it stopped, twelve days ago. *End of report.*"

"If it was that simple, you wouldn't be there," Guthrie said.

"Am I missing something?" Olsen demanded.

"Maybe that I ain't wasting breath on the obvious," Guthrie replied. "Bowman was snatched outside LMA—pretty sure you know the place. I can find all that out without asking you—"

"She was at LMA?"

"Sure."

Olsen sighed. "So maybe this is on me, then," he muttered.

"What's that?" Guthrie demanded.

"I was a busy man," Olsen said bitterly. "An important man. I left her alone. With time on her hands, she drifted back to what she did beforehand, now and then. I wasn't ever able to find fault with her for that."

"You're saying that wasn't something you did together."

"One time I went with her to that club, a long night I spent fending away drunken girls and prying hands loose from Cammie. Those youngsters are pretty forward, maybe to the point of already putting their clothes back on when you're finally coming to the point of taking your own off."

The little man laughed. "I had a look," he said. "But who knew about the gun? You did, and Bowman did. Who else?"

"Gettysburg! She practiced at Gettysburg, and Michelle always went with her. Maybe Michelle noticed something there. Talk to her—"

"Slow down there, Mr. Olsen. Michelle Tompkins knew about your gun. Michelle Tompkins came and went at Bowman's apartment. She had access to the gun—"

"Why would she do that?"

"Maybe she had some interest in you."

"She didn't like me. She tolerated me. She was Cammie's friend. So maybe she's my friend *now*. I guess we had a truce, a few months ago then. When Cammie decided to be serious about her schoolwork, maybe that's when Michelle's attitude changed. That's it, because she harped on that. She was real studious, a supernerd. She was the tagalong at the party."

"Cammie's party at LMA, you mean?"

"So now you need the obvious, then?"

"I'm not finding it so obvious. This could use some spelling out. Tompkins was along for the ride—in the party at LMA, and then at your party with Bowman, it seems. The three of you were together? I guess you can't call that a couple—"

"She was Cammie's friend," Olsen interjected.

"A friend who sat on the bed with you? Or did you notice when they switched out?"

"That's not true!"

The little detective let a long moment pass to see if Olsen would say more. "I admit I didn't find any pictures of it at Grove Street, but the suggestion came to me. Now would be a good time to get in front of it. What occurs to me most is that Tompkins knew about the gun, and she spent plenty of time at Grove Street. That gives me something to think about."

"After a few more years," Olsen said, "I might not be caught quite so off guard by the abruptness in this city, but I hope that won't mean I've come to match it." A moment's silence intervened. "Michelle didn't kill Cammie. She was the only one who was really her friend. She was the only one who didn't desert her."

"I hear you," the detective said.

The moment Guthrie cradled the phone, Vasquez said, "I don't think she did it. Why'd she send us looking if—"

"Does it matter what we think?" Guthrie asked tiredly. He stood, went to the coffeemaker, and poured a cup for himself. "Maybe Olsen was framed. But if we clear him, the next suspect is Tompkins. Then is she framed? Or maybe she did it, and now she's making it look good. Or maybe *he* did it. He should be as mad as a hatter after eight years in Afghanistan." He took the piece of paper from his desktop and handed it to her. "Read it."

Vasquez scanned the paper. "This's a job offer—a million a year for consultation," she said. "He don't need to be a lawyer."

"See the address—North Carolina. That's a private security firm. Really, they should be called mercenaries. The date there, Olsen was still in the hospital after having his hand sewed back onto his arm." The little detective nodded. "They want him bad—see where it says call for a follow-up offer? They don't want him because he does a good job of tying his shoes. Greg Olsen's covered in blood. Our question is this: How fresh is the *last* drop?"

That afternoon, they drove uptown to hunt for Ghost Eddy. The sun played hide-and-seek in some thin banks of clouds beyond the Hudson River, but the streets of Washington Heights and Morningside were still glowing hot. Vasquez drove. She cruised up and down the blocks while Guthrie cranked the old Ford's window up and down to hang out and fire words at the street people. He emptied a large cooler of drinks and sandwiches, and reused some tired jokes until they finally found the cemetery. Vasquez quickly lost count of the names the little detective shouted. Some of the vagrants threw annoyed looks and drifted away without talking, but most came to the old blue Ford and propped a hand on the top of the window frame while they drank a soda and bantered with Guthrie. The afternoon slid toward evening.

The little man's search revealed the same information again and again. Ghost Eddy had gone to ground. The gray-bearded drifter was as canny as a fox. No one knew where he came from or where he went to, but they saw him haunting the streets. The summertime sidewalks had a heavy burden of loiterers and passersby for Guthrie to sift, and eventually his voice faded to a croak. The street women claimed Ghost Eddy wasn't eating as much, but Guthrie figured that for wishful thinking. Others pointed out his cans in the 150's, and a liquor store he visited on 149th Street, east of Jackie Robinson Park. Guthrie jotted down a list of corners where Ghost Eddy was spotted, alleys he passed through, and stoops he sat on, but the long afternoon didn't get them a single glimpse of the gray drifter.

The sun got lost in the clouds late in the day, when dusk was hustling toward the city. Vasquez guided the old Ford south on Broadway like a slow bomb. Guthrie had already mentioned a break for supper, but he was tapping his pen softly on the dashboard while he scanned his notes.

"Okay, Rachel, what do we know?" he asked.

She shrugged. "Ghost is the right name for this guy."

"Sure, but he's leaving tracks."

"Where?"

"He's got money, ain't he? Enough to go to the package store, steady. But he's not hooking cans."

Vasquez nodded. "I see what you're saying, *viejo*. He robbed Bowman's body. Maybe that's where the money is coming from."

"Good. So, next time he calls, we ask Olsen how much pocket money Bowman carried. Then what?"

"Check the store for how much Ghost Eddy's spending." She

turned the old Ford left on 125th Street, then went down until she could turn back uptown on St. Nicholas. She gunned the old car hard into the turn, and grinned when Guthrie gave her a sour look. She felt better about looking for the drifter. Searching the blocks had been like looking for a needle in a haystack, but now they were luring a pet cat with cream.

The bodega on 149th Street had a dirty dark green facade, slanted inward to a recessed door. The display windows held stacks of canned beans and beef stew, topped with hanging tri cards promoting a cheery, fat-cheeked cook in a billowing apron. A little bell rang when they entered the dimness inside. The street was bright, even with dark approaching, and the inside seemed like a cave with cool, spicy air. One long shelf sliced down the middle of the narrow store. The liquor was behind the counter, like a wrinkled glass wall behind a tall old black man perched on a high stool. Wisps of white marked his mustache and beard, but his hair was still deep black.

Guthrie wandered around the long central shelf, leaving Vasquez to talk to the proprietor. Guthrie listened, and occasionally looked over to watch. The young Puerto Rican started slowly, shifting uneasily from foot to foot, but she built some momentum during her description of Ghost Eddy. The old black man, Jude Nelson, unfolded himself from the stool and leaned on the countertop, nodding when she finished. He was familiar with Ghost Eddy. The gray drifter usually had clean money, and something funny to say—unlike the other vagrants, who came in carrying grubby bills and cups of change, with a shifty look that turned easily into anger or begging. Nelson counted the drifter as a decent customer.

"So what's this about?" he asked. "It's not my business, except that you're asking me to pass another man's business."

Vasquez glanced at Guthrie, but he turned quickly away to study some jars of pickles. He raised his fedora like a shield to block his view of her—and to keep her from seeing his smile.

"Okay, then," Vasquez muttered before turning back to the proprietor. "About ten days ago, there was a killing. This guy we're looking for, he saw something, and we're wanting to follow up. He's kind of dodging, but he ain't got reason. We ain't cops. We just want to clear the guy the cops got, if he ain't the one, you know?"

Jude Nelson nodded. "That's an old story about maybe being good enough for jail," he said. "I understand that. But what can I do?"

Vasquez's smile was brighter than her red windbreaker. She played fill in the blanks with the proprietor to round out the interview. Ghost Eddy usually spent twenty or thirty dollars at a time, for something hard, something soft, and a handful of food. The past ten days, he'd been spending more—fifty or sixty—and buying more hard than soft. Lately, he wasn't talking, but Nelson didn't press customers for small talk when they didn't volunteer. He agreed to ask the drifter if he would have a talk with them, though, and pass the answer along. He shifted back to his stool, which made him seem even taller, and waved to Guthrie as they were leaving the bodega.

Once they were back in the Ford, Guthrie told her to drive up and down 151st Street a few times. He already knew where the manhole was that Black-haired John had mentioned, but he wanted to remind himself of the lot's situation. They paused to eat, then cruised the manhole a few more times as the light failed. The night began slow and hot. Guthrie checked his notes again before deciding to set up in the abandoned lot on 151st Street. He figured the manhole for a good maybe, and worth watching. If they saw Ghost Eddy going in or out, they would have a chance for a conversation.

Redbrick buildings crowded the lot from all sides except the street side, but an alley wandered from among them on one backside corner. The manhole was an old-style rectangular job that shouldered above the sidewalk and opened on top with a swinging lid. About half of the rectangular casing jutted beyond the sidewalk into the lot. The sidewalk boasted some fence posts with drooping triangles of rusting hurricane fence; layers of debris sheltered behind them in the dusty lot. Trails cut through the weeds from the alley in the back to the manhole and the cross corner of the lot.

Sometime in the past, the manhole had been secured. Since then, a long war raged between lockers and breakers, with the debris of battle scattered around the old battleship. The war appeared over. Every hasp welded on had been sawn, burned, or broken. Links of chain, long gone with rust, peeped from the dirt like old shell casings. A fiery deathblow warped the lid past the point of closing normally, leaving it to sit dark and silent like a boxer with a crooked jaw, wearing tattoos of slag and weld burn. The city maintenance workers' surrender was only an admission that they had no control over what was determined to emerge from the darkness beneath the city. Turning a blind eye was just easier.

Guthrie decided the lot had enough junk cluttering it to set up inside. He sent Vasquez to buy some cold food and leave the Ford parked down the street. When she came back, he was in the lot with some makeshift stools. He gave her a flashlight and a pair of quick-start railroad flares. Aboveground, the streetlights were numerous, but he thought they could end up going underground. One of the buildings blocked the western sky and passed for a cool wall.

After the light was gone, the city's noise seemed to fill the space left behind. Guthrie and Vasquez were invisible in their corner. Above them on the bricks, some of the windows leaked light through shades. Traffic on 151st was light, but in the dark silence it seemed to race over their laps while they waited. Every so often, someone hustled by on the street, or an elderly couple would tap by slowly. Vasquez developed a habit of checking her watch and dropping sighs. Guthrie laughed quietly at her, but she couldn't stop. The sound of a kicked bottle came from the alley a little after midnight, and a golden tomcat prowled the lot at two o'clock. He watched them distrustfully, then shook furry haunches at the bricks nearby. Morning tagged along an eternity after that.

"Tomorrow," Guthrie said when he stood up in the morning

light. His knees and back crackled when he stretched. "He'll be here tomorrow."

Vasquez snorted.

"It could happen," he said. "Let's get breakfast, and then I'll run you home."

CHAPTER TEN

Guthrie and Vasquez started late on the fifth of August. After a night of stakeout, the little detective was willing to sleep until lunch. The afternoon sky glowed like hot chrome above Columbia University, with no relief in sight. Vasquez parked the blue Ford in the east-side lot. Empty spaces outnumbered the parked cars jutting bright as gold teeth in the sunshine above new asphalt that stank of tar. They found a bench covered over with the shade of a maple tree, on the north side of McNamara Hall, and settled down to make calls.

Greg Olsen knew enough about the letter societies to outline obvious things when he'd roll-called the address books for Vasquez. The shade around the maple tree bloomed slowly to the east while the detectives used their phones and jotted notes. Most of the Columbia students wouldn't talk; they weren't interested beyond volunteering a good-guy or good-girl report, mixed with an occasional "Screw you": Bowman was dead, and Olsen wasn't worth talking about. The students were absorbed in what they were doing themselves. The detectives whittled the list and watched the campus.

Small groups of students hurried in the heat between the parking lots and auditoriums. They wore blue jeans, backpacks, and pastel shirts, with glittering wristwatches and sunglasses for accessories. The detectives were invisible on their bench because the students weren't looking.

Irene Locklear, a pushy organizer for Sigma Kappa, volunteered a gripe about Camille Bowman that stood out from the whitewash the others reserved for the victim. The detectives had inadvertently discovered someone who knew Michelle Tompkins better than she knew Camille Bowman. Locklear blamed Bowman for drawing Tompkins to the dark side of the sorority, into the clique of sisters obsessed with partying. The alignment lasted a year; then Bowman's abandonment of the party scene was quicker than Tompkins's switch from studious to possessed. The sorority erupted when the crown princess fled the palace, smoothing things over afterward with Tompkins on the outside again.

Sunlight splashing from the windshields of passing cars winked beyond the line of shrubbery masking the campus. The shade from the maple tree had all the effect of an illusion against the mid-afternoon heat. Vasquez scored the last point on the phone list. From other conversations, she pegged a second Sigma Kappa sister, Amanda Hearst, as being close to Bowman—enough that she held back from the infighting after Bowman's fall from grace. Hearst had nothing good to say about Olsen, and she volunteered sympathy for a Delta Psi brother, Justin Peiper, who held Bowman's eye before Olsen appeared. Destiny was averted, according to Hearst; Peiper and Bowman would've been the prettiest couple in the universe.

"Maybe she ain't had a look at Olsen," Vasquez said after the call.

Guthrie grunted. After looking Peiper up in the Columbia directory, the little detective had begun sifting for information. Peiper was a senior, and the registrar showed him attending summer classes. "This guy needs a look," he said finally. "He's carrying a temper. He pled no contest on two assaults in Utica in the past three years. Maybe there's something to him."

Finding Peiper proved little challenge.

Each time Vasquez paused to ask a passing student, she received a knowing smirk and a quick answer. Justin Peiper was a tourist attraction at the university. Within a quarter of an hour, she found him in the food court. The court was an upscale cafeteria with a veneer that couldn't hide the institutional background. Banks of plants softened two walls over rows of booths, looking out on an island of more booths, which were overshadowed by towering ficus trees. Bright light poured down from the translucent ceiling.

The students didn't seem to notice the effort to make the cafeteria comfortable. Some of them were in a burning hurry, so rushed that even five minutes spent gulping a handful of french fries was too much to spare. They ran in and out like hummingbirds, a new one appearing to replace every one who left. Some students sat alone, darting glances as they wolfed down their food.

One group filled two booths on the central island, lounging like castaways killing time. Their conversation was punctuated with hoots of laughter and the switching of seats. At a distance, Justin Peiper was small enough to be inconspicuous, dark-haired and clean-shaven, but the bigger, louder men were plainly circling around him. Vasquez compared him against his DMV photo and snapped her palmtop shut.

"Maybe he walks like a duck," she said. "He's a little guy like you, *viejo*. Too bad you aren't that pretty."

"I used to be. I had surgery to correct it." He took out his phone and pointed it at the crowded booths. "We need some decent pictures—preferably walking. Jeannette Overton might recognize him."

"Those are some stupid muchachos," Vasquez said.

"See? I knew you would be a good detective."

Vasquez laughed, and some of the young men at Peiper's table looked at her. Whispers and pointed fingers slid around the two tables. Two students stood for a better look, and then the tile floor cast hard echoes from a round of banter and laughter.

"Maybe this ain't the best time," Guthrie said. "Some of them are drunk, or just ordinarily stupid. Let's move a little bit." He stood up but kept shooting video with his phone.

"What do you mean?" Vasquez asked, throwing the detective a puzzled glance before turning her glare back to Peiper's table. The young men were slipping from their seats and walking toward them. "What're they going to do?"

"I thought you grew up on the Lower East Side," Guthrie muttered. "Or maybe you been watching too much TV. White don't mean soft unless you're talking about bread."

Vasquez scowled; she didn't run from boys. It was the other way around, ever since she was eleven. On Henry Street, the muchachos looked but didn't talk. That way, they were safer. By the time she was twelve, Vasquez learned she couldn't mention she liked some boy at school or in the neighborhood. Within a few days, he would be sporting the new style provided by her brothers: bruised and hurting. Even after Vasquez learned to be quiet, Indio and Miguel could get her friends to talk. They were tough muchachos. A glance and smile from Indio could make her girlfriends' tongues wag like a dog's tail. Then the new crush would get crushed.

Before middle school was over, Vasquez knew two things. First was that no boy dared speak to her—her brothers were loco and they would beat his stupid ass. Second was that this wasn't normal. Other girls had brothers who weren't stupid loco. Vasquez didn't think it was about sex. That was no big deal. She tried that the first time at her fifteenth birthday party. Hurried fumbling at clothes in a darkened room was not the big deal everyone was making it.

These young men at Columbia University didn't know her brothers, though, and they didn't have the usual respectful looks on their faces. Some were amused, others curious, and some suspicious. Justin Peiper was small, but some of the others towered over him, like defensive ends or rush linebackers surrounding a punter. "Are we gonna cut out?" she asked.

"Nah. I'll try to rattle him, but if things do get ugly, I don't want the exit strategy to be sliding under the table in the booth and shouting for cops." He panned his phone over the approaching crowd.

"Whatcha doing, old man?" a tall dirty-blond surfer asked. His eyes were invisible behind mirrored wraparound sunglasses; his shirt and jeans were sunbleached to the color of pale sand. The other young men ambled forward to nearly surround them. Other students, who had been hurrying, drifted to a stop like leaves striking the ground.

"Taking pictures for *National Geographic*," Guthrie said, taking a pan of Peiper at short range before slipping the phone into his pocket. The little West Virginian seemed toylike beside the big young men.

Justin Peiper had hair one shade short of black, and eyes that seemed a mix of green and blue. His features weren't overfine or pretty, but they suggested amusement and sensuality without coarseness. He had the cocky good looks that made Gary Cooper immortal, with a slim, muscular build flawed only by stature. He admired Vasquez and arched a perfect eyebrow. "You want wildlife, I know places," he offered, then nodded at Guthrie. "Seriously, check his phone."

The surfer took a step and leaned as if he was reaching for a wayward basketball, but Guthrie caught his wrist and stepped around him. Another of the big men snarled and pushed the little detective when he was bumped, but Guthrie rode the surfer into two more of them and they tangled. Guthrie stopped beside Peiper.

"Justin, there're cameras all around us in the cafeteria," he said softly, "but you want to worry about mine? Seriously?"

"You're right, man," Peiper said, holding up his hands. "My bad!" He flashed a grin that had stopped as much trouble as it ever started. The big men shifted around to leave some space. The surfer snatched off his sunglasses to glare down at Guthrie with dark eyes.

"Maybe you can tell me where you were at on Thursday, the twenty-third of July. Maybe you should pay special attention to the night hours."

"What the hell? You're a cop?" Peiper asked.

"Worse than that," Guthrie said. "The night Camille Bowman was murdered, where were you?"

"Greg Olsen is in jail for that, dumbass," Peiper said coolly. "Read the newspaper."

"That can change, Justin, especially now that the motives are getting clearer," the little detective said. "She dumped you for him. That's jealousy. Juries like jealous rivals who got spurned for war heroes. Right? Maybe you should get in front of this and talk to me, instead of making me dig for it." He glanced at the other men surrounding them. "Maybe I could find something on a lot of you. Are all of you Deltas? Been spending time at LMA?"

"I was doing something that night," Peiper said.

Guthrie laughed. "Studying? Or something better, that you got pictures of, and somebody willing to come forward?"

"No badge, no cop," the surfer said. "Dude's faking. You don't have to answer his questions."

The little detective shrugged. "I'm worse than a cop. I work for James Rondell, an ugly-ass lawyer on Wall Street. If making you look bad helps him talk to a jury, count it as done. I'm not so bad, myself. Convince me, and I vanish like a puff of smoke. If you don't answer, I dig; then I throw you to James Rondell. Maybe start with how many times you visited Bowman's apartment?"

"So what! A lot of guys went to that tramp's apartment," the surfer said.

"You got names?" Guthrie countered.

"Enough fun and games," Peiper said. "Talk to your lawyer. He can talk to my lawyer. They can get together and talk lawyer shit, late at night, and get pictures for show-and-tell." He shrugged, turning away. The surfer lingered until last, glaring, then followed the others. The food court was full of people but as quiet as a tomb.

"I thought you got to him," Vasquez said.

"We can call him later and see," Guthrie said. "Away from the audience, he might turn helpful."

CHAPTER ELEVEN

"I spent a long part of this morning thinking that if a man wanted me to call him, then he should answer his phone," Olsen said crisply. The speaker of Guthrie's cell phone was loud enough to fill the old Ford when the windows were cranked shut to use the air conditioner. Vasquez turned from Broadway to Ninth Avenue, going south. Early afternoon traffic shuttled smoothly.

"I apologize, Mr. Olsen," Guthrie said. "When I had you call before, I should've given you my cell instead of my office. You had trouble finding that?"

"A bit," the big man said. "I would be somewhat more comfortable if you would call me Greg. When I hear Mr. Olsen, or Captain Olsen, or Captain, the words are always coming from my men, and they're expecting me to take care of them. In this situation, I would rather find that shoe on the other foot."

The little detective nodded, then said, "I'll do that."

"Mr. Rondell provided your number, and that seemed to take some effort on his part," Olsen said. Faint metallic drumming rattled in the background, like a rushing, tumbling heartbeat. "I had a vague idea from Mr. Rondell that he believes you know some things he doesn't—and maybe I had that vague idea from his saying you might know some things he doesn't, in a tone that didn't suggest the idea that the two of you were all that cooperative with each other. Is something going on out there?"

"I suppose I am holding Mr. Rondell at arm's length."

"Then I have to say you have long arms for a little guy."

Guthrie laughed. "We do have a question for you," he said. "If you call every day, things will be a bit easier." He gestured to Vasquez.

"What?" she asked, before remembering. "Okay, when Bowman went out at night, how much money did she usually carry?"

Traffic was jammed up at Forty-first Street, where a delivery truck had tiptoed along the sides of some passing cars. Gawkers lined the sidewalks and horns blared into the mess of NYPD getting information from drivers and trying to decide what to do with the truck. The uniformed driver was sitting in a cruiser, leaning out against the open back door, adding more to a puddle of vomit on the street. The old blue Ford crawled by and they had a lingering look before Olsen replied.

"About three hundred dollars," he said. "She never spent the money—she used cards. I never understood that."

Vasquez frowned. Ghost Eddy had already spent more than that since the murder, in the bodega on 149th Street. Without Bowman's money, he spent ninety dollars of clean money every week. The drifter was a steady drinker.

"So that was important, then?" Olsen asked.

"I don't know yet," Vasquez replied.

"Linney warned me that intel would be a hard requisition," Olsen muttered. "So he wasn't lying, then, and the pair of you aren't talking to anyone. I'll try this the other way. Drive over to Westchester and check on Linney for me. On the phone, he says he's not drinking, but, naturally, I can't smell his breath. He was in a bad way before I was arrested. His mother was killed. Not much worse can happen to a man, for then he started drinking and he called me to bail him from jail. Is it strange that now I'm in jail?"

"I think I can manage that," Guthrie said.

"*That's* a different answer. Then you could take my calls for me, along with that. I've had a few bad months of late nights, but it hasn't been so terrible that a grave digger would notice. My men call, mostly late at night, when they're a klick past drunk and wondering where their hat was laid by. Linney did that. I spent years trying to leave the service, but even now the calls bring me back."

Vasquez turned onto Thirty-fourth Street and slid in behind a convoy of empty clothes racks. Switch-thin teenagers pushed one rack and pulled another behind, stepping along like ants escaping with jelly. Traffic going the other way idled, gunning forward a few feet at a time, and honked during the pauses.

"At first they ask questions. What happened to so-and-so? Or 'Did you really get smashed?' After they talk a bit, something comes out—a new job, a marriage. Somewhere along the way, all of the news turned bad. Cars crash, girls tumble down the stairs, junkies toke their last smoke, dying is written in fire across the sky. I haven't heard about a baby in months. Can you do that for me, then? Can you answer my phone for me and screen my bad calls?"

"I think you're in a morbid mood," Guthrie said. Vasquez whipped into a space fifty feet from the entrance of their building. "I won't say you don't have reason, but you have to look up. You know whether you're innocent, or guilty. I won't rest until I prove it to myself. Does that make sense to you?"

"That makes sense, but you know you're a voice on a phone, with hardly a face attached to it. I guess that's all you can give me, though." Olsen paused. "I smell a push-along, so I'll leave you. Do me that favor to check on Linney, like you said."

After Guthrie cut off the phone, Vasquez said, "You could've given him something. We have some angles."

The little detective grunted, climbed out of the car, and slammed the door. He walked fast. He was on the steps of the building before she caught up with him. The bright sunshine made her red jacket glow like fire.

———

That night, they watched the manhole on 151st Street again. They slipped into the lot at twilight and hid in the shadow of the redbrick building. Vasquez picked up her impatience right where she'd left it the previous night, as if there had been no break. The moon peered down from the cloudless sky, dark behind the streetlights. The waiting wore her down quickly, turning her inside herself.

At the beginning of May, her job with Guthrie was exactly what she needed. Carrying a pistol made her important, deadly serious, an immediate adult instead of a teenager with a summer job waiting tables. She needed that, because she was defying her father. No bullshit job could've given her enough strength for that, but the size of her paychecks, and the solid weight of *la pistola*, made her shoulders strong enough to shrug it off. Walking past Papì's frown was no joke. His disapproval was like gravity; he could nail her to the floor.

Even her loco brothers didn't make little of her choice. They knew it was tough to deal with their father. Miguel was glad she wasn't going to school. Indio wasn't sure, but he was with her because she was against Papì for a change. In three months, she had learned some of what they had faced for years. That wasn't easy. She wanted her life back to normal. She didn't want to need to steel herself for an argument every time she walked through the door at home.

Actually, she decided Indio and Miguel had it easier, despite their complaints about Papì. The old man rode them like horses on a merry-go-round; no matter how much they seemed to run, they never ended up very far from him. He shouted at them, but it was still easy to see that he was proud of them. He acknowledged their strength even when he punished them; he backed off after he pushed. He told them, "Think! Don't be stupid!" and clapped them roughly on the shoulder when they were pulling something from the refrigerator he'd put there for them, like the bottled water for Indio. "Who pays for water?" Papì yelled, but he kept buying it because Indio wanted it. Even when they were in trouble outside the house, a place still waited at the table for them, with yells if they missed a meal. "Don't be out all night! Don't worry your mother!" For her brothers, no matter how fiercely her Papì's anger burned, it was always cooled with acceptance.

Since the end of school, she'd been cut off from Papì. When she was lucky, there was grim silence instead of stormy outbursts. He made no secret of his displeasure. His daughter should go to school, and do even better than Roberto. She couldn't; the thought of more school made her sick. Then magically, another option came along, like something from a Márquez novel, as matter-of-fact as the sun rising one morning in May. And just like in the novels, not everything was what it seemed. A thousand jobs, with a thousand paychecks and a thousand pistols, couldn't convince Papì that she was anything but his little daughter, running along the beach at Coney Island and chasing butterflies until she fell into the water. His brooding scowl, and clenched fist tucked onto his hip, showed he was only marking time until he erupted again.

None of that made waiting any easier for Vasquez. The manhole never moved. Shadows from the streetlights never changed. Ten P.M., midnight, and 2:00 A.M. all looked exactly the same, except that at midnight, two drunks spent a handful of minutes shouting at one another in the alley before shattering a bottle against the brick wall, and then at two, the golden tomcat prowled. Guthrie named him "Piss," which seemed like an insult to go with the injury of waiting. She couldn't sneak over to the corner for relief. By the time night began lifting, Vasquez had fed her anger everything that would burn, and nothing remained but a bitter pile of ashes and coals in her belly.

Two small, grimy men stopped on the sidewalk. Both wore dark clothes that showed stains as light splotches, and their ratty mustaches split their pale faces into halves. One lifted the hinged top of the manhole, and the other climbed gingerly down. The first glanced around, missed seeing the detectives, then disappeared downward. The lid clanged shut after a rusty belch. Guthrie laughed softly, and Vasquez glared at him.

"Weitz hated stakeouts, too," Guthrie said. His back and legs crackled when he stood.

They flowed with the early traffic moving downtown. The morning was cool enough for cracked windows. Guthrie drove. He stopped at a diner in midtown for breakfast. His jokes couldn't lighten Vasquez's mood, because she was beginning to understand that a lot of Guthrie's work was like a stakeout, watching videos, or writing reports—slow and boring.

Peering over the top of scrambled eggs and bacon, she said, "We're not getting anything out of that manhole."

Guthrie grunted and shook his head. "We got the cat's schedule now. We can bag him any night we want. You don't know somebody who wants a piss yellow tomcat?"

"Shut the fuck up," Vasquez muttered. She rearranged eggs around a bite of bacon. "Be serious."

"Okay, we got the drunk in the alley. He's been there two nights in a row. Maybe he sees our ghost going in and out, even though he don't stay all night. I don't like him. The Gaines brothers are a better chance."

"Those two scruffy guys?"

"Sure. Lucky we saw them. They'd sell their sister for a dollar."

"Lucky because you want to buy their sister?"

Guthrie grinned. "See, you never know," he said. "And you're probably not going to believe this, but I first ran into them on a stakeout. I was tailing a guy I was trying to make smell bad, seeing what I could find on him."

"What d'you mean?"

"Politics is dirty business in the city." He tore off a big piece of bagel with his teeth and spoke around it. "My guy is going to the same place over in TriBeCa, night after night. I can't squeeze in, so I'm watching the entrance for each time he comes out—hoping there'll be a girl, or whatever. Then I can run him to ground.

"Along come two guys, these scruffy little nondescript mutts— the Gaines brothers, who I don't know at the time. They cut over from Hudson, on the far side of the street. Traffic's not moving much. I'm sitting there, so I can't miss them. They're shuffling along, maybe drunk, just two guys on a stroll, and all of a sudden they stop. They huddle up like the Giants trying to call a play. Then Ralph swings over to the door of the warehouse—a street door, not a roller door—and goes inside. A minute later, he pokes out; then Rodney goes in with him.

"This is so stupid." He paused to drink some coffee. "After a little while, they come out, just the same as they went in, and walk down the street. A half hour later, they come back and stop again at the door. Then they both go inside. I'm watching the club door, with a steady line of peacocks going in and out, so the thing across the street is just happening. As the night goes along, it happens so much that I can set my watch by the Gaines brothers. They need forty-five minutes each time they go inside, leave, and come back. By the time my guy pops from the club, they've already quit. On the last trip, Ralph Gaines slaps a lock on the door—he's closing up shop.

"That's on Friday. Saturday night is the same thing all night. I watch them take the lock off, in and out, forty-five-minute trips, and they lock up again before I follow my guy away from the club. They do the same thing all night Sunday. By then, I'm pretty sure I had them wrong—maybe they actually work there. But Monday night, I'm trailing my guy again, and the NYPD knocks on my window while I'm sitting outside the club. 'Hey buddy, whatcha doing?' I let him know, and they ask if I saw anybody break into the warehouse across the street and rob the loft upstairs.

"Ralph and Rodney emptied the poor bastard's refrigerator. They took his clothes, and a bunch of crap. They left his plasma, his computer, that stuff. I'm serious. They took the dirty clothes outta his hamper and all. Soap, toilet paper, everything—they cleaned out his domestic shit."

"They're going to help us how?" Vasquez asked.

Guthrie laughed. "I know, right? That metro princess in TriBeCa was screaming. They didn't touch anything that was insured. That killed him. But they know things, and they're always hot. They're going underground, so they'll know what's down there."

"Like Ghost Eddy." She pushed eggs around on her plate.

"I can get in touch with them because they're predictable."

Vasquez finished her toast after dropping a dollop of runny jelly on it. "Look, I can hear you explaining that stakeouts do the job—sometimes not even the job you're doing." She frowned. "How about the guy you were watching?"

"Ah, I never got him. Maybe he was clean."

The young Puerto Rican shook her head. "I don't like sitting still. I know, you don't have to say—I don't have to like it. I have to learn how to deal with it. Okay?"

"You could get somewhere with that attitude," Guthrie said.

Henry Street was already awake when the old Ford cruised up to the front of her parents' tenement. Garbage was going out, and brooms were dusting sidewalks. A few suspicious youngsters watched them, then ran off. Vasquez climbed out of the car and hitched at her gun belt before she went up the steps. The morning was cool. She paused and looked up at the building. Her long ponytail looked like a black stripe down her jacket, just another vertical line on a slim young woman. Nothing went sideways except the brim of her cap and the bunched-up sleeves of her windbreaker. She wasn't out of the ordinary. She went inside. She was right at home.

CHAPTER TWELVE

That afternoon, Guthrie ventured onto the Net, looking for Justin Peiper. Vasquez watched him fish out a SSN and a short list of credit cards with juggled balances. Peiper had trouble managing his finances—tossing debts from one card to another—but cleared all of his balances on the second of August. Most New Yorkers couldn't manage that. Guthrie searched dates, times, and places to cross-check with LMA, Washington Heights, Melrose, and the twenty-third of July. He reasoned that the districts near the crime scene might turn up a timely purchase, or give him proof whether the dark-haired man was at LMA the night Bowman was killed. He found nothing. Peiper was missing, so to speak, on the night of Bowman's murder. He registered credit-card bills for LMA and in places in the Heights infrequently, but credit-card charges didn't place him anywhere on the twenty-third.

"That would've been easy," Guthrie muttered. He searched court documents in Utica to examine the assaults. Both were pled down to misdemeanors from ABHAN, a felony that had sent both of Vasquez's brothers to Rikers before. Peiper didn't mind waiting for someone to turn their head before he started trouble. Vasquez went back to her own desk with a shrug. While the hunt was on, she'd watched over Guthrie's shoulder.

After that, the little detective propped his feet up on his desk, moving only to refill his cup of coffee. A succession of frowns marched across his face. He opened his notebook and slowly turned the pages, but it didn't seem as if he was reading what was there. "We need another look at him," he said finally.

"Justin Peiper?" Vasquez asked.

"Sure. We're going up to the university."

On the drive up Broadway, Vasquez discovered that Guthrie didn't mean to stalk Peiper. He called Michelle Tompkins to make sure that she would be on campus. The traffic was moving quickly. Tompkins was in a class, so they would spend a little time on campus waiting for her. They had a long look at a barricade of clouds piled high in the eastern sky. Some invisible wall had the relief penned away from Manhattan, which glowed with ruddy, distorted heat. The dog days were barking along.

The auditoriums of McNamara Hall huddled drunkenly around an atrium roofed with glass. Clever workmanship joined the smaller buildings into a whole but couldn't quite unite the scattered arrangement. The mezzanine bent in irregular lengths and lolled staircases out like tongues into a disjointed lobby. Guthrie and Vasquez strolled for a quarter of an hour before locating the second-floor door to Tompkins's auditorium. They waited, watching students also wait and wander. The classrooms attracted fewer customers than the food court, but they seemed the same—a mix of the busy pouring around the slack.

Michelle Tompkins came from the auditorium with a satchel over her shoulder, near the front of a small group of students. She wore a pleated khaki skirt that clung to her hips and revealed muscular calves tapering down to slender ankles. Her chocolate brown hair bounced in unruly waves above the collar of her short-sleeved button-down shirt. When she saw the detectives, her eyebrows knitted into an annoyed frown, but she strode quickly over.

"*You* have been busy," she said.

"We have," Guthrie said. "I believe I found the mess you warned me about."

Tompkins smiled bitterly. "Wasn't difficult, was it?" she asked quietly. "I suppose it's fortunate that most of it's gone—or unfortunate, since that was Cammie." She looked at them impatiently and took a hesitant step along the mezzanine. "Perhaps we should go somewhere off campus?"

"We like the idea of an audience," Vasquez said.

"Then you had a reason for the drama yesterday. I've already heard several versions, though, naturally"—she smiled again, but it looked like mockery—"only one call from Sigma. That was Amanda, in a panic." She walked over to the mezzanine rail and lowered her satchel to the carpeted floor. "I won't disagree that the method makes sense. You might frighten someone into foolishness. How is it that I can help?"

"You have an insider's view of what they were doing at LMA," Guthrie said. "So far, we have the story from witnesses standing too far away, or from witnesses who're busy trying to hide it."

Tompkins's eyebrows lifted in surprise, then drifted back downward into an annoyed twist. "I'm not sure what you think I can tell you. I didn't even know she was kidnapped outside LMA, until you told me—"

"Quit kidding me, Michelle. You've been trying to stay clear since the beginning, but you must've thought it was something sexual all along. You were running with her before she met Olsen. You met Olsen after she brought him in, but that's when your knowing the ropes at Columbia became important. You knew she was up to absolutely nothing before she met Olsen—and I bet she didn't go outside the Sigma set to bring in an alumna. You had to go to her. You knew what she was doing, because she was some use to you—"

"Okay, *I get it*! You're a detective!" Tompkins said. Some passing students slowed to listen when she raised her voice, but then hurried on when Guthrie gave them a hard look. Vasquez propped herself against the railing after peering over; a few faces in the lobby were turned their way.

"It's true. I went to Cammie. I saw how easily she moved around, and I sold her the idea that I would be useful to her." She smiled, but with a thoughtful look that tinged it with sadness. For a flashing moment, she was beautiful, but even when her expression changed, the image wouldn't go away. "That turned out to be true."

"What was the point of it?"

"Cammie was my way into LMA." She shrugged, leaned back against the railing, and stretched out a hand on either side of it. The relaxed pose plushed her curves to Hellenic proportions. "If it comes out, it comes out. I suppose it's too late to worry about exposure—there were too many pictures anyway to keep all of them from escaping." She laughed. "When I first came to Columbia, I didn't look like this. I could say that more clearly. I was undeveloped—I suppose I looked like you," she continued, glancing at Vasquez. "But I didn't have your face. I was introverted, an outcast forced upon the socially more adept; a plain, unattractive girl with no advantage but money. Despite what everyone might say, money doesn't make pain go away. When I was an undergrad, I dealt with it by focusing on school, and trying not to get trampled. By the time I realized I did want to be included, my role was already set in stone. I was the outsider.

"Then Cammie came to Columbia. The initial connection was a family one—I was supposed to look out for my cousin—and she was a Sigma legacy, too." She smiled bitterly. "But imagine anyone asking me to help watch out for Camille Bowman. There was nothing I could do for her."

"Maybe you're selling yourself short," Guthrie said. "She needed you for school."

"Not really," Tompkins said, and shook her head. "Cammie was smart, even if it wasn't easy to see past the face. She only had to apply herself. That wasn't how it unfolded, though. In the game the houses played, she could decide who played with whom. She could put me with the people I wanted, and that's where we started. It wasn't until after she met Greg that I saw she could be something more than that."

"Like what?"

"An adult."

"Olsen is your problem here," Vasquez said. "I think you have a thing for him, and that's why we're here. I know you said you didn't kill your cousin. You sold me on that. But everything we uncover points at you or Olsen. Do you—"

"That's crap," Tompkins said. "I didn't do it. Neither did Greg. Whether I like him really isn't an issue. The games might have made him look bad, maybe, but they were over before Cammie started with him—but not before they met. At first, they were classmates, like I told you. Once she realized she wanted to be with him, she left the games, but even then she had been following him around for weeks. He knew she was doing crazy things, and he knew that she stopped. He thought it was childish, he told her so, and left it at that. Greg is just cut from a different cloth."

Vasquez smirked. "That could convince his mother."

"Does it really sound that stupid?" Tompkins asked with a pained expression. "Then okay, he makes me stupid. I can't say I have a lot of sympathy for lucky people, like you"—she nodded at Vasquez—"or myself. You're looks-lucky and I'm money-lucky. I know I helped make this mess, but now I need a way out. Maybe lucky people need help sometimes, too."

"What's important is that you were rolling with Bowman before Olsen came along," Guthrie said. "We're not interested in the rest of it. Your eyes were on the inside. Who was she with before Olsen? Not hookups. I need to know who spent time at her apartment. Who felt territorial?"

"That could've been anyone from the G unit, but I think you already started with the top of the list—Justin Peiper."

Guthrie shook his head. "Who had a key?"

"I had one, and then there was 'the key.' It was passed around."

She shook her head at their frowns. "This time, it isn't what you think. Cammie's Greenwich Village apartment was the spot, but not always for her. My apartment on the West Side was our safe house. Grove Street was for playing around. A lot of sisters used it."

"You mean Sigma Kappa?"

"And Alpha Chi Omega. The boys, too."

Guthrie whistled. "That's what you mean by the G unit. Delta Psi fraternity, two sororities—"

"And Kappa Alpha, more guys. Two pairs of houses."

"I guess I don't need to tell you that a pass-around key is gonna make it hard to keep this quiet," he said. "Did she fight with any of them? Why did Olsen get the gun?"

"The sisters were scared of Cammie—they wouldn't cross her. She wanted the gun because of Peiper. He's real intense. She didn't tell Greg that, because he probably would've hurt Peiper. She fed him a story about a rash of break-ins." Tompkins frowned, pausing thoughtfully. "Greg was out a lot at night—he didn't sleep through nights—so a lot of times he wouldn't be there. But the gun was crazy. Peiper wasn't going to do anything to her. . . ." Tompkins dribbled to a stop.

"That don't sound right to me, neither," Vasquez said.

"Maybe that's the brick I need," Guthrie said. "Somebody's going to feel the pressure."

Tompkins scooped up her satchel and lifted it onto her shoulder. She put on a pair of plastic-framed glasses to hide her blue eyes, and suddenly she was anonymous again, mouselike and plain. Vasquez leaned against the mezzanine rail and watched her walk away.

"She's real sure you're gonna protect her, *viejo*," Vasquez said.

"It's something more than that," Guthrie said, "because she knew that all along. I think she don't believe we're gonna find out what she was doing."

The young Puerto Rican detective frowned. She looked again for Tompkins, who was walking unnoticed across the lobby. More eyes were aimed at the detectives than gave the graduate student even a passing glance. They followed her down the stairs, into the pool of hot sunlight pouring down from the transparent ceiling. Passing outside was like dropping from the pot into the fire. The sun was ascendant, and the clouds skulked in fear along the eastern skyline.

The Columbia campus seemed empty. When they left, they were immediately caught up in the movement of the city, like leaving an empty back bedroom where the coats were stacked to join a dinner party. All of the people of New York rubbed against one another in the streets, no matter how different they were. Going from one world to another could take a lifetime, or it could be as easy as passing through a door. Just when they walked on the streets, opposites could catch a glimpse of each other and dream, anytime they wanted.

Jude Nelson was distracted when Guthrie and Vasquez walked back into his bodega on 149th Street. The bell rang, and their eyes began adjusting from the brilliant sunshine of the street as if the sound were a signal. A half dozen middle school kids, dressed in tones of urban cool, drifted in the two narrow aisles of the bodega. Nelson stood at the counter, frowning, occasionally craning his neck when one of the youngsters rounded the end of the shelves in the back. The streaks of white in the old store owner's mustache and beard stood out sharply against his dark face.

Guthrie leaned against the counter for a minute, watching, then smiled. "All right," he announced. "All of you bring a drink and a candy bar to the counter. I'm buying."

The kids hesitated, gathering, and finally the biggest boy asked, "What's the matter with you?"

"Look, kid, I can't rob the place with a bunch of witnesses in here," Guthrie snapped. "Bring something on up here, then scram."

A stream of sodas and candy passed across the counter, and the kids hurried out. Only one lingered to stare for a moment through the window. Nelson settled back on his stool with a sigh. The kids had been nerving up for a half hour, preparing for one of child-hood's rites of passage—shoplifting. Watching was hard, even though he knew that it was just something kids would do, like throwing rocks or splashing their way through puddles.

Guthrie admitted to Nelson that he was a reformed shoplifter. A younger but not too much smaller version of himself usually pock-eted chocolate cupcakes. That was before he realized sugar was bad for him, he continued, while he paid for some cupcakes. The old store owner laughed. He'd lived down south when he was little, and he'd slipped into orchards and carried away peaches.

"Kids are gonna find something to steal, sure enough." Nelson shifted on his stool and smoothed his mustache. He nodded to Vasquez when she drew breath to ask a question, then said, "Ghost Eddy heard me out, but I don't know if it made much difference, considering that his hands didn't pause about going in his pockets.

"That big man is hard to read, with that beard covering most of his face, and wearing those mirrored aviators. Maybe he even keeps his eyes closed and smells his way back and forth." The old man grinned. "I suppose waiting those few days wound me up about it, and then my pitch sounded flat.

"He spent fifty-four dollars on vodka and Kahlúa, a tin of sar-dines, and some cheese crackers, in case you're interested, and he had new money, just like usual. He has a lot of pockets. I suppose when he's drunk, he might forget where he put the money. While he fished in his pockets, I talked. I've watched him do that a hundred times, and usually he don't pay it mind. He might have a particular order he goes about it."

Nelson grinned. "That was fun. Are you on your toes, young lady?" He didn't give Vasquez a chance to reply before he continued. "He didn't say anything, so I asked him if he didn't mind whether the wrong man might be sitting in jail. After he set out his money, he says, 'What makes you think they don't have the man I saw?'"

"So I say, 'What about you? Do *you* know?'"

"'That don't matter,' he says. 'Did a killing ever matter before, except when there was some money in it? Leave it be, old-timer.'

"Can you imagine?" the store owner said. "That big old man may not be quite as old as me—I can't always tell—but he's near it. So I says, 'You're old enough to know things *do* change. I own this store, and you're buying straight from my hands—how's that? Then look who's sitting in the White House. Things change. How can you leave a man in jail on maybe when you're holding for sure? Don't do that.'

"He heard me, but I couldn't read him. I'm sure I could've said more. You reminded me just now when you walked in on those kids. When I was a child, I stole peaches from white folks in Georgia, dreading what they might do. Now I got white kids stealing from me. The world moves on."

"But it ain't made him talk?" Vasquez asked.

"Afraid not," he said. "I suppose he had some of the right of it. Money's what's got you here. That man in jail's paying, else he would have no one on his side."

"America's ugly along that side of her face," Guthrie admitted.

CHAPTER THIRTEEN

Late in the afternoon, Guthrie and Vasquez parked across the street from New Albuquerque Pawn and Loan on Forty-seventh Street, which boasted a painting of a man wearing a blue-and-cream shirt with a tall hat, overshadowed by a saguaro cactus. The heat was oppressive, but down the street clouds were boiling like rice, rushing in from the Atlantic. The pawnshop was a low-rent crackhead dive. Scrawny humans of indeterminate sex vibrated in and out of the entrance, in various stages of pre- and post-score mania. A handful of junkies with nothing to sell orbited the entrance while worrying fingers through their matted hair, torn between running for a soft score or spending the afternoon begging from the more fortunate. The detectives walked the gauntlet to enter the pawnshop.

Ground-out cigarette butts filled the cracks between the sidewalk and the storefront. Inside, an off-on smell of old vomit waited like a lonely dog. Suggestive stains darkened the floor in front of the display guitars, where some junkie bent on a jones had paused to reconsider his bygone musical career. The counterman was a tall, fat heavyweight with body hair all of the way down to his fingertips.

A cigarette dangled from the corner of his mouth, and the eye above it was sealed shut from the heat. A dirty patch on his brown work-shirt said ROBBIE. Glassed counters and displays stretched past open doorways into more collections of used, grubby memorabilia.

"Ralph Gaines been in here yet?" Guthrie asked. The counter-man didn't blink, but he reached out to take the fifty that appeared in the little detective's hand.

"Nope."

"Tell him Clayton Guthrie was here asking."

Guthrie and Vasquez walked out. The heat on the street was a relief. They dodged through the traffic like they were making sure the smell of the pawnshop couldn't follow them without getting hit by a car.

"They'll run when they hear your name," Vasquez said, frowning, when she settled back behind the wheel of the Ford.

"Ain't but one way out," Guthrie said. "We wait. You go ahead and have that Smith in your pocket. Ralph's terrified of guns."

They rode low in the front seat and watched the New Albuquerque. The clouds rolled in from the east and darkened the afternoon into early twilight. A hard, thick shower swept through Hell's Kitchen like a whisk broom. Junkies scurried back and forth like startled cats, crouching in doorways. Once the rain blew through, they rolled the windows back down to enjoy the cool air chasing the rain.

The Gaines brothers came hurrying down Forty-seventh Street as the sky lightened again. Both men had bulging pockets and jack-ets stretched around misshapen packages. Rodney kept getting out in front, then pausing to wait impatiently while Ralph caught up with him. At some distance, Ralph's limp was pronounced. He swung a stiff right leg wide to the side before it would go forward, bouncing along like a disco dancer obsessed with practice. They disappeared into the pawnshop.

Guthrie and Vasquez climbed out of the old blue Ford and crossed the street. The junkies in front of the New Albuquerque watched, and their hollowed-out eyes turned dark with suspicion. They drifted away from the storefront. Guthrie posted Vasquez on the west side of the door, because the Gaines brothers had come from the east. The Gaines brothers spent some time bargaining for their score, and Vasquez started to get impatient.

"Ralph was always slower than Rodney," the little detective said. "That was how he ended up with the limp." He paused to step out to the sidewalk and glance down the street.

"Anyway, back when they were baby dirtbags, they ran out of places to make a score, but they still needed a bag—like that wasn't every day—but this time they had the bright idea to hit their mother. That was probably Rodney's idea. He's pretty stupid. They tore up the house looking for wherever it was that the money was stashed, and she came home while they were looking. She was a pretty tough old Brooklyn girl, and she kept a purse gun. When she came in, I guess she heard them rooting around, tearing up the kitchen. Rodney's got good ears; he dove out the window. Ralph tried behind him, but he was still hanging halfway when she came through the door with the gun out. Naturally, she couldn't recognize his ass end, so she plugged him right in the ass while he was trying to pull the rest of the way across the window ledge."

Vasquez was still laughing when the Gaines brothers hurried out. They stared at her, rushing, and plowed into Guthrie because they were trying to go back the way they'd come. A flurry of cursing ended when Vasquez flashed her pistol.

"Freeze, *chico*," she said.

"Ah, damn," Ralph Gaines said, and stopped wrestling against Guthrie's grip.

The brothers were about the same size as Guthrie: the middle of five feet and square in the 130's—right in the middle of Harlem. At a distance he might have passed as a third brother, but without the signature mustache and speckled clothes. The difference was in the face. The little old detective had a face as hard and flat as a brick; the Gaines brothers were younger, and their eyes darted like goldfish looking for a way out.

Guthrie doubled up his grip on Ralph Gaines's dirty black jacket and marched him across the street. Rodney Gaines mumbled a string of curses as he followed. Vasquez trailed them, hand burrowed into her jacket pocket. Guthrie pushed Ralph into the backseat of the old Ford, and Vasquez climbed into the driver's seat. Rodney stood outside the car for a few seconds, undecided, before he climbed into the passenger seat.

"Look, if it's about that place on Seventy-eighth, I can explain," Ralph said. "Anyway, you never said stay away from there."

"Ralph, you need to steal some toothpaste. If you find a place on Seventy-eighth with any, be my guest. And get some soap while you're at it."

Gaines sidled away on the bench seat as far as Guthrie's grip allowed. "Ain't nobody told you to touch me."

"This ain't about a score, Ralph. This's a chance for you to do me a favor, so don't blow it. I'll pay off, like usual."

"You mean quick money, or a get-out-of-jail-free card?"

"Your choice."

The brothers exchanged a sly glance across the car seat. "We'll take that upfront," Ralph said. "Never know where you'll be tomorrow, you know?"

"When you prove out, naturally, not for cooking up a good lie to feed me." Guthrie flashed a smile. "The other night I caught a look at the two of you dropping into the ground on One Fifty-first. You going someplace down there?"

"You're asking about the carousel."

"Tell me about it, then."

"A million years ago, the subway lines didn't all run the same as now. The old rail companies were always looking to beat each other—didn't even use the same kind of tracks. There was a Bronx line that came under the river, and back then it was for real special, but it got pushed under by another company—"

Guthrie twisted Ralph Gaines's jacket collar until he squeaked. "When you start studying history? Are you high already? You're cooking this up?"

"No, man! Take it easy! The man down there studies up on this shit. He runs the squat, and it's real cool. Some of them old leather cushions are still comfortable, you know?"

"If you're shitting me, this could go bad," the little detective said.

"Not our problem your people are on you," Rodney said. "That's your lookout for working for them."

"Shut up, Rodney. You're stupid," Ralph Gaines said. "He don't got to get it, Guthrie. I get it. The carousel was this fancy place for switching trains, with bars and kitchens and all. The man found it in a book, buried in a library somewhere. The place ain't really for lightsiders, you know? The man's got people. The families can come, and people can bring business, but his people will waste you. They'll wall you up in a hole and forget where they put you."

"Anybody can go there?"

"Yeah, but, you know." He glanced at Vasquez. "You two would stick out stupid, no offense."

"We'll fix that," Guthrie said. "I'm not looking for the place, see; I'm looking for a guy I know went underground. He was aboveground, all the way uptown on the river, but he's dodging. You heard of Ghost Eddy?"

"*That* guy's a nutcase. He don't want *nothing*—"

"Shut up, Rodney."

"What're you saying?" Guthrie demanded.

"All he does is sit in the dark and drink. No women, no dope, no cards. He could do his thing in an overturned trash can, if he could stand all that racket he makes when he's sleeping—"

"I don't think that evil son of a bitch sleeps," Ralph said. "I think he just pitches those fits when he's deep in the bottle."

"So he's down there?"

"Oh yeah," Ralph said. "I could point you where he lays, but I'm not getting my head twisted off for no money."

"You don't mind that part. I just need you to get me down in the carousel and give me some bearings."

"All right. Then drive on up to Trinity, and—"

"Not tonight. *Tomorrow* at midnight." Guthrie pulled a bundle of money from his pocket, peeled ten fifties slow enough for Ralph to count, and handed them to the grimy little man. "This is tonight, for talking. *Tomorrow*, midnight, I lay this on you five times."

Staring at the money, Rodney Gaines let out a yodel that startled the people walking by the old Ford on Forty-seventh Street. He jumped out of the car as soon as Ralph dragged his leg free from the backseat. The Gaines brothers hurried up Forty-seventh and Guthrie moved to the passenger seat. He left the door open to air out the stench.

On the way back to the office, they stopped at a secondhand store. The rain shower had wet the streets enough to dry the dust, but the heat glowed back through quickly. Guthrie bought a few sets of mismatched army fatigues and two pairs of boots in their sizes. The clothes and shoes were throwaways, because he wasn't sure what they would find underground. He knew enough dusty, unswept corners in New York to accept Ralph Gaines's story, without being sure how much faith to place in the description. He wanted to be ready. The darkness under the city wasn't inclined to forgive mistakes.

At the office, the little detective showed Vasquez his holdouts. On both wings of the back wall, the wainscoting was a facade covering lockboxes.

The little detective locked the outer door, drew the shades, and brought out a small toolbox. He used needle-nose pliers to draw the finish nails from the wainscoting, which lifted out to reveal a removable section of plasterwork that made the holdout sound solid. Guthrie used one lockbox for guns and the other for anything else.

"Wasserman used a gun cabinet, right over there by the window," he said. "He had a class-three permit—grandfathered automatic weapons and everything. He left the artillery behind, but I got rid of the cabinet." He pointed along the wall toward the windows looking down on Thirty-fourth Street.

"You would rather take the extra trouble," Vasquez said dubiously, studying the little man's tools and the carefully arrayed boards.

Guthrie shrugged. "That sort of paperwork attracts attention," he said, and smiled. "Then sometimes you shouldn't put something you want in a bank or storage. Maybe it ain't open when you need it. Maybe people watch you go back and forth, and check on what you're doing. Being a squirrel is a good thing when it gets you through a winter, but not if it's too easy to find the tree where you cut nuts."

Vasquez frowned. The little detective had a thing with animals, but that didn't always help her understand what he was trying to say. He compared the situation to Ghost Eddy's; the gray drifter had habits that made it possible to locate him. All people did predictable things, and you could discover anything if you watched patiently. Some things were just simpler than others, like with drug dealers. Whatever disguise they attempted, three things always stood out: The dope had to come from somewhere, it had to be stashed somewhere, and the money had to go somewhere. When people did things, they had a purpose. The dealer went to pick up his dry cleaning, went grocery shopping, or slipped over to his girlfriend's house. When he did something where the purpose wasn't obvious, or maybe did something obvious too often, a watcher found something.

"You make that sound too easy, *viejo*," Vasquez complained.

Guthrie laughed. "Drug dealers don't get caught, because nobody's really watching them," he said. "Anyway, hand me those laptops from Bowman's apartment in the village. They're going in the box with this hard drive." He unwired Bowman's hard drive from the office system and slid it into the strongbox. He stacked the laptops with it.

"What's the problem there?" she asked.

"Something Tompkins said about pictures, up at the university. She said there're pictures out there. Those files are huge—probably video, graphics, whatever—and the names were alphabet soup. *Then* I remembered, there was alphabet soup in the trash can in the Village. We could be talking about something somebody wanted."

"Then wouldn't they just take the drive?"

Guthrie shrugged. "Criminals ain't all supergeniuses. Sometimes you get the Gaines brothers. And sometimes a supergenius makes a mistake, just like Wily. I know a guy in Brooklyn who'll look at this stuff for me."

That night, Guthrie and Vasquez drove downtown to haunt Chinatown. The little detective wanted to stay on a night cycle, so he would be alert when the Gaines brothers took them to the carousel in the underground. He let Vasquez cut back and forth among the downtown business districts, switching between abandoned streets and those still thrumming with life. As the hours ticked by, he occasionally looked at his wristwatch and called out a distant address, timing how long Vasquez needed to drive there. He questioned her each time why she chose her route, like Seventh Avenue instead of Park, or the Manhattan Bridge when he sent her into Brooklyn. When he had introduced her to driving the Ford, he made her drive routes the same way, but in the daytime. After each outbound that night, he always sent her back to Chinatown. She guided the old blue Ford slowly through the quiet streets, watching. Sometime before dawn broke, like an egg yolk bleeding yellow into a dark pan, she discovered the difference between watching and watching *for* something. Suddenly, they were two different things, when before it had been impossible to tell them apart.

CHAPTER FOURTEEN

With their meeting with the Gaines brothers set for midnight, Guthrie and Vasquez didn't go into the office until six o'clock the next evening. The day's heat was beginning its slow slide down. The Garment District was still busy with rolling racks, and shouts accompanying last-minute deliveries. A message waited for them on the old-fashioned answering machine Guthrie kept in the office, signaling laconically with a blinking red light.

"Guthrie, this is Mike Inglewood. You remember me, right? The guy who works for NYPD in the big building downtown. Say hello to—what's her name, the new one? Vasquez! Say hello to Vasquez for me. Tell her she should go to the Academy if she wants to learn how to do real police work. Unless she likes that Peeping Tom stuff you got her doing." He laughed roughly. "I been trying to get hold of you all day, Guthrie. Too bad. I had to talk to your client—Olsen. Maybe you would've liked to be there to take notes, or something. I think Rikers agrees with him. People say the air is cleaner, but knowing what I know about the East River, I ain't so sure." He laughed again. "I don't know which one of him I talked to. I think it's the one that dummied up and asked for a lawyer. But like I was saying, we should get together. I'll be down at Mako's after hours. Come on by; we'll laugh at the Angels game. Talk shop. You know." More laughter was amputated by a disconnect.

"He's waving the other murders in my face," Guthrie said. "That don't really matter, though. He's asking us down there, so we go and have dinner on the city. We got time for an extra meeting in front of midnight."

Vasquez drove downtown and parked by the old Custom's House. They walked down to the sports bar off the park. People lounged like cats on the waterfront, catching a breeze off the bay to unwind. Mako's was dark inside, noisy with diners and a half-baked crowd jeering the Angels on the large screen behind the bar. The NYPD detectives had a booth in the back; Inglewood shouted and waved like a lunatic when he saw Guthrie. On the way to the back, the little detective slowed a waitress long enough to order steak sandwiches, fries, and a pitcher.

The little detective poured himself a mug of beer from the pitcher waiting on the table. Landry was there, too. He shot him a sour look, then scowled when Inglewood grinned and reached beneath the table to produce a folder. All of Inglewood's work was on paper. He was a man determined to avoid the computer revolution, along with anything else new, exciting, or championed by somebody under the age of forty. He pushed some dirty plates aside, dabbed at a puddle of beer with a napkin, then spread his folder on the table.

The front part of the folder held crime-scene pictures. A doll-like blonde, pretty in a battered way, was splattered with blood. Beneath her the ground was a mess of crumbled asphalt, dust, and gravel. Her blouse was messy with blood, dead center. She was faceup, with her legs bunched up but her arms askew. A second, less messy wound decorated the base of her neck between the collarbone and spine.

"Pictures of Camille Bowman?" Guthrie asked. "Before these, I've just seen glamour shots."

"She was a beauty," Inglewood said. He dipped a cold steak fry in sauce and folded it into his mouth. "Keep going."

Glaring light illuminated the photos. In each one, Bowman was very dead. Wound photos with measurements and layouts of the scene accompanied photos of trace evidence gathered by ISU. Guthrie became impatient and flipped photos faster. Soon he came to the point where the photos began a fresh sequence.

The second fashion show also starred a pretty young blonde—an eerie similarity that could've been a remake of the same movie. Guthrie extracted the topover shot of the second girl—body faceup, with bunched legs, arms askew, a messy wound in the center of the chest, and a second bullet hole in the base of her neck. Guthrie flipped back to find Bowman's matching picture. He grunted.

"GI Ken didn't have much reaction, either," Inglewood said, pushing his taped-together glasses back up his nose. "Anyway, I heard you found a wit didn't turn up on canvass. That right?"

"Sure," Guthrie said. "His handle's Ghost Eddy; it fits. I ain't cornered him yet, but I'm gonna get another interview to see if he eliminates my guy."

"Well now!" the ginger-haired detective said, then smiled. "Let me level with you, Guthrie. I got no feelings about GI Ken, myself. Then you're not even sure what your witness says? How's that gonna help?" He rapped a fingertip on the stack of pictures, then folded them away and tucked them beneath the table. "Now this is coming soon. Where are you?"

The little detective shook his head, and spent a few minutes making a steak sandwich vanish after the waitress set it on the table. The quiet at the table made the bar seem louder. To Vasquez, they seemed like a table of old guys studying hard on a draw of dominoes. The hard eyes, the scowls, and sharp glances were only missing a slam and a click to punctuate the points.

Guthrie shrugged after wiping steak sauce from his mouth with a napkin. "I should start at the beginning," he said. "Down there at Major Case, your guy Barber was never working the Bowman case.

He was working the other case all along. I know this because I'm working the Bowman case, and I got fresh trail. I think Olsen's clean. After I've looked around for a while, maybe I pinpoint him elsewhere when Bowman gets killed—I'm not even done with that much, Mike. You see where I'm going?"

"I never thought you were gonna lay down on it, Guthrie," Inglewood said.

"Here's my theory—somebody framed Olsen on sexual jealousy. Maybe this happens to be Barber's killer, who crossed paths with Olsen. Or maybe somebody lucked into a good copy while they were placing the frame. Those are guesses. What I'm not guessing about is this: some serious heavyweights are involved, from uptown. They're gonna line up for a crack at whoever fucked this one up. I don't think it ever goes to trial, unless the ADA has a sick desire to be kicked repeatedly where the sun don't shine." The little detective paused to finish his beer. "That brings me to my problem. If I give you a list of suspects, you could get stuff splattered all over you. It ain't gonna wash off easy if it goes in the air."

Inglewood shrugged. "I was born dirty," he said. "But I gotta say, if you don't want it out, you better find another way to clear Olsen."

"All right, Mike. We appreciate the beer and sandwiches. I'll let the bigwig get you next time."

Across the hazy bay, Brooklyn lay humpbacked and slumbering beyond Governor's Island. Daylight drained from the sky like bathwater. Standing outside Mako's, Guthrie called Justin Peiper. After a disjointed phone conversation loaded with exasperated pauses, the college student gave Guthrie an address for a midtown club where he would be available all night.

"I think that kid gets high," Guthrie said to Vasquez as they walked back to the Custom's House for the car. "Or maybe he's got some nervous tic."

The club was on Third Avenue. Coming into midtown, the big buildings hovered overhead like pregnant clouds. They towered above Everland, a redbrick building squatting behind a chain-link fence and a narrow parking lot. A row of loading-dock doors into a stepped-down sublot on one side suggested brewery. Fresh entrances had been carved through the brickwork, but paint and a smeared patina of decorations didn't hide the grilles of industrial windows near the roof.

Everland's vast interior space was wrapped in a mezzanine disguised as a crenellated wall, and crudely divided with rough-sawn lumber. Wide cloth banners drooped in ranks from the high ceiling, dampening the sound. The gamer club still had the bones of industrial machinery thrusting through its medieval facade like the knobby knees and heavy boots of giants. Banks of computers lined side bars and filled booths. Music washed over the crowd, but they were talking, not dancing.

Vasquez spotted Justin Peiper at a side bar, tapping flurries on a keyboard and talking to himself. A cheap tapestry of a dragon hung above his head on the high wall. He wore blue jeans and a collared shirt, but the crowd swirling around him was decked in medieval pageantry—gowned ladies, armored knights, bards, robed wizards—while two tall men in armor battered each other with padded staffs on a raised platform. The crowd hooted and jeered each blow.

Guthrie and Vasquez pulled chairs from nearby tables to sit on either side of Peiper, and discovered that his conversation was with an earpiece, not an invisible friend. Vasquez prodded him with a fingertip, but he only glanced at her before returning his attention to the computer.

"We need some answers, *chico*," she said. "Don't waste our time."

Peiper grimaced but didn't look away from his computer screen. "Shouldn't you bring somebody big to do the bruiser part?"

Guthrie ignored the jab. "Where were you on the twenty-third?"

"In there," Peiper replied, pointing briefly at the screen before turning to face Guthrie. A sly smile brightened his face, but even the hint of malice left him charming. "I think somebody wants to challenge you, Mr. Detective." His finger flicked at a crowd gathering around them like wings spreading from the two tall men wearing armor and visored helms. "You must've said something to the wrong lady on your way over here."

Guthrie glanced at the crowd, then turned back. "I ain't got time for nonsense, son," he said.

One of the armored men extended his staff and rapped the little detective on the side of his head. His brown fedora rolled beneath the table. Guthrie spun to his feet, scanning the crowd. The tall men held their padded staffs poised, while the crowd began chanting, "Joust! Joust! Joust!"

With their faces hidden in visored helms, the tall men were unreadable. One thrust his staff at Guthrie. The little detective swiveled his hips to dodge, and caught the tip of the staff in a firm grip; while they struggled for the weapon, Guthrie slid slowly closer along the smooth floor. The other jouster swished his staff like a bat. Guthrie's head rolled like a ripe melon. He doubled over, still clinging to his grip on the outstretched staff.

"O, foul!" one of the costumed ladies cried.

Vasquez caught Peiper's wrist when he tried to stand, and shoved him against the side bar. "No, *chico*, you stay here with me," she said.

He grinned, raising his other hand in mock surrender. "No problem." He leaned against the bar, watching, as the crowd scattered to avoid a wide slash from a padded staff.

The little detective unrolled a sloppy somersault on the floor, ramming the legs of one jouster. The other tall man jabbed with his staff, but he missed. Guthrie sprang to his feet, clinging to the leg of the man standing over him. Guthrie's punch connected solidly with the tall man's crotch, folding him onto the floor. The crowd groaned in sympathy.

Guthrie sidestepped to avoid a hammer blow. The jouster backpedaled, recovering his staff, while the little detective paused to wipe a thread of blood from his nose. His face wrinkled with a disgusted frown. A lady and her bard pelted the tall jouster with jeers and square leather cushions from a nearby bench.

The jouster slashed. Guthrie ducked, then sprang forward with a kick before the backswing began. The jouster fended him away with a cross-check, then tried a jab, but the little detective slipped inside and slapped his visor. The jouster landed on his ass amid a chorus of laughter. Guthrie kicked him in the chest and he slid into a sprawl.

"Another blow receives banishment!" A pair of hefty bouncers dressed as English foresters pushed through the crowd. The onlookers swirled and scattered, while the bouncers pulled the tall men to their feet. Guthrie crawled beneath the table to retrieve his fedora before looking them over once their helmets came off, but he didn't recognize them.

"You got plenty of friends, Justin," the little detective said, dusting himself off.

"I can't help that you piss people off, Mr. Detective," Peiper said. He shrugged.

Vasquez prodded the young man again. "That was your little man, *chico*, the one that fell down?" She pointed at the unattended computer.

"Fuck!" Peiper stepped to the computer, and his fingers blurred on the keyboard. "What happened to the clerics? Morons!" He dropped back into his chair, and the snarl vanished from his face. "Don't matter . . . just a game."

"Right now, you got real-world problems," Guthrie said, "besides playing games with me. You need to account for your time on the twenty-third of July."

The young man turned to face Guthrie, grinning nastily. "No problem, Mr. Detective. I was in my dorm room, raiding with my guild. They'll vouch. We popped a Quarm on Time on the twenty-third, and it was my drop. I had a buyer waiting with five hundred to buy costume jewelry to wear during chat." He pointed at the costumed gamers around them. "Like those. This's where it turns freaky, though. I stayed in the dorm because I was running another account, selling crack—clarity—in the Nexus. Usually I wear my headset, but that Thursday I didn't. It wouldn't work without tinkering every few seconds. I didn't feel like being bothered, so I ditched it."

"Usually your mates could hear your voice when you played, but that Thursday, not so much?" Guthrie asked.

"My guild can vouch," he repeated. "I'll send you names. Anyway, that freak Olsen used his own gun to kill Cammie—that's in the papers, Mr. Detective."

Guthrie nodded, handing over a business card. "Sure. The same gun he kept at the Grove Street apartment in the Village. You remember that place? How many times did you have the key?"

Peiper laughed without missing a breath. "Silver-spoon central, right? Who cares? So I've been there." He turned back to his computer.

Unsatisfied, the detectives left Everland; the midtown night was under way. Traffic on Lexington was like a swing orchestra, and people rushed like blood from beating hearts on the sidewalks. Vasquez paused after she started the old Ford. "You looked pretty good in there, *viejo*, after you warmed up."

Guthrie shot her a sour look and wiped his nose.

"He was real comfortable on that computer," she offered.

Guthrie nodded. "Maybe enough to leave it behind after he took what he wanted," he said. "We're lucky he gave us the alibi. We ain't cops, to beat it outta him. That piece of crap is dirty. I can smell it. Boxing him in a corner is gonna be the hard part."

CHAPTER FIFTEEN

The detectives drove crosstown to the office. Guthrie took his Colt revolver from the desk drawer and slid it into a shoulder rig beneath a ragged field jacket from the secondhand store. When Vasquez came from the bathroom after changing into fatigues, he handed her a small holstered pistol. She paid him with a puzzled look.

"It's just like the one you're already carrying," he said. "A Chief's Special, forty caliber, except this one's got blue bullets. They're plastic. Next to the other one, this one won't kick."

"What's it for?" she asked.

The little old man took a deep breath. "Sometimes you might want to give somebody a warning," he said. "The plastic stings, might even draw some blood, but it ain't doing permanent harm except maybe to an eye. You can use that pistol to hammer away, even in a crowd. Especially if I'm standing there. If something happens, I'll tangle them up and try to keep you out of it, so you can get a clean shot."

"The same way you did with Ralph Gaines," she said.

"Sure, like that. Just don't get too in love with the idea that you can weigh in with this particular argument. Weitz drew trouble for that a few times. Probably it's a good thing you didn't have this earlier." He handed her an extra clip, already loaded. "Put your pistols in your jacket pockets for tonight, so they'll be handy. Some of these underground types ain't friendly. I don't want you ending up like Stoop-O for not having a pistol out quick enough to back somebody off."

Vasquez drove them up Eighth Avenue to Harlem. The night was already deep and dark by the time they parked and locked the old Ford on 151st Street. August heat still lingered on the street and reached out from the redbrick buildings to slap at them while they waited. Expectation transformed the abandoned lot. As a porch on the doorstep of unknown lands, the manhole oozed uneasiness the way a jack-o'-lantern spills flickering light.

A half hour before midnight, the Gaines brothers lurched from the alley across 151st Street and rushed the manhole like a badly organized tag team. Rodney went straight for the manhole. Ralph craned his head as he swung along, until he spotted Guthrie. He became a fast limper when he wanted to be somewhere. The little detective reassured him about the money, but he had the ill grace of a deprived addict. They all joined Rodney at the manhole. He peeled open the warped iron door to reveal steep stairs, and they went down into darkness. The hatch closed with a squeal and a clang.

Rusty stairs dropped twenty feet to a dirty brick tunnel running north and south. Guthrie and Vasquez lit it up with big halogen broad lights, saw that it shrank back into dark holes in both directions, then switched to smaller handheld lights. Rodney had a penlight, but he slipped it back into his pocket. Empty light sockets hung on the walls like eyeless watchers, spaced among conduit and piping. The Gaines brothers blended smoothly with the rough graffiti on the bricks, the scorch marks from campfires, and old bottles, cans, and bags littered beneath the piping at the bottom of the walls.

The tunnel was stand-up spacious and wide enough for the Gaines brothers to walk side by side. Rodney paused to fortify himself from a pint bottle of cheap vodka, then led them south as he fumbled it back into his pocket. The brothers shuffled along mostly side by side, but, like on the street above, Ralph would fall behind and then Rodney would pause to wait. In the bright, stabbing beams of the flashlights, they often looked like headless bodies, with the dark tunnel only present underfoot and in the puddles and swoops of light reaching ahead. Guthrie came along last. They walked south, passing dark openings that yawned silently and stank of still water, relieved by an occasional whiff of the distant river. Old repairs showed like dirty bandages on the piping along the walls, while the bricks changed colors like strippers doing sets, and alternated between running and English bond.

"We coulda come in closer?" Guthrie asked after a few hundred yards of darkness were behind them. His voice was quiet but seemed loud and sudden against the backdrop of silence under the city.

Ralph grunted assent. "Harder climb down, though."

A stiff leg saved them a climb down a ladder, at the cost of a long detour in darkness. They walked south. Rodney turned left into the ninth clear-out, kicked a clutch of ringing bottles out of his way, and muttered something about rats and a beating. Sour beer and the smoke from a recent fire failed to mask the stench of the drain. A slope of rough and dirty steps allowed them to scramble down, then drop a handful of feet onto fine gravel that was moist with seepage. Their handheld lights illuminated the naked tails of rats, which scurried to put distance behind them before turning to glare with shining eyes. The drain ran downhill, angling away from the access tunnel, toward the Harlem River in the dark distance.

Up the slope, a ragged opening marred the rounded wall. The corners of jutting bricks emerged from the mortar like shattered teeth. The opening revealed a brick-walled room, roughened by the use of vandals and the passage of time. Trampled garbage carpeted the floor. A half-rotten piece of plywood leaned against the back wall. Rodney Gaines crossed the room, gripped one edge of the plywood, and tugged. With a squeal, it swung aside, revealing a dark opening.

The rotted plywood was only a faceplate on a spring-hinged

door, braced neatly into the opening. Guthrie paused to admire it, while Ralph waited to close it behind them. The brickwork was pierced with lines as smooth as saw kerfs. Waiting beyond, an earthen tunnel smelled of damp and old metal. Ralph tugged the door in an over and down motion to secure the latch, needing two tries to close the puzzle box.

"The man is crazy smart," Ralph Gaines whispered. "Like now, there was supposed to be people watching the door. They'll catch it for going off without leaving nobody."

"Crazy, all right," Guthrie muttered.

"He just likes the dark," Ralph said. "He don't never come top-side, they say. Anyway, when we come to the end of this tunnel, we gotta out the lights and holler. They'll splash us with a searchlight, so they get first look. You just go toward the lights."

The tunnel was nearly straight, beyond the necessity of veering around some large buried stones and one half pipe of brickwork that was tapered like a smokestack. Pick and shovel marks decorated the earthen walls, showing the slick glow of moisture in the beams of the handheld lights. The tunnel ended at another neatly pierced brick wall, with steps leading down. The space beyond sounded vast. Rodney's shout fell into it, and Ralph waved for them to douse their lights.

Rodney Gaines led them down the narrow steps. A searchlight puddled him in brightness, then washed each of them in turn as they went down. The loophole in the brickwork led down into an ancient train tunnel. The rails were rough with rust. They trudged toward the light on crunchy gravel. Behind them, the tunnel shrank down to darkness, and the loophole hung on its side like a crow on a perch.

"Wasn't nobody at the door," Rodney called when they were nearer to the light.

Silence answered for a moment, then a disembodied voice said, "All right. Two of you I seen before; you can go along. You others, listen up before you go. This's the laws down here. You use the toilets, that costs a dollar. You piss 'n shit anywhere else, you get a beating. You throw your trash in the cans, that costs a dollar. Throw trash anywhere else, you get a beating. You don't tear nor mark anything up, or you get a beating. You worry anybody that's peaceful about their business, you get a beating. You want to rent a place, you see the man. You don't like the laws, turn round before you get a beating." The litany was worn, but the voice held a lingering trace of venom that suggested any beatings would not be soon forgotten by their recipients.

The Gaines brothers made herky-jerky time up the tunnel. The lights snapped out. Guthrie and Vasquez turned on their flashlights, and the glow illuminated the vague shape of a broad box framed to the ceiling, with a catwalk running away from it. The watchers were invisible. A faint glow emerged from the distant end of the tunnel, and the quiet was grooved by a sound like splashing water. As they went closer, it assembled into voices, snatches of music, occasional shouts, and mechanical humming.

The tunnel flared open into a broad subterranean yard. Numerous lights made puddles in the darkness without banishing it. Coaches lined up on rail spurs, leaking lines of light from blacked-out windows or briefly opened doors. The vastness of the space was traced out by distant coaches and swinging arcs from flashlights as people moved around the yard. Dark spaces around the periphery suggested other tunnel entrances. The hum sounded like the working of machinery, with fits of stuttering when something drifted from alignment. The Gaines brothers crunched to a halt in the gravel.

"You're *here*, man," Rodney said. "This's the carousel. Man, you're on your own looking for that nutcase."

Ralph shrugged apologetically but edged closer to Guthrie. The promised money held him like a leash. The little detective pulled a roll of bills and slipped it to him.

"Try not to get killed," Guthrie said. "That shit you do can bust a heart."

Rodney grinned. "If we're lucky," he whispered.

Guthrie and Vasquez let the Gaines brothers tag along out into

the center of the yard. Ralph moved as if he had an important destination in mind. Guthrie looked around carefully, without moving
more than turning a small circle in the gravel. The number of people and lights surprised him. He pointed out some watermarks on
the bricks, and decided that the machinery sounds came from
pumps. The air smelled dry and musty, with a whiff of oil and a lot
of iron, but no exhaust.

An old man crunched up to them. He had no light. Once he came
close, the crustiness of his unwashed clothes sharpened the air. His
leer might've been intended as a friendly smile, but gaps in his teeth
made the remainder resemble bared fangs.

"You're new, huh?" he asked. "I can lead you along, for a few dollars. That's all. An old man needs money to piss ever so often. And
maybe drink a bit. I know the best cathouse here. . . ." His chatter
paused when he peered at Vasquez. "That ain't what brings you,
huh? Cards? Drugs? Sport?"

Guthrie flashed a fifty in the beam of his light, then folded it into
his fist as the old man reached. "Where're the flops?"

"You aim to lay up? Trouble up under the sun, huh?" He licked
his lips, almost hidden behind a gray mustache. "Them presidents
will get you something right nice. If I go along, I can keep it all
honest. I got friends here." His hollow eyes darted over them with
fresh intensity.

"What I need can be worth something to you—but only if I get
it," Guthrie said. "I need the flops that don't cost nothing, because
I'm looking for somebody who ain't spending."

"Who's that?"

Guthrie took a quick step forward and gripped the old man's collar. "Right now, you." He tightened his grip with a twist. "Just so
you don't get an idea to run away. You don't want to know my business and then tell it."

"Let me go! I'm peaceful! I got friends!" the old man screeched.
He twisted, wrestling at the little detective's arm.

"Sure you do," Guthrie said. He glanced at Vasquez. "Show this
man what he's won."

She pulled a pistol and pointed. The old man fell quiet and stopped struggling. She slid the pistol back into her pocket.

"How big a piece of trash can I throw away for a dollar?" Guthrie asked in an amiable voice, then gave the old man a little shake to make the threat sink home. "Now maybe you got friends, old man, but you can have some friends named Ulysses Grant and Benjamin Franklin if I turn satisfied. You see how that'll work?"

The old man nodded sullenly, and Guthrie continued. "I'm looking for a big gray-bearded drifter called Ghost Eddy. Usually he stays up top, but a little bit ago he moved underground. He might have a little money."

"I know who you're talking about," the old man whined. "He lays up in the fueling station." He squirmed. Guthrie let him go. "That big man is mean. I suppose you're gonna get rid of him, huh? He's hiding from something. There a reward?"

"Sure. Ulysses might have some extra cousins."

The old man grumbled, but he was pleased. He encouraged them to follow, and walked into the darkness. The gloom was oppressive. The old man never stumbled, because his eyes were adjusted to dim light. Guthrie and Vasquez slid in the gravel, and caught their feet on ties or track when they crossed spurs. They had to study the ground with their lights, while the old guy had to pause to wait for them. He navigated among the coaches without entering the pools of light, avoiding the other people in the carousel as easily as a cat winds around furniture.

Most of the people they saw were grimy enough to pass for vagrants on the streets above. Some were hard-eyed, armed with sticks and attitude, while others were drunk and indifferent. Snatches of laughter and music drifted from coaches when doors opened and closed. The old man paused and made them turn off their handheld lights when a dozen men with bright lights marched from another train tunnel. They crunched purposefully across the gravel. Their bright clothes were undirtied by the darkness, and they soon disappeared into a coach.

On the far side of the train yard, the roof swooped down to form a succession of archways, further broken up by low dividing walls. Heavy wooden trestle tables still held gear and parts. Flaps of hanging cloth created tents beneath some tables; laundry lines stretched between posts; fires winked at odd moments through gaps in the dividers. Faces appeared and vanished before they could be recognized, and the old man kept moving.

Beyond the open bays were the dark doorways of ancient storerooms. The air was wet and greasy. The old man led them like a string of fireflies, and unseen people rustled in the darkness beyond their sight. The old man stopped and pointed to a long loading bay alongside a loop of spur track. The tracks were empty. Crisscrossed heavy timbers supported the decking of the bay. Quiet still held, but without the succession of faces, the loading bay seemed abandoned.

"He lays under there," the old man whispered. "Likely watching right now."

Guthrie folded a half dozen fifties together and handed them to Vasquez. "Give him that when I get something," he said. "You stay put for a minute, old man, while I find if you're lying to me." He doused his light and walked slowly toward the wooden dock, not stopping until he was well outside the light from Vasquez's flashlight.

"Eddy, are you drunk?" he called out. Silence came back. "You ain't running from me, you know. You carried the ghosts with you. How many tours did you pull?"

Silence.

"How'd you keep from throwing up when you saw that little round-eye covered in blood? You swallowed enough vodka to forget?"

"Shut the fuck up, little man!" The drifter's rough voice boomed from beneath the timbers. Vasquez handed the old man the money, and he turned and ran for the flops.

"Who killed her, Eddy? I want an answer," Guthrie said.

Laughter floated out, and then quiet thickened the darkness.

The scrapes of someone big shifting to his feet followed faintly. "*I* want some *quiet.* Don't have me shut you up."

"You gotta talk to me, Eddy. People need this. If I go away, somebody else'll come instead."

"If I wanted to *talk* about it, I would see a doc-tor." The drifter's rough voice had a sarcastic edge. "You're not a doc-tor, are you? You gonna make me feel bet-ter?"

"I don't need you better—unless that's what you want? That's why you're making me chase you? First time in a while anybody's given enough of a fuck to look for you? Feels good?"

"You little son of a bitch! Shut the fuck up!"

"I got all night. And the next, and so forth. You're gonna be hearing from me. This ain't gonna change until you talk."

Low cursing beneath the dock accompanied some scraping. Guthrie pulled his big floodlight from the cargo pocket on his field jacket and snapped it on. The sudden glare caught movement among the heavy crisscrossed timbers. The little detective steadied his light and started jogging that way. Vasquez lit her big light and followed. The big halogen lamps were like miniature suns. Ghost Eddy hustled through the timbers beneath the dock like an anxious recruit rushing an obstacle course. He had a lead. Guthrie hurried to catch him.

The gray-bearded drifter burst from beneath the dock, then paused to hurl a bottle. The bottle sailed end over end, flickering in the lights. Guthrie dodged. Ghost Eddy sprinted again. The liquor bottle slashed gravel and rang like a chime on a rusty rail, but it didn't break. Vasquez ran along the rail spur, trying to make up distance. Her light cut sudden arcs, but the little detective kept the drifter pinpointed.

Beyond the loading dock, an archway yawned with a dark throat. Ghost Eddy lumbered toward it, and Guthrie gained distance. The smaller man was quicker. Vasquez turned off the spur, stretching her legs like a hurdler. The drifter disappeared into the archway, with Guthrie a few dozen feet behind. The archway swallowed his light like a fire-eater and spit out the sound of boots slapping stone.

Vasquez rushed through the archway and swept her light around the room. Coal dust blackened the floor, with a few faint scuffs aiming like an arrow at the far wall. A wide pan on the floor was fed by a chute. Her light swept across the chute in time to see Guthrie's legs disappearing as he climbed up the rusty shaft. She hurried to the base of the chute and shined her light into it. A moment of silence was followed by a soft curse from the little detective, then a booming clang, and finally rough laughter. Guthrie's boots scraped on the rusty metal.

"You're quick, little man. A regular round-eye Charlie." Hard iron walls magnified his menace.

"You got good tricks for a fat man," Guthrie rasped. "Cut and turn works."

"I'll kill you, you know," the drifter wheezed.

"Don't die on me, you fat bastard. When's the last time you ate a salad?"

"Fuck you. Sound like my daughter—a *girl*."

"'Cause I listen to 'em."

"Smart fuck."

"Don't hang on to it, Eddy."

"I got no help for you. Maybe it was *you*. It was a little fucker. Coulda been you. Now leave me the fuck alone!" The drifter's rough shout boomed in the iron shaft.

"I know people you might like, Eddy," Guthrie said conversationally. "They went back across the water."

Silence followed for a long moment. Then softly: "Shut the fuck up, little man."

CHAPTER SIXTEEN

On the eighth of August, the city woke up like a man with a fever. Dawn seemed as hot as dusk, enough to confuse anyone as to whether they should be getting up or going to bed. Guthrie waited outside Vasquez's tenement so long that he changed his mind twice about getting out and walking up to knock on her door. She came down, slid into the passenger seat, and ignored him while he started the Ford, then drove down until he could turn back onto Grand. The little man looked like he felt the same. They'd come out from underground early enough the night before that he wanted to start an ordinary day, but they were both in the position of their feet still trying to catch up with their good intentions. With the heat, they looked deep-fried. The morning sky above Manhattan glowed like a fresh lemon, but the air smelled like an old, dusty-dry garbage can.

By the time Guthrie drove past Union Square, Vasquez was testing the coffee and doughnuts. A sleepy frown twisted her eyebrows, and she kept glancing at Guthrie. Finally, she said, "That bothered me all night. What happened in the chimney?"

"You heard it," he said.

"Seriously?"

"You mean *before*?"

"Yeah," she said.

"He almost got me. You didn't hear that? The old bastard tried to splatter my brains with a pipe."

"I heard a clang," she said. "Lucky he missed. I don't think you can spare your head." She smiled. "You wouldn't make four feet without it, you know?"

The little detective shook his head. "Wasn't luck—I was listening. All of a sudden, I couldn't hear him, so I knew he'd stopped. I had just poked my head out the feed end of the chute, and I didn't hear him, so I drew back. He had that set up, running there with a pipe waiting. I drew back just as he swung."

"You *heard* he *wasn't* making noise? That don't sound right."

"Ain't it?" Guthrie grinned. "I used to chase things when I was little—don't say it—and rabbits got this sudden stop trick. When you're barreling along behind them in a rough patch, they'll stop. They cut the other way once you shoot past. You have to listen for them."

"Did the rabbits do something to you?"

He laughed. "I just wanted to see if I could catch them. That came along after seeing if I could *find* them."

The Garment District was in the early stages of waking up when Guthrie and Vasquez parked on Thirty-fourth street. A roll-up door slithered in its track like a rack runner call to arms, but the street was quiet when they went inside. While they finished coffee, they raided photos from Web sites, the DMV, and the video clip Guthrie had shot in the Columbia University food court. They mixed in extra faces, looked for candids to match the style of the video clip, and found driver's-license photos for some of the college students to make a credible lineup.

Guthrie and Vasquez drove down to the Village to see the Overtons. The front of their narrow town house on Grove Street was still wet from the hose. One of the steps was coated with a slick, shallow puddle. Phil Overton answered the door as soon as they knocked.

Jeannette had seen them through the window. Phil brought lemonade and cookies while they sat in the front room with Jeannette.

The old couple continued playing gin while Jeannette looked at the pictures. She studied them slowly, and Phil took advantage of the distraction to score some victories. Two piles of pictures grew on the edge of the card table. One was much larger than the other, but even the smaller pile had several prints. Afterward, she led them through the pictures she had chosen; all were of Greeks from Columbia University. "A few times," or "Often," or "I recall seeing him once," or "He reminded me of my cousin Bert," she said before she ended with a single picture in her hand: one of Justin Peiper.

"This one was very determined," she said. "He courted continually, until the good boy came along. Almost every day, this young man came to visit, even if it was only briefly. For a long time, I thought he had won her. Months."

Outside in the midmorning, the sky shone like polished silver, with the hot sun invisible but powerful overhead. The smoothly running engines of the city's cars purred in the distance, away from the quiet nieghborhood. Guthrie paused on the sidewalk in a puddle of shade to consider. The little detective was upset; Jeannette Overton had eliminated Peiper for the murder. After explaining to Vasquez that the old lady knew Peiper well enough that he couldn't be the deliveryman, he said, "He's dirty for something, and I'll find it out. That leaves me wondering about the computer. That's next."

Guthrie used a computer geek who worked in Brooklyn to do his programming and setups, like the kill switches in the palmtops and office computers. They made two stops on the way to Brooklyn. At the office, they took Bowman's hard drive from the strongbox, and then Guthrie stopped to buy two liters of Norwegian vodka at a package store. They crossed the Manhattan Bridge on the top deck, mixed into a motorcade of drivers packed up for Long Island, with their cars full of anxious kids. The dog days were melting the city, and people were heading to the beach.

Barney Miller's, the electronics store, was as dark as a cave. Out front, a faded, barely legible sign showed a blond boy in red coveralls offering an ancient radio. The boy had tiny projecting antennae on his head, like a 1930s pulp-book Martian. The interior of the store was divided into two bays. On the right, a roll-up door in the back admitted a corona of light, and a handful of men in dark coveralls crawled in, on, and under a chromed lowrider. The lowrider's system blared intermittently as the techs tested the installation, harried by shouts from a skinny black man with a long goatee and a row of shining silver stripes on the sleeves of his dark coveralls. Shelves crammed the remainder of that side, loaded with a junker's selection of system components, wire, fittings, conduits, and rows of dusty, archaic junk—analog televisions, cartridges for obsolete video games, refurbished toasters, and old record albums.

On the left, a second bay looked like an old pharmacy. The shelves held fire alarms, lightbulbs, remote controls, game controllers, headphones, and patent medicines in a mix of dusty packaging with ancient stickers and neatly printed handmade tags. A tattooed Latino kid wearing a brown skullcap and a ragged T-shirt was browsing the shelves and laughing to himself. In the back, a wire cage surrounded some hanging droplights that floated in a cloud of haze. The wire walls were blockaded by more shelves inside, all loaded with electronic components, with attached and detached cables bundled like sluggish snakes. A tan baseball cap with an upturned bill floated in the smoke like a sentry peering above the shelves.

Guthrie led Vasquez around the corner of the cage, where an opening served as a door. A gigantic Korean sat perched on a high stool at a worktable littered with components and supplies. Fat-Fat's arms were the size of an ordinary man's leg, and he had heavy shoulders to hold up a head like a small laundry basket. The ball cap sat high on his forehead like a joke. He glanced up when the detectives rounded the corner.

"Yo, Guth, what's up?" he said as his gaze dropped back to his work.

"Brought you something I need looked at," the little detective replied. He found an open spot on the table to lay the hard drive and vodka.

"Gotta finish this mission," Fat-Fat said. A circuit board rested on the palm of his wide hand, held beneath a circular magnifier clamped to the worktable. A hot iron smoked faintly in his other hand, held between his fingers like a cigarette as he rotated a chip under the magnifier to align it. A bank of flickering oscilloscopes on his left made his outline wink like a hologram, and his eyes were red slits against the haze of flux smoke, but his hands were deft. His iron tapped like a woodpecker, shifting and settling, rotating down his fingers like a Vegas shuffle each time he reached for test probes or a brush. After a short quarter hour he holstered his tools with a sigh.

"I gotta get out of here, Guth," Fat-Fat said.

"Now?" Guthrie asked suspiciously.

"No, man," the big Korean said, and grinned. "Just the usual. I keep dreaming about jumping off New York Life, and that's just crazy. Too short, and I don't figure I bounce back from that splat."

"So where you going?"

"I ain't done Angel Falls yet," Fat-Fat said. "I'm gonna base Angel Falls, just as soon as I get airfare."

"Then I got some help for you. If you get locked up in South America, though—"

"Don't call you? Come on, man. My dad keeps saying that, too. You old guys are all alike." He tugged open the brown paper bag from the liquor store and saw the glowing white necks of the vodka bottles. He rubbed his belly and grinned. "Must be something special, huh?"

"I ain't sure," the little detective said. "I want to know if somebody went into it and cut any files out."

The Korean's eyebrows shot up. "No idea what's on it?"

"Or what it is, beyond somebody told me the owner was careful."

"*Mystery*," Fat-Fat said softly. He picked up the hard drive. "Okay, this's a high-end case, about the biggest you can get on a desk." He undressed the machinery and looked it over with his magnifier. "Looks factory, but these pricey ones can come out clocked and all that now." He screwed the case back together carefully, wiping as he went, and winked at the little detective. "Speaking of going to jail, right?"

"I should've thought about that, Fat," Guthrie said. "Now I wish I'd asked you to put on gloves."

"Shit! Seriously?"

"That thing might end up being evidence, depending."

The big Korean frowned and wired the drive into his system. He had a bundle of cables for power and busing attached at the work-table, and a keyboard to prop in a space he swept clean with one huge hand. A monitor winked on when he flipped a switch. He scrolled through the directory, pronouced it normal, and then opened his toolbox to begin an examination. After a few moments of operations, Fat-Fat's monitor colored, and he whistled.

"This's something," he said. "Can't go in the ordinary way."

Fat-Fat's system emitted a low beep and then began repeating every few seconds. The monitor cycled color again. Fat-Fat killed the power to Bowman's hard drive, then began typing furiously on his keyboard.

"That thing's got teeth, Guth," he said when he stopped.

Guthrie grunted.

Fat-Fat typed some more, until his system stopped signaling. "That thing's lethal," he said. "I could try opening it from a couple of different software platforms to see if it has keys to attack them, but it's real slick. Somebody good put that together."

"So what won't it do?"

The big Korean shrugged. He repowered and gave the drive a string of commands from within the system. The files wouldn't open or delete. He tried a lock pick inside the system, and the pick ran without triggering a counterattack. "The hardware's been tin-kered with," he said. "I could maybe bypass by switching chips, but I knew a guy one time built a drive that made files only it could open, even after they were transferred. Like it has a special tool to signal the file—take out the chip, and the file wouldn't open because it doesn't hear the signal."

"That might be the case here?"

"It's something in the hardware," Fat-Fat replied. "Some of the hard-cores picked up on it a long time ago, like Jobs. You keep things proprietary by making sure the query and the mailbox are a hard fit, and that don't need much tinkering in the ROM. Wait, got something."

One of the alphabet-soup files ballooned open on the monitor, disgorging a multitude of tiny pictures, each wrapped in a line of text and numerals arrayed like a date, time, and names. Fat-Fat's cursor skittered on the screen, guided by his fingertip on the touch pad. "Some of these are small—here's a big one," he mumbled a moment before his selected image amplified.

"Ooh, party pictures!" He tapped some more at random, showing tables circled by drunken young people, dancers, and people clowning. "Looks like rave shit . . ." He hit one that expanded into an explicit shot of a young couple in suspended motion. A curvy young woman with short chocolate hair stood gripping the posts of a bed, with her near foot braced on the mattress, while a tall young man lined up with her from behind.

"Ooh, action!" Fat-Fat tapped again, and the photo smoothly became video, with accompanying moans and gasps. "Whoa, Guth! *She* knows the camera is rolling, but I don't think *he* does. I need a copy of that one—"

"Not a good idea," the little detective said. "You don't want your fingers pinched in that trap."

"For real?" The big Korean shrugged. "There's a lot there—maybe something different?"

"It ain't worth it. You can get better than that anyway."

"You're kidding, Guth. She's on fire."

Vasquez peered over Fat-Fat's other shoulder. "She looks to be enjoying it, true enough."

"Shit!" The big Korean killed the screen, then looked sheepishly at her. "Sorry."

"She ain't as mean as Wietz," Guthrie said.

"Not yet? You haven't pissed her off yet." He gave Vasquez a wary look. "Yeah, the vodka's good." He unplugged the drive from his system and cleaned his cache. "That good?"

"That's something you don't want coming back up from the sewer."

The big Korean raised an eyebrow. He kept erasing, and invited Guthrie to take turns. Rap music blared occasionally when the techs on the other side tested the system in the lowrider. The little detective gave him a handful of fifties and wished him good luck in Venezuela.

Guthrie and Vasquez drove back to the office on Thirty-fourth Street, and he locked Bowman's hard drive back in the strongbox. The day passed without any more success than that, despite some efforts in other directions. They were tired. Eventually they were both watching the clock, staying only to avoid sleeping too early.

Late in the evening, Guthrie checked his watch and pronounced it time. Vasquez pulled her windbreaker from the back of her chair, but he pointed at the phone. "Try Sand Whitten one last time," he said, "and then call LMA."

Vasquez sighed. Whitten's phone took messages; she'd left a half dozen already that day. Guthrie wanted to show her the pictures Jeannette Overton had studied. The unidentified Grove Street deliveryman had dark hair, and so did Whitten's persistent admirer from LMA, but the little detective hoped Whitten might pick a face from their stack of pictures. Vasquez delivered another annoyed message to the bartender's voice mail. Then she called the Long Morning After, and received an angry snarl from the man who answered when she asked for Whitten.

"I take it she's not there," Vasquez retorted.

"That's right. I'm filling in again. If she lays out tonight, too, she's fired. Tell her if you find her—who are you?"

"Rachel Vasquez."

"Ever pour drinks, Rachel?"

"I got a job."

The man growled in frustration. "Tell her to come to work, will you?"

"I got you, don't worry."

After she hung up, she and Guthrie sat for a minute. Then he shrugged. The day was over. In the morning, they would try again.

CHAPTER SEVENTEEN

"We got a problem," the phone said to Vasquez in an electronic imitation of Guthrie's voice. She fought the blanket for a moment, then sat up and swung her legs from the bed. Twilight leaked through the bedroom window, barely brighter than streetlights, but enough to reveal the disarray in her tiny bedroom.

"What time is it?" Vasquez mumbled to the phone.

"Oh-dark-thirty. I'm on my way. We got to look at something before it's spoiled, so be ready. I'll be there in ten or twenty minutes."

"What?"

"A bad robbery on the Upper West."

Vasquez switched on her bedside lamp, frowning. "All right," she said before she cut off the phone and reached for her pants.

Mamì was at the stove in the kitchen, wearing her old soft slippers and the tan robe Roberto had given her after he graduated from Fordham. She had worn that for half of Vasquez's life. *Cuchifrito* in the skillet for Papì's breakfast warred with the aroma of fresh coffee. Vasquez laid her jacket and gun belt across the back of a chair and poured a cup for herself. Her mother glanced at her, scraped *cuchifrito* onto a plate, and then cracked two eggs into the skillet.

"You haven't been awake this early in a long time," she said. One of the faucet taps in the bathroom groaned. Papì was awake.

"I gotta go to work early this morning," Vasquez said.

Mamì nodded. "I heard your phone." She tried unsuccessfully to tuck a lock of hair behind her ear. Her long waves could become curls and frustrate her; this one had escaped her loose ponytail. "You should eat something."

"Guthrie will have some doughnuts."

Her mother snorted in reply. "You remember that time Fatty Espada caught you with the bowl of sugar?"

Vasquez smiled into her coffee cup. Fatty Espada was one of Papì's old friends; he'd lived upstairs so long ago that the red-checked wallpaper on the walls of the kitchen hadn't yet faded to pink from being scrubbed so many times. When Papì ate breakfast, Fatty would come downstairs to sit on their fire escape, drink coffee, and talk through the window. On Saturdays, though, Papì slept late. Vasquez was so little that even kindergarden was just a threat in her future, and she had an idea, since a spoon of sugar helped a bowl of corn-flakes, that more could be better. The effort actually resembled a bowlful of sugar sprinkled with cornflakes. Fatty came from the fire escape before she could douse the bowl with milk.

"I remember," Vasquez said.

Outside, the old Ford's horn honked briefly on the quiet street. Vasquez downed the rest of her coffee, brushed at her mother's shoulder, then picked up her jacket and gun belt and rushed out.

Guthrie drove up Broadway as the morning brightened. Along the way, he explained the job to Vasquez. Henry Dallen, the investigator who'd worked for James Rondell, had been killed in a push-in robbery at a brownstone on the Upper West Side. Dallen had been night guard on an estate that was working through probate, and probably going to auction. Guthrie and Vasquez came into the picture because Dallen worked, however indirectly, for HP Whitridge. That made him important. George Livingston, Whitridge's hatchet man, called and explained that the old man wanted Dallen's killers found, and any stolen items recovered, with emphasis on the killers.

Guthrie often spent time chasing missing property, especially when the property was more important than unmasking the perpetrator. Sometimes the families didn't want to see the thieves on the police blotter. The process was mechanical. Stolen goods were sold or exchanged, resurfacing around sewer drains, usually, but sometimes in fancy places. The little detective had an enormous web of contacts and traveled in places the NYPD couldn't go. Afterward, the property could be backtracked to the thief, and the puzzle was solved.

A pair of patrol cars waited outside the old brownstone on 102nd Street near West End Avenue. Trees towered over the sidewalks like skyscrapers. A knot of men crowded the sidewalk and steps, drinking from Styrofoam cups of coffee and dropping cigarette butts to decorate the pavement. Uniformed patrolmen from the 24th Precinct brushed elbows with ISU techs from downtown. A knot of plainclothes NYPD detectives surrounded Rondell's day guard, the man who'd found Dallen's body. He was smoking hard and staring at the pavement, as if he was reconsidering his line of work. Sgt. Jack Murtaugh was the lead detective. Guthrie called him "Gentleman Jack"; tailored clothes, slicked-back black hair, and a good shave made him stand out from his rumpled colleagues.

ISU techs entered the brownstone first, leading the way with cameras. The front door hadn't been forced. The entry seemed like a knock-and-push. The lace runner on the sideboard in the foyer was askew, and some small picture frames were overturned and lay broken atop and beside it. The hint of violence didn't cover the smell of money. Blond woodwork and Abstract Expressionism rose brightly above a blond wooden floor accented with dark South Asian carpets the color of river mud and moss. The other rooms were more drawers in an expensive jewel box. In the back, a coppery smell tainted the air.

"Your guy gonna make it, Guthrie?" Sergeant Murtaugh asked, then glanced at Vasquez. He jerked a thumb in the direction of the front door, where the day guard was waiting.

Guthrie shrugged. "Another college boy trying to do real work." Then he looked at Vasquez and said, "She's East Side."

The little detective's joke brought a few reflexive chuckles, but the faces of the policemen were all grim. The smell coming through the kitchen door had persuasive powers, a mix of blood and shit making a graveyard cocktail. The kitchen matched the rest of the brownstone—bright and eye-catching. Speckled gray marble floors and countertops reflected from stainless-steel fixtures to magnify the space. A cloud of pans, utensils, and supplies floated above the central island on barely visible hanging racks.

A pool of blood peered from around the corner of the island, as out of place as a scrap of dirty cloth in a home and garden picture book. Dallen's body was beyond the island, hanging from the oven door by handcuffed wrists. Drained of blood, the middle-aged investigator was as pale as votive wax. Sergeant Murtaugh circled to peer at the body from the other angle.

"His face is marked up," Murtaugh said.

"Bad?"

"Just a bit." He pointed with a fingertip. "That's it. That's why the oven—it kept his hands in place near the stove."

"Why's that?"

"See, burned his fingers with something, probably held it to the stove, scorched him, let him watch it get red, so forth."

"Do you see the wound?"

"Uh-uh. Don't get that. He don't look touched." Sergeant Murtaugh stepped slowly back around the island, scanning the counters. "Okay, let ISU do their thing. We got a torture thing here. Fucking skels."

The detective sergeant plowed slowly from the kitchen, trailing a cloud of anger. He crooked a finger at Guthrie as he passed. Everyone followed him to the living room. The creamy fabric on the sofa and chairs and the studied placement of the artwork suddenly belonged to a different building.

"So how long will it take to catalog and find out what's missing?" Murtaugh asked.

Guthrie shrugged. "Rondell had an appraisal scheduled for this week. That's from the insurance list, but it has to be backtracked for anything recent. I didn't know the old guy who lived here, or whether he was a big buyer."

"They wanted Dallen to answer questions about something; that's plain. What's the chance he had some inside knowledge about the choice items here?"

"Zero," Guthrie replied. "I talked with Rondell this morning. The old guy was with the firm for eleven years, spotless reputation."

Murtaugh led a slow sweep of the brownstone. After a quarter of an hour, he was upset. The rooms all had a feel of precise order, without any disarrangement, as if the inhabitant had been too decrepit to shift anything. "Tell me something, Guthrie," he barked. "This feel right to you? This is an inside job, right? If something's gone, they knew exactly what they were after—because it don't look like they took nothing else."

"I don't get that, either," the little detective said. "Why do they need to ask the guard if they know what they want?"

"Maybe they were trying to cover with that," Murtaugh said. "It still stinks. The skels do murder, then leave the money behind."

"Maybe the blood changed their minds, when it started pooling like that," one of the other detectives offered.

Sergeant Murtaugh shrugged. "After all the screams and begging they squeezed out with torture didn't disturb them?" He slapped his notebook against his thigh in disgust. "Something stinks. We start by looking at everyone who knew this old guy who just died. One of them is probably our skel. Williams, you got the canvass."

Guthrie and Vasquez left the day guard to oversee the NYPD's comings and goings at the brownstone. He was capable of watching whether anyone left with an armload of antiques or artwork, and signing a reciept for any evidence. Discovering the body early in the morning, when he'd expected to find a sleepy middle-aged man, had unnerved him, and then he started thinking about how it could have happened to him instead. Guthrie watched the man smoke a cigarette to the filter while he stood looking at the ground, then clapped him roughly on the shoulder and walked away. The man was still thinking about it, because thinking was safer than doing.

Vasquez was quiet and pale as she drove back downtown. The slow crush of rush hour gave the detectives plenty of time to think. Guthrie watched her stew until they crossed Houston, then said, "Don't think about it too much. Thinking don't change nothing."

"What d'you mean, *viejo*?" Vasquez demanded. "I ain't—"

"Don't give me that. You're chewing your tongue and going around in circles, trying to solve something in your head. Then you get back to where you started, and do it again."

She scowled.

"This's the real world, Rachel. Reasons and explanations don't matter too much, for a lot of things. When some blocky bastard with a bad shave and dirt under his fingernails comes along, he ain't gonna argue with you. He don't care about reasons. He's gonna end that argument before it ever starts, by using his fists. Then afterward, he ain't gonna be thinking about why. He's gonna be spending what you had in your pocket."

"Then what are we gonna do about that?"

"Drive over to Queens," Guthrie said. "We're gonna see Henry Dallen's widow."

Dallen's neat white row house was tucked securely into a quiet middle-class neighborhood in Forest Hills. Inside, a minister was sitting with his widow. Marjorie Dallen was small and slight; her knuckles glowed like white prayer beads while she twisted and folded a handkerchief. Her living room was carpeted and neat, with clusters of books on corner shelves and framed photographs arrayed like soldiers on the painted walls. She accepted Guthrie's condolences quietly, and answered questions before coming to a sudden stop.

"You seem to be asking if something Henry did caused the trouble," she said. "Wasn't it a robbery? He was sitting for the lawyers."

Guthrie nodded. "That's the way the police are examining the matter," he replied. "As if your husband's death is a consequence, which it could be. I was asked to look for the killer, so I wonder if anyone would want to do him harm."

"Oh. Well, I don't think so. He wasn't a drinker or a gambler. He stayed home at night. If someone wanted to hurt him, they would be crazy."

"Was anyone calling him recently? Did he have visitors, or change his schedule?"

"No. He was sitting the house for the lawyers recently, but he didn't do that often—only a few nights each year. Otherwise, he was always here."

"Did he tell you where he was at, when he worked at night?"

She shook her head. "No. If I wanted to talk with him, I called him on his phone."

Guthrie and Vasquez exchanged a glance. Only Rondell's firm had known where Dallen was overnight. Guthrie gave the widow his card in case she remembered anything after they were gone, and they said polite good-byes. Vasquez drove back to the city through Williamsburg, then went downtown to Wall Street. The big buildings swallowed the sky that had been so wide over Queens and Brooklyn. A few light lines of clouds followed them back to Manhattan; something was moving in from the Atlantic.

Parking was easy to find on Wall Street; Sunday quieted the business district. The detectives waited outside Reed, Whitaker & Down until James Rondell's secretary arrived. Miss Helen Walterberg was a stern, no-nonsense woman with iron gray hair, past middle age but with an aura of competence. She was assigned to chaperone the young Wall Street partner's ascent to power. She seemed frustrated when she arrived, but not distracted. She had immediate answers for most of the little detective's questions: The lawyers could have known where Henry Dallen was overnight, along with two other settled, middle-aged investigators employed by the firm, and members of the clerical staff. The hired men they used during the daytime had also been given the address. She ticked off names on her fingers, naming them in their groups, and reached a total of forty-nine.

"Would all of these people have known specifically that Henry Dallen was there?" he asked.

Miss Walterberg frowned. "No," she replied. "Our policy was rotation. Our salaried investigators rotated the nights to prevent the duty from being burdensome. Even the other investigators might not have known more than that they weren't assigned, but I suppose Ms. Roscoe, the senior administrator, would have known that."

"Would you have a way of knowing if someone asked that question?"

"If the question came from inside the firm, we can ask Ms. Roscoe," she replied. "If the question came from outside the firm, we will need to be lucky." Reed, Whitaker & Down used a secretarial and reception pool for the junior partners, associates, and routine work. Miss Walterberg felt that some of them were less than competent; the use of computers was eroding office habits. She watched the phenomenon with James Rondell, who occasionally decided that he could, by computer, prepare a presentation or organize materials more efficiently than a secretary. She then found it necessary to open windows and air out the stink of flaming failure. The firm's pool had some similarly inclined members. Even education didn't seem capable of eradicating the belief in a labor-free shortcut. Miss Walterberg led them with the crisp stride of a martinet.

An old-fashioned memo spike held a sparse handful of messages. Walterberg sighed as she searched the messages, then offered one to Guthrie.

The note identified a plumbing service in Brooklyn—Lackland

Brothers—and detailed an inquiry on whether the firm would recommend Dallen as an investigator of someone they believed was defrauding them.

"Ms. Jenkins initialed the message," Walterberg said. "I have her number. Perhaps she will have more details."

On the phone, the secretary revealed that a foreign-sounding caller had asked for Rondell's investigator; she had given him Dallen's name because Rondell preferred him over the firm's other investigators. Then Guthrie called the number noted for Lackland Brothers, but reached a pizzeria in Gravesend. He listened to the pitch, then hung up without offering a reply.

After they left the quiet marble building on Wall Street and were walking down to the car, he dialed another number on his phone. He handed the phone to Vasquez. "Gimme the keys," he said. "You make friends with Sergeant Murtaugh from the two-four, and tell him what we got."

CHAPTER EIGHTEEN

Thirty-fourth Street was quiet when Guthrie and Vasquez returned to the office.

Guthrie ordered a pizza for lunch. Not long after, a shadow slid onto the frosted glass panel of the office door and the knob rattled. The sound fell into a lull where the detectives were both studying monitor screens, or chewing the ends of pens. The little old man frowned and sat forward in his chair.

The office door opened and a young blond man of about average height stepped into the office, followed by a heavyweight with a flattened face and wearing a wide-brimmed black Stetson. "Please to excuse me," the man said, "but I was recommended to inquire to engage your services. I believe someone is stealing from me."

The young man wore an earnest expression, but he glanced quickly around the office as he spoke, walking along the length of the oxblood couch toward Guthrie's desk. The heavyweight's eyes slid over Vasquez, then locked on Guthrie and didn't waver. He followed the smaller man along the couch.

"I think that's what I was missing," Guthrie said to Vasquez. He stood up, and his hand dropped onto the heavy glass paperweight on his blotter. He smiled and continued: "You two can have a seat while you tell me about it."

After he rounded the end of the couch, the blond man strode past Guthrie's desk. His hand dipped into the back pocket of his dark trousers to retrieve a flip knife and opened it: *tat-a-tat*. The heavyweight wearing the black Stetson grinned and rushed forward.

Guthrie lifted the paperweight from his blotter and threw it like a shortstop firing for first base. The heavy blob of glass collided with the big man's cheek and wiped away his grin. He missed a step while he shook off the blow, but his Stetson stayed square on his blocky head. A trickle of blood streaked down his face. Guthrie jumped up onto his desktop. Notepaper, pens, and paper clips showered onto the low coffee table framed inside the couches and desks.

The blare of horns from Thirty-fourth Street leaked through the windows. The blond man swerved around the coffee table without looking back at Guthrie. He wagged his gleaming knife blade at Vasquez and turned the corner of her desk with a rush. She spun from her chair, then flung it at his knees. He slashed at her ponytail as it whipped by his face, grinning as he disentangled his legs from the light chair and kicked it aside.

The big man swept Guthrie's computer monitor from the desk with one wide hand, roaring a guttural insult, and snatched for the little detective's ankle. Guthrie leaped from his desk to Vasquez's, scattering paper, coffee, and more pens, then bounced from the desktop to dive onto the blond man. The man's blue eyes flared wide with surprise.

The detective was too small to tackle him to the floor, but they collided with the wall. Guthrie kept his feet by hanging on to the larger man. The blond's hand whipped. Guthrie smashed elbows with him to stop the knife. They howled curses in different languages. The heavyweight charged through the mess between the desk and couches like a defensive end aiming at a scatback.

"Draw!" Guthrie shouted.

The little detective's shout startled Vasquez, but her hand moved automatically. For her first month, he had repeated the same command hundreds of times with a stopwatch in his hand. Each time, she used a thumb to hook aside the zipper of her windbreaker, slid her hand palm out around to her kidney holster, and drew her Chief's Special for five shots at short distance. After a pause to examine the target and reload, they did it again.

The small pistol fit Vasquez's hand perfectly. Her frown vanished when she stretched out her arm. Her first shot with the .40-caliber pistol froze the moment like a strobe light, but the sound was flat, not sharp. The bullet smashed into the side of the big man's head, lifting his Stetson over the furry brown couch. He staggered, plowed into the arm of the couch, and tumbled into an ass-up pile.

Vasquez grinned. The blond man muttered a curse and stepped to use Guthrie for cover while he dug at something tucked behind his belt, but the little detective dropped suddenly into a crouch. The blond dived for the furry brown couch, with gunshots chasing him. A hit wrung out a high-pitched scream.

"Fuckmother!" the blond man shouted from behind the couch. His shoes squeaked on the wooden floor as he crawled. The heavyweight untangled himself and stood up, then felt for his hat—or maybe to see how much of his head remained. A second trickle of blood decorated his face. The short black hair on his head was as stiff and matted as an unwashed goat. He looked around the office to take his bearings.

Vasquez switched gun hands and pulled her other pistol. Guthrie spun along the floor without leaving his crouch, grabbed her belt, and snatched her to the floor. He crawled across her legs like a monkey and turned the corner of his desk to open the big bottom drawer. Vasquez took aim from the floor and shot the heavyweight in the stomach with the soft-loaded .40-caliber. He yelped and folded. The slide on the Smith & Wesson locked open; the clip was empty.

The blond rose from behind the oxblood couch and fired two quick shots with an automatic pistol before he realized no one was standing. One bullet drilled a hole through Vasquez's computer monitor. He hissed a string of curses and rushed back down the length of the office. The tip of his pistol wavered between the two open doors flanking Guthrie's desk. The heavyweight rolled to his feet, silhouetted in the light of the street windows. He drew a large automatic pistol from beneath his jacket.

The hard-loaded .40-caliber boomed with a heavier sound than the young blond man's automatic; Vasquez fired three shots. The bullets drove the big man back to the window sash. His shoulder cracked a pane of glass before he slid down the wall and slumped forward. His hand brushed at the hardwood floor for a moment, as if he was smoothing a place to lay his head. The blond man turned the corner of Guthrie's desk while Vasquez was still firing. The little detective was lying on the floor, with his heavy Colt revolver in his outstretched hand.

"Fuckmother!" the blond shouted again, firing twice.

Guthrie's shot squeezed in between the lighter bullets like a zesty piece of roast beef sandwiched between two slices of plain light bread. The blond's first shot clipped splinters from the desk, and the second burrowed into the floor. The little detective's shot hammered the blond against the painted wall; he sneezed a spray of blood, then curled up on the floor, holding his pistol like a teddy bear.

The horns blaring on Thirty-fourth Street mixed with the wail of approaching sirens seemed quiet after the gunfire. Guthrie muttered curses as he rescued papers from the puddle of coffee on his desk. Vasquez laid her pistols on her desk and tucked her hands into her armpits. She stared at the crumpled heavyweight beneath the window. The body had fallen at an awkward angle, unrecognizeable at first glance as something human—like a picture in *National Geographic* meant for a reader to puzzle over before flipping the page to read the identifying caption. Flecks of blood on the painted wall looked like a heavy shake of red pepper. Guthrie walked over and righted her chair, rolled it behind her, and gently tipped her into it.

"Maybe now is a good time to give you a raise," he said.

For a long time, the approaching sirens were only an empty threat. The light from the windows dimmed under the weight of a heavy bank of clouds. Guthrie poured himself another cup of coffee and rummaged in his desk drawer for a card to give Vasquez. He left the computer monitor on the floor.

"We gotta cover a few things before the police get here," he said.

"They shot first! Kind of—"

"I'm not talking about that. Those guys were looking for us, the ones who killed Henry Dallen last night. I don't know what happened, but it's connected to James Rondell. We stirred something up, but I can't see what it is yet."

"So what do we do?"

"Somebody talked, or somebody noticed. We know some things that nobody else knows—they have to stay that way. Jeannette Overton, she's one. I think she saw our guy."

"The deliveryman," Vasquez said. "I got you."

"Right. And the sex pics. Maybe that's behind it, but we can't just throw it out. I warned Inglewood there was some dirt at Columbia, but now that I know what it is, it's worse."

Vasquez frowned. The sirens were on the street outside. "But that's probably who's behind it."

"Even so," the little detective said.

"So we're sitting on this?"

"That's it. Dummy up and call the lawyer on the card."

Quick footsteps sounded in the hall outside. The office door opened wide and a dark-uniformed patrolman pushed through behind an extended gun. Guthrie and Vasquez raised their hands. They took a ride to the Midtown South, courtesy of the NYPD. After a wait for the lawyers to drive into the city from Brooklyn, the questioning began.

Guthrie's lawyers were Italians, and they had sharp teeth. Guthrie and Vasquez accounted for their pistols but otherwise left the

NYPD detectives to guess. Guthrie let the lawyer suggest that the killing could be connected to the murder in the 24th Precinct, since there seemed to be a connection through James Rondell.

That brought Sergeant Murtaugh for a visit, and then a detective from Major Case named Wilkins. Murtaugh looked as neat as he had that morning: Even a murder couldn't get his hair out of place. Wilkins was a skinny black man a few years into middle age, and he shaved his head to hide oncoming baldness. He didn't like the idea that the 102nd Street killing might not have a robbery motive, and he liked it even less that Clayton Guthrie was mixed into it. The little detective was a bad stink in their squad room because of the Bowman murder investigation.

Wilkins sat, angrily silent, when the chief of detectives ordered Guthrie and Vasquez released. The canvass in the 24th Precinct had turned up witnesses for two suspects, roughly matching the bodies in the office, and Murtaugh had interviewed the secretary at Reed, Whitaker & Down. Unless something else came to light, the shooting was clean, and it was rolled together with the 102nd Street killing.

Guthrie's lawyers gave them a ride back to the Garment District. The lawyers surprised Vasquez by not being nosy; they looked her over, then talked about the Knicks. They walked up to the office with the detectives. The bodies were gone. Guthrie broke the yellow tape, took a look to see if ISU had touched anything they shouldn't, and brought out their palmtops. The good-byes were brief, because the air smelled like approaching rain. The clouds were as dark as iron, pushing fast over the city, chased by a cold wind from the Atlantic.

CHAPTER NINETEEN

"I think we made some progress," Guthrie said into the phone as he flipped it to speaker. "But I doubt you've heard anything on the news, unless you follow it close."

"What do you mean?" Michelle Tompkins asked.

"Henry Dallen was murdered last night," Guthrie said. "Did you ever meet Henry Dallen? No? He was one of the investigators who worked for Reed, Whitaker & Down. No bells yet? That's James Rondell's firm, the lawyer who's representing Greg Olsen."

Vasquez turned the old Ford onto the Bowery. They were going to Brooklyn. The rain began as a gentle speckling on the windshield, but before she could turn on the wipers, the drops whooshed into a hissing roar. The city around them faded behind gray curtains, while the wipers shaved helplessly at the sheet of water on the glass.

"I don't understand," Tompkins said.

"Are you sure?" Guthrie asked. "You've been doing a champion job of playing dumb since we started. I'm not a dentist. I'm not going to pull your teeth if you open your mouth."

"I'm studying," she said sharply. "I don't have time for jokes."

"I wish this was a joke. Two thugs from Brighton Beach tried to rub me out a little before lunch, and I bet you don't know anything about that, either. So let me help you. You asked us to find Camille Bowman's killer, or prove Greg Olsen didn't do it. Somebody doesn't want us to do that. I think they wanted to find out how much we know first—that being a good guess based on that they talked to Henry Dallen before they killed him. They tied him to an oven door and branded his hands with hot knives. Then I'm pretty sure they asked him for my name, because their next stop was my office."

"Oh God." For a long moment, the only sound was rain and the creak of the Ford's windshield wipers. Guthrie didn't press, because they had plenty of time. They were driving all of the way down to Flatbush. "You think somebody at the school did it?" she asked.

"You were doing something there that could get somebody shut up. Maybe it already got Camille Bowman shut up. What scares me is that they left the pictures behind. Maybe they took the ones that could damage them—" The little detective came to a sudden stop.

"What?" Tompkins asked.

"Tell me about Justin Peiper. I know already he was with Camille; what was he doing at Columbia? Is he connected to someone in the city?"

"No. Justin's a pretty face from upstate. His face unlocks doors."

"No money? How fast could he find eight thousand dollars, you think?"

"I don't . . ."

While a pause stretched on the phone, and the Ford waited at a light, Vasquez opened her palmtop. She had Peiper's credit-card statements in his file. The accounts were paid off on the second of August. The young Puerto Rican frowned. Guthrie was stalking a trail.

"Justin doesn't have money," Tompkins said. "He's a sponge. I think he carries summer classes so he can live on campus."

"So who knew about the pictures? Have you got a straight answer for that? And maybe you should volunteer everything connected to it," Guthrie added.

"Fuck," she said acidly.

"There was a strong resemblance."

"Everybody knew about the party pictures, but nobody knew about the action pictures." Tompkins paused, then continued. "Scratch that. Three people knew about the action, directly. After that, I can't say who told whom, beyond that my mouth stayed shut. Cammie's dead. Amanda Hearst knows. Cammie was a shutterbug, and that's how it started. She was always taking pictures. I think if she hadn't met Greg, she wouldn't have considered law. She was definitely following him, and eventually she would've regretted that decision. I think she would've gone for film."

"An aspiring actress?"

"Uh-uh. A director. The pictures were her idea. That became my position in 'the court.' I took the pictures."

"You starred in some of them."

"Cammie took those, or Amanda did after she came inside. Cammie had a streak of . . . I guess that was something we all shared. Anyway, we had the goods on one another. That way, everyone was covered, and anything went. Crazy stuff went on at Grove Street. I thought she had her pictures secure. A lot of people knew about the party pictures, and sometimes they freaked people out. When Cammie put people together, she wanted a trophy. Some of the pictures are pretty crazy. I guess you haven't looked through all of them."

"Not even close. Fat-Fat screened a bedroom video clip, and I decided I didn't want to look at anything else. Should I?"

"Shit. Who's Fat-Fat?"

"A computer wonk who knows he shouldn't cross me. You say she secured her pictures. Fat-Fat said that her machine was tinkered with. I didn't let him go all the way with it—I just wanted to find out if anything was erased. He said the machine had an attack system. That's what you mean?"

"I use the same system."

"Like Amanda Hearst?"

"Same system, but not as much info. She doesn't have anything on me. She barely had anything on Cammie."

"You don't think Cammie could've sold you out?"

"No. She played with Amanda, and everybody else, including Justin, but she never teased me like that." A pause was filled with the sound of raindrops. "I never thought about it that way before. She was my friend.

"I guess here's where it's complicated, though," she continued. "I don't know how many videos there were. Grove Street was like a circus sometimes. I don't think a 'complete copy' exists, except for the party pictures. She kept a court history. Every 'performance' hookup had a spread. The pictures were more or less docile, unless they were really drunk, or really into each other. But a minimum of a kiss and a fondle." Tompkins laughed softly. "Okay, when I say 'fondle,' I mean something that could probably make a cheap magazine, and thrill perverts to no end. And definitely spoil a Goody Two-shoes image."

"And at least one other person knows you have pictures," Guthrie said. "That would be Justin Peiper—and somebody knows enough to pay him off. Any ideas?"

"Shit. Are you sure?"

"He's dirty for something, but I don't like him for Camille's murder. This scheme fits, and he's good with a computer. Who would he hit?"

"Amanda," Tompkins replied. "Try Amanda. She was upset." Another pause stretched. "Can you do something about it?"

The little detective stared out the window at the wet, gray version of Brooklyn that was being scoured by the rain. "Sure. I'll see if I can find some tracks tonight," he said before he cut off the phone.

Vasquez rounded the plaza and they slid along Prospect Park. "Less than murder," she said quietly. As she turned onto Caton, the rain intensified. The sky seemed determined to make up for all the dry, hot dog days at once. Guthrie directed her to a nondescript storefront looking out onto the Parade Ground. Faded paint blended the narrow street entrance of Bob's Sports into the pavement. Next door, the windows were boarded, with a dusty COMING SOON sign marked with the empty promise of a restaurant.

The gutters were awash, and the sidewalks covered with splashing puddles. By the time Guthrie and Vasquez reached the door, they were soaked. An old-fashioned hanging bell rang when they went inside. The inside smelled musty; most of the lights were burned out, or buzzing at the end of an ill-used life. An old clerk looked up briefly when they came inside, then sighed and flipped a page on the magazine he had spread on the countertop.

Vasquez scanned the shelves as she walked along behind Guthrie. The sporting goods all looked used, including muddy baseballs and splintered bats. An ancient leather maskless football helmet leered at her, and she picked it up. The inside smelled like vomit, and the price tag said $4. She decided that her middle brother, Indio, needed to have it. She brushed some loose wet strands of hair away from her face and grinned.

"Don't bother the displays," the old clerk said wearily.

"You mean I can't buy this?" Vasquez demanded.

"Hey, I just work here, you know?" the old man said. He perked up on his stool, suddenly ready to talk.

"Can it, Mike," Guthrie said. "She's with me. Vincent here?"

The old man shrugged. "In back."

Vasquez kept the helmet and followed Guthrie into the back. The clerk gave her a martyred look. Beyond a swinging door, four old men were playing pinochle. Two looked up when the detectives came through the door. One old man's eyes looked huge behind thick glasses; even sitting down, he was a giant. He could hide his spread of cards behind his palm. His voice was a match, like gravel roaring down a chute.

"Vincent, we got company," he said.

"Just Guthrie. I *can* see him, you know."

"Sometimes . . ."

The back room was decorated with old junk and a flimsy card table. A door on the back wall was marked EXIT. Vincent wore a fisherman's cap and wire-rimmed spectacles. He peered at Vasquez, raising his chin because the glasses had slid down to the tip of his nose.

"Hey, that's not Wietz! Who you bringing in here, Guthrie?"

"I tried to tell you," the big man said. "You don't never listen."

"Vincent Pagliaroli, Salvatore Lucci, this's Rachel Vasquez," the little detective said. "These two are junk dealers—"

"*Bad* dealer," another old man said, flicking the spread of his cards with a fingertip. "Would you believe no marriage?"

"So?" Vincent asked. "That makes her good people? What's a name?"

"Names are words," Guthrie said. "She made bones a few hours ago. We need some replacements."

The old men set their cards down, and they all turned to stare hard at Vasquez. With her hair wet, her ears stuck out even more than normal, and she looked as narrow as a drenched cat. She reddened and held up the old football helmet. "I want to buy this for my brother," she said.

Vincent smiled. "You don't like him, huh? He won't keep his teeth wearing that."

"No, no, I like him. I'll just hide it in his room to make him clean it."

Sal laughed. "Wouldn't do no good for my brother," he rumbled.

"All right. Let's take a break, guys. I don't think Guthrie needs long. You know what you want?"

Guthrie nodded. The other two old men went out to the front of the store. Vincent opened the exit door, grumbled about the puddles, and handed umbrellas to everyone before he went into the alley. Sal followed Vasquez and Guthrie. Vincent opened the alley door to the side and they entered a stockroom piled with cans of tomato sauce, tomatoes, and paste. Sal came in last and locked the door.

Three wire cages stacked full of wooden crates waited beyond the stockroom's locked door. Each cage had to be unlocked and relocked. Cameras peered down from overhead into rooms kept uncomfortably cold, like a meat locker. Orange-scented cleaner didn't cover the sharp smell of oil and metal. The last room was full of standing steel cabinets: Even without couches and reading tables, it looked like a library.

"I need two more of those Chief's Specials," Guthrie said.

"Those were hers?" Vincent asked, then glanced at Vasquez. "You liked those? Forties, right? I got something with more pop, if you want."

Vasquez shook her head. The smell of the ancient football helmet was making her queasy. In the card room, she hadn't understood what Guthrie meant when he told the old Italians she had "made bones." The armory was as cold as a mortuary, and she realized the old men had stared to size her up.

Vincent opened a cabinet. The metal clanged like prison doors. "I only got one forty-caliber. You want to go up, or down?" He looked at Vasquez, one small pistol cuffed in his withered fist.

Her mouth stayed stuck shut for a moment. "What's bigger?"

"I got forty-five, forty-four Mag, forty-four Special, forty-one Mag—"

"Let me get the forty-five," she said.

The old man peered into the cabinet, drew out a second pistol and some empty clips. "Okay. You need something?" He glanced at Guthrie, then frowned. "This was a confirmation?"

"It'll be in the papers, Vincent. NYPD took all the iron. So I need a pair of forty-four Mags—Colt, Smith, Ruger, don't matter as long as it's four and three-quarters."

The old man had a pair of Trooper IIs and a handful of speed loaders. Guthrie bought a double shoulder rig and some boxes of ammo. Sal watched them through his thick glasses while they loaded cylinders and clips, then tucked away their purchases. Vincent marked tallies inside his cabinets.

"Well, Guthrie, you're ready for the army," Vincent said. He ticked items off on his fingertips. "That'll be thirty-two hundred. And another five for the helmet. I'd give it to you for free, but it used to belong to my mother's brother."

"The tag says four dollars," Vasquez said.

The old Italian gave her a surprised look. "You're cute. I gotta say that. The helmet's been sitting there since sometime in the 1970s. That's a lotta inflation. You want me to add it up?"

"No, thirty-two hundred five is good," Guthrie said. He pulled bills from one of his pockets.

"I tell you what you better give her," Sal said. "An umbrella. She ain't big enough she can afford to have anything else wash away."

Vincent grinned, peering at Vasquez through his spectacles again. "Okay, I throw in the umbrellas," he said.

On the way back to the city, Guthrie and Vasquez paused to buy a bag of snacks: the grab bag. The grab bag was the ritual that accompanied sitting in a park or on a street corner to watch Manhattan get a few hours older. In Vasquez's first three months, the grab bag was filled a few times a week. Back in the city, they drifted into a spot in Battery Park, looking out over the bay. The rain wore away to nothing, but the clouds didn't thin. Guthrie kicked a can several laps around the Ford, while Vasquez just sat in the driver's seat.

The first time with the bag, Guthrie hadn't said anything. He'd sat down on a bench in Tompkins Square Park and ignored Vasquez like she was a pesky fly for four hours. Then he peppered her with questions about what had happened while the time was passing. After she realized he was serious about wanting answers, she began to spin lies to fill the big silence of not having anything to say. The little old man laughed at her. The night before, he hid a camera in the tree beside the bench to catch her if she tried bullshit. On top of that, he knew she was snowing him, because he had been watching, and his eyes were always on record. The camera was just proof.

After the first few trips with the grab bag, the little detective had added a twist. He asked her to explain the people they saw: who they were, why they were there, what they were doing, and even why they did what they did the way they did. "Why'd he throw that can down?" he asked, pointing at a Yuppie in Gramercy Park who was tossing litter, with a trash can twenty feet away. Something like that could start a quarter-hour argument—with Guthrie still expecting her to watch at the same time.

Mixed into the mess were the videotapes. Vasquez got angry when he showed her a black-and-white video and asked her what color things were. That was impossible. Then he brought out a color copy and ran them side by side; he used two cameras just to ask her about the colors. "At night, it's hard to tell colors apart," he said, but that was one of his rare moments of explanation. He had loops of tape from robberies, suicides, car wrecks, and fires, with rapidfire strings of questions to go with all of them. Clayton Guthrie was crazy; he paid her to shoot a pistol and do nothing.

The high clouds drizzled softly on Battery Park now, shrouding Lady Liberty's secrets across the bay. Vasquez watched Guthrie grow tired of walking and settle back into the passenger seat of the Ford. He was brooding. His jaw clenched like he was chewing on something difficult, and his eyes weren't focused on anything she could see. Before the phone rang, Vasquez had decided that she had been wrong all summer long. Clayton Guthrie wasn't crazy. Rachel Vasquez just wasn't old enough to know what he was doing.

"Hello?" Guthrie said, pressing the speaker on the phone.

"Guthrie? This's Sergeant Murtaugh. Are you tucked away somewhere?"

"Battery Park." The rain falling on the old blue Ford was silent, but the wind was cold, and it hissed through the open doors like a sluice.

"Okay. I had to let you walk away from MTS without saying anything," Murtaugh said. "Major Case, and some of the brass, would like to have you for lunch, you know?"

"I ain't surprised," Guthrie said.

"You were solid this A.M., so I figured you were good for a heads-up. OC identified that bruiser in your office as Vitaly Kozlov, formerly of Brooklyn. The other guy has a name, but he just came over by way of France. Kozlov was connected to V.I. Maskalenko, a Ukrainian boss. Naturally, I wonder what the *mafiya* has against you. Any ideas?"

"I've been thinking about it all afternoon," Guthrie said. "I'll wager a few guesses, starting with its being connected somehow to the case I'm working. There's a dirty college boy, but I doubt he's got stones enough to reach out for the *mafiya*. I'd bet against that. On the other hand, I do know why Major Case wants to ball me up. The lawyer involved, Rondell, he's representing Greg Olsen."

"GI Ken! No kidding!"

"No kidding. Right now, I think they're running with the Barbie doll murders, seeing if they can fit him up—"

"And you're chipping away at the Bowman murder." Murtaugh laughed. "Those guys downtown crack me up. You're getting somewhere?"

"Maybe. Could be somebody tried to send me an urgent message, since they were looking for Rondell's investigator. That mess earlier had me stirred up, and I wasn't willing to help out. I should call Mike Inglewood, downtown. You know him? Anyway, they turned up a wit in Morningside, and I think she saw somebody. I got a stack of pictures now that I want to show her, but she's been missing for two days."

A pause was punctuated with a snapping finger, then the rustle of paper. "That wit have a name?"

"Sand Whitten."

"I'll pass that along for you," Murtaugh said.

CHAPTER TWENTY

Night came early and felt cold. The clouds over the city never broke; the afternoon was a long twilight with spates of drizzle and rushing wind. Guthrie took the keys and drove Vasquez back to Henry Street. He told her to warn her parents, though her name wouldn't be in the newspaper from the police blotter until the next morning. Overnight, he planned to stay in a hotel, and they would lay low for a few days. The little detective figured the *mafiya* to step back after a failure. Even if they meant to try again, they would wait.

Vasquez slid the warning to the back of her mind. She knew that if she wanted to sleep, fighting with her parents wasn't the way to get ready for bed. When she undid her ponytail to take a shower, she found a ragged lock of loose hair tangled in the band. Without her realizing, the Russian's knife had almost opened her scalp, leaving one lock of hair not long enough to reach her ponytail; now it swung loose at the edge of her jaw like a trophy. She was disgusted, but she pushed the thought away. The day had been too full. Right before she went to sleep, she wondered how much of a raise Guthrie would give her. Then suddenly it was morning, she was wide awake, and she could hear her mother in the kitchen.

"You're going to make this a habit again?" Mamì asked when Vasquez walked into the kitchen and poured a cup of coffee. "I could fry some more eggs."

Vasquez shook her head. "I gotta go."

"Too fast for sunny-side up eggs and a slice of melon? With pepper?" She knew how to tempt her daughter. Vasquez teetered on the edge until she continued. "You should eat breakfast with your father."

"No, I gotta hurry," she said. "Before I go, though, I gotta tell you something. It'll be in the newspaper today. A thing happened at the office." Her eyes cut, and beneath the table her feet were already shuffling for the door.

Mamì frowned. "What kind of thing?"

"Some shooting, some guys that tried a robbery uptown."

"So . . ." She hesitated, throwing one sharp glance at her daughter, then another toward the back of the apartment. "That's where you were hurrying yesterday."

"Yeah, the robbery."

"So it's over?"

"They were Russians," Vasquez said softly.

"Rachel!" Mamì's cry came out sotto voce, and she shot another glance at the back of the apartment. She attacked the eggs she had in the frying pan. Her spatula rang like a machete. "Okay, I'll tell him. You'd better go."

Vasquez finished her coffee, then pulled on her gun belt and windbreaker. As she slipped through the front door, her mother called softly, *Buena suerte.* She rushed downstairs to get away, then had to wait on the stoop. The morning was cool, and she was glad she'd drunk the hot coffee. She watched a grizzled old man hook cans from the garbage until Guthrie's old Ford rolled up to the front of the tenement.

The little detective wasn't talking. He drove uptown on Park Avenue, ticking along with the traffic. Above the city, the clouds were broken, admitting shattered bars of early sunshine. North of Mount

Morris, he turned to get on Eighth Avenue. Along the way he had to fight the traffic, because he seemed to be going no place in particular, while every other driver in Manhattan had someplace they needed to be. Eventually he drove down by the Harlem, and the old blue Ford slid up beneath the bridge where Bowman was murdered.

In daylight, the underpinnings looked less forbidding. Sunlight revealed reality: tired, dirty, and overlooked. Guthrie parked. He took a walk among the piers, his feet crunching on gravel and glass, then returned to sit in the driver's seat with the door open.

"You all right?" he asked. "You sleep?"

Vasquez frowned into the bottom of a cup of coffee that was becoming visible. "Me? How about you?"

The little detective grunted. "Not enough," he said. "Pieces have been trying to fit together all night. This's coming down to two things. Somehow the *mafiya* is worked into it, and Olsen's caught in a beautiful frame with that gun. Those college boys haven't got that kind of grudge against him. Looking into Bowman turned my head the wrong way."

"*Viejo*, we only figured that out because we went through it."

"I'm not saying we didn't need to—we gotta get at Peiper," Guthrie said. "But Wasserman wouldn't have missed this."

"He must've been a genius."

"Maybe. He was an old-school tough guy, even when he was old. He was in his sixties when I started. That seems like a long time ago. HP was still a youngster back then. George Livingston is the new right hand, but he only started a few years ago. Before Livingston was Mr. Morgan, a real sharp guy who was doing for the Whitneys since the *first* war. HP inherited him from the man he took over."

"Another Whitney?"

"That's right. Wasserman was Mr. Morgan's go-to guy. When I ran into HP in France, he put me together with Wasserman over here." The little detective frowned. "You weren't even born when Wasserman retired. I guess that means I'm really, really old. Anyway, he did just about everything at one time or another—divorce, bail jumping, repo—the old man would even chase lost dogs and cats.

"I had one big case with Wasserman. That was in '91. That case was ugly. After that, he went on about another six months; then he called Mr. Morgan and told him he was finished. He cradled the phone, fished the office keys out of his pocket, tossed them to me, and walked out. I felt like I burned a hole through the chair."

"What happened?"

Guthrie glanced out across the river, toward the Bronx. He scowled. "I'm still here."

"No, the case," Vasquez said.

The little detective frowned and looked at his watch, but then he settled back into the car seat and sighed. "That was in September. Everyone was wearing jackets—the heat was gone. Wasserman had a friend down in Chinatown, an old tong named Li Wei. He called at about nine o'clock in the morning, and Wasserman's face turned as grim as a rock. I knew Viet before I started with him, so I picked Cantonese up fast. The old man stressed languages.

"I had something better than a sprinkling by then, so I could follow the conversation. Li Wei didn't trust phones except for chitchat—he wanted Wasserman to come meet him on Fulton Street. That was outside his territory, which didn't sound good to Wasserman. Before we left, he took an extra pair of forty-fives from the cabinet, and he made me take an extra pistol.

"The Chinese are different like that. They don't call the police. Chinese gangsters will cut you to pieces, or shoot you a dozen times, then run outside and set off firecrackers to pretend they're having a party for their cousin. The gangs are the law, and nobody talks. We took the subway downtown—did I tell you Wasserman would rather ride the train than drive? Sure. Once we got there, the little old Chinese guy gives me a hard look, then props on his cane while he talks. Messengers went back and forth around us while he spelled it out.

"Early that morning, somebody snatched Li Wei's granddaughter—eldest daughter of eldest son, along those lines. In China, the girls aren't that important, but over here, the old men treat every girl child like she's spun from gold. See, the old men almost died out, because there weren't no women. Up until the second war, Chinese women couldn't emigrate to America unless they were prostitutes. An American-born girl child?" Guthrie nodded absently. Trucks rumbled on the bridge overhead, coming out of the Bronx, headed somewhere in the city.

"Li Wei wanted his granddaughter back. She was gold, tiger sign and everything, and that made it double bad. See, the triads do kidnapping for ransom, but not the way it's usually done over here. They run all of the usual scams—extortion, robbery, whatever— but kidnapping is their ultimate shakedown. The victim has to pay promptly. They don't ask for huge ransoms because they don't wait long. After twenty or thirty hours, maybe forty, it's over. First, they tell you when and where to pay. Then after a bit, if the victim acts stubborn, they do a warning—who they're holding gets beat half to death, or loses some fingers, or gets raped, with some pictures taken. There ain't no second warning—just a body, and maybe not that.

"Wasserman grilled him for the details, and it was your typical seam job. The kidnappers picked just the right moment, and whisked her away, only chopping one guy. The job seemed too clean. Li Wei believed they had somebody on his inside, but Wasserman said different. People just trust their routines too much. They agreed the girl had to be *outside* Chinatown, because nobody would keep quiet about Li Wei's granddaughter—he was an old gangster, with more favors in his pocket than pigeons in the park.

"Then they came to the tough part. Li Wei couldn't pay. If he pays, he loses face. The renegades take his face and go up the ladder. So he has to have the crew. He wants his granddaughter back, but the crew is more important.

"The renegades snatched Li Wei's granddaughter real early. That was bad for them. Wasserman taught me the trick with the street people. Inside the city, that's easy. Sure enough, a florist's van went screaming down James Street at half past seven. By midafternoon, drunks were happy on a path through downtown and we're sitting on a white florist's van: Trammel's Treasury. The renegades were in an old walkup on Rivington, just down from Alphabet City.

"I watched while Wasserman went to call Li Wei. One Chinese guy came out, but I didn't worry, because it'd only been eight hours." Guthrie laughed. Vasquez had a sour look on her face. "I told you, he never missed anything. Eight hours after the snatch, we were sitting on them. We almost reached their hideout before they did.

"Wasserman came back and explained that Li Wei wasn't coming. He figured the first Asian face on the street got his granddaughter chopped. Then Wasserman asked me which apartment they were sitting inside, and I got the sick feeling you get when you do something stupid. I'd been waiting for him to find out. He didn't say a thing. He just sat down and planted his hands on his knees. I had to sit and think for a minute.

"Some Spanish kids down the block were playing stickball. I bought a stack of newspapers and sent one of the kids door-to-door, passing free newspapers and pretending to sell subscriptions. I made sure he was real persistent at every door." Guthrie laughed. "On the second floor the kid found a pissed-off Chinese guy who didn't want a newspaper—apartment two C.

"I was proud, like a kid who made his first peanut butter sandwich. Wasserman didn't wait for me to settle down. He went right back up the stairs and kicked in the door of two C. When the door came open, the first thing I heard was a TV. I followed him through the door into a typical nothing little apartment. All of the doors lead out into one room, and the kitchen was on one side. Three Chinese guys were inside. The angry guy who didn't want a newspaper was watching TV. Another one was sitting on a stool to watch the street, eating pistachios and spitting the hulls onto the apartment floor. The last one was in the kitchen, boiling some horrible-smelling soup. Wasserman told me later that the soup was called 'tiger balls'—not really from a tiger, but supposedly serious *yang*. The renegades were about to do the warning on Li Wei's granddaughter. The man who left before Wasserman came back was a tip-off, but I neglected to tell him.

"The angry guy picked up right where he left off with the Spanish kid: raising hell. The one on the stool started laughing, but he slid off the stool, pulled a knife, and threw it at Wasserman. The old bastard started shooting. The gunshots covered the sound of another four rushing up the stairs. We walked into the building just ahead of them. That's what the man on the stool was laughing about."

Guthrie rubbed his chin and pointed through the windshield down toward the Harlem River at something that wasn't there. "The cook was wearing a white apron. He threw a saucepan full of hot something at me. I spun around to dodge and missed with a shot. We ended up facing each other. He had a boning knife and the saucepan. He cut the buttons off the sleeve of my suit coat and almost smashed my face with the pan, but I hit him in the belly with my second shot. He dropped.

"Then the rest of them barreled through the door. One rushed me. I caught an inside grip on his knife hand with the outside edge of my hand and stepped inside him to keep the hold. He circled around me and rammed the kitchen counter, and I stepped back out. One of the new ones was flying toward Wasserman's back like an ax dropping on stove wood. I shot him through the hips. He bent in half and lost his knife.

"Wasserman slid a little deeper into the living room. He switched pistols and kicked the coffee table at them. The living room was already a mess. The TV was dead, along with the angry Chinese guy. The other one was still standing by the window, but he was propped on the wall with both hands and covered with blood. The guy who went out and came back ran for one of the inside doors. I chased him. The one I rammed into the kitchen counter swung his knife as I was taking the first step. He split my suit coat open and it slid down my arms. Probably the leather strap on my shoulder holster saved my life.

"That knife-in-a-gunfight thing is crap, unless you're twenty feet away," the little detective said. "That Chinese guy notched four of my ribs. Wasserman shot him as he chased me across the living room. I wanted to duck when the old man swung that forty-five auto past me. I had three bullets left in my forty-four. Going by,

I shot the other little guy who was after Wasserman. He had on a button-down shirt and tan pants, with plastic-framed sunglasses and his hair slicked back 1950s style. The blade of his knife was as long as his forearm. His shirt turned bright red when the bullet hit him.

"The bathroom was cheap plaster, with a claw-foot tub and one pebbled-glass window up high. The tub was converted to a shower, with a stand-up brass railing, and Li Wei's granddaughter was hanging by her wrists, a gag in her mouth. She was a little marked up already. The triads like heavy knives, to cut off anything held up to ward them away—fingers, hands, even arms. The last one rushed to chop her.

"Li Wei's granddaughter was brave. He meant to chop her across the throat, but she lowered her chin and took it on the face. I shot him twice. She didn't look good, but I was out of bullets and couldn't shoot him again. Wasserman came in and cut her down. She slid down into a puddle in the tub, and then a few seconds later she stood right back up. She wanted the gag out, but even after, she couldn't talk. That girl was brave. She looked like the walking dead. We had to run out of there and dodge the cops." The little detective shook his head.

"You saved her."

"She saved herself. Or Wasserman did. I couldn't have found her that fast. I doubt I could even now."

Vasquez pretended to look out at the river with him, but she was watching the little man. She wondered why he needed to be perfect, why good enough wasn't quite enough. He began brooding again; his jaw worked like he was chewing something. He climbed out of the old Ford and walked down to the shore of the Harlem. After a minute, Vasquez followed him. The bank of the Harlem was a concrete retaining wall and sheet pilings wracked with rust. Instead of reeds or sedges, a litter of empty bottles slowly bobbed around an old tire with part of the sidewall missing.

"Things come out of the past," Guthrie said before turning

back to look at the bridge. "The killer had to hate Olsen. This's the beginning. He chose this spot for a reason. We have to look again."

"This can't be the beginning," Vasquez said. "It's gotta be the end. Whoever it is hates Olsen for something he did."

"We have to find what ties it together." The little detective walked slowly back toward the abutment. He paused several times, studying the bridge and the loop of asphalt beneath it. Empty trailers were massed in a transfer park on the far side. A bobtailed Mack growled softly, slipping between them as it moved back out toward the city. Beneath the bridge, a Dumpster was tucked tight against the retaining wall of the abutment, and a colonnade of piers supported the bridge on its way to arch over the Harlem. A loop of asphalt ran north beneath the bridge, connecting the transfer park to an alley onto Eighth Avenue.

The Mack hadn't used the loop—it headed south, directly into the city. The fence line along the transfer park was a strip of ragged weeds sprouting from an illicit dump. Old, rotten cardboard and pallets formed crooked stacks. Bottles and cans filled the creases above a litter of grimy multicolored pebbles made of shattered glass. Inside the colonnade, fire pits dotted the bases of the piers. The retaining wall and Dumpster were marked with graffiti in a multitude of colors. Jumbled together in overlay, they looked more like a visual grille than an attempt to communicate, obscure, or vandalize.

Guthrie paced the distance from the asphalt loop to the remnants of NYPD yellow crime tape for the body. Faint stains remained. The bridge arched above like a shield. The killing had happened ten or twelve steps from the Dumpster. The little detective grunted. No attempt had been made to hide Bowman's body, even by tipping it into the Dumpster. The murder was meant to be discovered—a confirmation—but the site itself was tucked away. The site required either a search or familiarity.

"The killer knew about this spot," Guthrie muttered.

"Someplace secluded, where nobody could see. No houses or

apartments nearby, no kids hiding nearby," Vasquez said, glancing out around them.

Guthrie pointed at the graffiti. "What's that stuff mean?"

She shrugged. "Ain't tags. Don't even look like words."

The little detective pulled out his phone and took several snapshots.

"I'll float it on the Net and see if we get a bite."

CHAPTER TWENTY-ONE

"Olsen asked me to check on you," the little detective said to Philip Linney. "He wanted to be sure you came out of it."

Linney's answering smile had a sad edge. "I think that shoe's on the other foot now."

The midday sun on St. Peter's Avenue in Westchester was bright and hot. Dust from shattered mortar hung in the air, and every other breath had an ozone bite from scorched metal. Linney was on lunch break from his labor job on a teardown. He slid into the backseat of the old Ford. Vasquez pulled away from the curb and the smell of reconstruction.

"My boys say Captain ain't acting straight himself. He told me some story about the cops fishing after more murders—and I can see that on TV," he said. A few smears of bright dust decorated his dark face. He opened his brown bag and pulled out peanut butter and jelly sandwiches. "Captain's too white-bread. All this shit's catching him by surprise."

Guthrie nodded agreement. He pulled a lukewarm Yoo-hoo from

the grab bag and handed it over the seat. Linney cracked the top and took a long drink.

"That's what you wanted to see me about?"

"Sure. I wanted to see where you were at," Guthrie said. "I ain't gonna dig around in something and make a mess, not if there's another way. Talking to you about it would just be faster."

Linney frowned. "I'm straight. Captain squared me away, just like over there. See the job? I ain't some bullshit kid that's too good to work. I know what real gangster is—and it ain't sitting on your ass, getting high, and faking hard. So what are you getting at?"

"You're a sharp guy. Last time, you figured I wasn't talking because I didn't want Olsen to know what I was doing." Linney nodded. "That's changed. Now it seems clear that Bowman's killing has to do with Olsen, not Bowman. Everything else is only clouding the picture. So now I'm connecting the dots—and you have something to do with Olsen, not Bowman."

"I ain't been running around with Captain, you know. He's got his world, I got mine."

"Thinking they were apart like that kept me from coming back to you sooner," Guthrie said. "Maybe it's a coincidence. I say somebody framed Olsen. Maybe the same person who wants bad things to happen to him wants bad things to happen to you, too."

"What the fuck, man!" Linney turned in his seat as if he wanted to get out of the car, but they were moving. Vasquez studied him in the rearview mirror. The dark-skinned man was flushed with anger.

"Maybe it's a coincidence," Guthrie continued. "Tell me what happened to your mother."

Linney didn't say anything for a few minutes. He finished his sandwiches, barely chewing. He drained the bottle of Yoo-hoo, then rolled down his window. He hurled the bottle out at a lamppost, but his curse was the only sound that wasn't lost behind them. "Now you got me thinking," Linney said softly after rolling up the window.

"Mama lived in a mixed neighborhood in Unionport. Black, white, Spanish, Asian, Indian, whatever, all crammed into the tenements together. People ain't watching over each other like they should.

Some stickup boys ran into the bodega where she's picking up groceries, and they were high or something, and they beat everybody. Moms was old—" His fists clenched, and then he started strangling his empty brown paper lunch bag. "Moms died from the beating."

Guthrie waited while Vasquez drove the long length of the block. "Who's the story from?"

"The cops," Linney said. "And Ms. Wilson—she lived down the hall from Moms. Who knows where she had it from, but it was about the same thing."

"I know somebody who works the precinct up there. I should be able to take a look at that." He turned to look over the seat and study Linney's face. "I know this stirred you up. Are you gonna be okay to go back to work?"

"I ain't doing nothing hard."

"You ain't gotta pay attention?"

Linney smiled. "It ain't sentry duty. Maybe I'll drop something."

Guthrie handed the grab bag over the seat. "Reach in there and get you something."

"You a strange dude, you know that?" Linney smiled, his hand rustling in the bag. "Like Halloween or something." A yellow bag of M&M's was bright in his dark hand, but his eyes were hard. "You gotta tell me if you think there's something to what you said, all right?"

"I gotta talk with you again, anyway," the little detective said.

Linney gave the detectives a puzzled look as Vasquez paused the Ford by his job site to let him out. "You're like Captain," he said. "His mouth don't move much unless he's got something to say." He climbed from the backseat. The cool from the rain was gone, and the pavement was like an oven heated by the sun. For the moment, the dust was settled, but an air gun was already blatting somewhere in the building. The face of the city changes slowly, but on the inside, things shift around all the time.

———

Outside the Unionport precinct house, sunshine was a broad stripe of fire in the middle of the street. Inside, screaming drunks filled the bottom floor. Tiny Laotians hurled insults at Indians, and Jamaicans pointed fingers at Dominicans. Partisans on both sides wore blood-speckled bandages, or carried ice bags in manacled hands. Shouted taunts and threats twisted into a melody. Early reports placed the beginning of hostilities upon an unexpected pregnancy, along with a casual suggestion that the father might be other than the devoted swain. After half-a-dozen assaults were docketed in the same Olmstead tenement, the captain ordered anyone who raised their voice brought into the station house for a cooldown. The paddy wagons stayed busy. Guthrie and Vasquez wormed through the tired officers and fuming citizens to question Robert Gennaro, the desk sergeant.

Gennaro, a dark, heavyset Italian with a mustache, was still short of middle-aged. He recognized the bodega robbery when Guthrie described it—it was still on the board, and he didn't see much chance of a solve. The stickup crew didn't match any of the pros they had working the area. He called upstairs for the detective assigned the case. Jonathan Sullivan came down, disinterestedly swallowed a story about insurance coverage, and gave them details and information on his few witnesses—the five assault victims in the robbery. Gennaro spent his time fending off requests from uniforms, and watching Vasquez. Once they were finished, the police sergeant drew breath for a speech, but he was interrupted by a sloppy handcuffed fistfight between an overweight Jamaican and a half-dressed Dominican. Guthrie and Vasquez slipped out.

The bodega on Turnbull Avenue was dimly lit and perfumed with fresh fruit and baked goods. The detectives were lucky. William Donovan, the cashier, hadn't drifted away from the job after the robbery. He was a middle-aged man who knew he wouldn't get away from stupid people and stupid things by moving someplace else. He had a mop of faded red hair and a tired face. The bottoms of old blue jeans showed beneath his red work apron. He wasn't interested in talking about the robbery, but Guthrie slid a fifty-dollar bill across the dark wooden counter. Donovan took it, smiling sadly. The new floor man watched curiously as he swept; the man he'd replaced had quit because he was beaten badly in the robbery.

"How much did they get?" Guthrie asked.

The cashier shrugged. "Few hundred. It was early on a Tuesday. That's usually our worst day."

"That ain't sounding right. How many were there?"

"Four white guys in ski masks. One watched the door."

"Okay, I guess that's better. But they didn't know the good day?"

"They're crooks. They're stupid," Donovan said. "Or maybe they were high." He frowned. "I was ringing up when they came inside. Usually I look up, but I was counting, and then two were at the counter."

"Four?" Guthrie seemed surprised.

"Yeah, I know. How many dumbasses does it take to rob a bodega? Two came to the counter with their guns out, one stayed at the door, and one went to the back. They didn't say much. I pulled the money from the register. The last one comes from the back, pushing our kid along with his gun—that used to work here."

"So how'd the crazy part start?"

"I dunno. One of them said, 'Wallets!' and the one with the bag goes around. Nobody made a fuss. The one from the back put up his gun and pulled a bat. After the old lady handed over her wallet, he snatched her by the jacket collar and tapped her on the head. She drooped down onto her knees, and he hit her again. The one at the door, the other two, they didn't say a thing. The bagman kept after the wallets.

"He was a little guy. Maybe he had a complex or something. He just started nailing everybody. I couldn't believe it. They got their bag, but now he wanted to beat everybody's ass. The kid made a break for it, but the little guy was quick. He creamed Alonzo into the potato chips. When he came back to the counter, he didn't even seem excited. He came behind the counter and hemmed me up. I shouted in his face the whole time, but I don't think he noticed."

"How many times did he hit you?"

"I dunno. He was fast, like something out of a movie—Jet Li with a stick. I had lumps on my head and knots on my arms. I couldn't straighten my left elbow out for two weeks."

Guthrie nodded. "How many times did he hit the old woman?"

"Twice." Donovan frowned. "I couldn't believe she was dead."

"Ms. Linney was pretty old, I think," the little detective said. "Did you remember her from any other time? She shopped here?"

"A few times. I'm okay with faces. She wasn't here every week, maybe only every month or so."

"I want you to do something for me," Guthrie said. "Show me how he hit Ms. Linney, the old woman who died."

The cashier looked dubious, and Guthrie slid him another fifty. The bodega had only two customers, and both were more interested in the conversation than in their shopping lists. Donovan came from behind the counter, dusted his hands on his apron, and used Guthrie to demonstrate how the robber had gripped Althea Linney's jacket collar, close to the left shoulder. Vasquez watched. Donovan mimed a blow and tugged the little detective until he thought he was in the same position on his knees. Donovan frowned in concentration, shifting his feet until he was partly behind him, then mimed another blow. Vasquez moved to the other side, then made him do it again.

After he went back behind the counter, Donovan said, "I didn't see it like that before. Maybe he hit her on the back of the neck."

The first time Guthrie appeared at the door of her parents' tenement apartment on Henry Street to offer her a job as a private detective, Vasquez thought that would mean puzzling from clues who did what to whom. After they left the bodega in Unionport, they drove down to the city. They sat in La Borinqueña in Spanish Harlem, ate chips and chiles rellenos, and played connect the dots in the Olsen case, without enough dots to make a picture. Like watching videos and sitting in parks, trying to see a solution without enough to work from wasn't what she had imagined.

Guthrie squashed the notion of returning to the Bronx to question Philip Linney again. He thought they'd pushed the man too far already. He had grown up around veterans. Bad things happened fast when they were stirred. So they sat and thought about it, making outlines on their palmtops of places they'd gone, people they'd seen, and things they'd done, hoping that something would suddenly match. Guthrie showed Vasquez the electronic trail he'd found connecting Amanda Hearst to Peiper's newfound fortune, a ten-thousand-dollar spike that matched the date Peiper paid off his credit cards. For the little detective, the money was a smoking gun, but he hadn't decided what to do about it. The café was tranquil around them, a mix of quiet Spanish conversation and soft guitar music on the radio.

Late in the afternoon, Black-haired John called. The call was too short for Guthrie to be sure if the drifter wanted to meet immediately, because he only named a place. The little detective figured he meant later that afternoon, because now he was probably hooking cans with his family.

Guthrie couldn't be sure of what John might want. Sometimes the drifter worried about the police and wanted someone from the everyday world to reassure him he wasn't in trouble. Other times, he found something that he couldn't deal with. Once, he found a car abandoned. Its doors were open and there was a load of groceries inside. Black-haired John wasn't a drunk. He worried that someone had run away and left their groceries—the car was of no interest to him because his family couldn't fit inside it to sleep.

After Guthrie and Vasquez finished eating, they drove up to the north end of Highbridge Park. Vasquez cut the engine. The afternoon was roasting hot and muggy. Before they could begin walking, Little Tony jogged up to the Ford. Tony was the eldest kid in John's family, a seventeen-year-old black kid small enough to pass for a twelve-year-old. Usually he was lookout or scout, because he had a smooth voice and no one thought he was up to something if he suddenly started singing. At night, he could be almost invisible, since he was extremely dark; even during the daylight, the dark clothes he wore made him seem like a patch of shadows. He led them along one of the footpaths into the park. Past the end of a retaining wall, he turned uphill and they had to slog. Leaf litter and old sticks rattled off like firecrackers.

The kids were scattered around the top of the hill. They stared at Guthrie and Vasquez as they passed. Black-haired John was sitting at a charcoal fire with Cindy, roasting marshmallows on coat hangers. That was the first time Vasquez had ever seen him being still, but he stood as soon as he noticed the detectives. Each time he made a revolution around the fire, the late-afternoon sunshine caught his eyes and they flashed icy bright.

"Ghost Eddy is dead," Black-haired John said.

The night before, a rumor had surfaced on the north end of the city that the big gray-bearded drifter had been shot to death. Black-haired John asked around after he heard that, and discovered the source of the rumor was Stoop-O. He was traveling everywhere he could reach, telling anyone who would stand still long enough to listen. Stoop-O was glad to be the herald of Eddy's death, because the big man had punched out his teeth. Black-haired John had three thoughts upon hearing the news. Stoop-O might be saying what he hoped was true, or saying it because people were asking about Eddy but might stop if they thought he was dead. Stoop-O was enough of a crab to beg a man he hated and feared for liquor. Then, also, it could be true.

Black-haired John decided to hear it directly from Stoop-O. Being lazy and stupid, the drunk was easy to find. Men besides Guthrie had asked about Ghost Eddy on the street, but they were less friendly. They didn't listen when somebody said "I don't know." They squeezed until an answer popped out, a finger pointed at someone to ask, or a place to go. They almost seemed to be following Guthrie. A few drifters took car rides until they ran out of things to talk about and places to go, then got rolled from the car without the courtesy of a stop. They were white men with foreign accents, maybe Russians, though Black-haired John refused to say that for sure. His family was lucky. No one was grabbed, because all of that started after they stopped looking for Eddy and were lying low.

Busy walking around the fire, the drifter didn't notice Vasquez fuming. Her face was almost as red as her windbreaker. Cindy offered her a coat hanger and some marshmallows. Once the young Puerto Rican settled by the fire, Cindy tried unsuccessfully to tuck her hanging lock of hair behind her ear. Vasquez shrugged. She toasted marshmallows while Black-haired John continued.

They'd found Stoop-O on 137th Street a few hours after midday, bragging sloppily through his broken teeth. He was drunk. His lies were polished with repetition, and he cycled through them like a jukebox each time he caught a laugh or some encouragement. One version was that Stoop-O had helped the killers find Ghost Eddy to get even, while another was that the gray-bearded drifter had been too stupid to heed Stoop-O's warnings about stealing from dangerous men. The searchers caught up with Eddy in the underground and shot him as he fled. Stoop-O's lies made Black-haired John doubt him on details, even though the men stopped searching for Ghost Eddy. Plainly, he was dead, or they had given up on finding him.

"I say he's dead, John," the little detective said. "You gotta be careful for a while."

Black-haired John paused in mid-stride, smiled, and then kept moving. He was a mutt that didn't need advice on when to scratch or lie still. "You know something, huh?" he prodded.

"They were Russians," Guthrie replied. "A pair tried to shut us up yesterday."

The drifter threw a sharp glance at Vasquez, who was sitting with a wire hanger in hand. "Don't matter. I didn't ask Stoop-O. I only nodded and smiled to keep him lying, then hooked right up the street."

As the sun sank lower, the campsite atop the hill under the scrub trees cooled. The little charcoal fire was like a sharp needle requiring careful movement to avoid. Cindy hung cans to heat water and fry slices of turkey in butter. Kids drifted up to crowd the top of the hill. Guthrie and Vasquez walked back down in silence. The little detective counted on his fingers, reciting to himself the number of people he'd told about Ghost Eddy, then cursed quietly that he had told anyone at all.

CHAPTER TWENTY-TWO

In front of Vasquez's tenement, Henry Street was quiet and still. On a usual summer afternoon while the day cooled, kids played football and music blared from parked cars: muchachos swaggered on the sidewalk, spitting bad raps or worse, *piropos*. Quiet didn't exist on a summer afternoon. Above the street, the old people sat watching from the fire escapes, like usual. Faint tinny music from their old radios floated down onto the street like tired confetti. Across the street from the stoop, a chromed-out lowrider sat silently like a brooding tarantula. Four muchachos inside the car dangled cigarette hands out over piles of spent butts. They watched without interest as Guthrie's old Ford glided up to the tenement and Vasquez climbed out. The young Puerto Rican detective paused on the stoop, giving the street a once-over puzzled scan. Down the block in both directions, life was normal.

A note waited on the refrigerator in the empty apartment. Her parents were gone to sit with Maria Lopez, whose husband had died. Friends were taking turns to help while the relatives were gathered. Martin Lopez and Papì had been old friends. The note finished by saying they wouldn't be back until late and that she should heat the beans left over from two nights ago and roll them in a tortilla.

Vasquez wasn't hungry. She took a shower, cleaned the bathroom, and tried to decide what to do about her hair. She was full of nervous energy. She walked from room to room, pausing to look from the windows. She tired of tucking her hair behind her ear, and let it hang. The apartment seemed small. She would rather have been driving. When the streetlights lit outside, Miguel came home.

Vasquez's youngest brother was the shortest but most powerfully built of her three brothers. Papì joked, when he watched the Giants play on TV, that Roberto would be quarterback, Indio a tight end, and Miguel would be stuck as fullback. Miguel had a neat chin beard, with tattoos on cinnamon skin that he could hide beneath long sleeves when he wanted. He smiled when he saw her, like always, being her favorite brother, but then he darkened with anger. That caught Vasquez by surprise.

Miguel stalked into the kitchen. His anger drew questions from Vasquez like a magnet. While he made coffee, rattling the jars in the refrigerator door to get an apple, their voices amplified from a quiet beginning to a thunder that filled the empty apartment.

"Don't play you ain't seen our riders outside, or notice we cleared the street. You're the smart one! You ain't supposed to be doing this shit. A shoot-out with the mob? Those ain't kids, Rachel. We ain't worried about a drive-by. We worried they gonna come right up in here and get you. What the fuck you think you *doing*?"

"I'm doing my job!"

"Indio should be talking to you," Miguel growled. "He's better at this. You piss me off, then I want to pull your hair like I did when we were little. Make you holler for Papì."

"What about Indio? Three months ago this was *mucho*, now this?"

"That old man knew shit was coming! That's why he got you the *pistolita*," Miguel said. "Damn, we got an easier way of doing this."

"Easier way of what? You think you can beat that old man up? I ain't in school no more! You think you're gonna keep doing that shit to me my whole life? You ain't!"

Miguel grinned. "What are you gonna do, holler for Papì?"

"I ain't hollering for nobody," Vasquez spat.

An old plug-in clock sat on the counter behind her. She yanked it from the outlet, stepped forward, and hit Miguel over the head with it. He was frozen with surprise. The clock was tough; his head didn't do much to it. A thread of blood raced down his nose, and he tried to grab the clock.

Vasquez was quick. She hit him again. Unable to catch the clock, he grabbed her. They slammed into the table. The blood on his face made her decide to abandon the clock. She dropped it, grabbed him, and bit his shoulder. He shouted while they crashed around the kitchen, but she wouldn't let go.

"Fucking let go!" he shouted. He caught her ponytail and started yanking. She growled curses, dug her feet into the floor, and bit harder. He slammed her against the counter. Dishes showered onto the floor from the sink drainboard. Glass crunched beneath them. Punches flailed.

"Stop! I'm bleeding, damn it!" Miguel shouted. "I quit!" He let go of her and held up his hands like a beaten criminal. She let go and jumped back, spitting out the taste of his shirt. They were both breathing fast and wearing spots and streaks of blood like Christmas trees flaunt tinsel.

"Damn! You're crazy," Miguel panted. The kitchen was a mess around them. The table blocked the doorway to the living room.

"You ain't gonna fuck with me no more, Miguel. You or Indio. You should've known that when I wouldn't listen to Papì. I'm done with that shit."

"Look at you—you look like an animal or something."

"Me?" She shook her head. "You're still bleeding. Go to the bathroom." He pulled the table out of the doorway, then pulled off his shirt as he walked. He craned his neck to examine the bite mark on his shoulder. Blood oozed from an egg-size mark. He swore softly. Vasquez pressed clean rags to his scalp in the bathroom and stopped the bleeding from the shallow cuts. He held a pad of gauze to his shoulder.

A few times while they cleaned up, they started to say something, but only shook fingers or snorted instead. They didn't want to start fighting again. She went back out to straighten the mess in the kitchen. After he changed, he came back to sit at the table and watch her. She poured him a cup of coffee to drink while she finished. They watched each other, piecing together what they wanted to say. After the kitchen was reassembled, Vasquez sat down again.

"You ain't never done anything like that before," Miguel said finally.

"I ain't never been this serious."

They sat at the table and stared at each other over their cups of coffee. The apartment seemed too quiet. The traffic was distant and faint. Outside the windows, darkness suggested the city was gone, and they were all alone.

"You know I'd do anything for you, right?" Miguel asked. "But what you're doing is crazy. You can't be doing stuff that brings shit down on Mamì."

"What're you saying? I'm not supposed to do this because I'm a girl? If I was another brother, I could be a criminal and you wouldn't say nothing."

"I wouldn't tell a man not to be a man," Miguel said. "But you're my sister. There ain't but one of you. Me and Indio were finished from the beginning. We always knew it didn't matter. You're the one gonna go somewhere for us."

"You're wrong," she said softly. Her brothers had always picked on her about school, joking that she had an alien brain. She called them stupid, even after she discovered they knew answers they pretended they didn't. They failed classes because they cut and clowned, not because they couldn't do it. They were loco. More firmly, she continued: "You're wrong, Miguel. You could've done whatever you wanted. You don't get to make me do something by pretending you can't. I get to do what I want, too. I like this job."

"You want to run out and get yourself killed. We ain't got no other sisters."

"That's what makes it okay for you and Indio? Mamì would still have Roberto? You want me to be like Roberto? He's full of shit."

"Okay, nobody likes Roberto! He's an ass, but you don't got to be like him that way. You know I'm talking about the big-time desk job, the suburbs—and get away from this."

He gestured, a casual flip of the hand that could've meant the kitchen and its faded wallpaper, Henry Street's long row of tenements, or the entire city.

"That's what you want," she said. "Or maybe what Papì wants. I been doing that my whole life—what somebody else wants. Maybe I don't know for sure what I want, but I know I want to figure it out for myself. You want a desk job? You're smart enough. Do it."

"*Chica*, you're smart, but you're blind. Look at you. Nobody's ever gonna tell you 'no.' One look at you and they're trying to figure out how to say 'yes.' Me? I ain't gonna make it through like that."

Vasquez frowned. "You think I'm gonna get somewhere on my looks? *Guthrie* don't give a shit about that. I don't know yet what he started with. That's different. That's a place to start."

Miguel smiled. "When that old man came to the door with that job, you know what I thought? At least this *blanco* gets her off the Lower East."

"What the fuck?"

"See, you can't see it, because you are who you are. Me and Indio figured it out a long time ago. You don't get the looks we get. Doors swing open for you instead of slamming shut. That's how the world works. We're *morenos*, nobody wants us. You're *la blanquita*. Maybe in the city you're just another Puerto Rican girl, but if you stopped with the hat on the side of your head, you could be one of them."

"That's what you want? You want me to go away?" Tears slipped from her eyes, even though crying wasn't a thing she usually did.

"No, you don't understand. I want you to have something. You just ain't gonna ever have anything here."

"But I got something already," she said softly, even though she understood what he meant. The same complaint had floated around her for years, from anyone who didn't think they had a fair chance. He couldn't see it from her angle, though. She had looked through some of the doors that closed in his face, to see the same world on the other side, only with different people. Listening to Miguel let her see it again. Roberto was unhappy because he was tricked into thinking a difference existed between the two worlds. All his life was filled with promises of how good everything would be, and then everything was the same after all. Discovering the truth without being able to go back made Roberto sick.

"What you got?" Miguel demanded. "Some bullshit job in the city gonna get you killed? That ain't good enough."

"I got a fucking family—a fucked-up family—but a family," she said. "I got a job that could go somewhere. You can't see that because you're not there. Right now that's good enough."

"That ain't good enough. We ain't done all this so you can stay in the city and be stuck in the same mess everybody else is in. You gotta go free."

"You done what?" Vasquez demanded. "Run around banging? That was for me? Beat up every boy ever looked at me? That was to make me happy? I did good in school because I didn't have anything else to do. You and Indio are *loco*. Now you don't want me doing this? I should be doing girl things? You took that away from me!"

"That fucking trash ain't good enough for you!" Miguel snarled. "Some piece of shit in this neighborhood, not wanting no job, lining up another baby-momma just as soon as you show blue—we'll kill all of them!"

Vasquez sat quietly for a minute, swallowing her anger. She made another cup of coffee for herself. When she sat back down, she said, "You're saying *you* ain't good enough for me, Miguel. *You* bang. That's stupid. But you been doing that forever. When did you get the idea to do that?"

He scowled. "*You're* stupid. I don't handle *chicas* that way. Papì would kill me. What you don't know is when you were little, you were white. You didn't even get *that* dark until we went back to the island a few times. People thought Mamì was sitting you for somebody else. You never saw how people treated you."

"How the fuck old were you? Or was it Indio? He did this?"

Miguel shrugged. "You can't blame Indio. I hit him first, then Indio kicked him." He laughed. "That was easier than falling down. We never even talked about it, until the first time we had to lay for one of them. That was when you started middle school."

"You did that thinking it would make me happy?"

Miguel frowned. "I never thought about it," he said. "I didn't think I needed to. This's the Lower East. I mean, we make jokes about how fucked up this is. Now I'm wrong to want you out of this. But I see what you're saying.

"You don't want to leave if you gotta leave us behind. I know that, too. I would never leave Mamì and Papì here alone. So this is the first time in my life it's true: I'm stupid."

"Shut up, Miguel," Vasquez said. "Stupid people should be quiet people. Only reason I gotta keep telling you that is because you're stupid."

Miguel turned away, smiling about the worn-out old joke. Outside the kitchen window, the night was dark. The apartment was quiet. They waited, and eventually Vasquez went to bed. The Russians didn't come, even though Miguel waited all night. Vasquez slept like the dead. In the morning when she woke up, she had a black eye from one of her brother's punches.

CHAPTER TWENTY-THREE

Guthrie drove to the office in the morning after picking up Vasquez. Before then, while the muggy night cooled, he spent a few hours in the Garment District trying to find nonexistent Russians. The little detective admitted to some paranoia. After years spent watching people in the city, a feeling sometimes crept onto him that the city watched in return. That morning, he and Vasquez cleaned the office, scrubbing away bloodstains and aligning the furniture. Guthrie replaced Vasquez's dead desktop monitor, but his own was still functional. They finished up by ordering pizza. Trahn brought a mouthful of conversation with two pizzas. On his last trip, he'd sold the pizzas to the police, but they wouldn't let him see the office.

The little Vietnamese's curiosity matched him up with Tommy Johnson. Guthrie called Tommy, reaching for an update on NYPD's efforts to fit Olsen for the Barbiedoll murders. Tommy invited himself to lunch. The tall young man wore mirrored sunglasses and his NYPD jogging suit; he walked a lap around the office, craning like a tourist, as soon as he came through the door.

"We scrubbed the blood up this morning," Guthrie said.

"C'mon, Guth, you could've let me get a look first." He peeled the mirrored sunglasses from his face and reached into the pizza box, coming out with a narrow slice.

"It ain't as entertaining as you think."

The young man laughed. "It's got 'em talking in the big building." He noticed Vasquez's black eye. "Oh shit!"

She scowled. She started to rough up his ears, but Guthrie stopped her. He asked her to walk Tommy through the shooting and take the shine from the story. The young man was learning his job as he went. Comparing the scene she described to the photos would help him. The little detective listened while Vasquez pointed out where the Russians had fallen, how they had rushed between the desks and couches, and mimicked the blonde's disordered cursing. After two run-throughs of crawling and barrages of shots, Tommy was watching her instead of staring at the office, a slice of pizza dangling from his hand.

Guthrie watched Tommy Johnson stumble for a minute, then said, "They didn't come here to kill us. They came here to ask a question. What was it?"

Vasquez snorted. "They wanted to know if we had a good lead." She rescued a piece of pizza from the box and sat down at her desk.

"Sure, but that would be a lot of talking for muscle. Maybe they had a specific question."

Tommy sprawled on the brown fur couch. "I don't know about that," he said, "but this shooting caused a scene downtown. The Barbiedoll murders are hush-hush, but this splattered. They argued in the halls."

"I would've liked to hear that," Guthrie said.

"I think they're done with 'GI Ken,'" Tommy said. "The gossip says he's ruled out on time and place, 'cause of a receipt or something—"

"When were we gonna hear that?" Vasquez demanded.

"After they didn't need it for leverage," Guthrie said, and frowned at her. He waved Tommy Johnson to go on.

"And Bowman's a separate homicide, no connectivity beyond the resemblance. The other vics got no motives or whatever on them—missing, turned up dead, no suspects."

"They had a take on the Russian shooters?"

Tommy downed a bite of pizza hurriedly. "Freelance. There's a lot of money around the Bowman case, no offense."

"Major Case is squat. Somebody's cleaning up loose ends and they're not suspicious?" Guthrie darted a glance at the young Puerto Rican, then continued, "Let me get quiet. That's not worth talking about yet."

"They got Olsen," Tommy said, and shrugged.

The little detective nodded. "That helps," he said. "All we have to clear is the Bowman murder. Fill in the blanks for me, though. Tell me what you know about the Barbie dolls."

"I only know a few details on one vic—Cara Woodson. She was blond, two shots, no rape, found in Essex County at the edge of a scenic stop. She didn't have a vehicle. They couldn't find witnesses to place her anywhere, but the missing person report suggested shopping or the local honky-tonk."

"She was the May seventeenth victim," Guthrie said. "Essex? That's way upstate."

"Yeah. A long way from the city. They wanted it to stick together. The sex angle pushed them, too, but now the gossip is going the other way. Maybe there is no Barbiedoll killer."

"Tell that to the newspaper," Guthrie muttered.

"The differences were little things," Tommy Johnson said. "Not all of the vics were blond. One vic was missing her underwear, and her blouse was open, but still no sexual assault."

"You're safe to talk about that?" Guthrie asked.

"It's gossip," Tommy said, and shrugged. He slid forward to reach for another slice of pizza, and glanced at his watch. "Oh shit! Lunch is over. See ya, Guth." The office door closed on his heels with a rattling slam.

Once he was gone, Vasquez frowned and said, "I don't get it, *viejo*. We're off the hook for the other murders, but—"

"I don't like that they changed their minds," Guthrie said. "All of a sudden, they don't figure it as a serial killer? Why?"

"I got you," Vasquez said with a smile. "Because I thought of something. Inglewood's pictures showed the legs bunched up. At that bodega on Turnbull yesterday, when the cashier showed how the old woman was killed—I think she would've dropped the same way."

Guthrie frowned. "So you think the victims were kneeling? We can get pictures from the robbery and take a look." He looked toward the window. "You think we should do that?"

"Don't play with me, *viejo*. We'd better do that."

The little detective smiled. "This doesn't change anything, you know. The case is about Olsen—because of the gun. We have to concentrate on Olsen. I'll give it to you that the switch-up looks funny. I'll even go so far as to put it back on the table. Today we're gonna reach out to find what's connecting Olsen and Linney. I'll try the FBI along with that to see if we come up with something connecting them."

The little detective used the telephone to do the dirty work that afternoon. The office became his war room, and the telephones his subordinates. He used four simultaneously, juggling them to see if he remained on hold in Arlington, Virginia, or Washington, D.C. The local calls went quickly, but on the long-distance ones, he managed a multipartner bureaucratic courtship, complete with layers of flattery and devoted listening.

During pauses, he explained to Vasquez that using people would sometimes be part of the job—a task that could be as filthy as a garbage can. Informants could get hurt or killed. Ghost Eddy was another name that Guthrie had to add to the list of people he had screwed badly, without mentioning lost jobs, broken relationships, and money down the drain. Contacts sometimes ran a risk to answer a question, like Tommy Johnson. Detective work wasn't the shiniest job in the world, even when you had the excuse of pulling a man from jail when you were sure he was innocent.

Guthrie shrugged, making a call downtown to Police Plaza. The detectives didn't want to talk, but other people worked in the big building. Monica e-mailed the crime-scene photos of the bodega robbery. Guthrie stored the pictures in his palmtop behind Fat-Fat's kill switch, which operated like a puzzle box. Whenever the computer came on, or woke from a nap, a sequence of keystrokes was required to access the hidden part of its memory. Snapping it shut put the palmtop to sleep. Althea Linney's knees were bent, but not bunched, in the NYPD photographs.

After studying the pictures, Vasquez said, "Tommy said all of the Barbie dolls weren't identical."

"He also said there might not *be* any Barbie dolls," Guthrie said.

Long-distance calls consumed most of the afternoon, and the little detective showed the pressure as the end of the business day crept closer. Administrative assistants in a dozen offices heard corny "aw, shucks" jokes and thick layers of backwoods "Yes, ma'am" or "Yes, sir" as a veil over insistent questions and requests. Guthrie shifted positions behind his desk—propped up his feet, spun his chair, bent over an important doodle, and waved like a semaphore signaler for fresh coffee—and then wandered around the office. Even bathroom breaks didn't stop his chatter. His targets were in the Pentagon and FBI headquarters, but he also called people to help him apply pressure: bankers and lawyers on the southern tip of Manhattan, some hillbillies in West Virginia who made him show off his hog calling before they agreed to help, and a smooth-voiced woman in the nation's capital who sounded like she managed a chorus of dancers. Vasquez watched and listened, moving through her own evolutions of boredom, fascination, and amusement. The little detective was determined. More than that, he had style. By late afternoon, his efforts secured a pair of appointments. The detectives would have to fly to Virginia, because neither man would say anything on the phone.

While Guthrie and Vasquez were arguing about which flight to take to Virginia, someone knocked on the office door. A big shadow loomed beyond the frosted glass. Guthrie frowned, drew a revolver, and held it below his desktop. The door opened, and Detective Inglewood from Major Case limped through.

"Jeez, Mike, you scared the shit out of me," Guthrie said. "Call next time, will you?" He slid his revolver back into the shoulder holster.

Inglewood laughed and straightened his glasses on his nose. "Ain't no Russians woulda knocked on a second visit," he said. "Woulda been *rat-a-tat-tat*, and maybe *boom*!"

"That's real funny. Something bring you to midtown besides the smell of cold pizza? Couple of slices left there." He nodded at the box on the coffee table in front of his desk.

Inglewood settled his bulk down on the oxblood couch and looked the pizza over disdainfully. "I been driving, but I ain't that hungry. Stopped here on my way back downtown."

"This ain't starting out good," Guthrie said.

"I feel I gotta save you some shoe leather. A wit in the Olsen case surfaced upstate—Sandra Whitten. She's dead." The ginger-haired detective wagged a finger. "Before you *even* get started, it's *unrelated*. That comes from the experts. No motive, see? So don't try to roll it up with Bowman."

"Are you kidding me?"

Inglewood sighed, and paused like he was counting to himself. "Different MO. Some kind of blade, with a deep stab wound to the chest. Then, what's missing? Her panties. Okay, different MO?"

"Maybe she walked around with the package unwrapped. She's a wit on *another* homocide, with *another* connected body, and almost a few more—"

"Pure coincidence."

"Ain't a cop on this planet believes in coincidence!"

Inglewood pointed at himself. "Do you see me here? You know me? I'm on the job, right? Bowman's in our jurisdiction. That's closed. Whitten? Okay, she lived in the Bronx, fine. She went upstate for some fun that went bad. *Not* in our jurisdiction. I went and took a look, professional courtesy. Different MO. *Not* in our jurisdiction. The Bowman case is unrelated, and it's closed. Okay?" He pulled a folded piece of paper from inside his suit coat, then opened and smoothed it on his thigh. His face was so red with blood that his hair seemed ashy blond.

"Come on," Inglewood said, glancing at Vasquez. "You get one look." He stood and walked around the coffee table to Guthrie's desk and waited for her to come over. Then he laid a color photocopy of a picture on the desktop, keeping two fingers pressed heavily on one corner.

Sand Whitten was only recognizable because of her stainless-steel jewelry and skate-short black hair. Otherwise, her face was a mass of welts, with bright blue irises glowing in bloodred eyes. A precise slash on her throat revealed her spine from the front of the body, but her blouse sported only a few drops of blood, beyond a narrow stab wound between her small breasts. Her blood was spread on the ground like an abandoned apron beyond her legs—one bunched beneath her, the other bent. Her naked thighs glowed sharply white, and a short black skirt clung to her hips without exposing her. Waffle-soled hiking boots seemed out of place, blooming from her slender ankles.

Inglewood pulled the picture from the desk and struck a lighter. He held the flame to a corner of the picture. Several long seconds passed as it caught fire and was consumed.

"I ain't been here," the ginger-haired detective said. "I ain't talked to you. I ain't showed you no picture. *What* picture? I was on a piss break." He glanced down at the coffee table as he turned to go. "I ain't ate no pizza." He took a slice and then limped from the office. The door clattered behind him.

CHAPTER TWENTY-FOUR

Guthrie booked a late flight to Arlington, Virginia. That left the evening free, and he called Philip Linney. The veteran was off work, killing time in his Westchester flop, and he was available for a supper with a side of conversation. He chose the destination: Albert's Café on East 177th Street, about where it crossed Powell in Westchester. The nighttime crowd was local—a mix of drivers, stockers, and mop jockeys, sprinkled with hopeful students and a few secretaries. The dining room was a square, set off from the bar by a porch with a walk-up order window for street traffic. They ate at a small round table, encircled by the other customers. Guthrie took a long look around after they sat, and perched his fedora on the edge of the table.

"Well, it's cheap," Linney said. His smile was bright on his dark face.

"I can spring for quiet," Guthrie said.

"That's something I didn't ask," Linney said. "Who's paying? I guess I thought Captain had some bread held back, to go with disability. But PIs ain't cheap, are they?"

"Olsen makes friends easy," Guthrie said.

The veteran's eyes flicked over Vasquez. They ordered a round of grilled chicken on toast, home fries, pie, and coffee. The waitress had a fleecy mop of hair held back by a headband. She was tall, slim, and light-skinned. The café had heavy cream-colored ceramic coffee mugs that rested comfortably in a hand. Guthrie tipped a spoonful of ice into his coffee and stirred slowly, like a cow ringing a bell, before he drank.

"When did you get assigned to Alpha Strike?" Guthrie asked. "Ain't that actually Task Force One one two seven?"

"Yeah. Been talking to Captain, huh?"

Guthrie shook his head. "I'm a detective. I know things." The information was inside Olsen's military record, some dry but informative reading.

"Right at the end of '06, after the elections. I transferred down from the north, the toughest truck driver Afghanistan ever seen. I grew up fast then."

"How'd you wind up in Alpha? Your stretch was TDY, right?"

"Yeah. Everybody was TDY in Alpha. CENTCOM does that shit over there, something they supposedly got from the Germans, moving people and attaching them like that. I ain't seen no Euros doing it, though. They're all alike, German or not—soft. They split when something pops off. Hop in the armored car and zoom!" Linney made a flying motion with one hand above the tabletop. "Me, I was a truck driver, fresh from the street. I was a G with a machine gun. Ain't nobody happier than a G with a machine gun and plenty of bullets." He laughed.

"Then they assigned you to Alpha because you wanted to shoot?"

"Say tricked me, and then you got it. I was a driver. The other guys in convoy wanted to push past roadblocks, or turn aside and let the escorts take it. They wanted to duck and run whenever some stray Pashie sent a 'To whom it may concern' via AK mail. Me, I'm *strapped*. I want to take a look, get some chop in. Then one time I chased some shooters, I chop, they chop, I chase some more. I pulled a piece of the convoy after me, with the LT screaming on the radio.

That was crazy, but I winged one of them and followed the blood. I was lucky. He ditched his AK but failed a residue test. I wore a reprimand for ignoring the LT, but a guy from district went to bat for me. He said I had good instincts, the steadiness required of good infantry—he laid that on thick, before asking me if I wanted to go south."

"You volunteered," Guthrie said, and shook his head.

"You know it. Everybody's a volunteer. You got enough gray on your head to know that. You volunteer, and then you don't get to unvolunteer. That's when I got educated on real gangster. Captain is a G, all business, and Alpha was all Gs. That business down south in Afghanistan is what the Euros don't want no part of. There's nothing but Pashies down south. Everybody else is just passing through. Up north, you got Hazaras, Turks, Tajiks, they just want to do their thing. Pashies? Their thing is fighting."

The waitress came back and loaded the table, sneaking glances at Linney. The sandwiches had the sharp, hot smell of food that would keep Albert's open for fifty years, unless some unlucky bastard choked on a cockroach. Guthrie snagged the catsup and poured a pool beside his fries.

"Good scenery at Albert's, huh?" Guthrie asked after the tall waitress hurried away.

"She's all right," Linney said. "Kinda bright, but that's okay." He worked on his sandwich until it was almost ready to say good-bye. "Alpha wasn't a regular unit—it was a task force. That's the name, but most of them come and go. Alpha stayed around so long that CENTCOM ended up treating it like a regular unit. See, mostly a task force goes like this—a convoy is rolling out of Kabul, and it's gotta go through Helmand, and they gotta have escorts—see, they got a task, and now they build a force. They pinch platoons off the units stationed around the depot, they're tasked to the convoy commander, and they ride out and ride back. Down south, that can get ugly. Fifty trucks go out and maybe twenty make it through the ambush—or two.

"We figured they did that because of the Guard units. If they sent a Guard unit, and every fucker in Missouri got his balls blowed off on the same day, that would be a nightmare for CENTCOM. Captain was a genius at convoy, and that's part of what ended up screwing him—and Alpha—into being treated like a regular unit. When Captain rode convoy, the trucks went through, but then if we were sitting around on stand-down, they would pinch us like regulars, probably hoping it would rub off. Not without Captain.

"Mostly we did sweeps, nets, response. Alpha was active. I figured part of it out pretty fast, even if they tricked me in the beginning with that 'good soldier' shit. They push everybody to pick up Pash. That makes it easier, when you know what they're saying, right? And you can give 'em orders, go here or there, stop, whatever. By the time I went south, I had some handfuls of words and phrases, and an intelligence LT pushing me to learn more. Down south, I saw it for what it was. If you sling good Pash, you get stopped. So I shut up quick."

"You mean stop-lossed?" Guthrie asked around a bite of sandwich.

"Yeah, exactly. Captain had good Pash, the best I ever heard except for Slip. Slip could sing that shit. That was crazy. But that almost got Captain. He was gone except for the stop, and then he almost got wasted. He should've been back here, chilling."

They ate until most of the meal was gone. Vasquez looked around the square dining room and caught the stares aimed at their table. Guthrie was the only white person in Albert's Café. Seen through the big glass window at the front, the sporadic traffic on 177th Street seemed to indicate a sleeping city, instead of an early summer evening in the Bronx that had pumped the café full of people.

"Alpha was active. Most of the regular units are passive, like artillery parks, firebases, depots, airstrips, whatever. If AQT—another name for the Taliban—touches anything, the active units drop on it. Like, snipers gathered up on a depot, an active unit cleans them out. CENTCOM liked to run shit off the carriers or airstrips and just have it waiting up there. Then it would drop down like a big splat of bird shit on anything that caught their attention." Linney frowned. "Sounds good, right?

"Sometimes we chased snipers," Linney continued. "Sometimes we dropped bombs on them. One or two Pashies with AKs get rained on with a flight of A-eighteens. Hoo-ya! So maybe not as many fire-fights as you'd think. Captain didn't drop the whole hand on everything. You missed plenty of action if your number wasn't up. Captain paid attention like that. Maybe we spent a lot of time up when we were netting something. That could be bad on the nerves."

The dark veteran shrugged. He sipped some cold coffee and tried the apple pie. "The Pashies'll kill you in a second. They're full of crazy ideas. You could be doing something that ain't had nothing to do with them, and then they're saying your shadow fell across the udder of their goat. Thirty minutes later, the fucker's crouching behind a rock, shooting at you. Checkpoint, sitting in an OP, anything could get a shot took at you. And they were worse on each other. Damn, they liked to fight, and they never stopped keeping score. We weren't out there watching all of the time. When we weren't, playtime! That's what started the really dumb shit."

"How's that?"

"In the beginning they thought they'd stamped out the Taliban. How dumb was that? They could've turned off the lights and pretended there wasn't no cockroaches about as easy. To me, all the Pashies is Taliban. They got one set of clothes for when you're looking, and another for when you're not around, AK included as a free accessory. You leave somewhere, everything's cool, then come back in the morning and find a row of headless bodies lined up in an or-chard, with flies poured on them like syrup. With the heads gone, or the faces beaten in, you don't know if they were the ones you talked with the day before or not—unless you talk to them again *that* day. Which ones are the good guys? That's the shit that put the brass to thinking we should try to watch them all the time.

"The knock was they was doing that because they ain't felt they could trust us to be there and back them up, so they went back to the

Taliban. That was stupid. They went back to the Taliban because they hated us. That's common sense. You don't roll with Gs if you hate Gs—you cross to the other side of the bridge. The brass wanted a better explanation than that, like they couldn't believe anybody could really have a problem with the good ol' US of A. So the super-genius bright idea that would fix everything was tying units to the villages—embedment. That's when Afghanistan turned weird."

"That shit already sounds weird," Vasquez muttered.

Linney nodded. "See, you a civilian, just like I was before I went over. A civilian got a whole different concept of reality—no offense—and these people do, too." He pointed, taking in the customers in Albert's before stopping his finger at Guthrie. "Maybe this old guy here has different ideas. I can't put you in Afghanistan. If I show you a picture, it's still like TV. You can't smell it. A typical civilian don't want nothing to do with that dirty shit there. A typical Pashie smells like ass, feet, goat shit, and gunpowder. What's coming out of his mouth is *unbelievable*, baby. He's carrying a chopper, and a sword to save bullets. He likes to save bullets. A typical GI wants a shower every day, a Game Boy, a skin mag, and as much food at one meal as a Pashie eats in a week. Pashies and GIs are like oil and water. Giving the Pashies a close look at a GI didn't gain any respect. The brass wasn't thinking.

"Notice, though, that I say 'typical.' Alpha Strike was different." The veteran ate quickly for a minute, pausing to say, "Let's get the fuck out of here." He finished his pie and drank the dregs of his coffee. Vasquez was long finished. Guthrie dropped a fifty on the table before they went to the register.

Outside, the city was passing the point where the sidewalks were hotter than the sky and creeping slowly down toward stillness. Traffic pulsed around them as they turned the corner to reach the car. A skinny mutt, marked like a cross between a rottweiler and a Doberman, sniffed the rear tire of the old Ford, then hiked a leg.

"Sure, why not," Guthrie muttered.

The veteran laughed. "Next time, you get some barking to go

with it," he said. "Enjoy your stay in the Bronx." After he climbed into the backseat, he rolled both windows down.

"See, that's what really changed for me," Linney said. "I came back to the city with new eyes. Before Afghanistan, I thought this shit was hard. I came back and I could see it was just fronting. My Moms tried to educate me to reality, but I wasn't interested in listening to her. Now? You know, that's what made Alpha different—and Captain different. No fronting. He just did the shit." He shrugged. He watched the street slide by for a minute, with the neon and streetlights standing out starkly against the darkness.

"Alpha got embedded in this little pile of shit called Khodzai. I couldn't understand for a long time why shit was so fucked-up, everywhere we rolled on mission, because the shit worked great for us. We bulked up, broke a bunch of new guys in, had more downtime. That was the best time I had over there. I was on the inside, and it was smooth. The Pashies would line up at Captain's door, straight respect. On top of that, they loved Slip. You could hardly tell him from a Pashie anyway, and if he put on pajamas, forget it. Slip settled in harder than the rest of us; we couldn't cross over like that, but he just fit. We would ride him about it; then he would give us a 'Don't worry, brother' on his way out the door. Slip ain't talked much, unless he was clowning. Then he could spit with anybody I ever heard. But he got a girl. We all knew about her."

Linney cut his eyes at the look Guthrie threw over the back of the old Ford's bench seat. "Yeah, big-time no-no. Against the rules. That's the only time I ever heard Captain use the voice on Slip. Fucker could freeze your blood, not even shout. Then Captain dropped it. That shit was major leverage. Everything was really smooth while that was going.

"Then it went down. That was in October '08. The Pashies got a holiday, something about murdering goats. We got tapped—" The dark veteran frowned. "*This* shit is secret, right, Leavenworth secret. These fuckers are spooks. I ain't told you this part, and if anybody asks you, you get to do your good-detective routine. The spooks are everywhere over there, supposedly looking for AQTs. The spooks tapped Alpha when they needed muscle for dirty work, to run a net or a sweep where they thought AQT was squatting. When Alpha bulked up, they wanted to tap us all the time.

"Anyway, the spooks drift in that October, and they want to squat on *Khodzai*. This's our living room, and they're saying AQT is eating from our table—or we're eating from AQT's table. Either way, the shit is disrespectful. Captain is hot, right off, because he never got along with the spooks. When he went looking for Taliban, he did it one man at a time. The spooks did their thing the other way—once they put an eyeball on a target, they called in birds to drop shit. Don't matter about the splatter."

Linney smiled, then shook his head before he continued. "If you kill somebody close to a Pashie, forget about him forever. He hates you, and he never forgets. Every chance he gets, he shoots at you. The bird shit, that's American bird shit—everybody American did that. You could walk around Afghanistan and catch a suntan from the love and admiration. Captain was different. He killed fuckers one at a time. Alpha killed fuckers one at a time. The Pashies respected Captain because they saw how he worked. That took a long time to come around, but they saw it. So Captain didn't get along with the spooks, probably because of that. He waved birds off, even pushed rifles into a hot zone to get an abort. The spooks didn't like him neither, but they were scared to fuck with him.

"The spooks wanted to net and sift Khodzai. No matter how we handled it, there was gonna be hard feelings. We rolled on it and started, with the usual screaming, shaking fists, insults, like a circus, and then bird shit dropped right from the sky. They nailed the compound where a Pashie boss lived. The spooks were waiting on someone to squawk when the search started, triangulate, and drop shit. The net and sift was a trick to pull the squawk. I got that from a corporal that was standing there when Captain went off on the spooks. They made busy with an explanation while he threatened them.

"Slip freaked. His girl was in the compound the shit dropped on.

Spooks were picking through the wreckage, pillar of smoke, haze, children crying. The Pashies were stunned, like they couldn't believe we just done this to them. Captain detailed four troopers to keep Slip off the spooks until they could do their thing and split." Linney's hands drifted to a stop, coming down on the seat. "After that, it was over. What can you say? Takes one bad break."

"So this guy Slip, his girl got killed?" Vasquez asked. Her eyes bored into Linney in the rearview mirror.

"Yeah. He was pissed. He hated everybody then—kind of like a Pashie. I guess stuff rubs off on you, huh?"

"What's his name?"

"He had a weird name—sounded weird and spelled worse. One of those French names from down south, I think. Gagneau. Captain called him Sergeant, and the rest of us called him Slip."

Vasquez was impatient. She almost blurted her question before he finished. "So you know when he came back?"

"Came back? Nah, the fucker got killed."

Guthrie shook his head and laughed, then told her to drive up to the zoo. He knew a place by the park with good ice cream, and they had a little more time before they needed to drive to La Guardia.

CHAPTER TWENTY-FIVE

The detectives landed at Reagan National Airport late at night but never crossed the Potomac River to go to the capital. Fog covered the Virginia shoreline the next morning. As Guthrie drove to the first meeting, the suburban landscape materialized from the fog in front of the nose of their rental car. Delta Marine Salvage and Supply wasn't yet open when they eased into the cramped parking lot. They watched a pair of older men open up, waited fifteen minutes, then went inside.

An old warehouse served as the supply and service center, with sections of the wall that faced the Potomac ripped out and leading along breezeways to moorings on the river. Even with outside light, the interior was dim. The ceiling trusses looked like spiderwebs, hidden in the darkness behind shrouded droplights. Lines of shelves, tubs, and bins were toylike in the vast space. One of the old men watched them from behind the counter while they drifted along the dusty aisles, then returned to reading an unfolded newspaper. Every few minutes he slurped noisily at coffee to remind them he was waiting. The other old man turned wrenches on a manifold attached to a hanging motor, grumbling curses about rust and stupidity.

Guthrie and Vasquez dirtied their hands on old merchandise for a half hour before a tall old white man with a salt-and-pepper fade strode through the door. He wore a government-issue dark blue business suit cut to fit and polished shoes with a special license to repel dust. Closer, his face had enough age to make him a grandfather, but his hooked nose and cleft chin suited him. At a distance, a tapered build down from wide shoulders marked him for younger.

"Kid, you didn't need to call the Rice brothers," he said to Guthrie when he swallowed the smaller man up with a handshake and hearty hug. "You know I would've heard you through."

"I got a sore throat from arguing with that roadblock you're using for a secretary," Guthrie said.

The tall man cut eyes at Vasquez and frowned. "Who's she?"

"Rachel Vasquez. She started working for me this summer."

The tall man looked her over again. "She doesn't stick out too much?"

"Not except for her ears," Guthrie said, and grinned. "Maybe she shines a little outside the city."

"Well, you're outside the city."

"And maybe you could tell me what you're talking about?" Vasquez demanded.

"You catch eyes easy to be a detective," the tall man said. "Not like that one, but that adds to the picture." He studied her again. "Those're *more* bruises?"

"She's an East Side girl—she likes to fight," Guthrie said, then turned to Vasquez. "The old guy's name is Robert McCall, in case you want to turn him in to the proper authorities for being nosy."

"I haven't heard from you in a while, kid," McCall said. "You look prosperous." He lifted Guthrie's fedora and looked. "I suppose I could stop calling you kid, since you've grown some gray hair on your head."

"Maybe."

McCall smiled. "It's good to see you. It's churning up memories. You remember the summer Kenny taught you that shit? What year was that? Seventy-five, I think. You were about the size of a wet raccoon—"

"Kenny? Teach me? He was just drunk and having fun. I was too young to know any better. That wasn't martial arts—"

The tall old man cut him off with a laugh. "Tell that to Angel! I remember, one time he ticked you off, and then he bent over the fire down in the gorge, and you kicked him in his ass. He flipped right over the fire and landed on his feet with beer still in his cup! *That* was '77."

"Ah, Kenny had me convinced. Kicking Angel like that was luck."

The smile faded from McCall's eyes. "Long time ago, kid. You sounded serious on the phone. *Better* be serious if you're asking what I think."

"I just need names, addresses, pictures—"

"For Task Force One one two seven," the old man said. "I heard that part loud and clear—too loud and way too clear. That's not supposed to be on the intercept list, but the left hand may not know what the right foot is doing. I suppose you don't know what I mean, so let me clarify: You'd better have a damn good reason."

Guthrie paused for a moment, and McCall said, "You look like you're dreaming up a lie, kid."

"Not this time." The little detective didn't seem amused, but he smiled anyway.

"Come on," McCall said. "I have to get a coil."

Guthrie and Vasquez followed him deeper into the maze of shelves. Filthy, dusty parts crammed the shelves, each with a neat handwritten tag. McCall studied the items on offer on a shelf of heavy copper coils, selected one, and retrieved it gingerly with a white handkerchief.

"That task force had an officer from Tenth Mountain attached," Guthrie said. "He's in Rikers on a murder that I think is connected to his service."

McCall shrugged. "You have to give me more than that."

"It's complicated enough that it's not a sure thing. My client was framed. The perp used his gun, and since then, he's rubbed out witnesses. I think I have an eyewitness who can finger a picture. She's a real sharp old lady in the Village. My connection to the unit is another veteran in the city. His mother got killed recently. I don't think it's coincidence."

"You think somebody in One one two seven didn't like them," the old man said softly. "What was disagreeable about them?"

"Don't know that."

McCall frowned. "You remember Phoenix, from Nam?"

"Read some stuff," Guthrie said. "A CIA project to liquidate Vietcong, right?"

"Close enough. We've come back to that. This task force has the Activity's fingerprints all over it. They have presidential authority to liquidate, wherever, whenever, however, in the war on terror." He smiled sadly. "Didn't know that, did you? It's not even secret, kid; it's just not talked about. On the other hand, if you poke around that nest, you can get stung."

"Can you get the pictures?"

"I can. My question is whether it sends up flags in SOCOM. If I need to go carefully, it'll come out in pieces. Either way, I'll talk with you after six." He pulled a folded paper from his pocket and handed it to Guthrie. "This'll be the place." He hefted the coil again. "Give me a half hour before you leave here, kid. And stay off the telephones around here, will you?"

McCall marched briskly up to the counter to pay for his coil. The old warehouse was still quiet, even though a few early customers were searching the shelves. The detectives waited. A half hour's caution seemed worthwhile after hearing those few letters early in the alphabet: CIA.

After the fog burned through, the sun rolled over northern Virginia like a glowing ball of iron. Guthrie and Vasquez killed time while they waited for lunch. The young Puerto Rican didn't have skeletons in her closet to share—she was too young. That left the little man from West Virginia doing most of the talking. He let her drive around the suburban landscape and recover from getting lost while he tried to distract her.

One side trip sent Vasquez most of the way to Harper's Ferry before she caught on and turned around. After she took the mistaken turn, the little detective grinned like a shark and told her that Mike Inglewood hadn't always walked with a limp. Listening to anyone normal, the story that followed would've had something to do with Inglewood's feet. With Guthrie, the search for the punch line was how he kept Vasquez's head turned.

When Inglewood was a uniform fresh from the Academy, he worked midtown. One of Guthrie's stakeouts coincided with Inglewood's shift. Guthrie notified the watch commander he was running an operation, but as usual for the little detective, he gained a better view of the club's pool deck by climbing a billboard across the street—technically illegal. He wanted to catch the fraud he was trailing while he used the pool. Inglewood decided Guthrie was more of a Peeping Tom than a detective. Along the span of seven days, the green patrolman ran Guthrie into the precinct house three times for trespassing. Truce talk and a big chicken dinner settled the business: Stakeouts should stay in the car, but *sometimes* a man had to go where he could see.

"Happily ever after, huh?" Vasquez asked.

"Sure," Guthrie said. He pointed at a road sign as they whizzed past. "Maybe you would rather I take a nap while you drive to West Virginia?"

Even with turnarounds, the detectives reached their lunch meeting early. Guthrie had found Agent Rackers by way of a third-party introduction. The FBI agent had standing reservations at an Arlington restaurant, La Dame. When Guthrie saw the manicured parterres around the entrance and the neat gold calligraphy on the windows, he paused and sighed. The window dressing was served up alongside a healthy dose of American commercialism—a jet-stream boulevard raced in front of the windows, and a horseshoe mall, complete with parking lots and a bus stop, provided a ghastly mirror image.

Inside La Dame, the maître d' took a moment to study the scruffy pair before honoring them with a table as far from the front as he could find. Their small round table had a dark green cloth and a basket of fresh rolls, with a saucer of butter alongside it. Guthrie was mollified after a few bites, but Vasquez continued fuming. Reservations were not enough. Grudgingly, she removed her Yankees cap after the maître d's second visit. Agent Rackers arrived before hostilities escalated; he fit perfectly, wearing a dark blue Italian suit, a fresh shave, and a hundred-dollar haircut. His expression darkened with each step the maître d' led him away from the front windows, and then his eyes lit with dawning recognition when he saw Guthrie and Vasquez.

"I suppose we're not the crackerjack detectives you expected," Guthrie said.

Rackers smiled. "Perhaps I was misled by the society bona fides," he said. "Some people in New York spoke highly of you."

"I guess we'll be keeping our jobs, then," Guthrie said.

"I'd prefer to clarify my position at the beginning," Rackers said as he glanced at the menu. "Naturally, FBI policy allows no comment on an ongoing case. We're not actually discussing an investigation." He smiled. "Ours is a discussion of unrelated topics."

"I thought the field office—" Guthrie began.

"The SAC held a different view from the beginning. The Manhattan office briefly entertained a competing idea, but the special agent's opinion matters more."

"We're talking about the same thing?" Guthrie asked. "I got a couple of dead girls around the city. That's what you're talking about?"

"We should eat first," Rackers said. "Then we can use the lounge. I recommend anything that includes fish. They use Brittany-coast recipes here."

Guthrie nodded. They made small talk. Rackers entered the FBI, and the Behavioral Science Unit, as an academic. The psychologists often trailed behind the field investigators, with notepads full of suppositions based on patterns, looking for motive from the physical evidence. Rarely did they point their fingers at a place to start. That distinction was reserved for the senior agents, with decades of field experience and an academic feather in their caps. Without saying so, Rackers made it plain that he wanted to point a finger at New York. The meal was good, but it vanished in the purposefulness of their talk.

La Dame's lounge was U-shaped, with a bar on the short wall facing the door. One middle-aged man sat at the bar with a cocktail, but the lights were too bright to encourage hard drinkers. They ordered coffee and settled into a leather-benched booth. Rackers studied the detectives again, then interrupted Vasquez as she began to take offense.

"Serial killers are commonplace enough that I shouldn't lecture," he said.

"Just like on TV, right?" Vasquez said.

"Exactly. We have a definition, and we search for what fits. Part of the Behavioral Science Unit at Quantico culls data, looking for patterns and geographical clusters. That is my specialty. I search for footprints, then guess whether they add together to prove that someone has walked through. Our basic assumption begins with a certain type of person being required to commit serial murder."

"You don't agree? I thought it worked just that way," Guthrie said.

"I *do* agree," Rackers said, then made a sour face. "Only perhaps not this time. I have collected a signature for an unsub who doesn't commit sexual assault."

"That's required?"

"The *absolute* answer is no, but the correct answer is yes, when the unsub is regenerative. An impulse to murder requires a powerful motive; sex is such a motive. Serials kill to satisfy an urge—our analysis accepts that as a given. The corollary requires the killer to be sick. He fails to match societal norms—he's aberrant. He becomes addicted, escalates, grows careless, and is caught." He smiled. "I'm lecturing."

"Then you're not talking about our guy in Rikers," Vasquez said.

"I do know that you're working on a case in New York, but I don't have details on suspects." Rackers shrugged. "Officially, this is not a case. No suspect is necessary because no case file exists to close."

Guthrie smiled and finished his cup of coffee. "So you don't know about our case. Do you know about the New York killings?"

Rackers nodded. "Serials have a signature, a methodology for their crimes that allows them to satisfy their motivating urge. The commonality can include a weapon, or a particular type of victim. A signature can be very subtle. The Bowman killing in New York, and others in the area, match the signature I have collected. Officially, there is no such signature, and therefore no killer."

"Why the hell is that?" Vasquez blurted.

"Simply put, they're afraid," Rackers replied. "Part of the Behavioral Science Unit culls data, as I said. Certain victims fit the definition for potential serial victims—at risk, roadside dumps, rape-murders—unless motive clarifies quickly for a local suspect. The United States generates a fairly constant number of these types of murders each year, suggesting a stable population of serial predators. Within certain bounds, the unit expects to catch them as they reach a certain point in their development—when they become sloppy. That number for an individual serial in the United States isn't high. A half dozen or dozen is typical. Elsewhere, the typical number can be far higher, where data exists. In China, a hundred may be typical. They're afraid because my signature is larger than that. The number is high enough that it is pressuring our numeric baseline—" Rackers gave Vasquez a sharp glance. "You've heard this before?"

"*No*. I just—" Vasquez began.

"I think she just realized we got a suspect," Guthrie said. "Well, we did. He died. We had a witness. He died. There was another witness. She died. Now we're looking."

"You have a line on something?" Rackers asked.

"I gotta admit that when I walked in here, I was crossing a *t*," Guthrie said, "or maybe I was dotting an *i*. I followed this angle because suddenly my client is *off* this particular hook. I know that sounds perverse, but I'm working for the defense." The little detective grinned.

"You *didn't* believe this was relevant to your—" Rackers flushed.

"Now it's time to deal," Guthrie said. "You don't even want to know my suppositions—they're out there. I need more information, and you have more bodies. Give me the information on your victims. Then I can cross-check them."

"Wait!" Rackers said fiercely. "First, in exchange for what? Second, what could you cross-check them with? Data is what I do—give yours to me, and it'll go faster."

Guthrie shook his head. He raised one finger. "I point you in the direction I'm looking." He added a second finger. "You got no case—so you're talking. If I give you something that turns it into a case, you *stop* talking. I would be back at the beginning, with nothing. That means you pay off first."

Rackers groaned, then settled back into the leather bench. The man at the bar spared them a glance and signaled the bartender for another drink. "I've been picking at this problem for fourteen months—almost since the beginning. The signature begins only four months before that," he said. "So I want him. If he exists. No serial has ever killed so many so quickly. He doesn't have a cooldown. He just kills."

"If he exists," Vasquez said softly.

"That's correct." The FBI agent reached inside his suit coat and produced a palmtop. He opened it and fed it a disc. "I can't give you anything you couldn't get somewhere else. Fortunately for you, that's a great deal. Every coroner in the country has a link to the national database. What I'm saving you is the trouble of sifting the data—for which you should be forever grateful." His fingers worked, feeding files to be copied.

The detectives waited silently until Rackers slipped the disc from his palmtop and slid it across the table. He smiled as Vasquez took the disc and hid it in her pocket. "You're difficult to deal with, but that could be a New York motto," he said.

"The Bowman murder matches your signature, right?" Guthrie said. "I got, or had, witnesses proving my client was framed—that's personal motive. While I'm looking, two witnesses in the Bowman murder get killed, and an investigator—"

"A police officer was killed?"

Guthrie shook his head. "A house detective for the lawyer. They were actually after us." He gestured with a fingertip at Vasquez and himself.

"That's him!"

"*Them*. Russian mobsters."

"A Russian. That explains the body count."

"Here's the rest, Mr. Rackers. Althea Linney was killed in a Bronx robbery. She won't be on your list, but she should be."

Guthrie and Vasquez parked on the grass at Easy Acres, a produce market existing in the blurry transition between suburban Arlington and the rural countryside of northern Virginia. A few dozen cars and trucks were scattered on the shoulders of the rural route and lined carelessly in the grassy farmyard beneath old oaks with thick, outstretched limbs. On one side of the barnyard, a farmhouse swirled more like a party in progress than a place of business. Pavilions shrouded the barnyard, covering produce stalls that overflowed from the barn. A second kitchen in the remodelled barn served as a cannery, pouring forth an aroma of apples and cinnamon that washed down to the road. A dozen people in hairnets peeled, sliced, sorted, and washed apples, while more stirred vats, loaded juicers, and scraped pans full of sauce, syrup, and diced apples.

The stall owners were friendly; the market was a cooperative. Inside the barn, dry goods were offered alongside cheese, fruit, and vegetables. Guthrie shopped, and Vasquez followed him back and forth to the rental car as he tucked away spices, jars of honey and preserves, and a sack of oats. She asked him if he was going to buy a pig, prompting him to wonder whether she thought the trunk was large enough to hold a small one. After a trip to carry a bag of shelled hickory nuts back to their car, Robert McCall whistled at them as they marched back through the barnyard.

"Kid, you haven't changed a bit," McCall said. He studied the two cantaloupes he held in his oversized hands and gave them a sniff.

"Well, what're you doing here, then?"

"Not making an ant of myself," the tall old man said, and grinned. "You aren't going to believe how lucky you are."

"I don't feel lucky."

"This might do it: One one two seven isn't a SOCOM operation—it belonged to CENTCOM. They wrapped up their own piece of the special-ops thunder, and they—well, that's Pentagon stuff. I doubt it's what you want, even if it's entertaining." McCall grinned again, looking boyishly happy with the two melons in his hands. "SOCOM was getting all of the ribbons and gold stars, while CENTCOM was eating crap for all of the mistakes. See, CENTCOM has operational responsibility for every asset in the theater. Fuckups go directly up the chain of command. SOCOM borrowed assets when they needed them, but with zero accountability because they were liaising. Fuckups are on the actual commander, not the little bird riding his shoulder."

"This is supposed to be good for me?"

"Absolutely," McCall said. "SOCOM doesn't have a finger in the task force, and so I don't need to worry about the Activity calling me. One one two seven was a test unit for insurgent-control tactics. The big brains have been analyzing everything from the beginning. Everything you wanted was on a long pass-around list."

"So Uncle Rob's ass is covered, you mean."

"That's not good?" the old man asked. "You're hesitating, kid. Some kind of chickenshit is coming."

"You said *was* a test unit?"

"Was," McCall confirmed. "I checked out your Tenth Mountain officer, Olsen. Some of that's beyond my reach. The big brain word is *exemplary*. The task force was built around him, and didn't survive after him. The task force bulked up at a certain point, and after that a pissing contest went on between CENTCOM and SOCOM. The Activity tagged them as an asset, with the usual accountability issues."

"Somebody outside the unit could be interested?" Guthrie asked. "Tell me something about that."

Robert McCall shrugged, considered the melons again, and placed one back in the basket. "Jealousy, maybe. SOCOM continuously poaches personnel. If anyone was fragged, that would be in the field." He frowned. "You like Olsen for a target? He never had any complaints filed by his men."

"We're looking at it," Guthrie said. "What about the Activity?"

"That's Intelligence Support Activity. They do something new—they make solutions. I told you before, there's authorization for anyone, anytime, anywhere. The Activity locates the time, the place, the person—and then they solve it."

Vasquez crossed her arms and looked at Guthrie. "That's who Linney was talking about," she said. "But I don't think that's who we're looking for."

"You'd better hope so, kid. The Activity does things the CIA never dreamed about." The tall old man pulled a disc from his pocket. "This's a cut and paste from about a dozen sets of files—

names, addresses, photos, dates—but don't think it's not dangerous because it can't be sourced."

Guthrie took the disc and slipped it into his pocket.

"You know you owe me now, right?"

The little detective nodded.

"Good. Tell Danny Rice he owes me a year of whiskey."

CHAPTER TWENTY-SIX

Guthrie and Vasquez flew back to New York City and landed at La Guardia late at night. After a night's sleep, they drove into the Garment District before it woke for business. Bleary-eyed teenagers idled outside the loading gates, nursing cups of coffee in the shadowless world before dawn. The detectives had their own form of wide awake: two computer discs. They opened the office with a flurry—starting coffee, devouring doughnuts, checking printers for paper and ink—then became almost silent. Movement was fingers on keyboards or eyes scanning monitors. The street noise rose slowly, with shouts and whistles before the blare of horns lifted, all competing with the quiet whir of printers.

"That's a lot of pictures," Vasquez said after a pair of piles accumulated.

"An infantry company has a lot of soldiers," the little detective said. "Then it was larger, for years. Add transfers, short-timers, casualties. . . . We have a lot of pictures." He didn't seem happy.

"You're not sorting them?"

He shook his head. "It's gonna be easier just to do them all. Maybe one catches Jeannette's eye. Otherwise, we're in trouble."

Vasquez frowned. "What you mean?"

"Last night, I kept waking up thinking about it. What if our guy wasn't in Alpha? We know he's out there, sure, but what if he's Activity? It's far-fetched—"

"You're gonna drive me crazy, *viejo*," Vasquez said.

"You? That's why our first move is taking pictures to the Village. If he was in Alpha and she picks him out, we got him."

Vasquez shook her head, then turned to look again at the map of the United States she had taped to the wall behind her desk. Dots of red from a marker indicated locations of murders from the list of signature victims Rackers had provided. During her study of each file, she turned and marked the murder on the map. Clusters were forming around Chicago, and in Southern California and the Northeast corridor. Other specks were haphazardly scattered on the map. She paused to study the map after each additional mark, like a diviner studying a Rorschach test.

By the time the printer finished, the neighborhood was in full swing. A steady traffic of clothes racks clogged the street, accompanied by the usual symphony of annoyed horns. Guthrie gathered his pictures and tossed Vasquez the keys to the Ford. Outside, the air was thick and humid. Lines of high clouds marched along in a battle with the open sky. Vasquez took Seventh Avenue south to the Village.

Jeannette Overton smiled when she saw the stack of pictures. Her husband, Phil, suggested it included pictures of every man in the city. With pauses to check the quiet street outside her window and encourage Vasquez as she was demolished in game after game of gin, the little old lady examined the stack of pictures. By lunchtime, she chose a photograph. Guthrie frowned when he read the caption on the photo, then handed it to Vasquez.

She read it, then asked, "You *sure*?"

"Even an old woman would never forget an ear like that, my dear," Jeannette Overton said. "That is the deliveryman. I suppose

I should have known he was in the military by the way he walked. He had such a smooth step. That reminded me of Philip when he came home from the war."

The man in the photo wore a brush-top military haircut a bit shorter than Robert McCall's, but all of his hair was still dark. His eyes were green behind long dark lashes, and his skin was a wind-polished olive or tan. He might've been Italian, Puerto Rican, or Greek, but the faint smile stamped on his face suggested that he knew he would be admired. He was pretty, in the way a lean young wolf is pretty after some shampoo and a brushing, but merely wolfishly handsome with a toothy grin at any other time. Below the photo was a typescript caption: SFC Marc Lucas Gagneau.

The detectives drove to Rikers Island over the Queens causeway. Guthrie spent the time thinking, passing through excitement, relief, and anger, while Vasquez drove. The ritual of entering the jail calmed the little West Virginian until he seemed detached, but his hand kept visiting the printed photograph in the pocket of his suit coat, like a worried dog checking repeatedly a bone recently buried. The interview room was sterile, overly bright, gleaming with hard surfaces, and tainted with the exhaled breath of apathy and wasted resistance. Beyond the echoes of steel and concrete waited sullen silence.

A pair of burly guards escorted Greg Olsen into the interview room. The guards eyed Guthrie and Vasquez; added together, they weighed less than Olsen alone. Their warning to the big veteran was phrased in glares, arm-twisting while they removed the handcuffs, and a shove for assistance in finding his chair. Guthrie watched silently. After the door sealed with a steel click, he drew the picture of Gagneau from his pocket and laid it on the tabletop.

They argued, because Olsen believed Gagneau was dead. The big man turned red with the anger of denial and clenched his hands into heavy fists. Without raising his voice or standing, he still seemed to grow larger, but the detectives answered with grim reasoning. Guthrie rotated his fedora on the steel tabletop while he spoke, emphasizing with a jabbing forefinger. Vasquez folded her arms, making her hands disappear into the red of her jacket, and paced back and forth from her seat to the door. With her scowl, the fresh black eye over her faint, faded bruises seemed more like makeup than disfigurement. Olsen glared and argued, but he had only what he wished was true, while the detectives had facts.

Having identified the killer was a success tempered by Gagneau's being officially dead. The NYPD wouldn't look for him; officially, he didn't exist. Already, the police had simplified their accusations by removing the Barbie doll victims, leaving Olsen on the hook for one murder they felt sure of proving. A wild story about a faked death wouldn't change that position. Even Olsen didn't want to believe Gagneau's corpse, dismembered by an IED and unrecognizable except for tags, had been a fake. The big man would serve prison time for his fiancée's murder if they didn't unmask Gagneau completely.

"We'll catch him," Guthrie insisted angrily. The hinted suggestion otherwise was an insult to the detective's pride. "He was in the city—he left footprints. Maybe he ran a red light, or used an ATM. Maybe we find his face in someone's Web page scrapbook. But we'll find him, because he's still in the city, watching what happens to you. We'll catch him."

"I believe you, then," Olsen said. "Just like I believe in Gagneau. He won't be easy to catch, especially when he sees you're looking. Then you're just like the sergeant, judging by the look on your face. His jaw was set that way for about half of each day. The other half of the day he was easy to get along with."

Vasquez pulled out her chair and sat down. She dropped her Yankees cap onto the table beside Guthrie's fedora and let her shortened lock of hair swing free. She looked tired. "*El viejo*'s right. He's out there watching right now," she said. "He don't want to kill you, *chico*. I been thinking about that. He's a muchacho with a serious grudge. Killing ain't enough. You're lucky you ain't got no sisters. He could've killed you a long time ago. He wants you to stay in jail—killing your girl wasn't enough. He done killed more to keep you here. You see that?"

"So I can do something, then?" Olsen demanded.

"Sure," Guthrie replied. He jabbed the picture with his finger. "Tell me how to catch Marc Lucas Gagneau. You know him, Greg. My first problem is his being dead. Worse, he ain't alone. Tell me how he's got the Russian mob in his pocket. They don't crew up with outsiders. Is that something you did over there?"

The big blond man snorted and rubbed at the tabletop with his good right hand. "I see you've been saving up questions for the last few days," he said. "So I doubt I know him as well as I thought. The letter of condolence I sent his parents came back to me stamped 'Return to sender.' His home address was a chicken-processing plant outside Baton Rouge, a lie from the beginning, before he ever met me. All along, he had something to hide then."

"That's what you *don't* know," Guthrie said. "Tell me what you *do* know."

"A guy like Gagneau isn't common," Olsen said. "He was pretty like a girl, and small, but vicious enough to balance that out. He said he lost a brother in New York, and volunteered after nine/eleven. I never thought about that, though, beside the fact he came from Louisiana and carried an accent that sounded like a man talking around a mouthful of loose thread. Gagneau was quick and quiet. No one noticed him unless he wanted them to pay him mind.

"After a week of watching him, I had realized that he could tell me what I wanted to know about something, if I sent him to take a look at it for me. His eyes were like cameras, and he could spin details until a picture filled, without adding something wished for or taking away. That's a good scout. Then he didn't have a need to take a shot, or get something started, so people would notice him. Gagneau was satisfied with seeing; he was good at staying out of the way, staying alive."

Olsen frowned. "Over there, some of the men had their hands dirty. Even before I commanded Alpha, I began overlooking what didn't ruin a soldier. A man can't stop the wind from blowing. I never noticed Gagneau involved in trouble, except when he married Jaime-jan. After we embedded in Khodzai, he fell in love with Nawar Akrami's daughter.

"Nawar Akrami was one of the local lords. . . ." The big man paused, studying the look on Guthrie's face. "This story isn't new to you, then?"

"The girl was killed by a bomb. Linney told us."

The big man nodded, rubbing his chin. "Linney might not have known all of it. I don't know how much Pashtun he ever learned. That's what leads to the Shorawi—Russians. The opium goes north in the hands of the Chechens. Even under the Taliban, the drugs never stopped. Too many of the lords were involved indirectly. Nawar Akrami's cousin, Jarul Akbar, borrowed men during the autumns to protect his shipments."

"Gagneau knew the drug lord?"

"He sat beside me, drinking tea in *jirga* with Nawar and Jarul, enough that I can't remember all of the conversations."

The big veteran fell silent and watched Guthrie brood on his words. Vasquez stood and returned to pacing. After a minute, Olsen asked, "So that wasn't a help, then?"

"Maybe," Guthrie replied. "That explains how he would have connected with the Russians. Jarul Akbar called in a favor.

"I suppose I hoped he'd spoken about his places and things here, but you say he claimed to come from Louisiana. I can't add that up with the man losing a brother on nine/eleven. You're saying he never mentioned the city? He wasn't a talker?"

"Gagneau was quiet, mostly. I got along with him not needing to talk. I'll go awhile myself with nothing to say, then not worry if no one else is talking."

The little detective nodded. "Maybe that leaves me with only the Russians as a place to start. Searching the city, I might find a track, and then I'll find him. Maybe after a while of looking." He frowned.

"If I had you out of here, I would show you a puzzle and see if you solved it, or I would use you to pull him in. He's after you."

The big man scowled as he listened but then nodded slowly. He could play bait.

After they drove back into the city over the Triborough, Guthrie and Vasquez ate a late lunch at La Borinqueña. Across the table they held a slow council of war. Gagneau wouldn't be found easily on a cold trail, no matter how many tracks he left in the city. Their leads were sparse, and the city was full of unknown people. They held two advantages: Gagneau thought he was anonymous, and despite needing a false identity, he had no reason to conceal his face from anyone on the street.

Guthrie and Vasquez drove back to the office on Thirty-fourth Street. The street was clogged with rack runners, and Vasquez had to park down the block. Michelle Tompkins was waiting for them inside the lobby downstairs, clutching a laptop and a textbook. She looked plain, wearing thick-rimmed glasses, a loose T-shirt, and faded old blue jeans with deck shoes.

"Greg said you know who killed Cammie," she said, hurrying to join them as they climbed the stairs.

"Sure," Guthrie replied.

While Vasquez unlocked the office door, Tompkins said, "He didn't seem very enthusiastic, either. Did you really solve the murder, or just find another suspect?"

The little detective let Tompkins come inside and invited her to take a seat. He handed her the picture of Gagneau, then slid out of his suit coat and dropped his fedora onto his desk. The young woman studied the picture but seemed disappointed.

"He's prettier than Justin Peiper," she said softly, and set the photo down on Guthrie's desk. "Can't we get Greg out of jail?"

"I would if I could. This's going to be a tough job without help, and needing to move slow enough not to spook him." He pointed at the photo and paused. "What about you? Maybe you have two million and seven?"

Tompkins flushed, and her eyes dropped. "Not yet," she said. "In a few years."

"The trust fund hasn't opened wide enough yet?" Guthrie asked.

"*You* shouldn't be smug about Whitney money," she said.

"Then we're stopped, and moving slow," the little detective said, "unless you think your uncle will do it on what we've got."

The tracery of facts, spoken aloud, seemed as thin as the clouds above Manhattan. While murdered witnesses might prove that someone meant to stifle Guthrie's search, the remaining witness had chosen a dead man's picture. Until then, Jeannette Overton had been convincing; afterward, maybe glib but senile. Michelle Tompkins shook her head. The detectives didn't have enough to convince her uncle, but they did have an avenue left to explore. The material from Arlington hadn't been cross-checked. Taking the pictures from Alpha to Overton had seemed simpler.

So the detectives began comparing the lists. Guthrie marked blue dots on Vasquez's map to show home addresses from Alpha. Vasquez continued marking murders. Michelle Tompkins haunted the far end of the office, floating between the windows, where she could watch the traffic and commotion on Thirty-fourth Street, and the office door behind the oxblood couch, where she could trace the reverse of the gold lettering on the frosted glass. Her book and laptop sat unattended on the coffee table.

A direct comparison of the lists provided no connections. The soldiers from Task Force 1127 were all men; the victims of Agent Rackers's signature were all women. Given time to read and mark the map, the addresses began to align in a rough approximation with the locations of the murders. The detectives enjoyed a few minutes of mounting excitement before Tompkins padded over from the windows.

"If you had two random samples of men and women in America," she said, "it might end up looking the same." She studied the map. "Lots of people live in Chicago. So you have two soldiers and two victims from Chicago. That's an easy coincidence. You could make an argument about that pair in Iowa, though."

Guthrie shrugged. "Good thing we had someone here with a college education," he muttered. "We ain't got time to go out to Iowa and dig through that. Not right now. It's time to get on the telephones."

He split the list of military records, calling attention to the contact numbers for next of kin. The cold calls would begin with a line of chatter about a survey. They wanted deaths in the last eighteen months, corresponding with the list Rackers had provided. Guthrie fashioned an officious pitch for a Veterans Administration survey, and then they practiced the chatter for a few minutes to smooth out kinks.

The task force list contained over four hundred names. Unanswered rings and quick hangups outnumbered conversations, but in four hours they dredged up a hundred names, finding thirty-two deaths. Six dead men they set aside. Twenty-six mothers, sisters, daughters, wives, girlfriends, and nieces were dead from car accidents, fatal robberies, drunken falls, overdoses, and other morbid circumstances, both unexpected and expected; including one elderly woman who died of cancer, and one infant girl who choked to death at night on a toy rattle that wasn't supposed to be in her crib. None appeared to be victims of deliberate murder.

Guthrie failed to reach the family in Iowa despite three tries, but the coincidences were numerous. With deaths in the task force to compare, Rackers's signature list placed twenty bodies nearby, each within a few days and a hundred miles. Guthrie tried Iowa again, then slapped the cell phone onto his desk after twenty rings.

"One man could do all that?" Tompkins asked softly.

"According to Greg Olsen, this little guy is a force of nature," Guthrie said. "But I guess you got me again, college girl. Let's put a time line together for the killings."

"All of them?" Vasquez asked.

"All of them."

Outside, Thirty-fourth Street was rolling up, signaled by the sound of loading doors sliding down with slams. The Garment District had made another day's money. Bright sunshine reflected from the window ledges and doorways on the gray marble across the street. Inside, more work waited. Late-night calls to the West Coast could continue into the small hours. Guthrie handed Tompkins a phone and a list. He didn't mind if she walked while she talked, but he'd had enough of bright ideas without work.

CHAPTER TWENTY-SEVEN

By the end of a weekend spent making phone calls, the coincidences were impressive. Iowa produced a second body to pair with the victim Rackers provided. Even with a long list of murders, the killer never needed to be in two places at the same time. Comparably, New York City was Gagneau's sparsest hunting ground. Across the country, he killed two or three people every week, but his hunting in the city was slower and more calculated. Michelle Tompkins didn't need the matched lists to convince herself; she intended the proof for her uncle. Late Sunday night, they finished their calls, having found crossover bodies on most of the signature murders. George Livingston gave them an appointment with HP Whitridge for early Monday morning.

The old man's office was in a museum on Park Avenue in the sixties. An exclusive suite perched high atop the building like an eagle's aerie, with access through the museum below. Guthrie and Vasquez looked like weekend sightseers who had wandered astray from viewing the collection. The little detective could pass a casual glance in his rumpled suit, if he held his off-colored fedora out of sight behind his back, but Vasquez still looked like a grade-school tomboy on a summer jaunt, maybe with a frog and a handful of mud in her pocket to match up with the black eye and tilted cap. Michelle Tompkins led them upstairs, like an escort uniformed in dark blue Armani, with her dark hair held tightly by combs. Whitridge's office was cool, wrapped in dark woodwork and the smell of old leather. Broad, high windows looked down on Park Avenue.

The little detective outlined their proof against Gagneau, and then Tompkins pitched for Greg Olsen's bail. Whitridge studied her in a long pause after she finished, then slowly shook his head.

"I don't suppose I ever noticed before how much you resemble your aunt Nancy," he said gently. "Your great-aunt. Sometimes a resemblance skips a generation. Aunt Nancy was a crusader, and you have that same determined look."

Tompkins flushed with anger. "You would leave him in jail?" she demanded. "He doesn't deserve to be in jail! Don't say you don't believe what we've told you."

The silver-haired old man sighed. He settled into his wing-backed chair. "I believe I told you how long I've known Clayton Guthrie," he said. "I also know he's done what was asked: He found the killer. The police can do the rest, or perhaps the FBI is more likely." He paused to study his niece again. She was standing angrily with her hands on her hips. He continued before she lost her patience. "I don't know Greg Olsen, while you do. That doesn't mean I dislike him if I don't rush to take his side. I can see him for what he is, which isn't far different from the man who killed Camille. Both of them are soldiers from the same elite unit of killers. Gagneau is a loose cannon; he's out in the street exacting vengeance for the death of his fiancée. Greg Olsen isn't a stray cat you'll take home and feed from a dish. If I put Greg Olsen on the street, what do you think he'll do?" Whitridge emphasized his point with a frown.

Tompkins started to speak, but she was shocked. Her mouth closed and the hand she had lifted suddenly dropped, deprived of a gesture.

"That's right," he continued. "He would run out into the street, bent on taking revenge for Camille. She was your friend, too. That's what you want?"

"That's not fair," Tompkins said softly. "That's not what I was thinking."

Vasquez cleared her throat and caught Whitridge's eye. "I gotta admit I thought of that," the young Puerto Rican said. "That first thing, he would kill Gagneau. I thought of that, and I didn't think it was a bad thing. Gagneau needs to be dead *now*, not a year from now, or however long it takes to convince the NYPD to look for him. I spent the past few days looking at women he's killed. Gagneau's not gonna stop. He's killed almost two hundred *women* over the past year or so. Maybe a man don't find that much to worry about. Mister, he don't *need* another year, or even another week."

Whitridge frowned, leaning forward. He glanced at Guthrie but then turned back to Vasquez. "You can't find Gagneau?" he asked. "If Olsen comes out, he can help you do it?"

"I don't know," she replied. "I'm new at this. Maybe *el viejo* works some more magic and finds him—but he don't sound hopeful. Maybe we find him faster with Olsen's help. He knows Gagneau."

Whitridge glanced at Guthrie, noted the grim look on the little man's face, and leaned back in his chair again. "Michelle, are you determined about this?" he asked. "Are you prepared to accept the consequences?"

"What do you mean?" she asked.

"I think you have more in this than wanting Camille's killer caught," he said. "Is that worth risking? Because you will be, whether you understand that or not."

Tompkins seemed bewildered, but she nodded.

"Then I'll call James Rondell and tell him to arrange bail."

On the ride back into the city from Rikers Island, Greg Olsen sat quietly in the backseat of Guthrie's old Ford and watched the streets slide by through the glass. Thick clouds darkened the sky. Michelle Tompkins sat beside him, clutching a knapsack of his things gathered from the Grove Street apartment like a teddy bear. Crossing the Triborough, she held it out to him silently.

Vasquez drove through Harlem as the big man sifted through the knapsack. At the bottom, he found a bag of butterscotch candies. A shadow of a smile crossed his face, and he doled out pieces of candy.

"So this's a peace offering, then?" he said.

"I don't remember declaring war," Tompkins replied.

"What you wrote on my paper for Professor Markham's class wasn't friendly, though."

Tompkins grinned. "Someone needed to kick that pile of leftist propaganda. The ghost of Neville Chamberlain might've whispered that into your ear."

"Whatever," he said. He fussed with the bag for a moment, pocketed a few butterscotches, and then handed the bag to her. "I appreciate you helping. A lotta guys wouldn't have reached out to a guy, with a friend being murdered and all."

"I knew you didn't do it," she said, turning to look from the window. Drizzle floated down from the clouds, slowly speckling the glass with tiny droplets.

Philip Linney stayed close behind them like a ground-bound storm cloud, copiloting a black Escalade driven by a young black man he called "Little Prince." The lunch-hour traffic gathered and disappeared repeatedly around them as Vasquez cut around blocks alongside the Harlem River. They passed three Macks and a Freightliner coming from the transfer park. The Escalade tailgated them along the hurricane fence, where the stacked cardboard and pallets looked like miniature apartment blocks, darkening under the slow rain. Vasquez parked away from the abutment, where the rusted sheet pilings looked like ragged teeth on the shore of the river.

The Escalade pulled past the Ford, parking closer to the abutment beneath the bridge. Little Prince left the door of the Cadillac open, scowling at the grimy hardscape while he walked around his vehicle. A long black duster topped with a flat-brimmed black cowboy hat made him seem lanky, but he was a few inches shorter than Linney when they stopped side by side. Traffic buzzed on the bridge overhead, with pauses like long, slow breaths. Olsen, Guthrie, Vasquez, and Tompkins crunched through the gravel and glass as they walked along the underside of the bridge. The little detective looked as sober as a churchman in his dark suit; the two young women in blue jeans and sneakers made him seem misplaced.

Olsen stopped suddenly. "The thought of coming here gave me a bad feeling," he said. He pointed at the piers and then at the Dumpster. "You see it, Linney?"

"I see it, Captain," Linney said softly. "Still can't read it."

The big blond man stepped away from them and scooped an unbroken wine bottle from the ground. A wide, thick circle of shattered glass surrounded one of the piers; he threw the bottle like a tomahawk at the pier and shouted a curse. Fragments of glass showered around it. Linney found a bottle, threw it, and cursed.

Olsen answered the little detective's questioning look with a glare. "He did it," Olsen barked. "Despite that I didn't want to believe you when you said that, Gagneau did this." He pointed at the Dumpster again. "Right about there I'm sure he killed her." He stalked over to the Dumpster. Tompkins followed a few steps behind him.

"Says it right there: one dead, one dying," he said. Angular lines of white spray paint were stacked like slashes on the green Dumpster's face. He scanned the ground, striding back and forth; Tompkins kept pace with him and tried to bring him to a stop. His feet couldn't stop moving, but he began circling around her.

Vasquez and Guthrie exchanged a glance. The marks on the Dumpster were as incomprehensible as the other graffiti scattered under the bridge. "That's some sort of writing?" Guthrie asked.

"That—" Olsen began, gesturing at the Dumpster.

"Slip was crazy," Linney said. Little Prince paused beside him and punched his hands down into the pockets of his long duster. "He had every rifle in Alpha calling everybody 'brother.' When I first shipped in, I thought them dudes was fucking with me."

Olsen pointed again, this time at a pier. "That—"

Linney nodded. "Yeah, I see it. Looks like two-rum. That's the one I know: 'Are you one?' That's what Slip asked, then you say, 'I am that.' He wanted to know if *you* were a brother," he said conversationally. His eyes darkened with sadness, watching Olsen. The big blond man looked like a towering bomb with a racing fuse. Tompkins's hand closed on his forearm, and his feet fell still, but his chest was heaving.

"Hardrock thought Slip was talking about that WW Two thing," Linney continued softly, "the band of brothers, but it was something else. He said killing a brother was a waste of time; even cutting him in ten pieces only left you deviled by ten brothers. The rifles was crazy for that shit. Slip was spooky sometimes. The way his feet moved on the ground wasn't natural."

Olsen cleared his throat and pointed again. "That was something Gagneau made up," he said roughly. "He used those marks when he scouted, so when I trailed him I would know what he saw, or something that had happened, or his intentions. Dead-and-dying marked when he saw AQT casualties."

Vasquez shook her head. "Ain't you said he was from Louisiana?" She looked around at the other graffiti. "Some of that paint's old, *chico.*" She pointed at more slashes of paint in different colors, and scratches marring the concrete or patches of paint around them. "Do those say something?"

The big man started looking. Tompkins studied his face. Concentration softened the fierce anger marked there. A gust of wind whipped drizzle under the bridge, then rain began to fall.

"Some of those are different," Olsen whispered. "But some are the same, like the curse pole. See there?" He pointed, then strode over to trace a flaking pattern done with red paint. "It means 'Where're you coming from?'"

"That's *old*," Vasquez said, peering at the paint. A legion of other scrawls was massed beneath the old red mark in a riot of colors, scratches, and forms, often overlaid.

"He can't have done all of this," Olsen said. His eyes darted from mark to mark, and he walked along to look at them. Tompkins followed him. The big man went from pier to pier, muttering. "Some of this must be names. Gagneau didn't use names when he marked the patterns over there—whatever he was saying, he was saying to me. A pattern on the tailgate of a burned-out Toyota always meant something, but some of these are 'Screw you.'" His fingertip flicked, stabbing at mark after mark. "Then these are the same thing over and over, but not like the greeting pole. Two trees."

Guthrie laughed. "That's it," he said.

"What?" Olsen asked. Linney and the big man turned on the detective.

"Twin Oaks in Essex County," Guthrie said. "A pair of bodies already turned up there."

"So he's going to be up there then?" Olsen asked.

"One of the old great lodges up there in the Adirondacks goes by that name. If a man wanted a place to stash away from the city, but close enough, that would be a spot. I think I'm gonna start there."

"I don't see going up there empty-handed, though," Olsen said, tracing out the shape of a rifle with his hands. Anger drifted across his face like the gusts of wind carrying splashes of rain beneath the bridge.

"We're gonna need to talk about that," Guthrie said.

Tompkins glanced down at her feet. The tips of sneakers showed beneath the hems of her blue jeans. "I guess I should get my boots," she said.

"You won't need any boots in class," Olsen said.

"I am *not* staying here while you—"

"What are you going to do if we find him?" Olsen challenged.

"Don't be stupid," she hissed. "Or don't you remember that I always went with Cammie when she practiced shooting? I'm a better shot than she was, and—"

"I know she was your friend." The big man wrapped his long hands around her shoulders and shook gently. Her blue eyes widened in surprise. "Gagneau won't spin at seven meters, Michelle. He was my scout in Afghanistan for *years*. He's a killer."

"I didn't—" she began, but then she stopped. She glared at Vasquez. "*She's* going."

"I'm getting paid," Vasquez said. "That means don't try it at home." She squared her feet and thrust out her chin, but she knew what Tompkins was thinking. She was stuck being a girl.

"Michelle, this isn't going to be a dialogue," Olsen said. "At times, talking with you, I've thought you could reason anything out, given time. You made me realize we could do something in Afghanistan, if we went about it a better way. But Gagneau won't do much talking. He was never much of a talker, for being too much like a stone. That was the one way he didn't fit with the Pashtuns—he didn't *laaf,* if you don't mind another silly pun."

"He didn't boast. I get it," she said softly. "But everything is a dialogue."

"You bet," he said, "but this one will be a material dialogue." His hands slipped from her shoulders, but she didn't move away. She nodded. She knew Olsen had reasons. They were different from the ones that had sent him to war for eight years.

Rain hissed quietly on the old broken asphalt beyond the bridge and made the Bronx a gloomy shadow beyond the Harlem. The sky above Manhattan was dark and gray.

CHAPTER TWENTY-EIGHT

Clayton Guthrie was willing to accept being lucky. Tough cases needed luck. The graffiti at the crime scene was luck, and saved the hard work of watching V.I. Maskalenko to see if Gagneau liked to visit. After Tompkins took a cab back downtown, Vasquez drove them back to the office. Slow rain fell on Fifth Avenue, and the little detective watched the park slide by past his window.

"If this lead don't pan out, we're gonna watch Brooklyn," he said. "That was the plan until she came along with bail."

Vasquez laughed. "Brooklyn? All of it, or just Flatbush?"

"Sure, that's a good joke, right?" he said. "That's our other lead, but I'm not in a hurry to mix with the Russians." He looked over his shoulder at the Escalade still trailing them. "Greg, I gotta ask you to clear that up for me."

The blond veteran looked, then nodded. Linney's interest in Gagneau didn't need an explanation—his mother was involved. The younger man wasn't so different. Before Linney joined the army, Althea Linney plucked Little Prince from the street. He became younger brother and younger son. Linney left the gang behind when he joined the service, but Little Prince stepped right into his shoes. Linney hadn't made much progress changing Little Prince's mind about the gang since he'd returned from Afghanistan. Day labor wouldn't put rims on an Escort, and forget about a Cadillac. Olsen shrugged. Linney was struggling his way forward with Little Prince, and outside help was actually interference.

The Garment District was in full swing. In the rain, the runners had to hold plastic over the clothes. They doubled up—more trips, more jammed traffic, and more chaos. Vasquez parked a block away, but the rain wasn't heavy enough to drench them before they reached the office. Guthrie ordered pizzas. The little detective flipped through the phone book while Olsen and Linney argued about whether Linney should go back to work, and where Olsen should stay the night.

"Quiet," Guthrie said when he picked up the phone to dial. "The calls go on speaker, so you gotta be quiet."

The Park Service kept an information center and ranger station outside Blue Ridge, near Twin Oaks. Guthrie fed one of the rangers a story about an estranged family, with worried parents looking for assurance that their youngest son was alive and functional, and being led to Twin Oaks by a comment from one of the young man's friends. The ranger offered that the campsites below the old great lodge were a transient haven. Electricity was available in a camper park that boasted a collection of tin-pot trailers and slackers, along with a heavy dose of late-summer campers, nature lovers, and wandering retirees. The campgrounds were a miniature city away from the city. Guthrie clipped a copy of Gagneau's picture from his computer to send by phone, and asked the ranger to have a look. The first ranger didn't connect him, but the second, who regularly pushed through the campsites, claimed to recognize him from the camper park. Guthrie drew the rangers into a conspiracy of silence by claiming to need pictures for the worried parents. He cradled the phone and shrugged.

"If you weren't working to help me, I think I might have some reason to worry," Olsen said. "Then, I know some other guys who would see it the other way."

Linney laughed. "You's a *serious* liar."

"So when we gonna go get him?" Little Prince asked.

The little detective looked from face to face in the office, waited a few seconds, and nodded. He stood up and peeled off his suit coat, revealing the pistols holstered under each arm. "I ain't going to jail with the rest of you," he said quietly. "So you're about to make a choice: You step out of the office and don't come back unless I call you, or you do what I say, when I say, and how I say. All of you follow that?"

Blank stares and silence answered him from around the office, with one angry scowl from Little Prince. The traffic outside seemed loud.

"See, this ain't Afghanistan. When you shoot someone in New York, that's homicide. If you plan in advance to do it"—he indicated all of them with a roving fingertip—"that's murder. You already conspired, just now."

"Yo, P-Lo, what's up with this dude?" Little Prince said.

"Shut it, Prince," Linney said, aiming a frown at the young man and then at Guthrie. "Old man, you got to make that clearer."

"All right. Greg's on bond for the Bowman murder. We figure Gagneau for the killer. What if we can't prove it? Greg goes back to jail on the murder. The first item on my list is getting around that. But let's say we have proof—and then one of us shoots Gagneau. I'm seriously not explaining to the NYPD how I came to be in that position; to wit, I searched for the man, found him, approached him with a firearm, and, in some ensuing altercation, shot him dead. In New York, that's murder. Arguing that he killed your mother beforehand is only getting you an injection. Your fiancée?" he said, looking at Olsen now. "Same thing. Am I getting through here?"

"Fuck that shit," Linney muttered. Olsen's face turned as red as blood, but he folded his hands in his lap and said nothing.

"See, it don't matter what Gagneau did, or even if we can prove it. You kill him, that's murder. Explain why you killed him, that's evidence against you for being a dumbass. Hide the body and cover up the shooting, and Greg here goes away for the Bowman murder. That's to make sure everybody understands. Vasquez, you made a speech to HP that puts you in the fire if you happen to be the shooter. You remember that?"

"You made your point, *viejo*!" she snapped. "We can't touch him! So what are we doing?"

"We're waiting on pizza," Guthrie said. "We don't do anything else until after we eat."

On the drive north to the park, Vasquez stayed on the east side of the Hudson River. The rise and fall of the Catskills folded the city away into a distant box after they slipped past Yonkers and Mount Vernon. A neat manicure and ranks of ancient estates polished away the wildness of the mountains, leaving it like a well-behaved dog wearing a ribbon and hat and refusing to go out to play. Olsen slept in the backseat of the Ford. Linney and Little Prince trailed them in the Escalade. Guthrie brooded quietly in the passenger seat, watching the road signs and fences.

Farther north, the Escalade became a comfort to Vasquez because it reminded her of the city. The boroughs were straight lines and hard surfaces. She was a child of the city; when she said *concrete*, she wasn't talking about philosophy. The Adirondacks shimmered like a hallucination when gusts of wind swept the edges of trees and shrubbery into motion. Dim light from the cloudy sky left the countryside colorless and distant, except when the road was swallowed by dips in the ground or surrounded by an onslaught of trees. Everything was too far away. When Vasquez was little, her family flew down to Puerto Rico for vacations, but they never ventured far from Barranca, Papì's village on the coast. Driving into the park took her farther from the sea than she had ever been in her life.

Earlier, Guthrie had used the ritual of eating to make sure that everyone was calm before questioning the two veterans about Gagneau. After the pizza boxes were empty, the little detective asked, "Do you suppose Gagneau's armed?"

Linney laughed; the two veterans looked at each other, and both nodded. "The real question is whether he's got a chopper," Linney said. "Slip loves full auto."

"He's a fair shot?" Guthrie asked. "Would he go for a head shot?"

Olsen shook his head. "Once I gave him all day to line up on a cow, and then he shot her in the ass. I never saw him miss the long side of a cream-colored Toyota in the dark, though."

"Captain, you tripping," Linney said.

The big man grinned. "So maybe he could be a little better than that."

"This ain't time for jokes," the little detective said. "If he's a good shot, we'll need to do things differently."

"No, then," Olsen said glumly.

"How does he eat and sleep?"

"Slip *eats*," Linney said. "Always had candy in his pocket, too."

"He wanted to stay in the rack late. He hated A.M. roll-outs," Olsen said.

The little detective grunted and searched the computer file from Arlington for a minute, then shrugged. "Too bad. He ain't a diabetic." He'd peppered them with questions about Gagneau's personal habits for almost an hour, without seeming satisfied. None of the answers provided a breakthrough.

During pauses, Guthrie gathered equipment. He cornered Little Prince and tricked him into handing over his pistol "just for a look"—a Glock with an obliterated serial number—then wouldn't give it back. Little Prince's appeal to Linney fell on deaf ears, getting a shrug and a comment: "You knowed he was a liar, all right?"

Guthrie stuffed the trunk of the old Ford with equipment. Besides camping gear and food, he had a box of wireless walkie-talkies, handcuffs, Tasers, and pepper spray. Little Prince grumbled some insults about "police shit," but changed his tone when the little detective handed him a model 1911A1 Colt. Five Colt pistols and five M1 Garands came from the holdout while Little Prince and the veterans went to pick up food. On the way out of the city, they stopped to get body armor and blue bullets for the firearms.

Vasquez drove into Essex County around the northern tip of Lake George. A wild tangle of mountains rose in the northwest, with the sun dropping slowly down onto their green ridges through thinning clouds. From a distance, the slopes were velvet-smooth, but they blocked the path to Mount Marcy like walls. Twin Oaks nestled within a small, split ridge, an old lodge built as a summer house by a rail baron in the nineteenth century. The lodge had endured through family convulsions until finally drifting into disuse and obscurity. Long Island stripped the city vacationers from the Adirondacks once vacations became less about getting away and more about being seen, but a web of campsites still surrounded the secluded valley, scattered along winding country roads.

Deep in the park, past the first ridgeline, they were enclosed in green space. Trees thickened around the road, then disappeared like suddenly swept curtains when the road turned corners and looked down upon hollows. Sunshine lit the open meadows, but beneath the arching trees was cool, dim twilight that summer couldn't erase. Olsen woke and sat up in the backseat when the road began snaking back and forth. Guthrie handed him a thermos of coffee over the seat.

The Park Service station was a small information center and visitor bathroom, with a narrow parking lot overshadowed by trees. Guthrie rented campsite number three, perched on the mountainside above the camper park, which sat on a horseshoe of flatter ground. They collected some brochures containing simple maps of the surrounding campsites and connecting roads, with pictures to entice the visitors, and a fee schedule for the wary.

With a few hours of late-afternoon sunshine remaining, Little Prince took a video camera to the camper park to film license plates. The young thug had the only face that Guthrie was sure Gagneau wouldn't recognize; the risky job was his by default. Guthrie filled his ears with repeated warnings about not making anyone suspicious, and took his pistol to make sure he wouldn't get reckless.

Campsite number three perched well above the camper park, with access along a secondary road that wound around a shoulder of the mountain and hugged narrow crevasses on both sides. The camp pitched above the road on the shoulder of a narrow shelf. The Park Service had installed rough wooden foundations to make the sloped site more useful. The view of the valley was clear, but the area was exposed to wind and sun.

The mountainside loomed above them. Beyond the ridgeline, a narrow lake divided the hollow from the true crest. A generous patron had dignified the cleft with the title of valley; the lake it contained was the focus of the great lodge, called Twin Oaks—first as a hunter's haven, then for the fishing, and finally for swimming and lounging. While it was far smaller than Tear of the Clouds, that was a point in favor for a man with a fortune smaller than Rockefeller's. Guthrie and Olsen studied maps and looked over the ground while the sun slowly sank behind the mountain above them.

The Escalade rumbled up the hill to the campsite before nightfall. Vasquez and Linney had raised a pavilion on one of the wooden foundations and wrapped it with cheap mosquito netting. A charcoal brazier provided their campfire. During the afternoon of waiting, Vasquez had practiced following Guthrie around Manhattan electronically, using his license plate for the starting resource. The little detective used cash for almost everything, but the data companies still had his fingerprints. E-Z Pass and ATM withdrawals pinpointed him, while skeleton keys provided by Fat-Fat could pull pictures from their security cameras. No one stayed invisible in the city.

A cloudy sky and lingering damp made the evening cool, but the insects in the north woods gathered like an army as the light failed. In the wilderness, they had an edge, and often won their arguments. Guthrie and Vasquez studied videotape, writing down license tags, while Olsen and Linney grilled steaks. Eventually, the detectives sat in small pools of light cast by the screens of their laptops, and quiet conversation swirled around them, almost disembodied.

"This kid Slip been crazy when you met him?" Little Prince asked.

"Nah," Linney said. "He was solid when I landed in Alpha."

Crickets screamed outside in the darkness, trying to match volume with frogs. "Then after all this happened, it occurred to me what drove the sergeant crazy," Olsen said.

"Captain, you the slowest fucker I ever met," Linney said.

The big man chuckled, but his voice was serious when he spoke again. "He told me he lost a brother on nine/eleven. So he goes to war. What happens when Uncle Sam bombs his girl, then?"

"*Bitch.*"

"You bet."

"Slip been real serious, real quiet," Linney said. "Street legend stuff. The rifles used to go, 'You know what Slip did?' Like that. I can't put him together with killing a girl. That don't make no sense to me. Like this: My second rotation after I broke in with Alpha, I went with recon. I thought he was outta his mind. Slip never said shit. He's like, 'Stand here, and look that way. Squawk if you see anything move.' Then he splits."

"For real?" Little Prince asked.

"Word. Ain't say shit. Don't blow it. He's watching you, or somebody watching you, until he trusts you gonna do what he said. I prove out on OP, and then he's ready to see me on sweeps.

"Okay, like the Pashies did a hit-and-run on a village post in Marshan in oh six and we went after them. That was a blistering hot day—not a cloud, unless you count dust. Slip pulls two pair of fire teams and we bounce a hundred meters at a time. I get the idea at the beginning he wants to get in front of them, and he knows where he's going, but he drags us through every bush and pile of rocks on the way. Makes it a memorable experience, right? We go up a cliff and down a crazy dirt-bike trail on the other side."

"You're talking about Mar Sharif," Olsen said. "Oh six was the second time we rolled over that ground."

"I don't get it," Little Prince said. "You ain't had trucks? Helicopters?"

"You ain't never gonna catch no Pashie like that—too much noise," Linney said.

After half a minute, the crickets sounded thick. "Been a hot-ass day," Linney muttered.

"Yo, what happened?"

Linney shrugged. "We freaked that shit. They'd been working for the devil long enough; we made 'em pay the taxes. How many rifles we took?"

"Twenty-three," Olsen said. "That was four less than the time we rolled over Mar Sharif in oh five."

"You took they guns?"

"No shit, we took they guns. See, new fuckers being born all the time, but they only so many guns—and they ain't free."

The veterans told stories as the darkness thickened into night, taking turns correcting and adding details. The detectives tracked lists of license plates culled from Little Prince's video of the camper park. They muttered briefly about each dead end they uncovered. Long past nightfall, Guthrie stood up and stretched. His back crackled. "Run this one," he said, and handed Vasquez a scrap of paper.

"What is it?" Olsen asked.

"Let her study behind me," Guthrie said.

He floated forward into the soft light thrown by the grill. He stripped the wrapper from a candy bar and spitted it on a wire, then roasted it above the charcoal. He drew it back and caught a bite when the chocolate started to sizzle.

"Yo, gimme one of them," Little Prince said. Linney and Olsen crowded the grill with him.

"That thing's been rolling around in my head since we had that conversation, Greg," the little detective said.

"About what?"

"Gagneau. I know why he kills those girls. I don't reckon it matters, but that FBI agent in Virginia wanted this. He's looking for Gagneau, without knowing who he's looking for. His bosses in the Bureau don't believe Gagneau exists, because he's not a sex killer.

They can't believe anybody would kill that many people for anything but sex. So he can't exist. He's a figment of our imagination.

"Anyway, the Bureau guy puts about a hundred bodies on Gagneau, without looking at all the other bodies we've connected to him. But I'm not sure he's crazy." He warmed the candy bar for another bite. "I remembered there was another man used to run through here who killed for the same reason as Gagneau. Might've killed someone right where we're standing."

Little Prince laughed. "You got ghost stories, right?"

"You wish," Guthrie said. "This was three or four hundred years ago. Some of the old names don't translate so well, but my great-uncle called him 'Cuts Through Bone.' The old people said he killed half a hundred in fair combat, and more than that by murder."

"Indian, right?" Little Prince asked. "That ain't like now. Back then, they murdered for nothing."

Guthrie shook his head and finished off his candy bar. "They did things different, but not for nothing. But the old people told the story, I think, to point out he did something wrong. Cuts Through Bone was a big man for the Onondaga. I guess I forgot most of the story, since I used to could say it out right, the way it was said to me. My great-uncle started like this: 'The brother of Cuts Through Bone was killed in the dark of the moon of Falling Leaves.'

"Back then things were different, right enough. When a man got killed, his woman was entitled to a replacement, because it really was the other way around. He belonged to her. So Cuts Through Bone's brother was killed, and his sister-in-law wanted a new man. There had to be some sort of resemblance. Maybe they sounded alike, or walked alike, or ate the same things, or liked the same jokes. That was a mark from the spirits that they would become similar in all ways. The selection took time—months or years, even, because the new man had to learn his responsibilities, even if he was replacing a chief or a shaman.

"While that learning was going on, if anybody got dissatisfied with him, that was that. He could sing his death song. They're gonna kill him. A terrible kind of death that an imposter deserves— burned alive or cut slow in little pieces. And Cuts Through Bone killed his adopted brothers. He killed so many that nobody wanted to be his brother—forty, fifty times. He might wait until they started the ceremony to finish the adoption, then rush in and knock him.

"My great-uncle said he ain't done it from malice," the little detective said. "Sure, when he wound a man's guts around a stick, he meant it to hurt. But he killed them because he was sure they weren't his brothers. Even though he tried, again and again, to let the spirits bring his brother back. So I thought that would be why Gagneau keeps killing the girls. He tries to let one get close, then realizes she's an imposter and loses it."

"*Bitch*," Linney muttered.

"You bet," Olsen echoed.

"I don't see what you're talking about," Vasquez said. A frustrated frown marked her face, dimly lit by the glow of the computer screen. She tapped slowly at the touchpad.

"Okay, what have you got?" Guthrie dusted his hands on his pants.

"A black Volvo registered to Michael Watson in Brooklyn," she said. "Buyer info has an SSN and an address in Brooklyn. Receipts stack up, with nothing today. You were talking about this?"

Guthrie nodded. "Where're the receipts?"

Vasquez recited names and addresses—bodegas, laundries, gas stations, pharmacies, liquor stores. She shrugged.

"Ain't about every one of those addresses in Little Russia?"

Her eyes fastened on the screen again and her finger tapped. "Damn," she muttered.

"So check the DMV. What's he look like?"

"I don't—" Vasquez shot him a glance. Her hands grew busy, then she said, "*Viejo*, why you put me through that? No, wait—I know. I'm a smart girl. I'll figure it out."

"He's down there," Guthrie said. "In the morning, we'll go take a closer look."

The two veterans rushed over to see Vasquez's computer screen. Michael Watson's DMV photograph looked a lot like Marc Lucas Gagneau.

CHAPTER TWENTY-NINE

"You understand we're going down there to have a look," Guthrie said. He didn't look up from the coffeepot heating on the charcoal grill. The cool twilight was unbroken, though sunrise approached.

Olsen and Linney exchanged a sour glance.

"Michael Watson ain't committed any crimes, unless it's illegal to own a foreign car, live in Brooklyn, or go camping," he continued softly. "We know that's Gagneau, but that don't matter."

The coffeepot hissed, and the men fingered their empty mugs expectantly. Olsen grunted, then said, "So this could be the time where you share a general idea of your intended operational procedure that concludes with—"

"Like that, but faster," Linney interjected.

"We trick him into the first move," Guthrie said.

"No, don't tell me you saying we give the fucker first shot," Linney said.

The little detective shrugged. He poured himself a cup of coffee. During breakfast, he checked his watch repeatedly, and finally made a phone call. He rented a Land Cruiser to serve as an OP, then called Fat-Fat in Brooklyn to offer him money to drive it up from the city. The big Korean had already gone to Venezuela; his answering machine had a message suggesting to call back next month. Guthrie grumbled for several minutes. Without Fat-Fat, he was forced to call Wietz, who had quit working for him before the Christmas holiday. After a short conversation, she agreed to drive the Land Cruiser up to the park with a load of surveillance equipment, but the little detective hadn't wanted to ask.

Little Prince crawled from the backseat of his Escalade, ate a breakfast of champions—candy bars and cola—and nosed out Guthrie's plan for the day. A stakeout rubbed up the young man's impatience, but Linney gave him a long, slow walk and lecture. Vasquez kept quiet. Waiting didn't suit her any better than it suited the young thug, but she had already seen it produce results. Real life just didn't rush along as fast as a one-hour TV show.

By lunchtime, Wietz found Blue Ridge and called for better directions to the campsite on the mountainside. The clouds were gone and the sunshine was bright. The Land Cruiser nosed up to campsite number three like a sleepy cow. Wietz parked, then opened the side door so she could roll her Ducati down a two-by-ten from the cabin behind the driver's compartment.

Wietz was a slim young woman about a decade older than Vasquez, with dark hair cut shorter than Sand Whitten's. She had a cocky bounce in her stride. She took a quick look around the campsite while she pulled on her riding leathers. She had to go back to the city to get some sleep. She was watching a car lot in Brooklyn, waiting for some hit-and-run thieves; that kept her busy at night. She spent her longest looks on Vasquez and Olsen, then had a brief conversation with Guthrie before she rode back down the mountain on her motorcycle.

Guthrie drove the Land Cruiser down the mountain to the camper park. He made a circuit of the park, searching for the site they'd rented. One looping road surrounded a grid of dusty dirt roads, with the campers jammed close together. Suburban trailer parks had more privacy. Unevenly spaced oak trees provided pools of shade, but there were no lines of hedges or other windbreaks. In the front, Winnebagos lined up as neatly as the infield at a racetrack. Smaller campers mixed under the trees with pop-ups surrounded by crowds of kids. Farther from the entrance, the campers became old and ratty, often no more than a dusty chrome bubble fit to be towed behind a station wagon or light truck. A pair of square bathhouses squatted on concrete pads to one side in a tangle of pine trees. The early-morning arguments about Gagneau had been wasted. By the time Guthrie found the site and parked the camper, he had rolled slowly along every road in the park. The black Volvo was gone.

The little detective ignored complaints for a half hour while he arranged surveillance equipment inside the big Land Cruiser. A tinted cupola behind the driver's compartment gained a hastily built ledge for the cameras; he spiraled the wires into a thick cable stretching to an array of monitors and recorders in the middle cabin. He held back a handful of wireless cameras to be positioned and tested at night in the trees around the Land Cruiser.

By the time Guthrie finished, Little Prince's complaints were sullen silence and stormy looks. The little detective made a cup of coffee and sat down, watching the young man. The veterans waited uncomfortably. Vasquez sat in the driver's seat of the camper and looked from the window at two old couples in nylon stretch pants playing pinochle at a folding table.

"I know he went back to the city," Guthrie said.

"So I doubt you expect we'll pick him up with these cameras, then?" Olsen asked.

"I'm not gonna play stalk with him in the city, Greg. He's gonna be looking for you, or setting something up. When he gets tired of that, he'll come back here. We got his bolt-hole, here. If we chase him in the city, it's gonna be who spots who first. I ain't gotta roll them dice."

"How long do we wait, then?"

"Until I got him," Guthrie said. "This spot right here, I think I got a trick that puts him away. Just be patient. Anybody wants out, now would be a good time." He looked pointedly at Little Prince and stirred his coffee.

"No, man, I good," the young thug growled, but he stood and stomped from the trailer. The cheap door didn't make a very satisfying slam behind him.

Once the detectives settled in to watch, the camper park seemed quiet around them. Retirees played slow card games and dozed in the sunshine. Busy mothers hustled strings of kids along the assembly line of nature walks. Orderly leisure kept the wilderness around them as antiseptic as a suburban living room. Even the boys were neatly collared and chained by game machines; they formed silent circles where movement consisted of fingers trembling on buttons, and shrugs of triumph or disgust. The detectives were trapped inside the rented trailer. Only Little Prince could go out without wrapping up in hat and glasses. Everyone else played solitaire, drank coffee, or cleaned and loaded weapons.

As the afternoon declined, the suburbanites lit charcoal grills and sprayed bug repellent. In the back of the park, bearded men stacked council fires. Rusted cars roared to life and prowled around the park like muscleheads strutting the beach. Before she heard the engines purr, Vasquez pegged the heaps for scrap and wondered why the sunburned men bothered to lift the hoods and tinker. While the retirees settled down for radio shows and packaged dinners, guitars appeared around the bonfires. The young Puerto Rican watched continuously, fascinated by the transformation.

A few youngsters slipped over from the suburban campers, with furtive backward glances like Middle Americans crossing railroad tracks, but they hurried back before full darkness. Dancers that began at one fire wandered to the next to throw bottles in drinking contests. Their drunken choruses were audible at a distance. Pots swung above the fires, tended as carefully as newborn babies. When the stars came out and the men were drunk, they fought like tom-cats. Insults and wars of words were followed by punches, curses, dire threats, foot chases, and thrown rocks, before being settled by the intervention of women. The warm night wrapped around them like an endless velvet blanket.

Guthrie slipped from the camper when the air cooled. People were still gathered around the fires, but they had mellowed into peacefulness. Quiet music and storytelling had replaced dancing. The little detective climbed trees and placed his cameras, and Vasquez told him what she could see as he adjusted each placement. At the back of the encircling road, where the Volvo had been parked, two old chrome trailers sandwiched a large new towed camper. He figured the new camper for Gagneau's. He placed two of his four cameras to watch it.

Parked beside one of the old trailers, in front of a small mountain of pallets, a rusted tow truck nestled in a bed of weeds. Like a shadow, Guthrie slid over and filmed the license plate. Little Prince hadn't been able to get it from the road. On the Internet, they discovered that the tow truck had a salvage title originating in Louisiana. The owner, Oriel Robataille, had no driver's license.

By morning, the waiting drew the watchers' nerves thin and tight like wires. Every movement drew attention and comment. Little Prince kept his angry glances hidden behind dark glasses, but his mood was infectious. Arguments he had with Linney didn't reduce the pressure, because he didn't trust Guthrie. The little detective spent his time playing solitaire, watching the video monitors, and using the phone. Linney and Little Prince ate peanut butter sandwiches at lunch while listening to Guthrie recruit Joe Holloway, one of the house detectives who'd worked with Henry Dallen. The little detective wanted to bring him up to join the surveillance and was pulling on the idea that the house detective would get to take Dallen's killer. Little Prince listened with unconcealed disgust.

"Fuck it, then," Linney said after watching the young thug across the table for several minutes. "Get out. Don't be back. I heard and seen enough of this to the point where I ain't dealing with no more bitch shit."

Little Prince seemed surprised for a moment. "No, fuck *this*. This slow-ass soft shit has got me tripping, and it about over. You forgetting you ain't the only one got something in this—"

"And what? Moms took you in, so you feel some kind of way. That don't give you rights to blow this."

"Blow *what*? The *plan*? I don't see nothing but some soft motherfuckers sitting around waiting on a car to roll back down the block. The fucking car ain't been here since that night. I could have every set in the city scanning the bricks for the motherfucker right now. That's where he at, and that's where we should be." Little Prince shot a venomous glance toward the back. Guthrie was laughing into his telephone.

"You just as stupid as them motherfuckers I made you leave in the city. Wild West and Drop couldn't find they ass. Soft?" He looked at the driver's compartment, where Olsen sat in the passenger seat, daydreaming through the windshield. "You too used to that street shit, Prince. You ain't know what hard is. *Ain't* emptying a clip at some motherfucker running down the bricks. What I'm thinking, since you pressing the issue, is that some stupid motherfucker done slipped when they came in here and got the tags, and he's on we know about this. That's what I'm thinking, and I'm kicking myself for using stupid motherfuckers to do a man's work. If I wasn't holding you back, you would've rolled out there last night flashing them silly-ass gold teeth and spit everything you know as soon as you drunk and looking to impress some bitch over there."

"Fuck you!"

"No, fuck you. How many fuckers you killed, Prince? How many? Ain't know shit for sure because you ain't never been by yourself. Always three, four stupid motherfuckers throwing shots. Whose body? Every stupid motherfucker claims it at the same party. You lucky you ain't in prison. *That* been what Moms talked about, worrying for your stupid ass. What's worse? *I* put you there, from following me. I done told you about Slip. We gotta get lucky. We gotta catch him slipping, or that fucker gonna run up the score."

The young thug was quiet for a minute, his eyes dropping to

study the narrow tabletop. "What you even call me for in the first place?"

"'Cause I need your eyes," Linney said. "But I need your brains, too. You gonna have to think, Prince, and leave that street shit behind. This a new world you seeing, and maybe it a chance for you to come on up."

"I ain't going in no army."

"I ain't said that."

"Then you ain't said nothing."

Linney snorted. "This ain't time to build, if you ain't seeing the foundation around you." The dark veteran laid out another slice of bread and twisted the lid from the peanut butter.

"All right," Little Prince said. He stood up and dug the keys of his Escalade from his pocket. "I gonna be back."

"Be sure to leave that bitching with some sisters, then."

"Fuck you."

After the trailer door clicked shut, Olsen asked, "So you don't think that'll turn into a problem, then?"

"No," Linney said. "Child just got too much knowledge, without enough reality."

The rented camper seemed quiet and empty with Little Prince missing. A lazy summer afternoon drifted past the windows, livened only by an argument from the two old couples angry about a pinochle game. The cards waited on their folding table until they returned with lemonade and shrugs. The dog days were over, but the summer was still hot. The black Volvo almost slipped past them without being noticed, even though they could watch a long stretch of the encircling road from their front windshield. They rushed to the windows, staring, and then to the monitors. They watched the Volvo park in front of the overgrown tow truck. A small dark-haired man climbed out and stretched. The veterans agreed that the driver was Gagneau. He walked smoothly over to the door of the large trailer and went inside without knocking. The killer was home.

Olsen and Linney began strapping on holsters, but Guthrie

stopped them. He wanted more patience, because he had more backups to place. First, he called Joe Holloway again. He and David Lieberman had agreed to come up from the city for a grab. Lieberman hired on at the law firm after chasing bail jumpers for several years, when he was ready for a slower job. Guthrie expected they could help corner Gagneau.

The little detective didn't mind a risk that Gagneau would drive away before they were ready. Clean beat fast on takedowns, and he felt sure Gagneau would keep returning to the camper park, even if he left again. Another more important piece of his plan remained in the city. Mike Inglewood owed him an old favor; he burned it by asking the NYPD detective to come up to Essex County. The phone conversation was short and simple; Guthrie asked him to take lost time to come up and talk him through a personal problem. A pause threatened after Guthrie finished, but then Inglewood's response was clear: "I'm on the way." The little detective grinned as he turned off his phone.

Before nightfall, everyone was assembled. Gagneau joined the crowds at the fires while they waited; Vasquez and the two veterans spied on him like suddenly avid bird-watchers. The house detectives didn't press for an explanation after Guthrie told them he was still waiting for another man. Seam jobs were tricky, but they were also common enough in divorce and custody cases. Private detectives caught plenty of dirty work. After Inglewood arrived, Guthrie pitched his evidence with a delivery as smooth as Sandy Koufax's. Inglewood was the insurance policy, and his part was simplest. He would watch the monitors and then call the police if Gagneau fired shots.

"You know, Guthrie, you're maybe a little bit crazy," Inglewood said after he listened to the plan.

Guthrie shrugged. "Your boss down in the big building don't want him, and those people in Virginia don't believe he exists. What else am I gonna do?" he asked.

"I'm just saying maybe you would try something different if you were the one gonna knock on the door," Inglewood said. He looked at Olsen and pushed his taped-together glasses back up his nose. "Right?"

The big blond man tightened a strap on his bulletproof vest. "You bet," he muttered.

CHAPTER THIRTY

Gagneau floated around the camper park like a windblown leaf. He swirled circles around each bonfire, pulled by conversations, food, and drinking. The night darkened while they watched him, though Olsen and Linney warned the others that Gagneau wouldn't settle for sleep until the small hours. Early in the vigil, Inglewood saw their quarry for the first time, standing in firelight, arguing with a woman. Gagneau pushed her away and then she screamed at him until he drifted away to another fire.

Inglewood looked around at the other men in the camper, making incredulous gestures at Olsen, Holloway, and Lieberman, who were all big men. "That guy's about your size, Guthrie," the NYPD detective said. "You called enough plumber butt up here to surround him, you think?"

"If you come along, we might be able to box him in," Guthrie said.

"With these feet? That guy's too quick; he'll just get by me." Inglewood slumped on the bench seat, staring at the monitors.

The displays didn't cover the entire camper park. Guthrie hadn't installed that many cameras. Vasquez went from window to window with video binoculars to watch Gagneau in the blind spots. The trailers in the back near the tow truck had the best coverage; two cameras crossed over them. They watched as the nightly celebration slowed.

Gagneau went in and out of his trailer a few times, and once, the young woman he had argued with tried to follow him inside. Another screaming fight ensued, until an older couple pulled the young woman away. The older man stood quietly outside afterward, looking disappointed, his hands on his hips. He had a bushy black beard and a chest like a beer cooler, without a belly beneath it. At 4:45 A.M., Gagneau disappeared into his trailer and didn't return. Guthrie watched the clock for a half hour, then was satisfied.

The early morning felt cold after hours spent cramped in the trailer. A slice of moon lit the ground enough to keep it from disappearing beneath their feet. The watchers looked like a string of shadows; Guthrie threaded them between campfires and trailers to avoid sleepy people. On the monitors, filters made the images bright, but the ground around Gagneau's trailer was dark. The nearest campfire was about forty yards along the encircling road, closer to the front entrance of the camper park. The little detective sent Linney and Vasquez behind the trailer, and the rest paused to allow them to settle.

"Door back here," Linney whispered on the radio. All of them wore headset walkie-talkies and bulletproof vests, and they carried Tasers, pepper spray, handcuffs, and firearms loaded with blue bullets. The older men had one magazine each of hard bullets for their pistols. "Two windows."

"All right," Guthrie said. "Maybe he wants to bolt from the door, so be sure to mention he's surrounded."

"You bet," Olsen muttered.

The big veteran marched up to the trailer door with a Garand slung over his shoulder. Guthrie crept along the length of the trailer and stopped outside the window closest to the door. Lieberman, Holloway, and Little Prince stood back, waiting. Olsen pounded on the trailer door after a glance at the little detective. His task was simple: goad Gagneau into violence, using himself as the bait in the trap.

Olsen pounded heavily on the door again. The blows rocked the trailer. "Open this door, Sergeant! You been working for the devil long enough! Now it's time to pay the taxes! Alpha's ghosts are out here surrounding you, Sergeant! Come on out!" The big man stretched the words out with a parade-ground voice. The crickets fell silent around the trailer, leaving the night eerily quiet when he paused. The trailer creaked. A question made wordless by distance drifted from the group at the nearby fire.

"Captain, you a brave man," Gagneau called from inside his trailer. "But you should not have come here."

"Come on out of there, then!" Olsen roared, and pounded on the flimsy trailer door.

The killer answered with a fusillade. Muffled shots emitted holes around and through the door. Olsen dived into the dirt, cursing. Guthrie shattered the window glass with a hard rap from his can of pepper spray, then began spraying blindly into the interior of the trailer. Shouts rang out from the campfire. People rushed toward Gagneau's trailer. The sleepy summer morning erupted; lights snapped on in every direction, followed by outraged voices.

"That's enough, Guthrie," Inglewood said on the radio. "I'm on the phone to the Essex County sheriff. Just back off and hold him."

The little detective kept spraying into the broken window. Olsen rolled and found cover beneath the edge of the trailer. People rushed up, coming to sudden halts when they saw the house detectives and Little Prince waiting in the darkness. Tall oak trees stretched their limbs above the trailer from the back, blotting out the sky. The big black-bearded man emerged from the gathering crowd. His plaid shirt looked almost black without the light filters on the computer monitors.

"Here, what's you're doing there?" he demanded.

A young woman darted glances at the waiting detectives and

shouted, "Marc! Marc! Here's people out here!" More men rushed up. Their shouts blended into a basso chorus of anger.

The window on the other end of the trailer shattered and an arm snaked out, holding a pistol. Gagneau fired at Guthrie. The little detective ducked for the bottom edge of the trailer. Little Prince drew his Colt and fired a string of shots at the dark window. Gagneau dropped his pistol and his arm whipped back through the window. Running feet hissed through the dusty leaves all around them as some of the onlookers scattered, but even more rushed forward to replace them.

"Under the trailer, Marc!" someone shouted.

A shot boomed into the air, then a slim, longhaired man in the crowd leveled a pistol at the house detectives. "Here's enough now!" he shouted. "Get on away, you!"

Little Prince turned and fired at the longhaired man. His gunshots lit the night like strobe lights, capturing images of scattering gawkers, shocked faces, upraised pistols, and returning shots. Shooters dived for cover and hid behind trees, while the unarmed scattered. A few people in the darkness paused to hurl stones, adding curses to keep the silence at bay. On the radio, Inglewood swore softly, watching the riot on the video monitors.

"Ah jeez," Holloway said. "Forget a vest—shoulda brought my bulletproof underwear."

"You hit?"

"Ah jeez," Holloway repeated.

Hovering trees darkened the ground behind Gagneau's trailer to invisibility. The aluminum trailer floated like a long, pale boulder of limestone on dark water. Vasquez broke from behind the tree she was using for cover and trampled through the light underbrush to reach the trailer. Linney hissed at her. She ignored him and peered through one of the trailer windows. She hammered the glass out with the barrel of her Garand. The sound seemed lost in the gunfire and shouting beyond the trailer. Linney hissed again as she leaned the rifle against the trailer. She coughed a few times, then hauled herself through the window. The dark veteran cursed as her feet disappeared.

Under the front edge of the trailer, Olsen unslung his rifle and then rolled back onto his stomach. The Garand was loaded with blue bullets, but they still carried a knockout punch. Along the encircling road, shouts and screams formed a melody for the bass line of cranking engines. Some of the visitors had decided to leave. Pistol shots cracked like misplaced drumbeats.

Little Prince threw shots at a line of underbrush along one of the camper lots, but Olsen didn't see anyone there. The big man shot a bare-chested man as he flourished a pistol, aiming at one of the detectives on the other side of the road, and snapped another pair of shots at crouching shadows. The shooter and the shadows fled, yelping in pain. The rifle had a big sound, with a muzzle flash like a fog light.

Guthrie slid along beneath the edge of the trailer and rose to a crouch at the door. He tested the knob; it was unlocked. He grinned at Olsen while the big man reloaded his rifle. Escaping visitors raced in the depths of the park, their headlights crossing like sword blades. A band of half-dressed youths crept from among the campers beyond the encircling road, threw rocks, and faded back into cover. Little Prince cursed, and his pistol fell silent as he spun to his hands and knees.

"Maybe you oughta get out of there, Guthrie," Inglewood suggested.

Lieberman banged away with his Colt at some creeping shadows, where muzzle flashes had winked a few moments before. Wood smoke drifted on the cool morning breeze. The camper park was a crazy quilt of darkness, dim sides of trailers and vehicles, and blotches of greenery that drank the light from faint pools cast by campfires and lamps beyond windows; rushing arcs of headlights made fleeing people wink like fireflies as they ran through slices of light. The house detective could've been shooting at ghosts, but the strobe of his muzzle flashes pinpointed him. Gagneau poked the tip of an AK from his window and sprayed a burst—the chopper had found a place to land. Lieberman pitched over.

"Ah jeez," Holloway groaned, and fired at the window.

Pepper spray tainted the air inside Gagneau's trailer. Vasquez slithered over the sink onto a carpet of glass on the tiny kitchen floor. Both windows in the kitchen were broken. A partial wall screened the rest of the camper. One narrow door was open on the front side, and a countertop opening doubled as the kitchen table and a breakfast nook in the middle room. The young Puerto Rican detective rose to a crouch, pulled her Colt, and extended the gun over the countertop. Gagneau was kneeling at the window on the other side of the front door, peering along the length of his AK, partially silhouetted by faint light from the window. His cough sounded like a stutter.

Vasquez shot Gagneau. The blue bullets flung the little man away from the window; he tumbled like an acrobat, disappearing behind a couch along the back wall of the middle room. His curses were interrupted by a fit of coughing. Then he slid from behind the other end of the couch and sprayed the kitchen wall with the AK. Vasquez dived back onto the glass-covered floor, deafened. Guthrie peeled the front door open and fired his Taser across the small room. The probes caught in the corner of the couch. Gagneau opened the door to the back room and rolled through as the little man drew his Colt and coughed.

Inglewood cursed steadily on the radio as Olsen spaced five shots slowly, pausing to aim. Four screams erupted. The shadows vanished. Honking horns joined the chorus of gunfire, racing engines, and shouts. The riot stopped as suddenly as it had begun, deprived of fresh people to fill with anger. Holloway crawled over to check on Lieberman and Little Prince. The stunned house detective clutched a bleeding, paralyzed arm. The young thug had a bloody knot on his head above his ear. He had recovered his pistol but couldn't fit his flat-brimmed cowboy hat back on his swollen head.

Inside the trailer, Guthrie charged the door to the back room as Vasquez scrambled to her feet in the kitchen. The little man ricocheted from the locked door and smashed a small table in the corner. A fit of coughing swallowed his curse of frustration. The back door of the trailer swung wide with a creak, and Linney aimed into the interior. The dark veteran's eyes were adjusted, and he braced himself with the help of a tree. A grenade sailed through the doorway. Linney stared in puzzlement. The detonation was a flash of light and a concussion like a punch. Linney fired blind, reflexively, as Gagneau tumbled through the door. The little man paused; his AK stuttered. Guthrie and Vasquez threw themselves flat inside the trailer, but Gagneau was aiming at Linney. The heavy bullets whipped the veteran to the ground, and then the killer rushed through the ring of underbrush into the deep darkness under the trees.

The sudden return of quiet seemed like deafness. Guthrie kicked through the locked door, and Olsen low-crawled beneath the trailer. They found Linney by flashlight after calling his name produced no response. His vest had stopped most of the bullets, but a single stray had found his neck. Death made him so still and quiet that he seemed to be part of the ground.

"He got through us, Mike," Guthrie said on the radio as he peered into the darkness under the trees. Along the back of the encircling road, the hillside rose sharply.

"The kid's wearing a knot on his head the size of a pumpkin," Holloway said. "Dave's in shock, and I got a few ounces of lead in my ass. We're done around this side."

Inglewood sighed. "This's the middle of nowhere. I called the deputies. What're you gonna do?"

"I'm going after him," Guthrie replied.

Vasquez frowned, glancing into the absolute darkness beneath the trees before studying the little detective's face. Olsen slung his rifle and grunted disapproval.

"What?" Guthrie demanded.

"The sergeant was always a careful planner. He would have more than a little in mind here, and without some night vision a guy could stumble around until he caught up to his own ass." The big man studied Guthrie's face and frowned. "So you're half a cat, then?"

"No, I just do some things the old-fashioned way," the little detective said. "Maybe he has a plan—or maybe he's circling or waiting. I won't know until I look. Dawn ain't far off anyway."

"So I'll be right behind you," Olsen said.

The little detective shook his head. "Mike, maybe you got a reason to take a look in his trailer, right?" he asked.

"I could do that," Inglewood said, "but I think maybe you should rethink going after this skel. He almost wiped out your crew already. Ain't but three of you left, and I ain't in no shape to climb no mountain—"

"Mike, give it a rest," Guthrie snarled. He bent, scooped a small handful of leaf litter, and crumbled it. He sprinkled the dust on Linney's body. "I'm gonna get this bastard," he whispered.

The little detective posted Olsen at the back door of Gagneau's aluminum trailer to watch uphill for lights or movement. He took Vasquez with him, telling her to watch and keep quiet. She followed him blindly for the first minute, concentrating just to keep him in sight, before her eyes could pick out other shapes in the darkness. She listened but couldn't hear his footfalls even when she stopped moving herself. At a distance, the ground seemed as smooth as a blanket, but in the dark, every footstep was treacherous.

Faint gray light trickled into the sky from the east, but Vasquez used Gagneau's trailer to position herself. Guthrie walked a slow semicircle behind the trailer, pausing with each step to kneel and gently run his fingertips over the leaf litter. Several times, he hissed at Vasquez when she took a step or shifted while he listened. The young Puerto Rican fumed but watched him carefully. Guthrie went only about half around the semicircle before he paused and moved away from the trailer. He led the way with his fingertips, brushing soundlessly among the leaves. His footsteps were quiet; he balanced his rifle on his left knee each time he swept at the ground with his right hand. Slowly, he crept a few dozen feet uphill, then stood and looked ahead.

Vasquez looked, too. Trees were slowly emerging from the darkness. She and Guthrie were climbing the eastern side of a broad, tall ridge. Beyond the ridgeline, Twin Oaks waited. She wondered if the little man was crazy, dribbling around on the ground like an old drunk chasing a fallen bottle in the dark. Then Guthrie moved again, taking long steps before bending to test the ground with his fingers again. Every few steps, he stopped to peer again, but he moved faster.

After a few minutes, the little detective crept up to a large forked tree. He stopped Vasquez, then swept a gentle circle around the tree before returning to the trunk. He found a Kalashnikov almost at her feet, with a length of twine and an empty trash bag.

"His first stop," he muttered. He pointed up the hill. "Then he went that way." He studied the tree, then tapped a plastic disk nailed to it.

"Seen anything, Greg?" Guthrie asked on the radio.

"Not a thing."

"Found his cache," Guthrie said. "He left the machine gun and kept going uphill. What's above us?"

"A few campsites, then that old lodge. Two roads run along the mountainside." The big man paused. "So you're sure he's going up, then? He left a note explaining he didn't mean to circle?"

The little detective sighed. "He'll make the top of the mountain by midmorning. He was moving fast. You come on up here. Shine a light up the hill. There's a reflector on the cache."

A flashlight beam washed over them briefly from downhill, then winked out. Olsen began slashing uphill through the leaves. The light was richer; the details of the forest floor were emerging from the darkness at their feet.

"Why you so sure, *viejo*?" Vasquez whispered.

"It ain't the where he was going; it's the how," he answered softly. Once Olsen joined them, the little detective pointed the way

Gagneau had gone, then played his flashlight briefly in that direction. A tree trunk twinkled. The killer had blazed the trail to make it useful in the dead of night.

Olsen checked the assault rifle and found the clip empty. The big man let out a hiss of breath. "He'll have more weapons somewhere," he said. "That's when he'll turn on us."

"We still need him alive, Greg. We follow him as best we can, and maybe get ahead of him." Guthrie looked east at the patches of sky faintly visible through the trees. "I'll be sight-tracking in another half hour. This ground holds sign as good as any in West Virginia. I might puzzle out where he's headed when I can see it."

"*Viejo*, you're crazy," Vasquez said.

"You bet," Olsen echoed.

CHAPTER THIRTY-ONE

In the predawn darkness, the vast mountain towered above the detectives, with Gagneau already vanished, seeking a hole of his choice that they must find by blind chance. Guthrie's slow woodcraft, guided by brushing fingertips, felt like an ant crawling behind a fleeing blue jay. Faint shapes of trees and underbrush sharpened into focus at arm's length, carrying a clinging scent, almost rotten but sweet and moist. The dry, dusty top of the leaf litter hid a cool, slick layer patrolled by an army of mutant insects. The darkness made everything else invisible.

Vasquez struggled behind Guthrie. The little man was silent, but she made a sandpaper racket with every step. Olsen did no better following her. Fortunately, no trap waited; their creeping fear of ambush disappeared as Guthrie's hunch proved true. Gagneau was racing for the ridgetop. They climbed into the descending edge of dawn as the sun peeked above the ridge to the east, lighting the western side of the valley as it rose.

With light, Guthrie moved more swiftly. The killer's boot prints were as plain to him as words on a written page. They climbed past

campsite number three, close enough to see the rough wooden platforms, and disappeared into the mountain's cupped hand. The
stone surrounding them resembled a mass of broken knuckles and
twisted fingers, with oak and maple trees emerging like splinters
thrusting upward toward a sky hidden by greenery. Guthrie paused,
finding on the mountain's bony knee a perch to see its shaggy crest.
He pointed at a notch high above them.

"He's going there," Guthrie said. "That's contrary, on account
that the saddle southeast is lower and quicker." He pointed again.

Olsen scanned the ridgetop, then said, "If a guy meant to guess,
he would suppose that notch fell directly above the spread on the
other side, do you think?"

"Sure," Guthrie replied. "Your sergeant would do that?"

"Dirty and direct was Alpha SOP," he replied.

Guthrie looked again. "I don't reckon that's quicker."

The big veteran grunted. "So if he decided to turn aside, you
don't think it would matter, then?"

The old man removed his fedora and wiped his forehead with his
sleeve. He worried at the brim for a moment. "He might be a half
hour ahead, striking hard with your head down, but I reckon he's
less. We won't make up time trailing to that notch."

"So we have to split up," Olsen said. "I can pass that saddle and
turn back to the resort, but I can't see what you're looking at on the
ground. You'll have to follow him to the notch so he can't turn aside,
then."

"Can you hit his knees?" the little detective asked with a frown.
"Can you shoot low?"

"I'm a fair shot," Olsen replied.

The little detective pulled some short, square Garand magazines
from his jacket pockets. The bullets inside were tipped with brass,
not blue. He pressed two into Olsen's hand, and a third into Vasquez's.
He watched them reload their rifles. The gray limestone made the
hollow as cold as a graveyard, even on a warm summer morning.
Guthrie pointed out the quickest way along to the saddle, then
turned to follow the killer's trail before Olsen passed from sight.

Gagneau's trail up the mountainside was short and hard, clinging to defiles and washes that gave purchase even when they were steep. The coolness of the morning disappeared in a few hours of hard hiking. The detectives ended up in a wash gully leading sharply upward to the notch. Even Vasquez could see the fresh scuffs marring the bare earth, and caked pebbles loose atop dry leaves. At the top, Gagneau's trail continued across a wide, shallow bowl that drained into the gully. Tall pines filled the bowl, lifting a dark green umbrella above a smooth cinnamon carpet. The mountain fell away from the bowl's western side; an oak tree stood guard on a circle of ground, with pines threatening. The trail ended at a parachute cord tied to the oak's trunk.

Along the ridge, the western side fell away repeatedly in cliffs and draws cut into the mountaintop with a giant's pick and shovel. Trees danced up to the edge, before the ground fell away into nothingness. Morning's shadow remained like an unshaved beard even late in the morning. Some open country lay below, old gardens and lawns for the abandoned great lodge visible in breaks between the treetops on the broad terrace below them.

The parachute cord dropped into a rounded hollow. The slope was steep and smooth for a few hundred feet. Mature trees nestled on the slope in several places, but mostly it was bare except for slick curtains of stone, ferns, and lines of leaf litter trapped in creases like gutters. A thick tangle of oak and maple trees crowded their shaggy heads together in whispered conversations. Guthrie and Vasquez lost their view of what lay below, becoming like ants on the mountainside again. Twin Oaks waited at the end of a quarter-hour downhill plunge, for anyone in a hurry, but it was invisible in the folds of stone and crowds of trees. Guthrie sprang along like a hungry goat, his attention split between Gagneau's tracks and the way ahead. Then two rifle shots slashed the quiet mountainside; all the birds abandoned their gossip.

"Missed him," Olsen reported, his voice broken with movement and punctuated by the thud of his boots. "A guy could've hit a belly shot something easier."

Guthrie and Vasquez ran. The little detective needed no more caution. The killer was somewhere ahead, running from Olsen, and they were behind the chase. Guthrie picked a sure path, but the rough, pitching ground gave wild slides down leafy slopes and hard pounding on sudden upturns. The wide emptiness of the mountainside ignored their haste, staying stubbornly in their path.

"Think I can get another shot," Olsen added, measuring his breath. "Need to pass that fence line." More pounding boots were followed by an afterthought. "Didn't see a weapon."

Guthrie and Vasquez raced. She didn't quit, even though she couldn't catch the little man. Steady running earned grudging passage from the trees, but the waist of the mountain was a long, jumbled cloth, where each bend revealed only one more space to rush across.

Another pair of rifle shots cracked, followed by a curse from Olsen. The big man was breathing hard. "He made it into the big building." His footfalls were heavier, slower.

"East side?" Guthrie asked.

"Yeah. I'll enter south side. Must be more doors."

"Wait on us. We're getting close."

Olsen's breath whistled. "Negative." The sound of his footfalls vanished.

Guthrie and Vasquez ran, and the sky opened above them as if the sun had lifted the lid of their leafy green box. Breaks and bends marred the open ground, but in sometime past, gardeners had carefully smoothed out lawns and fields. The Twin Oaks great lodge wore a facade of massive joined timbers under high-pitched roofs cut to display windows, like a circle of Victorian gentlemen gathered around a card table without removing their top hats and frock coats. A string of muffled semiautomatic shots encouraged them to go faster. On the smoother ground, they were swift. They found a small doorway on the eastern side in time to hear another fusillade of semiautomatic fire. None sounded with the sharp, authoritative crack of a Garand.

Guthrie and Vasquez rushed through a doorway without a door

into the middle of a long kitchen. The dark slate floor wore a doormat of dirt and windblown leaves, and it betrayed their boots with a clatter. A large double door stood ajar on the interior wall, opening about midway into a long corridor.

"Tricked him," Olsen said softly on the radio, then coughed.

"Where are you?" Guthrie hissed.

"Courtyard inside," Olsen answered. "Building's wrapped around it."

Wide swing doors faced the kitchen from across the hall, spilling light through porthole windows to match the kitchen doors. One door clung to the frame like a leaning drunk, failed by a broken hinge. Dusty boxes and stacks of lumber, buckets, and sacks lined the corridor, with unstirred dust as opaque as paint hiding peeling labels on supplies meant for a long-abandoned remodel. The undamaged door squealed like a jilted lover before revealing a formal dining room. Vasquez brushed past Guthrie as he paused to listen. Tall windows filled the dining room with light. She hurried around the end of the long table to reach a broken door.

The door to the courtyard slapped back into place after Vasquez pushed through. Two tiers of wraparound balconies surrounded the long, narrow courtyard, propped up by ornate wooden pillars; doorways and windows yawned like a tired audience, revealing dark shadows but no teeth. The young Puerto Rican rushed along the back wall, watching the far side of the courtyard. Olsen waited, reclining against the wall on the left end. Guthrie slipped from the dining room as Vasquez reached Olsen. The big man smiled when she bent over him; blood crept silently from his body. His Colt was locked open in his left hand, and a spent magazine lay in his lap. Blood welled from holes in his right arm and leg, wetting his clothes like a man snatched from water.

"Tricked him," he said again. "Pretty sure I hit him, once maybe."

Guthrie stopped by Vasquez, and Olsen gestured weakly at the far end of the courtyard with his empty pistol. The little detective nodded and turned away. He moved quickly, scanning the balconies without lifting the muzzle of his rifle.

"You ain't tricked him, *chico*," Vasquez muttered. "He fucked you up." She pulled at the lapel of his jacket. "What do I do?"

"Stuff the holes, wrap them, then tie them," the big man said. Vasquez laid her rifle beside him. While she worked, he continued: "I *did* trick him. He didn't expect the pistol."

Guthrie found a blood trail at the far end of the courtyard, glowing like a neon arrow. The splatters spread like silver dollars where Gagneau had paused to open doors, but they narrowed and scattered where he'd moved along. Scuffs along the floors of two large, bare rooms underlined the blood, before leading through a wide doorway onto a flagstone terrace. Olsen's voice on the radio followed the little detective as he stalked, twisting with indrawn breaths or emerging through clenched teeth as Vasquez dressed his wounds.

"Caught him in the entry out front. Almost had him then. Too quick." Scuffling sounds and breathing interrupted his soft voice. "Has a Beretta."

A juniper hedge wearing a thick wig of honeysuckle lined the far side of the flagstone terrace. Guthrie rushed along the blood trail with his rifle clamped to his shoulder, then turned the corner of the hedge.

"Figured him for my rifle butt," Olsen muttered. "There, when we took an AQT all alone, he would wait until the butt of the man's rifle lined with him. That's a long, slow swing—too late to come around." He coughed. "So I drew my pistol and cradled the rifle on my left elbow—pistol pointed down the butt."

"That's you tricking him?" Vasquez asked softly. "Your leg, your hip, your arm—"

Olsen cursed. "But not my heart or my head."

"Yeah, you would miss those."

"You bet. I got him, though. Didn't I get him? Guthrie?"

More curtains of shrubbery waited beyond the juniper, with shadows speckled beneath. Wet blood glowed on the dry leaf litter. A row of boxwood draped with morning glory hid a small, rough circle of bloodstained leaves and some scraps of rag. The trail continued along the boxwood without blood; Gagneau had paused to dress his wound.

Tangled, overgrown parterres edged with flagstone sealed the end of the hedges. The lines of stone left thread-thin paths between overhanging trees, gloomy with shadow and choked by dust. The parterres flanked the overgrown lawns in front of Twin Oaks; once it left the dense thicket, Gagneau's trail turned like an arrow for the front of the lodge. Guthrie cursed. The trick had been too easy, returning in a circle to finish wounded quarry. The little detective spit a warning into the radio as he ran for the front of Twin Oaks.

Vasquez saved Olsen by accident; watched by the crowd of dark windows and doorways in the courtyard while she dressed the big man's wounds, she filled with paranoia. Guthrie was silent. Olsen's bloody fatigues quietly stole her assurance. The young Puerto Rican detective opened the nearest door, then dragged the big man inside with strength born of fear.

Shutting the door darkened the room like a theater awaiting the final act of a play. A small dirty window glowed enough to show a rough worktable cobbled from unfinished lumber, a door in the far wall, and some wooden crates jammed into the corners. The air was silent and heavy with dust. Vasquez watched the courtyard from her window, crouching needlessly. From the courtyard, nothing in the room could be seen, but a wide highway of Olsen's blood, like a smear of crimson icing, showed where he hid.

Gagneau came from the front of the lodge and looked out into the courtyard. He paused to study the blood trail and stare at the small window beside the door, but the panes of glass sucked light like tar paper. The killer's instincts were deep—he balked at the risk of crossing the open space. He turned aside and circled through the halls of the great lodge to approach from the other side.

Gagneau arrived before Guthrie's warning. Olsen was muttering softly when the killer crept to the door. The faint light wasn't enough for him to study the room through the crease of the door, and it creaked when he moved it. Vasquez whirled to her feet, pulling her Garand with her by its forestock. The jumpy teenager caught Gagneau by surprise. She was partly hidden behind the opening door, with Olsen in sight on the floor on the other side, but the sound of her feet made him leap back.

Vasquez fired. The Garand lit the room and the hallway; the heavy bullets plumed geysers of plaster from the walls with each shot. Gagneau sprayed shots with his Beretta and fell onto his ass in the hallway, rolling among some old glass bottles. Vasquez shot the walls on both sides of the door, but the killer was too low.

The gunfire startled Olsen fom his daze. He fumbled a clip of blue bullets from the pocket of his fatigue pants. The Colt slid from his lap. Vasquez squeezed the Garand's trigger twice more after it stopped firing, while Gagneau scrambled upright outside the door. Bottles skittered away from his feet like squeaking mice.

Vasquez dropped the rifle and drew her hard-loaded Chief's Special as Gagneau sprang into the room. The strobing shots had revealed the worktable; he dived and rolled beneath it, firing as he came. Vasquez rushed her shots. Together they made a drumroll, announcing the killer to the detective, face-to-face, with pistols locked open on spent clips. Olsen patted at the floor, searching for his Colt. Vasquez dropped the empty Special and reached for her soft-loaded backup.

Olsen found his Colt, even without gunshots for light, then realized his damaged hand couldn't seat the clip. Gagneau stepped forward and chopped Vasquez with his empty pistol; in the darkness, the bloody gash on her face looked black. He followed like a dancer as she stumbled back, sliding her pistol from the kidney holster.

Gagneau chopped her wrist as she whipped her hand forward to fire. The pistol discharged, caught on her finger for a moment before flying against the plaster wall. Olsen clamped the Colt between his nerveless right hand and his thigh and angled the clip into the butt. Vasquez threw a sloppy jab with her left hand that glanced from the killer's shoulder.

Gagneau stepped forward again, fully visible in the weak light from the window, and seized Vasquez's ponytail. She tried to step away, but he jerked her off balance and spun her into the wall. She bounced roughly. He chopped again with the pistol, catching her on the corner of the jaw. Vasquez sagged to her knees, dazed, suspended in Gagneau's grip.

The killer dropped his pistol and drew a heavy knife from his belt. The steel had a gleaming curve like a tiger's fang and seemed as large as a sword in the small man's rising hand. The Colt's action snapped shut on a blue bullet. Olsen's left hand shook as he lifted the heavy pistol.

"Sergeant Gagneau!" he barked.

The killer turned his head to see the big man, but his hand kept moving.

Guthrie dropped the rifle and drew his revolver as he rushed up the front steps of Twin Oaks. The heavy door was ajar. A sweeping staircase overlooked the rough-timbered entry. Gloomy oak arches led past flanking pairs of doors, ending in a wide double that opened into a salon. Fireplaces at each side faced silent judgment from ghostly courts of furniture wrapped in dusty shrouds. High, narrow windows admitted light from the courtyard. A thunder of muffled shots greeted the little detective when he looked out.

Olsen's blood marked his hiding place. The little detective rushed past a couch, rammed the courtyard door, and stumbled outside. More gunshots boomed as he sprinted across the courtyard but fell silent before he threw his shoulder into the door. The door banged open, slamming into Olsen's feet as he aimed his Colt.

Vasquez reached for the hand gripping her hair. From the corner of her eye, she could see Gagneau behind her, swinging his heavy knife. Guthrie was so close behind the killer that the swinging muzzle of his revolver brushed Gagneau's hair. Guthrie fired once. The bullet smashed Gagneau's elbow, and the knife embedded point-first in the worktable. Then Guthrie took a quick step and kicked Gagneau in the face with his dusty walking boot.

"*Fuck*," Vasquez said.

The rattle of handcuffs seemed quiet after the gunshots. "He shot you?" the little detective asked.

"No."

"We got lucky," Guthrie said softly. "He could've killed us all, with the breaks the other way." Gagneau groaned, coming to as Guthrie wrapped his shattered elbow.

"So I got him, then?" Olsen asked.

"Sure, you got him."

CHAPTER THIRTY-TWO

The city cooled quickly in September. The Atlantic whisked a steady supply of clouds and rain across Long Island to erase the summer; the waning days were gloomy. Trinity Cemetery in Washington Heights felt like the flat bottom of a shallow bowl, with the hardscape surrounding it snapped shut by a gray sky. A slow rain drizzled from tired clouds. Two people stood at a graveside in the empty, chilly cemetery. Guthrie wore a long black overcoat. Wietz stood beside him, holding an umbrella. She watched him uneasily. She wore running boots beneath a long green skirt, along with a vest and button-down shirt. The little detective arranged some flowers on a neat column headstone, shifting them a few times before deciding where they suited best. He stepped back to stand beside her, carefully avoiding the cover of her umbrella, and worried the brim of his old brown fedora while the slow rain speckled his grizzled hair.

"I appreciate you coming along for this," Guthrie said, looking at the gray headstone with a frown. The slender bouquets were tilted at different angles. "I didn't want to do this by myself."

"It's all right," she said. She studied the headstone. "She died young—1993."

"An accident. Maybe you expect someone with a guardian angel will live forever, but it ain't the case."

The sky was quiet except for rushing wind. The traffic seemed far away. "This's why he wouldn't leave," she said, making the words a statement instead of a question.

"As far as I can gather," Guthrie said. "He fell off the map then, too. I suppose his daughter was all he had left. After that, Eddy was the ghost."

The rain thickened. Guthrie clapped his hat onto his head. Wietz glanced around the graveyard, like she was looking for someone trying to overhear. For a detective, suspicion was a habit. She was older than Vasquez, her features more rounded than angular, but equally striking.

"How's the new girl?" she asked.

He shrugged. "Her jaw was bad. She's out of the hospital, at least. Olsen's still mending his bullet holes."

"It worked out, right?"

"They got Gagneau in jail, squeezing him for answers. It'll come out."

"So what's the new girl gonna do?"

Guthrie shrugged again.

"I got something else I need a little help with," he said. "A college boy needs some toys taken away from him, and taught some manners."

She slid a glance at him, her green eyes lighting up. "Since when have you ever needed help with anything, Guthrie?"